D1267749

THE GAMBLER
AND OTHER STORIES

THE NOVELS OF FYODOR DOSTOEVSKY

Translated from the Russian by CONSTANCE
GARNETT, Crown 8vo,

FYODOR DOSTOEVSKY

♦

THE
GAMBLER
AND OTHER STORIES

*Translated from
the Russian by*
CONSTANCE GARNETT

NEW YORK
THE MACMILLAN COMPANY
1950

CONTENTS

THE GAMBLER

A NOVEL

(From the diary of a young man)

CHAPTER I

AT last I have come back from my fortnight's absence. Our friends have already been two days in Roulettenburg. I imagined that they were expecting me with the greatest eagerness; I was mistaken, however. The General had an extremely independent air, he talked to me condescendingly and sent me away to his sister. I even fancied that the General was a little ashamed to look at me. Marya Filippovna was tremendously busy and scarcely spoke to me; she took the money, however, counted it, and listened to my whole report. They were expecting Mezentsov, the little Frenchman, and some Englishman; as usual, as soon as there was money there was a dinner-party; in the Moscow style. Polina Alexandrovna, seeing me, asked why I had been away so long, and without waiting for an answer went off somewhere. Of course, she did that on purpose. We must have an explanation, though. Things have accumulated.

They had assigned me a little room on the fourth storey of the hotel. They know here that I belong to the *General's suite*. It all looks as though they had managed to impress the people. The General is looked upon by everyone here as a very rich Russian grandee. Even before dinner he commissioned me, among other things, to change two notes for a thousand francs each. I changed them at the office of the hotel. Now we shall be looked upon as millionaires for a whole week, at least. I wanted to take Misha and Nadya out for a walk, but on the stairs I was summoned back to the General; he had graciously bethought him to inquire where I was taking them. The man is absolutely unable to look me straight in the face; he would like to very much, but every time I meet his eyes with an intent, that is, disrespectful air, he seems overcome with embarrassment. In very bombastic language, piling one sentence on another, and at last losing his thread altogether, he gave me to understand that I was to take the children for a walk in the park, as far as possible from the Casino. At last he lost his temper completely, and added sharply: "Or else maybe you'll be taking them into the gambling saloon. You must excuse me," he added, "but I know you are still rather thoughtless and capable, perhaps, of gambling. In any case, though, I am not your mentor and have no desire to be, yet I have the right, at any rate, to desire that you will not compromise me, so to speak . . ."

"But I have no money," I said calmly; "one must have it before one can lose it."

"You shall have it at once," answered the General, flushing a little; he rummaged in his bureau, looked up in an account book, and it turned out that he had a hundred and twenty roubles owing me.

"How are we to settle up?" he said. "We must change it into thalers. Come, take a hundred thalers—the rest, of course, won't be lost."

I took the money without a word.

"Please don't be offended by my words, you are so ready to take offence. . . . If I did make an observation, it was only, so to speak, by way of warning, and, of course, I have some right to do so. . . ."

On my way home before dinner, with the children, I met a perfect cavalcade. Our party had driven out to look at some ruin. Two magnificent carriages, superb horses! In one carriage was Mlle. Blanche with Marya Filippovna and Polina; the Frenchman, the Englishman and our General were on horseback. The passers-by stopped and stared; a sensation was created; but the General will have a bad time, all the same. I calculated that with the four thousand francs I had brought, added to what they had evidently managed to get hold of, they had now seven or eight thousand francs; but that is not enough for Mlle. Blanche.

Mlle. Blanche, too, is staying at the hotel with her mother; our Frenchman is somewhere in the house, too. The footman calls him "Monsieur le Comte." Mlle. Blanche's mother is called "Madame la Comtesse"; well, who knows, they may be Comte and Comtesse.

I felt sure that M. le Comte would not recognise me when we assembled at dinner. The General, of course, would not have thought of introducing us or even saying a word to him on my behalf; and M. le Comte has been in Russia himself, and knows what is called an *outchitel* is very small fry. He knows me very

2

well, however. But I must confess I made my appearance at dinner unbidden; I fancy the General forgot to give orders, or else he would certainly have sent me to dine at the *table d'hôte*. I came of my own accord, so that the General looked at me with astonishment. Kind-hearted Marya Filippovna immediately made a place for me; but my meeting with Mr. Astley saved the situation, and I could not help seeming to belong to the party.

I met this strange Englishman for the first time in the train in Prussia, where we sat opposite to one another, when I was travelling to join the family; then I came across him as I was going into France, and then again in Switzerland: in the course of that fortnight twice—and now I suddenly met him in Roulettenburg. I never met a man so shy in my life. He is stupidly shy and, of course, is aware of it himself, for he is by no means stupid. He is very sweet and gentle, however. I drew him into talk at our first meeting in Prussia. He told me that he had been that summer at North Cape, and that he was very anxious to visit the fair at Nizhni Novgorod. I don't know how he made acquaintance with the General; I believe that he is hopelessly in love with Polina. When she came in he glowed like a sunset. He was very glad that I was sitting beside him at the table and seemed already to look upon me as his bosom friend.

At dinner the Frenchman gave himself airs in an extraordinary way; he was nonchalant and majestic with everyone. In Moscow, I remember, he used to blow soap bubbles. He talked a great deal about finance and Russian politics. The General sometimes ventured to contradict, but discreetly, and only so far as he could without too great loss of dignity.

I was in a strange mood; of course, before we were half through dinner I had asked myself my usual invariable question: "Why I went on dancing attendance on this General, and had not left them long ago?" From time to time I glanced at Polina Alexandrovna. She took no notice of me whatever. It ended by my flying into a rage and making up my mind to be rude.

I began by suddenly, apropos of nothing, breaking in on the conversation in a loud voice. What I longed to do above all things was to be abusive to the Frenchman. I turned round to the General and very loudly and distinctly, I believe, interrupted him. I observed that this summer it was utterly impossible for a Russian to dine at *table d'hôte*. The General turned upon me an astonished stare.

3

"If you are a self-respecting man," I went on, "you will certainly be inviting abuse and must put up with affronts to your dignity. In Paris, on the Rhine, even in Switzerland, there are so many little Poles, and French people who sympathise with them, that there's no chance for a Russian to utter a word."

I spoke in French. The General looked at me in amazement. I don't know whether he was angry or simply astonished at my so forgetting myself.

"It seems someone gave you a lesson," said the Frenchman carelessly and contemptuously.

"I had a row for the first time with a Pole in Paris," I answered ; "then with a French officer who took the Pole's part. And then some of the French came over to my side when I told them how I tried to spit in Monseigneur's coffee."

"Spit?" asked the General, with dignified perplexity, and he even looked about him aghast.

The Frenchman scanned me mistrustfully.

"Just so," I answered. "After feeling convinced for two whole days that I might have to pay a brief visit to Rome about our business, I went to the office of the Papal Embassy to get my passport *viséed*. There I was met by a little abbé, a dried-up little man of about fifty, with a frost-bitten expression. After listening to me politely, but extremely dryly, he asked me to wait a little. Though I was in a hurry, of course I sat down to wait, and took up *L'Opinion Nationale* and began reading a horribly abusive attack on Russia. Meanwhile, I heard some-one in the next room ask to see Monseigneur; I saw my abbé bow to him. I addressed the same request to him again; he asked me to wait—more dryly than ever. A little later someone else entered, a stranger, but on business, some Austrian; he was listened to and at once conducted upstairs. Then I felt very much vexed; I got up, went to the abbé and said resolutely that as Monseigneur was receiving, he might settle my business, too. At once the abbé drew back in great surprise. It was beyond his comprehension that an insignificant Russian should dare to put himself on a level with Monseigneur's guests. As though delighted to have an opportunity of insulting me, he looked me up and down, and shouted in the most insolent tone: 'Can you really suppose that Monseigneur is going to leave his coffee on your account?' Then I shouted, too, but more loudly than he: 'Let me tell you I'm ready to spit in your Monseigneur's coffee! If you don't finish with my passport this minute, I'll go to him in person.'

"'What! When the Cardinal is sitting with him!' cried the abbé, recoiling from me with horror, and, flinging wide his arms, he stood like a cross, with an air of being ready to die rather than let me pass.

"Then I answered him that 'I was a heretic and a barbarian, *que je suis hérétique et barbare,*' and that I cared nothing for all these Archbishops, Cardinals, Monseigneurs and all of them. In short, I showed I was not going to give way. The abbé looked at me with uneasy ill-humour, then snatched my passport and carried it upstairs. A minute later it had been *viséed.* Here, wouldn't you like to see it?" I took out the passport and showed the Roman *visé.*

"Well, I must say . . ." the General began.

"What saved you was saying that you were a heretic and barbarian," the Frenchman observed, with a smile. *"Cela n'était pas si bête."*

"Why, am I to model myself upon our Russians here? They sit, not daring to open their lips, and almost ready to deny they are Russians. In Paris, anyway in my hotel, they began to treat me much more attentively when I told everyone about my passage-at-arms with the abbé. The fat Polish *pan,* the person most antagonistic to me at *table d'hôte,* sank into the background. The Frenchmen did not even resent it when I told them that I had, two years previously, seen a man at whom, in 1812, a French *chasseur* had shot simply in order to discharge his gun. The man was at that time a child of ten, and his family had not succeeded in leaving Moscow.

"That's impossible," the Frenchman boiled up; "a French soldier would not fire at a child!"

"Yet it happened," I answered. "I was told it by a most respectable captain on the retired list, and I saw the scar on his cheek from the bullet myself."

The Frenchman began talking rapidly and at great length. The General began to support him, but I recommended him to read, for instance, passages in the "Notes" of General Perovsky, who was a prisoner in the hands of the French in 1812. At last Marya Filippovna began talking of something else to change the conversation. The General was very much displeased with me, for the Frenchman and I had almost begun shouting at one another. But I fancy my dispute with the Frenchman pleased Mr. Astley very much. Getting up from

5

the table, he asked me to have a glass of wine with him.

In the evening I duly succeeded in getting a quarter of an hour's talk with Polina Alexandrovna. Our conversation took place when we were all out for a walk. We all went into the park by the Casino. Polina sat down on a seat facing the fountain, and let Nadenka play with some children not far from her. I, too, let Misha run off to the fountain, and we were at last left alone.

We began, of course, at first with business. Polina simply flew into a rage when I gave her only seven hundred guldens. She had reckoned positively on my pawning her diamonds in Paris for two thousand guldens, if not more.

"I must have money, come what may," she said. "I must get it or I am lost."

I began asking her what had happened during my absence.

"Nothing, but the arrival of two pieces of news from Petersburg: first that Granny was very ill, and then, two days later, that she seemed to be dying. The news came from Timofey Petrovitch," added Polina, "and he's a trustworthy man. We are expecting every day to hear news of the end."

"So you are all in suspense here?" I asked.

"Of course, all of us, and all the time; we've been hoping for nothing else for the last six months."

"And are *you* hoping for it?" I asked.

"Why, I'm no relation. I am only the General's step-daughter. But I am sure she will remember me in her will."

"I fancy you'll get a great deal," I said emphatically.

"Yes, she was fond of me; but what makes *you* think so?"

"Tell me," I answered with a question, "our *marquis* is initiated into all our secrets, it seems?"

"But why are you interested in that?" asked Polina, looking at me dryly and austerely.

"I should think so; if I'm not mistaken, the General has already succeeded in borrowing from him."

"You guess very correctly."

"Well, would he have lent the money if he had not known about your 'granny'? Did you notice at dinner, three times speaking of her, he called her 'granny'. What intimate and friendly relations!"

"Yes, you are right. As soon as he knows that I have come into something by the will, he will pay his addresses to me at once. That is what you wanted to know, was it?"

6

"He will only begin to pay you his addresses? I thought he had been doing that for a long time."

"You know perfectly well that he hasn't!" Polina said, with anger. "Where did you meet the Englishman?" she added, after a minute's silence.

"I knew you would ask about him directly."

I told her of my previous meetings with Mr. Astley on my journey.

"He is shy and given to falling in love, and, of course, he's fallen in love with you already."

"Yes, he's in love with me," answered Polina.

"And, of course, he's ten times as rich as the Frenchman. Why, is it certain that the Frenchman has anything? Isn't that open to doubt?"

"No, it is not. He has a château of some sort. The General has spoken of that positively. Well, are you satisfied?"

"If I were in your place I should certainly marry the Englishman."

"Why?" asked Polina.

"The Frenchman is better looking, but he is nastier; and the Englishman, besides being honest, is ten times as rich," I snapped out.

"Yes, but on the other hand, the Frenchman is a *marquis* and clever," she answered, in the most composed manner.

"But is it true?" I went on, in the same way.

"It certainly is."

Polina greatly disliked my questions, and I saw that she was trying to make me angry by her tone and the strangeness of her answers. I said as much to her at once.

"Well, it really amuses me to see you in such a rage. You must pay for the very fact of my allowing you to ask such questions and make such suppositions."

"I certainly consider myself entitled to ask you any sort of question," I answered calmly, "just because I am prepared to pay any price you like for it, and I set no value at all on my life now."

Polina laughed.

"You told me last time at the Schlangenberg that you were prepared, at a word from me, to throw yourself head foremost from the rock, and it is a thousand feet high, I believe. Some day I shall utter that word, solely in order to see how you will pay the price, and, trust me, I won't give way. You are hateful to me, just because I've allowed you to take such liberties, and

7

even more hateful because you are so necessary to me. But so long as you are necessary to me, I must take care of you."

She began getting up. She spoke with irritation. Of late she had always ended every conversation with me in anger and irritation, real anger.

"Allow me to ask you, what about Mlle. Blanche?" I asked, not liking to let her go without explanation.

"You know all about Mlle. Blanche. Nothing more has happened since. Mlle. Blanche will, no doubt, be Madame la Générale, that is, if the rumour of Granny's death is confirmed, of course, for Mlle. Blanche and her mother and her cousin twice removed—the Marquis—all know very well that we are ruined."

"And is the General hopelessly in love?"

"That's not the point now. Listen and remember: take these seven hundred florins and go and play. Win me as much as you can at roulette; I must have money now, come what may."

Saying this, she called Nadenka and went into the Casino, where she joined the rest of the party. I turned into the first path to the left, wondering and reflecting. I felt as though I had had a blow on the head after the command to go and play roulette. Strange to say, I had plenty to think about, but I was completely absorbed in analysing the essential nature of my feeling towards Polina. It was true I had been more at ease during that fortnight's absence that I was now on the day of my return, though on the journey I had been as melancholy and restless as a madman, and at moments had even seen her in my dreams. Once, waking up in the train (in Switzerland), I began talking aloud, I believe, with Polina, which amused all the passengers in the carriage with me. And once more now I asked myself the question: "Do I love her?" and again I could not answer it, or, rather, I answered for the hundredth time that I hated her. Yes, she was hateful to me. There were moments (on every occasion at the end of our talks) when I would have given my life to strangle her! I swear if it had been possible on the spot to plunge a sharp knife in her bosom, I believe I should have snatched it up with relish. And yet I swear by all that's sacred that if at the Schlangenberg, at the fashionable peak, she really had said to me, "Throw yourself down," I should have thrown myself down at once, also with positive relish. I knew that. In one way or another it must be settled. All this she understood wonderfully well, and the idea that I knew, positively and distinctly, how utterly beyond my reach she was, how utterly impossible my mad dreams were of fulfilment—that thought, I am convinced, afforded her extraordinary satisfaction; if not, how could she, cautious and intelligent as she was, have been on such intimate and open terms with me? I believe she had hitherto looked on me as that empress of ancient times looked on the slave before whom she did not mind undressing because she did not regard him as a human being. Yes, often she did not regard me as a human being!

I had her commission, however, to win at roulette, at all costs. I had no time to consider why must I play, and why such haste, and what new scheme was hatching in that ever-calculating brain. Moreover, it was evident that during that fortnight new facts had arisen of which I had no idea yet. I must discover all that and get to the bottom of it and as quickly as possible. But there was no time now; I must go to roulette.

CHAPTER II

I CONFESS it was disagreeable to me. Though I had made up my mind that I would play, I had not proposed to play for other people. It rather threw me out of my reckoning, and I went into the gambling saloon with very disagreeable feelings. From the first glance I disliked everything in it. I cannot endure the flunkeyishness of the newspapers of the whole world, and especially our Russian papers, in which, almost every spring, the journalists write articles upon two things: first, on the extraordinary magnificence and luxury of the gambling saloons on the Rhine, and secondly, on the heaps of gold which are said to lie on the tables. They are not paid for it; it is simply done from disinterested obsequiousness. There was no sort of magnificence in these trashy rooms, and not only were there no piles of gold lying on the table, but there was hardly any gold at all. No doubt some time, in the course of the season, some eccentric person, either an Englishman or an Asiatic of some sort, a Turk, perhaps (as it was that summer), would suddenly turn up and lose or win immense sums; all the others play for paltry guldens, and on an average there is very little money lying on the tables.

9

As soon as I went into the gambling saloon (for the first time in my life), I could not for some time make up my mind to play. There was a crush besides. If I had been alone, even then, I believe, I should soon have gone away and not have begun playing. I confess my heart was beating and I was not cool. I knew for certain, and had made up my mind long before, that I should not leave Roulettenburg unchanged, that some radical and fundamental change would take place in my destiny; so it must be and so it would be. Ridiculous as it may be that I should expect so much for myself from roulette, yet I consider even more ridiculous the conventional opinion accepted by all that it is stupid and absurd to expect anything from gambling. And why should gambling be worse than any other means of making money—for instance, commerce? It is true that only one out of a hundred wins, but what is that to me?

In any case I determined to look about me first and not to begin anything in earnest that evening. If anything did happen that evening it would happen by chance and be something slight, and I staked my money accordingly. Besides, I had to study the game; for, in spite of the thousand descriptions of roulette which I had read so eagerly, I understood absolutely nothing of its working, until I saw it myself.

In the first place it all struck me as so dirty, somehow, morally horrid and dirty. I am not speaking at all of the greedy, un-easy faces which by dozens, even by hundreds, crowd round the gambling tables. I see absolutely nothing dirty in the wish to win as quickly and as much as possible. I always thought very stupid the answer of that fat and prosperous moralist, who replied to someone's excuse "that he played for a very small stake," "So much the worse, it is such petty covetousness." As though covetousness were not exactly the same, whether on a big scale or a petty one. It is a matter of proportion. What is paltry to Rothschild is wealth to me, and as for profits and winnings, people, not only at roulette, but everywhere, do nothing but try to gain or squeeze something out of one an-other. Whether profits or gains are nasty is a different question. But I am not solving that question here. Since I was myself possessed by an intense desire of winning, I felt as I went into the hall all this covetousness, and all this covetous filth if you like, in a sense congenial and convenient. It is most charming when people do not stand on ceremony with one another, but act openly and above-board. And, indeed, why deceive oneself? Gambling is a most foolish and imprudent pursuit! What was particularly ugly at first sight, in all the rabble round the roulette table, was the respect they paid to that pursuit, the solemnity and even reverence with which they all crowded round the tables. That is why a sharp distinction is drawn here between the kind of game that is *mauvais genre* and the kind that is permissible to well-bred people. There are two sorts of gambling: one the gentlemanly sort: the other the plebeian, mercenary sort, the game played by all sorts of riff-raff. The distinction is sternly observed here, and how contemptible this distinction really is! A gentleman may stake, for instance, five or ten louis d'or, rarely more; he may, however, stake as much as a thousand francs if he is very rich; but only for the sake of the play, simply for amusement, that is, simply to look on at the process of winning or of losing, but must on no account display an interest in winning. If he wins, he may laugh aloud, for instance; may make a remark to one of the bystanders; he may even put down another stake, and may even double it, but solely from curiosity, for the sake of watching and calculating the chances, and not from the plebeian desire to win. In fact, he must look on all gambling, roulette, *trente et quarante,* as nothing else than a pastime got up entirely for his amusement. He must not even suspect the greed for gain and the shifty dodges on which the bank depends. It would be extremely good form, too, if he should imagine that all the other gamblers, all the rabble, trembling over a gulden, were rich men and gentlemen like himself and were playing simply for their diversion and amusement. This complete ignorance of reality and innocent view of people would be, of course, extremely aristocratic. I have seen many mammas push forward their daughters, innocent and elegant Misses of fifteen and sixteen, and, giving them some gold coins, teach them how to play. The young lady wins or loses, invariably smiles and walks away, very well satisfied. Our General went up to the table with solid dignity; a flunkey rushed to hand him a chair, but he ignored the flunkey; he, very slowly and deliberately, took out his purse, very slowly and deliberately took three hundred francs in gold from his purse, staked them on the black, and won. He did not pick up his winnings, but left them on the table. Black turned up again; he didn't pick up his winnings that time either; and when, the third time, red turned up, he lost at once twelve hundred francs. He walked away with a smile and kept up his dignity. I am positive he was raging inwardly, and if the stake had been two or three times as much he would not have kept up his dignity but would have betrayed his feelings. A Frenchman did, however, before my eyes, win and lose as much as thirty thousand francs with perfect gaiety and no sign of emotion. A real gentleman should not show excitement even if he loses his whole fortune. Money ought to be so much below his gentlemanly dignity as to be scarcely worth noticing. Of course, it would have been extremely aristocratic not to notice the sordidness of all the rabble and all the surroundings. Sometimes, however, the opposite pose is no less aristocratic—to notice—that is, to look about one, even, perhaps, to stare through a lorgnette at the rabble; though always taking the rabble and the sordidness as nothing else but a diversion of a sort, as though it were a performance got up for the amusement of gentlemen. One may be jostled in that crowd, but one must look about one with complete conviction that one is oneself a spectator and that one is in no sense part of it. Though, again, to look very attentively is not quite the thing; that, again, would not be gentlemanly because, in any case, the spectacle does not deserve much, or close, attention. And, in fact, few spectacles do deserve a gentleman's close attention. And yet it seemed to me that all this was deserving of very close attention, especially for one who had come not only to observe it, but sincerely and genuinely reckoned himself as one of the rabble. As for my hidden moral convictions, there is no place for them, of course, in my present reasonings. Let that be enough for the present. I speak to relieve my conscience. But I notice one thing: that of late it has become horribly repugnant to me to test my thoughts and actions by any moral standard whatever. I was guided by something different . . .

The rabble certainly did play very sordidly. I am ready to believe, indeed, that a great deal of the most ordinary thieving goes on at the gaming table. The croupiers who sit at each end of the table look at the stakes and reckon the winnings; they have a great deal to do. They are rabble, too! For the most part they are French. However, I was watching and observing, not with the object of describing roulette. I kept a sharp look-out for my own sake, so that I might know how to behave in the future. I noticed, for instance, that nothing was more common than for someone to stretch out his hand and snatch what one had won. A dispute would begin, often an uproar, and a nice job one would have to find witnesses and to prove that it was one's stake!

At first it was all an inexplicable puzzle to me. All I could guess and distinguish was that the stakes were on the numbers, on odd and even, and on the colours. I made up my mind to risk a hundred guldens of Polina Alexandrovna's money. The thought that I was not playing for myself seemed to throw me out of my reckoning. It was an extremely unpleasant feeling, and I wanted to be rid of it as soon as possible. I kept feeling that by beginning for Polina I should break my own luck. Is it impossible to approach the gambling table without becoming infected with superstition? I began by taking out five friedrichs d'or (fifty gulden) and putting them on the even. The wheel went round and thirteen turned up—I had lost. With a sickly feeling I staked another five friedrich d'or on red, simply in order to settle the matter and go away. Red turned up. I staked all the ten friedrichs d'or—red turned up again. I staked all the money again on the same, and again red turned up. On receiving forty friedrichs d'or I staked twenty upon the twelve middle figures, not knowing what would come of it. I was paid three times my stake. In this way from ten friedrichs d'or I had all at once eighty. I was overcome by a strange, unusual feeling which was so unbearable that I made up my mind to go away. It seemed to me that I should not have been playing at all like that if I had been playing for myself. I staked the whole eighty friedrichs d'or, however, on even. This time four turned up; another eighty friedrichs d'or was poured out to me, and, gathering up the whole heap of a hundred and sixty friedrichs d'or, I set off to find Polina Alexandrovna.

They were all walking somewhere in the park and I only succeeded in seeing her after supper. This time the Frenchman was not of the party, and the General unbosomed himself. Among other things he thought fit to observe to me that he would not wish to see me at the gambling tables. It seemed to him that it would compromise him if I were to lose too much: "But even if you were to win a very large sum I should be compromised, too," he added significantly. "Of course, I have no right to dictate your actions, but you must admit yourself . . ." At this point he broke off, as his habit was. I answered, dryly, that I had very little money, and so I could not lose very conspicuously, even if I did play. Going upstairs to my room I succeeded in handing Polina her winnings, and told her that I would not play for her another time.

"Why not?" she asked, in a tremor.

"Because I want to play on my own account," I answered, looking at her with surprise; "and it hinders me."

"Then you will continue in your conviction that roulette is your only escape and salvation?" she asked ironically.

I answered very earnestly, that I did; that as for my confidence that I should win, it might be absurd; I was ready to admit it, but that I wanted to be let alone.

Polina Alexandrovna began insisting I should go halves with her in to-day's winnings, and was giving me eighty friedrichs d'or, suggesting that I should go on playing on those terms. I refused the half, positively and finally, and told her that I could not play for other people, not because I didn't want to, but because I should certainly lose.

"Yet I, too," she said, pondering, "stupid as it seems, am building all my hopes on roulette. And so you must go on playing, sharing with me, and—of course—you will."

At this point she walked away, without listening to further objections.

CHAPTER III

YET all yesterday she did not say a single word to me about playing, and avoided speaking to me altogether. Her manner to me remained unchanged: the same absolute carelessness on meeting me; there was even a shade of contempt and dislike. Altogether she did not care to conceal her aversion; I noticed that. In spite of that she did not conceal from me, either, that I was in some way necessary to her and that she was keeping me for some purpose. A strange relation had grown up between us, incomprehensible to me in many ways when I considered her pride and haughtiness with everyone. She knew, for instance, that I loved her madly, even allowed me to speak of my passion; and, of course, she could not have shown greater contempt for me than by allowing me to speak of my passion without hindrance or restriction. It was as much as to say that she thought so little of my feelings that she did not care in the least what I talked about to her and what I felt for her. She had talked a great deal about her own affairs before, but had never been completely open. What is more, there was this peculiar refinement in her contempt for me: she

14

would know, for instance, that I was aware of some circumstance in her life, or knew of some matter that greatly concerned her, or she would tell me herself something of her circumstances, if to forward her objects she had to make use of me in some way, as a slave or an errand-boy; but she would always tell me only so much as a man employed on her errands need know, and if I did not know the whole chain of events, if she saw herself how worried and anxious I was over her worries and anxieties, she never deigned to comfort me by giving me her full confidence as a friend; though she often made use of me for commissions that were not only troublesome, but dangerous, so that to my thinking she was bound to be open with me. Was it worth her while, indeed, to trouble herself about my feelings, about my being worried, and perhaps three times as much worried and tormented by her anxieties and failures as she was herself?

I knew of her intention to play roulette three weeks before. She had even warned me that I should have to play for her, and it would be improper for her to play herself. From the tone of her words, I noticed even then that she had serious anxieties, and was not actuated simply by a desire for money. What is money to her for its own sake? She must have some object, there must be some circumstance at which I can only guess, but of which so far I have no knowledge. Of course, the humiliation and the slavery in which she held me might have made it possible for me (it often does) to question her coarsely and bluntly. Seeing that in her eyes I was a slave and utterly insignificant, there was nothing for her to be offended at in my coarse curiosity. But the fact is that though she allowed me to ask questions, she did not answer them, and sometimes did not notice them at all. That was the position between us.

A great deal was said yesterday about a telegram which had been sent off four days before, and to which no answer had been received. The General was evidently upset and pre-occupied. It had, of course, something to do with Granny. The Frenchman was troubled, too. Yesterday, for instance, after dinner, they had a long, serious talk. The Frenchman's tone to all of us was unusually high and mighty, quite in the spirit of the saying: "Seat a pig at table and it will put its feet on it." Even with Polina he was casual to the point of rudeness; at the same time he gladly took part in the walks in the public gardens and in the rides and drives into the country. I had long known some of the circumstances that bound the

Frenchman to the General: they had made plans for establishing a factory together in Russia; I don't know whether their project had fallen through, or whether it was being discussed. Moreover, I had by chance come to know part of a family secret. The Frenchman had actually, in the previous year, come to the General's rescue, and had given him thirty thousand roubles to make up a deficit of Government monies missing when he resigned his duties. And, of course, the General is in his grip; but now the principal person in the whole business is Mlle. Blanche; about that I am sure I'm not mistaken.

What is Mlle. Blanche? Here among us it is said that she is a distinguished Frenchwoman, with a colossal fortune and a mother accompanying her. It is known, too, that she is some sort of relation of our Marquis, but a very distant one: a cousin, or something of the sort. I am told that before I went to Paris, the Frenchman and Mlle. Blanche were on much more ceremonious, were, so to speak, on a more delicate and refined footing; now their acquaintance, their friendship and relationship, was of a rather coarse and more intimate character. Perhaps our prospects seemed to them so poor that they did not think it very necessary to stand on ceremony and keep up appearances with us. I noticed even the day before yesterday how Mr. Astley looked at Mlle. Blanche and her mother. It seemed to me that he knew them. It even seemed to me that our Frenchman had met Mr. Astley before. Mr. Astley, however, is so shy, so reserved and silent, that one can be almost certain of him—he won't wash dirty linen in public. Anyway, the Frenchman barely bows to him and scarcely looks at him, so he is not afraid of him. One can understand that, perhaps, but why does Mlle. Blanche not look at him either? Especially when the Marquis let slip yesterday in the course of conversation—I don't remember in what connection—that Mr. Astley had a colossal fortune and that he—the Marquis—knew this for a fact; at that point Mlle. Blanche might well have looked at Mr. Astley. Altogether the General was uneasy. One can understand what a telegram announcing his aunt's death would mean!

Though I felt sure Polina was, apparently for some object, avoiding a conversation with me, I assumed a cold and indifferent air: I kept thinking that before long she would come to me of herself. But both to-day and yesterday I concentrated my attention principally on Mlle. Blanche. Poor General! He

16

is completely done for! To fall in love at fifty-five with such a violent passion is a calamity, of course! When one takes into consideration the fact that he is a widower, his children, the ruin of his estate, his debts, and, finally, the woman it is his lot to fall in love with. Mlle. Blanche is handsome. But I don't know if I shall be understood if I say that she has a face of the type of which one might feel frightened. I, anyway, have always been afraid of women of that sort. She is probably five-and-twenty. She is well grown and broad, with sloping shoulders; she has a magnificent throat and bosom; her complexion is swarthy yellow. Her hair is as black as Indian ink, and she has a tremendous lot of it, enough to make two ordinary coiffures. Her eyes are black with yellowish whites; she has an insolent look in her eyes; her teeth are very white; her lips are always painted; she smells of musk. She dresses effectively, richly and with *chic*, but with much taste. Her hands and feet are exquisite. Her voice is a husky contralto. Sometimes she laughs, showing all her teeth, but her usual expression is a silent and impudent stare— before Polina and Marya Filippovna, anyway (there is a strange rumour that Marya Filippovna is going back to Russia). I fancy that Mlle. Blanche has had no sort of education. Possibly she is not even intelligent; but, on the other hand, she is striking and she is artful. I fancy her life has not passed without adventures. If one is to tell the whole truth, it is quite possible that the Marquis is no relation of hers at all, and that her mother is not her mother. But there is evidence that in Berlin, where we went with them, her mother and she had some decent acquaintances. As for the Marquis himself, though I still doubt his being a marquis, yet the fact that he is received in decent society—among Russians, for instance, in Moscow, and in some places in Germany—is not open to doubt. I don't know what he is in France. The say he has a château.

I thought that a great deal would have happened during this fortnight, and yet I don't know if anything decisive has been said between Mlle. Blanche and the General. Everything depends on our fortune, however; that is, whether the General can show them plenty of money. If, for instance, news were to come that Granny were not dead, I am convinced that Mlle. Blanche would vanish at once. It surprises and amuses me to see what a gossip I've become. Oh! how I loathe it all! How delighted I should be to drop it all, and them all! But can I leave Polina, can I give up spying round her? Spying, of course, is low, but what do I care about that?

I was interested in Mr. Astley, too, to-day and yesterday. Yes, I am convinced he's in love with Polina. It is curious and absurd how much may be expressed by the eyes of a modest and painfully chaste man, moved by love, at the very time when the man would gladly sink into the earth rather than express or betray anything by word or glance. Mr. Astley very often meets us on our walks. He takes off his hat and passes by, though, of course, he is dying to join us. If he is invited to do so, he immediately refuses. At places where we rest—at the Casino, by the bandstand, or before the fountain—he always stands somewhere not far from our seat; and wherever we may be—in the park, in the wood, or on the Schlangenberg—one has only to glance round, to look about one, and somewhere, either in the nearest path or behind the bushes, Mr. Astley's head appears. I fancy he is looking for an opportunity to have a conversation with me apart. This morning we met and exchanged a couple of words. He sometimes speaks very abruptly. Without saying "good-morning," he began by blurting out:

"Oh, Mlle. Blanche! . . . I have seen a great many women like Mlle. Blanche!"

He paused, looking at me significantly. What he meant to say by that I don't know. For on my asking what he meant, he shook his head with a sly smile, and added, "Oh, well, that's how it is. Is Mlle. Pauline very fond of flowers?"

"I don't know; I don't know at all," I answered.

"What? You don't even know that!" he cried, with the utmost amazement.

"I don't know; I haven't noticed at all," I repeated, laughing.

"H'm! That gives me a queer idea."

Then he shook his head and walked away. He looked pleased, though. We talked the most awful French together.

CHAPTER IV

TO-DAY has been an absurd, grotesque, ridiculous day. Now it is eleven o'clock at night. I am sitting in my little cupboard of a room, recalling it. It began with my having to go to roulette to play for Polina Alexandrovna. I took the hundred and sixty friedrichs d'or, but on two conditions: first, that I would not go halves—that is, if I won I would take nothing for myself; and secondly, that in the evening Polina should explain to me why she needed to win, and how much money. I can't, in any case, suppose that it is simply for the sake of money. Evidently the money is needed, and as quickly as possible, for some particular object. She promised to explain, and I set off. In the gambling hall the crowd was awful. How insolent and how greedy they all were! I forced my way into the middle and stood near the croupier; then I began timidly experimenting, staking two or three coins at a time. Meanwhile, I kept quiet and looked on; it seemed to me that calculation meant very little, and had by no means the importance attributed to it by some players. They sit with papers before them scrawled over in pencil, note the strokes, reckon, deduce the chances, calculate, finally stake and—lose exactly as we simple mortals who play without calculations. On the other hand, I drew one conclusion which I believe to be correct: that is, though there is no system, there really is a sort of order in the sequence of casual chances—and that, of course, is very strange. For instance, it happens that after the twelve middle numbers come the twelve later numbers; twice, for instance, it turns up on the twelve last numbers and passes to the twelve first numbers. After falling on the twelve first numbers, it passes again to numbers in the middle third, turns up three or four times in succession on numbers between thirteen and twenty-four, and again passes to numbers in the last third; then, after turning up two numbers between twenty-five and thirty-six, it passes to a number among the first twelve, turns up once again on a number among the first third, and again passes for three strokes in succession to the middle numbers, and in that way goes on for an hour and a half or two hours. One, three and two—one, three and two. It's very amusing. One day or one morning, for instance, red will be followed by black and back again almost without any order, shifting every minute, so that it never turns up red or black for more than two or three strokes in succession. Another day, or another evening, there will be nothing but red over and over again, turning up, for instance, more than twenty-two times in succession, and so for a whole day. A great deal of this was explained to me by Mr. Astley, who spent the whole morning at the tables, but did not once put down a stake.

As for me, I lost every farthing very quickly. I staked

straight off twenty friedrichs d'or on even and won, staked again and again won, and went on like that two or three times. I imagine I must have had about four hundred friedrichs d'or in my hands in about five minutes. At that point I ought to have gone away, but a strange sensation rose up in me, a sort of defiance of fate, a desire to challenge it, to put out my tongue at it. I laid down the largest stake allowed—four thousand gulden—and lost it. Then, getting hot, I pulled out all I had left, staked it on the same number, and lost again, after which I walked away from the table as though I were stunned. I could not even grasp what had happened to me, and did not tell Polina Alexandrovna of my losing till just before dinner. I spent the rest of the day sauntering in the park.

At dinner I was again in an excited state, just as I had been three days before. The Frenchman and Mlle. Blanche were dining with us again. It appeared that Mlle. Blanche had been in the gambling hall that morning and had witnessed my exploits. This time she addressed me, it seemed, somewhat attentively. The Frenchman set to work more directly, and asked me: Was it my own money I had lost? I fancy he suspects Polina. In fact, there is something behind it. I lied at once and said it was.

The General was extremely surprised. Where had I got such a sum? I explained that I had begun with ten friedrichs d'or, that after six or seven times staking successfully on equal chances I had five or six hundred gulden, and that afterwards I had lost it all on two turns.

All that, of course, sounded probable. As I explained this I looked at Polina, but I could distinguish nothing from her face. She let me lie, however, and did not set it right; from this I concluded that I had to lie and conceal that I was in collaboration with her. In any case, I thought to myself, she is bound to give me an explanation, and promised me this morning to reveal something.

I expected the General would have made some remark to me, but he remained mute; I noticed, however, signs of disturbance and uneasiness in his face. Possibly in his straitened circumstances it was simply painful to him to hear that such a pile of gold had come into, and within a quarter of an hour had passed out of, the hands of such a reckless fool as me.

I suspect that he had a rather hot encounter with the Frenchman yesterday. They were shut up together talking for a long time. The Frenchman went away seeming irritated, and came to see the General again early this morning—probably to continue the conversation of the previous day.

Hearing what I had lost, the Frenchman observed bitingly, even spitefully, that one ought to have more sense. He added— I don't know why—that though a great many Russians gamble, Russians were not, in his opinion, well qualified even for gambling.

"To my mind," said I, "roulette is simply made for Russians."

And when at my challenge the Frenchman laughed contemptuously, I observed that I was, of course, right, for to speak of the Russians as gamblers was abusing them far more than praising them, and so I might be believed.

"On what do you base your opinion?" asked the Frenchman.

"On the fact that the faculty of amassing capital has, with the progress of history, taken a place—and almost the foremost place—among the virtues and merits of the civilised man of the West. The Russian is not only incapable of amassing capital, but dissipates it in a reckless and unseemly way. Nevertheless we Russians need money, too," I added, "and consequently we are very glad and very eager to make use of such means as roulette, for instance, in which one can grow rich all at once, in two hours, without work. That's very fascinating to us; and since we play badly, recklessly, without taking trouble, we usually lose!"

"That's partly true," observed the Frenchman complacently.

"No, it is not true, and you ought to be ashamed to speak like that of your country," observed the General, sternly and impressively.

"Excuse me," I answered. "I really don't know which is more disgusting: Russian unseemliness or the German faculty of accumulation by honest toil."

"What an unseemly idea!" exclaimed the General.

"What a Russian idea!" exclaimed the Frenchman.

I laughed; I had an intense desire to provoke them.

"Well, I should prefer to dwell all my life in a Kirgiz tent," I cried, "than bow down to the German idol."

"What idol?" cried the General, beginning to be angry in earnest.

"The German faculty for accumulating wealth. I've not

been here long, but yet all I have been able to observe and verify revolts my Tatar blood. My God! I don't want any such virtue! I succeeded yesterday in making a round of eight miles, and it's all exactly as in the edifying German picture-books: there is here in every house a *vater* horribly virtuous and extraordinarily honest—so honest that you are afraid to go near him. I can't endure honest people whom one is afraid to go near. Every such German *vater* has a family, and in the evening they read improving books aloud. Elms and chestnut trees rustle over the house. The sun is setting; there is a stork on the roof, and everything is extraordinarily practical and touching. . . . Don't be angry, General; let me tell it in a touching style. I remember how my father used to read similar books to my mother and me under the lime trees in the garden. . . . So I am in a position to judge. And in what complete bondage and submission every such family is here. They all work like oxen and all save money like Jews. Suppose the *vater* has saved up so many gulden and is reckoning on giving his son a trade or a bit of land; to do so, he gives his daughter no dowry, and she becomes an old maid. To do so, the youngest son is sold into bondage or into the army, and the money is added to the family capital. This is actually done here; I've been making inquiries. All this is done from nothing but honesty, from such intense honesty that the younger son who is sold believes that he is sold from nothing but honesty: and that is the ideal when the victim himself rejoices at being led to the sacrifice. What more? Why, the elder son is no better off: he has an Amalia and their hearts are united, but they can't be married because the pile of gulden is not large enough. They, too, wait with perfect morality and good faith, and go to the sacrifice with a smile. Amalia's cheeks grow thin and hollow. At last, in twenty years, their prosperity is increased; the gulden have been honestly and virtuously accumulating. The *vater* gives his blessing to the forty-year-old son and his Amalia of thirty-five, whose chest has grown hollow and whose nose has turned red. . . . With that he weeps, reads them a moral sermon, and dies. The eldest son becomes himself a virtuous *vater* and begins the same story over again. In that way, in fifty or seventy years, the grandson of the first *vater* really has a considerable capital, and he leaves it to his son, and he to his, and he to his, till in five or six generations one of them is a Baron Rothschild or goodness knows who. Come, isn't that a majestic spectacle? A hundred or two hundred years of continuous toil, patience, intelligence, honesty, character, determination, prudence, the stork on the roof! What more do you want? Why, there's nothing loftier than that; and from that standpoint they are beginning to judge the whole world and to punish the guilty; that is, any who are ever so little unlike them. Well, so that's the point: I would rather waste my substance in the Russian style or grow rich at roulette. I don't care to be Goppe and Co. in five generations. I want money for myself, and I don't look upon myself as something subordinate to capital and necessary to it. I know that I have been talking awful nonsense, but, never mind, such are my convictions."

"I don't know whether there is much truth in what you have been saying," said the General thoughtfully, "but I do know you begin to give yourself insufferable airs as soon as you are permitted to forget yourself in the least . . ."

As his habit was, he broke off without finishing. If our General began to speak of anything in the slightest degree more important than his ordinary everyday conversation, he never finished his sentences. The Frenchman listened carelessly with rather wide-open eyes; he had scarcely understood anything of what I had said. Polina gazed with haughty indifference. She seemed not to hear my words, or anything else that was said that day at table.

CHAPTER V

SHE was unusually thoughtful, but directly we got up from table she bade me escort her for a walk. We took the children and went into the park towards the fountain.

As I felt particularly excited, I blurted out the crude and stupid question: why the Marquis de Grieux, our Frenchman, no longer escorted her when she went out anywhere, and did not even speak to her for days together.

"Because he is a rascal," she answered me strangely.

I had never heard her speak like that of De Grieux, and I received it in silence, afraid to interpret her irritability.

"Have you noticed that he is not on good terms with the General to-day?"

"You want to know what is the matter?" she answered

dryly and irritably. "You know that the General is completely mortgaged to him; all his property is his, and if Granny doesn't die, the Frenchman will come into possession of everything that is mortgaged to him."

"And is it true that everything is mortgaged? I had heard it, but I did not know that everything was."

"To be sure it is."

"Then farewell to Mlle. Blanche," said I. "She won't be the General's wife, then! Do you know, it strikes me the General is so much in love that he may shoot himself if Mlle. Blanche throws him over. It is dangerous to be so much in love at his age."

"I fancy that something will happen to him, too," Polina Alexandrovna observed musingly.

"And how splendid that would be!" I cried. "They couldn't have shown more coarsely that she was only marrying him for his money! There's no regard for decency, even; there's no ceremony about it whatever. That's wonderful! And about Granny—could there be anything more comic and sordid than to be continually sending telegram after telegram: 'Is she dead, is she dead?'? How do you like it, Polina Alexandrovna?"

"That's all nonsense," she said, interrupting me with an air of disgust. "I wonder at your being in such good spirits. What are you so pleased about? Surely not at having lost my money?"

"Why did you give it to me to lose? I told you I could not play for other people—especially for you! I obey you, whatever you order me to do, but I can't answer for the result. I warned you that nothing would come of it. Are you very much upset at losing so much money? What do you want so much for?"

"Why these questions?"

"Why, you promised to explain to me . . . Listen: I am absolutely convinced that when I begin playing for myself (and I've got twelve friedrichs d'or) I shall win. Then you can borrow as much from me as you like."

She made a contemptuous grimace.

"Don't be angry with me for such a suggestion," I went on. "I am so deeply conscious that I am nothing beside you—that is, in your eyes—that you may even borrow money from me. Presents from me cannot insult you. Besides, I lost yours."

She looked at me quickly, and seeing that I was speaking irritably and sarcastically, interrupted the conversation again.

24

"There's nothing of interest to you in my circumstances. If you want to know, I'm simply in debt. I've borrowed money and I wanted to repay it. I had the strange and mad idea that I should be sure to win here at the gambling table. Why I had the idea I can't understand, but I believed in it. Who knows, perhaps I believed it because no other alternative was left me."

"Or because it was quite *necessary* you should win. It's exactly like a drowning man clutching at a straw. You will admit that if he were not drowning he would not look at a straw as a branch of a tree."

Polina was surprised.

"Why," she said, "you were reckoning on the same thing yourself! A fortnight ago you said a great deal to me about your being absolutely convinced that you could win here at roulette, and tried to persuade me not to look upon you as mad; or were you joking then? But I remember you spoke so seriously that it was impossible to take it as a joke."

"That's true," I answered thoughtfully. "I am convinced to this moment that I shall win. I confess you have led me now to wonder why my senseless and unseemly failure to-day has not left the slightest doubt in me. I am still fully convinced that as soon as I begin playing for myself I shall be certain to win."

"Why are you so positive?"

"If you will have it—I don't know. I only know that I *must* win, that it is the only resource left me. Well, that's why, perhaps, I fancy I am bound to win."

"Then you, too, absolutely *must* have it, since you are so fanatically certain?"

"I bet you think I'm not capable of feeling that I *must* have anything?"

"That's nothing to me," Polina answered quietly and indifferently. "Yes, if you like. I doubt whether anything troubles you in earnest. You may be troubled, but not in earnest. You are an unstable person, not to be relied on. What do you want money for? I could see nothing serious in the reasons you brought forward the other day."

"By the way," I interrupted, "you said that you had to repay a debt. A fine debt it must be! To the Frenchman, I suppose?"

"What questions! You're particularly impertinent to-day. Are you drunk, perhaps?"

"You know that I consider myself at liberty to say anything to you, and sometimes ask you very candid questions. I repeat, I'm your slave, and one does not mind what one says to a slave, and cannot take offence at anything he says."

"And I can't endure that 'slave' theory of yours."

"Observe that I don't speak of my slavery because I want to be your slave. I simply speak of it as a fact which doesn't depend on me in the least."

"Tell me plainly, what do you want money for?"

"What do you want to know that for?"

"As you please," she replied, with a proud movement of her head.

"You can't endure the 'slave' theory, but insist on slavishness: 'Answer and don't argue.' So be it. Why do I want money? you ask. How can you ask? Money is everything!"

"I understand that, but not falling into such madness from wanting it! You, too, are growing frenzied, fatalistic. There must be something behind it, some special object. Speak without beating about the bush; I wish it."

She seemed beginning to get angry, and I was awfully pleased at her questioning me with such heat.

"Of course there is an object," I answered, "but I don't know how to explain what it is. Nothing else but that with money I should become to you a different man, not a slave."

"What? How will you manage that?"

"How shall I manage it? What, you don't even understand how I could manage to make you look at me as anything but a slave? Well, that's just what I don't care for, such surprise and incredulity!"

"You said this slavery was a pleasure to you. I thought it was myself."

"You thought so!" I cried, with a strange enjoyment. "Oh, how delightful such *naïveté* is from you! Oh, yes, yes, slavery to you is a pleasure. There is—there is a pleasure in the utmost limit of humiliation and insignificance!" I went on maundering. "Goodness knows, perhaps there is in the knout when the knout lies on the back and tears the flesh. . . . But I should perhaps like to enjoy another kind of enjoyment. Yesterday, in your presence, the General thought fit to read me a lecture for the seven hundred roubles a year which perhaps I may not receive from him after all. The Marquis de Grieux raises his eyebrows and stares at me without noticing me. And I, per-naps, have a passionate desire to pull the Marquis de Grieux by the nose in your presence!"

"That's the speech of a milksop. One can behave with dignity in any position. If there is a struggle, it is elevating, not humiliating."

"That's straight out of a copybook! You simply take for granted that I don't know how to behave with dignity; that is, that perhaps I am a man of moral dignity, but that I don't know how to behave with dignity. You understand that that perhaps may be so. Yes, all Russians are like that; and do you know why? Because Russians are too richly endowed and many-sided to be able readily to evolve a code of manners. It is a question of good form. For the most part we Russians are so richly endowed that we need genius to evolve our code of manners. And genius is most often absent, for, indeed, it is a rarity at all times. It's only among the French, and perhaps some other Europeans, that the code of manners is so well defined that one may have an air of the utmost dignity and yet be a man of no moral dignity whatever. That's why good form means so much with them. A Frenchman will put up with an insult, a real, moral insult, without blinking, but he wouldn't endure a flip on the nose for anything, because that is a breach of the received code, sanctified for ages. That's why our Russian young ladies have such a weakness for Frenchmen, that their manners are so good. Though, to my thinking, they have no manners at all; it's simply the cock in them; *le coq gaulois*. I can't understand it, though; I'm not a woman. Perhaps cocks are nice. And, in fact, I've been talking nonsense, and you don't stop me. You must stop me more often. When I talk to you I long to tell you everything, everything, everything. I am oblivious of all good manners. I'll even admit that I have no manners, no moral qualities either. I tell you that. I don't even worry my head about moral qualities of any sort; everything has come to a standstill in me now; you know why. I have not one human idea in my head. For a long time past I've known nothing that has gone on in the world, either in Russia or here. Here I've been through Dresden, and I don't remember what Dresden was like. You know what has swallowed me up. As I have no hope whatever and am nothing in your eyes, I speak openly: I see nothing but you everywhere, and all the rest is naught to me. Why and how I love you I don't know. Perhaps you are not at all nice really, you know. Fancy! I don't know whether you are good or not, even to look at. You certainly have not a good heart; your mind may very well be ignoble."

"Perhaps that's how it is you reckon on buying me with money," she said, "because you don't believe in my sense of honour."

"When did I reckon on buying you with money?" I cried.

"You have been talking till you don't know what you are saying. If you don't think of buying me, you think of buying my respect with your money."

"Oh no, that's not it at all. I told you it was difficult for me to explain. You are overwhelming me. Don't be angry with my chatter. You know why you can't be angry with me: I'm simply mad. Though I really don't care, even if you are angry. When I am upstairs in my little garret I have only to remember and imagine the rustle of your dress, and I am ready to bite off my hands. And what are you angry with me for? For calling myself your slave? Make use of my being your slave, make use of it, make use of it! Do you know that I shall kill you one day? I shall kill you not because I shall cease to love you or be jealous, I shall simply kill you because I have an impulse to devour you. You laugh. . . ."

"I'm not laughing," she answered wrathfully. "I order you to be silent."

She stood still, almost breathless with anger. Upon my word, I don't know whether she was handsome, but I always liked to look at her when she stood facing me like that, and so I often liked to provoke her anger. Perhaps she had noticed this and was angry on purpose. I said as much to her.

"How disgusting!" she said, with an air of repulsion.

"I don't care," I went on. "Do you know, too, that it is dangerous for us to walk together? I often have an irresistible longing to beat you, to disfigure you, to strangle you. And what do you think—won't it come to that? You are driving me into brain fever. Do you suppose I am afraid of a scandal? Your anger—why, what is your anger to me? I love you without hope, and I know that after this I shall love you a thousand times more than ever. If ever I do kill you I shall have to kill myself, too. Oh, well, I shall put off killing myself as long as possible, so as to go on feeling this insufferable pain of being without you. Do you know something incredible? I love you *more* every day, and yet that is almost impossible. And how can I help being a fatalist? Do you remember the day before

28

yesterday, on the Schlangenberg, I whispered at your provocation, 'Say the word, and I will leap into that abyss'? If you had said that word I should have jumped in then. Don't you believe that I would have leapt down?"

"What stupid talk!" she cried.

"I don't care whether it is stupid or clever!" I cried. "I know that in your presence I must talk, and talk, and talk—and I do talk. I lose all self-respect in your presence, and I don't care."

"What use would it be for me to order you to jump off the Schlangenberg?" she said in a dry and peculiarly insulting manner. "It would be absolutely useless to me."

"Splendid," I cried; "you said that splendid 'useless' on purpose to overwhelm me. I see through you. Useless, you say? But pleasure is always of use, and savage, unbounded power—if only over a fly—is a pleasure in its way, too. Man is a despot by nature, and loves to be a torturer. You like it awfully."

I remember she looked at me with peculiar fixed attention. My face must have expressed my incoherent and absurd sensations. I remember to this moment that our conversation actually was almost word for word exactly as I have described it here. My eyes were bloodshot. There were flecks of foam on my lips. And as for the Schlangenberg, I swear on my word of honour even now, if she had told me to fling myself down I should have flung myself down! If only for a joke she had said it, with contempt, if with a jeer at me she had said it, I should even then have leapt down!

"No, why? I believe you," she pronounced, as only she knows how to speak, with such contempt and venom, with such scorn that, by God, I could have killed her at the moment.

She risked it. I was not lying about that, too, in what I said to her.

"You are not a coward?" she asked me suddenly.

"Perhaps I am a coward. I don't know. . . . I have not thought about it for a long time."

"If I were to say to you, 'Kill this man,' would you kill him?"

"Whom?"

"Whom I choose."

"The Frenchman?"

"Don't ask questions, but answer. Whom I tell you. I want to know whether you spoke seriously just now?"

She waited for my answer so gravely and impatiently that it struck me as strange.

"Come, do tell me, what has been happening here?" I cried. "What are you afraid of—me, or what? I see all the muddle here for myself. You are the stepdaughter of a mad and ruined man possessed by a passion for that devil—Blanche. Then there is this Frenchman, with his mysterious influence over you, and—here you ask me now so gravely . . . such a question. At any rate let me know, or I shall go mad on the spot and do something. Are you ashamed to deign to be open with me? Surely you can't care what I think of you?"

"I am not speaking to you of that at all. I asked you a question and I'm waiting for an answer."

"Of course I will kill anyone you tell me to," I cried. "But can you possibly . . . could you tell me to do it?"

"Do you suppose I should spare you? I shall tell you to, and stand aside and look on. Can you endure that? Why, no, as though you could! You would kill him, perhaps, if you were told, and then you would come and kill me for having dared to send you."

I felt as though I were stunned at these words. Of course, even then I looked upon her question as half a joke, a challenge; yet she had spoken very earnestly. I was struck, nevertheless, at her speaking out so frankly, at her maintaining such rights over me, at her accepting such power over me and saying so bluntly: "Go to ruin, and I'll stand aside and look on." In those words there was something so open and cynical that to my mind it was going too far. That, then, was how she looked at me. This was something more than slavery or insignificance. If one looks at a man like that, one exalts him to one's own level, and absurd and incredible as all our conversation was, yet there was a throb at my heart.

Suddenly she laughed. We were sitting on a bench, before the playing children, facing the place where the carriages used to stop and people used to get out in the avenue before the Casino.

"Do you see that stout baroness?" she cried. "That is Baroness Burmerhelm. She has only been here three days. Do you see her husband—a tall, lean Prussian with a stick? Do you remember how he looked at us the day before yesterday? Go up to the Baroness at once, take off your hat, and say something to her in French."

"Why?"

"You swore that you would jump down the Schlangenberg; you swear you are ready to kill anyone if I tell you. Instead of these murders and tragedies I only want to laugh. Go without discussing it. I want to see the Baron thrash you with his stick."

"You challenge me; you think I won't do it?"

"Yes, I do challenge you. Go; I want you to!"

"By all means, I am going, though it's a wild freak. Only, I say, I hope it won't be unpleasant for the General, and through him for you. Upon my honour, I am not thinking of myself, but of you and the General. And what a mad idea to insult a woman!"

"Yes, you are only a chatterer, as I see," she said contemptuously. "Your eyes were fierce and bloodshot, but perhaps that was only because you had too much wine at dinner. Do you suppose that I don't understand that it is stupid and vulgar, and that the General would be angry? I simply want to laugh; I want to, and that's all about it! And what should you insult a woman for? Why, just to be thrashed."

I turned and went in silence to carry out her commission. Of course it was stupid, and of course I did not know how to get out of it, but as I began to get closer to the Baroness I remember, as it were, something within myself urging me on; it was an impulse of schoolboyish mischief. Besides, I was horribly overwrought, and felt just as though I were drunk.

CHAPTER VI

NOW two days have passed since that stupid day. And what a noise and fuss and talk and uproar there was! And how unseemly and disgraceful, how stupid and vulgar, it was! And I was the cause of it all. Yet at times it's laughable—to me, at any rate. I can't make up my mind what happened to me, whether I really was in a state of frenzy, or whether it was a momentary aberration and I behaved disgracefully till I was pulled up. At times it seemed to me that my mind was giving way. And at times it seems to me that I have not outgrown childhood and schoolboyishness, and that it was simply a crude schoolboy's prank.

It was Polina, it was all Polina! Perhaps I shouldn't have behaved like a schoolboy if it hadn't been for her. Who knows? perhaps I did it out of despair (stupid as it seems, though, to reason like that). And I don't understand, I don't understand what there is fine in her! She is fine, though; she is; I believe she's fine. She drives other men off their heads, too. She's tall and graceful, only very slender. It seems to me you could tie her in a knot or bend her double. Her foot is long and narrow—tormenting. Tormenting is just what it is. Her hair has a reddish tint. Her eyes are regular cat's eyes, but how proudly and disdainfully she can look with them. Four months ago, when I had only just come, she was talking hotly for a long while one evening with De Grieux in the drawing-room, and looked at him in such a way . . . that afterwards, when I went up to my room to go to bed, I imagined that she must have just given him a slap in the face. She stood facing him and looked at him. It was from that evening that I loved her.

To come to the point, however.

I stepped off the path into the avenue, and stood waiting for the Baron and the Baroness. When they were five paces from me I took off my hat and bowed.

I remember the Baroness was wearing a light grey dress of immense circumference, with flounces, a crinoline, and a train. She was short and exceptionally stout, with such a fearful double chin that she seemed to have no neck. Her face was crimson. Her eyes were small, spiteful and insolent. She walked as though she were doing an honour to all beholders. The Baron was lean and tall. Like most Germans, he had a wry face covered with thousands of fine wrinkles, and wore spectacles; he was about forty-five. His legs seemed to start from his chest: that's a sign of race. He was as proud as a peacock. He was rather clumsy. There was something like a sheep in the expression of his face that would pass with them for profundity.

All this flashed upon my sight in three seconds.

My bow and the hat in my hand gradually arrested their attention. The Baron slightly knitted his brows. The Baroness simply sailed straight at me.

"*Madame la baronne,*" I articulated distinctly, emphasising each word, "*j'ai l'honneur d'être votre esclave.*"

Then I bowed, replaced my hat, and walked past the Baron, turning my face towards him with a polite smile.

She had told me to take off my hat, but I had bowed and

behaved like an impudent schoolboy on my own account. Goodness knows what impelled me to! I felt as though I were plunging into space.

"*Hein!*" cried, or rather croaked, the Baron, turning towards me with angry surprise.

I turned and remained in respectful expectation, still gazing at him with a smile. He was evidently perplexed, and raised his eyebrows as high as they would go. His face grew darker and darker. The Baroness, too, turned towards me, and she, too, stared in wrathful surprise. The passers-by began to look on. Some even stopped.

"*Hein!*" the Baron croaked again, with redoubled gutturalness and redoubled anger.

"*Ja wohl!*" I drawled, still looking him straight in the face.

"*Sind sie rasend?*" he cried, waving his stick and beginning, I think, to be a little nervous. He was perhaps perplexed by my appearance. I was very well, even foppishly, dressed, like a man belonging to the best society.

"*Ja wo-o-ohl!*" I shouted suddenly at the top of my voice, drawling the *o* like the Berliners, who use the expression *ja wohl* in every sentence, and drawl the letter *o* more or less according to the shade of their thought or feeling.

The Baron and Baroness turned away quickly and almost ran away from me in terror. Of the spectators, some were talking, others were gazing at me in amazement. I don't remember very clearly, though.

I turned and walked at my ordinary pace to Polina Alexandrovna.

But when I was within a hundred paces of her seat, I saw her get up and walk with the children towards the hotel.

I overtook her at the door.

"I have performed . . . the foolery," I said, when I reached her.

"Well, what of it? Now you can get out of the scrape," she answered. She walked upstairs without even glancing at me.

I spent the whole evening walking about the park. I crossed the park and then the wood beyond and walked into another state. In a cottage I had an omelette and some wine; for that idyllic repast they extorted a whole thaler and a half.

It was eleven o'clock before I returned home. I was at once summoned before the General.

Our party occupied two suites in the hotel; they have four

33

rooms. The first is a big room—a drawing-room with a piano in it. The next, also a large room, is the General's study. Here he was awaiting me, standing in the middle of the room in a majestic pose. De Grieux sat lolling on the sofa.

"Allow me to ask you, sir, what have you been about?" began the General, addressing me.

"I should be glad if you would go straight to the point, General," said I. "You probably mean to refer to my encounter with a German this morning?"

"A German? That German was Baron Burmerhelm, a very important personage! You insulted him and the Baroness."

"Not in the least."

"You alarmed them, sir!" cried the General.

"Not a bit of it. When I was in Berlin the sound was for ever in my ears of that *ja wohl*, continually repeated at every word and disgustingly drawled out by them. When I met them in the avenue that *ja wohl* suddenly came into my mind, I don't know why, and—well, it had an irritating effect on me . . . Besides, the Baroness, who has met me three times, has the habit of walking straight at me as though I were a worm who might be trampled underfoot. You must admit that I, too, may have my proper pride. I took off my hat and said politely (I assure you I said it politely): *'Madame, j'ai l'honneur d'être votre esclave.'* When the Baron turned round and said, *'Hein!'* I felt an impulse to shout, *'Ja wohl!'* I shouted it twice: the first time in an ordinary tone, and the second—I drawled it as much as I could. That was all."

I must own I was intensely delighted at this extremely school-boyish explanation. I had a strange desire to make the story as absurd as possible in the telling.

And as I went on, I got more and more to relish it.

"Are you laughing at me?" cried the General. He turned to the Frenchman and explained to him in French that I was positively going out of my way to provoke a scandal! De Grieux laughed contemptuously and shrugged his shoulders.

"Oh, don't imagine that; it was not so at all!" I cried. "My conduct was wrong, of course, I confess that with the utmost candour. My behaviour may even be called a stupid and improper schoolboy prank, but—nothing more. And do you know, General, I heartily regret it. But there is one circumstance which, to my mind at least, almost saves me from repentance. Lately, for the last fortnight, indeed, I've not been feeling well: I have felt ill, nervous, irritable, moody, and on

34

some occasions I lose all control of myself. Really, I've sometimes had an intense impulse to attack the Marquis de Grieux
and . . . However, there's no need to say, he might be offended.
In short, it's the sign of illness. I don't know whether the
Baroness Burmerhelm will take this fact into consideration when
I beg her pardon (for I intend to apologise). I imagine she will
not consider it, especially as that line of excuse has been somewhat abused in legal circles of late. Lawyers have taken to
arguing in criminal cases that their clients were not responsible
at the moment of their crime, and that it was a form of disease.
'He killed him,' they say, 'and has no memory of it.' And
only imagine, General, the medical authorities support them—
and actually maintain that there are illnesses, temporary aberra-
tions in which a man scarcely remembers anything, or has only
a half or a quarter of his memory. But the Baron and Baroness
are people of the older generation; besides, they are Prussian
junkers and landowners, and so are probably unaware of this
advance in the world of medical jurisprudence, and will not
accept my explanation. What do you think, General?"

"Enough, sir," the General pronounced sharply, with surprised indignation; "enough! I will try once for all to rid
myself of your mischievous pranks. You are not going to
apologise to the Baron and Baroness. Any communication with
you, even though it were to consist solely of your request for
forgiveness, would be beneath their dignity. The Baron has
learnt that you are a member of my household; he has already
had an explanation with me at the Casino, and I assure you
that he was within an ace of asking me to give him satisfaction.
Do you understand what you have exposed me to—me, sir?
I—I was forced to ask the Baron's pardon, and gave him my
word that immediately, this very day, you would cease to be a
member of my household."

"Excuse me, excuse me, General—did he insist on that
himself, that I should cease to belong to your household, as you
were pleased to express it?"

"No, but I considered myself bound to give him that satisfaction, and, of course, the Baron was satisfied. We must part,
sir. There is what is owing to you, four friedrichs d'or and
three florins, according to the reckoning here. Here is the
money, and here is the note of the account; you can verify it.
Good-bye. From this time forth we are strangers. I've had
nothing but trouble and unpleasantness from you. I will call
the *kellner* and inform him from this day forth that I am not

35

responsible for your hotel expenses. I have the honour to remain your obedient servant."

I took the money and the paper upon which the account was written in pencil, bowed to the General, and said to him very seriously—

"General, the matter cannot end like this. I am very sorry that you were put into an unpleasant position with the Baron, but, excuse me, you were to blame for it yourself. Why did you take it upon yourself to be responsible for me to the Baron? What is the meaning of the expression that I am a member of your household? I am simply a teacher in your house, that is all. I am neither your son nor your ward, and you cannot be responsible for my actions. I am a legally responsible person, I am twenty-five, I am a graduate of the university, I am a nobleman, I am not connected with you in any way. Nothing but my unbounded respect for your dignity prevents me now from demanding from you the fullest explanation and satisfaction for taking upon yourself the right to answer for me."

The General was so much amazed that he flung up his hands, then turned suddenly to the Frenchman and hurriedly informed him that I had just all but challenged him to a duel.

The Frenchman laughed aloud.

"But I am not going to let the Baron off," I said, with complete composure, not in the least embarrassed by M. de Grieux's laughter; "and as, General, you consented to listen to the Baron's complaint to-day and have taken up his cause, and have made yourself, as it were, a party in the whole affair, I have the honour to inform you that no later than to-morrow morning I shall ask the Baron on my own account for a formal explanation of the reasons which led him to apply to other persons—as though I were unable or unfit to answer for myself."

What I foresaw happened. The General, hearing of this new absurdity, became horribly nervous.

"What, do you mean to keep up this damnable business?" he shouted. "What a position you are putting me in—good heavens! Don't dare, don't dare, sir, or, I swear! . . . There are police here, too, and I . . . I . . . in fact, by my rank . . . and the Baron's, too . . . in fact, you shall be arrested and turned out of the state by the police, to teach you not to make a disturbance. Do you understand that, sir?" And although he was breathless with anger, he was also horribly frightened.

"General," I answered, with a composure that was insufferable to him, "you can't arrest anyone for making a disturbance before they have made a disturbance. I have not yet begun to make my explanations to the Baron, and you don't know in the least in what form or on what grounds I intend to proceed. I only wish to have an explanation of a position insulting to me, *i.e.* that I am under the control of a person who has authority over my freedom of action. There is no need for you to be so anxious and uneasy."

"For goodness' sake, for goodness' sake, Alexey Ivanovitch, drop this insane intention!" muttered the General, suddenly changing his wrathful tone for one of entreaty, and even clutching me by the hand. "Fancy what it will lead to! Fresh unpleasantness! You must see for yourself that I must be particular here . . . particularly now! particularly now! . . . Oh, you don't know, you don't know all my circumstances! . . . When we leave this place I shall be willing to take you back again; I was only speaking of now, in fact—of course, you understand there are reasons!" he cried in despair. "Alexey Ivanovitch, Alexey Ivanovitch . . ."

Retreating to the door, I begged him more earnestly not to worry himself, promised him that everything should go off well and with propriety, and hastily withdrew.

The Russian abroad is sometimes too easily cowed, and is horribly afraid of what people will say, how they will look at him, and whether this or that will be the proper thing. In short, they behave as though they were in corsets, especially those who have pretensions to consequence. The thing that pleases them most is a certain established traditional etiquette, which they follow slavishly in hotels, on their walks, in assemblies, on a journey . . . But the General had let slip that, apart from this, there was a particular circumstance, that he must be "particular." That was why he so weakly showed the white feather and changed his tone with me. I took this as evidence and made a note of it; and, of course, he might have brought my folly to the notice of the authorities, so that I really had to be careful.

I did not particularly want to anger the General, however; but I did want to anger Polina. Polina had treated me so badly, and had thrust me into such a stupid position, that I could not help wanting to force her to beg me to stop. My schoolboyish prank might compromise her, too. Moreover, another feeling and desire was taking shape in me: though I might be reduced to a nonentity in her presence, that did not prove that I could not hold my own before other people, or

that the Baron could thrash me. I longed to have the laugh
against them all, and to come off with flying colours. Let them
see! She would be frightened by the scandal and call me back
again, or, even if she didn't, at least she would see that I could
hold my own.

(A wonderful piece of news! I have just heard from the
nurse, whom I met on the stairs, that Marya Filippovna set off
to-day, entirely alone, by the evening train to Karlsbad to see
her cousin. What's the meaning of that? Nurse says that she
has long been meaning to go; but how was it no one knew of
it? Though perhaps I was the only one who did not know it.
The nurse let slip that Marya Filippovna had words with the
General the day before yesterday. I understand. No doubt
that is Mlle. Blanche. Yes, something decisive is coming.)

CHAPTER VII

IN the morning I called for the *kellner* and told him to make
out a separate bill for me. My room was not such an expensive one as to make me feel alarmed and anxious to leave the
hotel. I had sixteen friedrichs d'or, and there . . . there perhaps was wealth! Strange to say, I have not won yet, but I
behave, I feel and think like a rich man, and cannot imagine
anything else.

In spite of the early hour I intended to go at once to see Mr.
Astley at the Hôtel d'Angleterre, which was quite close by,
when suddenly De Grieux came in to me. That had never
happened before, and, what is more, that gentleman and I had
for some time past been on very queer and strained terms. He
openly displayed his contempt for me, even tried not to conceal
it; and I—I had my own reasons for disliking him. In short,
I hated him. His visit greatly surprised me. I at once detected
that something special was brewing.

He came in very politely and complimented me on my room.
Seeing that I had my hat in my hand, he inquired whether I
could be going out for a walk so early. When he heard that I
was going to see Mr. Astley on business, he pondered, he
reflected, and his face assumed an exceedingly careworn
expression.

De Grieux was like all Frenchmen; that is, gay and polite

when necessary and profitable to be so, and insufferably tedious when the necessity to be gay and polite was over. A Frenchman is not often naturally polite. He is always polite, as it were, to order, with a motive. If he sees the necessity for being fantastic, original, a little out of the ordinary, then his freakishness is most stupid and unnatural, and is made up of accepted and long-vulgarised traditions. The natural Frenchman is composed of the most plebeian, petty, ordinary practical sense—in fact, he is one of the most wearisome creatures in the world. In my opinion, only the innocent and inexperienced—especially Russian young ladies—are fascinated by Frenchmen. To every decent person the conventionalism of the established traditions of drawing-room politeness, ease and gaiety are at once evident and intolerable.

"I have come to see you on business," he began, with marked directness, though with courtesy, "and I will not disguise that I have come as an ambassador, or rather as a mediator, from the General. As I know Russian very imperfectly I understood very little of what passed yesterday, but the General explained it to me in detail, and I confess . . ."

"But, listen, M. de Grieux," I interrupted; "here you have undertaken to be a mediator in this affair. I am, of course, an *outchitel*, and have never laid claim to the honour of being a great friend of this family, nor of being on particularly intimate terms with it, and so I don't know all the circumstances; but explain: are you now entirely a member of the family? You take such an interest in everything and are certain at once to be a mediator . . ."

This question did not please him. It was too transparent for him, and he did not want to speak out.

"I am connected with the General partly by business, partly by *certain special* circumstances," he said dryly. "The General has sent me to ask you to abandon the intentions you expressed yesterday. All you thought of doing was no doubt very clever; but he begged me to represent to you that you would be utterly unsuccessful; what's more, the Baron will not receive you, and in any case is in a position to rid himself of any further unpleasantness on your part. You must see that yourself. Tell me, what is the object of going on with it? The General promises to take you back into his home at the first convenient opportunity, and until that time will continue your salary, *vos appointements*. That will be fairly profitable, won't it?"

I retorted very calmly that he was rather mistaken; that

perhaps I shouldn't be kicked out at the Baron's, but, on the contrary, should be listened to; and I asked him to admit that he had probably come to find out what steps I was going to take in the matter.

"Oh, heavens! Since the General is so interested, he will, of course, be glad to know how you are going to behave, and what you are going to do."

I proceeded to explain, and he began listening, stretching himself at his ease, and inclining his head on one side towards me, with an obvious, undisguised expression of irony on his face. Altogether he behaved very loftily. I tried with all my might to pretend that I took a very serious view of the matter. I explained that since the Baron had addressed a complaint of me to the General as though I were the latter's servant, he had, in the first place, deprived me thereby of my position; and secondly, had treated me as a person who was incapable of answering for himself and who was not worth speaking to. Of course, I said, I felt with justice that I had been insulted; however, considering the difference of age, position in society, and so on, and so on (I could scarcely restrain my laughter at this point), I did not want to rush into fresh indiscretion by directly insisting on satisfaction from the Baron, or even proposing a duel to him; nevertheless, I considered myself fully entitled to offer the Baron, and still more the Baroness, my apologies, especially since of late I had really felt ill, overwrought, and, so to say, fanciful, and so on, and so on. However, the Baron had, by his applying to the General, which was a slight to me, and by his insisting that the General should deprive me of my post, put me in such a position that now I could not offer him and the Baroness my apologies, because he and the Baroness and all the world would certainly suppose that I came to apologies because I was frightened and in order to be reinstated in my post. From all this it followed that I found myself now compelled to beg the Baron first of all to apologise to me in the most formal terms; for instance, to say that he had no desire to insult me. And when the Baron said this I should feel that my hands were set free, and with perfect candour and sincerity I should offer him my apologies. In brief, I concluded, I could only beg the Baron to untie my hands.

"Fie! how petty and how far-fetched! And why do you want to apologise? Come, admit, *monsieur . . . monsieur . . .* that you are doing all this on purpose to vex the General . . . and perhaps you have some special object . . . *mon cher mon-*

sieur . . . pardon, j'ai oublié votre nom, M. Alexis? . . . N'est-ce pas?"

"But excuse me, *mon cher marquis*, what has it to do with you?"

"*Mais le général . . .*"

"But what about the General? He said something last night, that he had to be particularly careful . . . and was so upset . . . but I did not understand it."

"There is, there certainly is a particular circumstance," De Grieux caught me up in an insistent voice, in which a note of vexation was more and more marked. "You know Mlle. de Cominges . . .?"

"That is, Mlle. Blanche?"

"Why, yes, Mlle. Blanche de Cominges . . . *et madame sa mère*. You see for yourself, the General . . . in short, the General is in love; in fact . . . in fact, the marriage may be celebrated here. And fancy, scandal, gossip . . ."

"I see no scandal or gossip connected with the marriage in this."

"But *le baron est si irascible un caractère Prussien, vous savez, enfin il fera une querelle d'Allemand.*"

"With me, then, and not with you, for I no longer belong to the household . . ." (I tried to be as irrational as possible on purpose.) "But, excuse me, is it settled, then, that Mlle. Blanche is to marry the General? What are they waiting for? I mean, why conceal this from us, at any rate, from the members of the household?"

"I cannot . . . however, it is not quite . . . besides . . . you know, they are expecting news from Russia; the General has to make arrangements . . ."

"*A! a! La baboulinka!*"

De Grieux looked at me with hatred.

"In short," he interrupted, "I fully rely on your innate courtesy, on your intelligence, on your tact . . . You will certainly do this for the family in which you have been received like one of themselves, in which you have been liked and respected . . ."

"Excuse me, I've been dismissed! You maintain now that that is only in appearance; but you must admit, if you were told: 'I won't send you packing, but, for the look of the thing, kindly take yourself off.'. . . You see, it comes almost to the same thing."

"Well, if that's how it is, if no request will have any influence

41

on you," he began sternly and haughtily, "allow me to assure you that steps will be taken. There are authorities here; you'll be turned out to-day—*que diable! Un blanc-bec comme vous* wants to challenge a personage like the Baron! And do you think that you will not be interfered with? And, let me assure you, nobody is afraid of you here! I have approached you on my own account, because you have been worrying the General. And do you imagine that the Baron will not order his flunkeys to turn you out of the house?"

, "But, you see, I'm not going myself," I answered, with the utmost composure. "You are mistaken, M. de Grieux; all this will be done much more decorously than you imagine. I am just setting off to Mr. Astley, and I am going to ask him to be my intermediary; in fact, to be my second. The man likes me, and certainly will not refuse. He will go to the Baron, and the Baron will receive him. Even if I am an *outchitel* and seem to be something subordinate and, well, defenceless, Mr. Astley is a nephew of a lord, of a real lord; everyone knows that— Lord Pibroch—and that lord is here. Believe me, the Baron will be courteous to Mr. Astley and will listen to him. And if he won't listen, Mr. Astley will look upon it as a personal affront (you know how persistent Englishmen are), and will send a friend to call on the Baron; he has powerful friends. You may reckon, now, upon things not turning out quite as you expect."

The Frenchman was certainly scared; all this was really very much like the truth, and so it seemed that I really might be able to get up a scandal.

"Come, I beg you," he said in a voice of actual entreaty, "do drop the whole business! It seems to please you that it will cause a scandal! It is not satisfaction you want, but a scandal! As I have told you, it is very amusing and even witty —which is perhaps what you are aiming at. But, in short," he concluded, seeing that I had got up and was taking my hat, "I've come to give you these few lines from a certain person; read them; I was charged to wait for an answer."

Saying this, he took out of his pocket a little note, folded and sealed with a wafer, and handed it to me.

It was in Polina's handwriting.

"I fancy that you intend to go on with this affair, but there are special circumstances which I will explain to you perhaps later; please leave off and give way. It is all such silliness! I need you, and you promised yourself to obey me. Remember

42

the Schlangenberg; I beg you to be obedient, and, if necessary, I command you.—Your P.

"P.S.—If you are angry with me for what happened yesterday, forgive me."

Everything seemed to be heaving before my eyes when I read these lines. My lips turned white and I began to tremble. The accursed Frenchman watched me with an exaggerated air of discretion, with his eyes turned away as though to avoid noticing my confusion. He had better have laughed at me outright.

"Very good," I answered; "tell Mademoiselle that she may set her mind at rest. Allow me to ask you," I added sharply, "why you have been so long giving me this letter. Instead of chattering about all sorts of nonsense, I think you ought to have begun with that . . . if you came expressly with that object."

"Oh, I wanted . . . all this is so strange that you must excuse my natural impatience. I was in haste to learn from you in person what you intended to do. Besides, I don't know what is in that note, and I thought there was no hurry for me to give it you."

"I understand: the long and the short of it is you were told only to give me the letter in case of the utmost necessity, and if you could settle it by word of mouth you were not to give it me. Is that right? Tell me plainly, M. de Grieux."

"*Peut-être*," he said, assuming an air of peculiar reserve, and looking at me with a peculiar glance.

I took off my hat; he took off his hat and went out. It seemed to me that there was an ironical smile on his lips. And, indeed, what else could one expect?

"We'll be quits yet, Frenchy; we'll settle our accounts," I muttered as I went down the stairs. I could not think clearly; I felt as though I had had a blow on my head. The air revived me a little.

Two minutes later, as soon as ever I was able to reflect clearly, two thoughts stood out vividly before me: the *first* was that such trivial incidents, that a few mischievous and far-fetched threats from a mere boy, had caused such *universal* consternation! The *second* thought was: what sort of influence had this Frenchman over Polina? A mere word from him and she does anything he wants—writes a note and even *begs* me. Of course, their relations have always been a mystery to me from the very beginning, ever since I began to know them;

but of late I have noticed in her a positive aversion and even contempt for him, while he did not even look at her, was absolutely rude to her. I had noticed it. Polina herself had spoken of him to me with aversion; she had dropped some extremely significant admissions . . . so he simply had her in his power. She was in some sort of bondage to him.

CHAPTER VIII

ON the promenade, as it is called here, that is, in the chestnut avenue, I met my Englishman.

"Oh, oh!" he began, as soon as he saw me. "I was coming to see you, and you are on your way to me. So you have parted from your people?"

"Tell me, first, how it is that you know all this?" I asked in amazement. "Is it possible that everybody knows of it?"

"Oh, no, everyone doesn't; and, indeed, it's not worth their knowing. No one is talking about it."

"Then how do you know it?"

"I know, that is, I chanced to learn it. Now, where are you going when you leave here? I like you and that is why I was coming to see you."

"You are a splendid man, Mr. Astley," said I (I was very much interested, however, to know where he could have learnt it), "and since I have not yet had my coffee, and most likely you have not had a good cup, come to the café in the Casino. Let us sit down and have a smoke there, and I will tell you all about it, and . . . you tell me, too . . ."

The café was a hundred steps away. They brought us some coffee. We sat down and I lighted a cigarette. Mr. Astley did not light one and, gazing at me, prepared to listen.

"I am not going anywhere. I am staying here," I began.

"And I was sure you would," observed Mr. Astley approvingly.

On my way to Mr. Astley I had not meant to tell him anything of my love for Polina, and, in fact, I expressly intended to say nothing to him about it. He was, besides, very reserved. From the first I noticed that Polina had made a great impression upon him, but he never uttered her name. But, strange to say, now no sooner had he sat down and turned upon me his

44

fixed, pewtery eyes than I felt, I don't know why, a desire to tell him everything, that is, all about my love in all its aspects. I was talking to him for half an hour and it was very pleasant to me; it was the first time I had talked of it! Noticing that at certain ardent sentences he was embarrassed, I purposely exaggerated my ardour. Only one thing I regret: I said, perhaps, more than I should about the Frenchman. . . .

Mr. Astley listened, sitting facing me without moving, looking straight into my eyes, not uttering a word, a sound; but when I spoke of the Frenchman, he suddenly pulled me up and asked me, severely, whether I had the right to refer to this circumstance which did not concern me. Mr. Astley always asked questions very strangely.

"You are right. I am afraid not," I answered.

"You can say nothing definite, nothing that is not supposition about that Marquis and Miss Polina?"

I was surprised again at such a point-blank question from a man so reserved as Mr. Astley.

"No, nothing definite," I answered; "of course not."

"If so, you have done wrong, not only in speaking of it to me, but even in thinking of it yourself."

"Very good, very good; I admit it, but that is not the point now," I interrupted, wondering at myself. At this point I told him the whole of yesterday's story in full detail: Polina's prank, my adventure with the Baron, my dismissal, the General's extraordinary dismay, and, finally, I described in detail De Grieux's visit that morning. Finally I showed him the note.

"What do you deduce from all this?" I asked. "I came on purpose to find out what you think. For my part, I could kill that Frenchman, and perhaps I shall."

"So could I," said Mr. Astley. "As regards Miss Polina, you know . . . we may enter into relations even with people who are detestable to us if we are compelled by necessity. There may be relations of which you know nothing, dependent upon outside circumstances. I think you may set your mind at rest—to some extent, of course. As for her action yesterday, it was strange, of course; not that she wanted to get rid of you and expose you to the Baron's walking-stick (I don't understand why he did not use it, since he had it in his hands), but because such a prank is improper . . . for such an . . . exquisite young lady. Of course, she couldn't have expected that you would carry out her jesting wish so literally . . ."

"Do you know what?" I cried suddenly, looking intently at Mr. Astley. "It strikes me that you have heard about this already—do you know from whom? From Miss Polina herself!"

Mr. Astley looked at me with surprise.

"Your eyes are sparkling and I can read your suspicion in them," he said, regaining his former composure; "but you have no right whatever to express your suspicions. I cannot recognise the right, and I absolutely refuse to answer your question."

"Enough! There's no need," I cried, strangely perturbed, and not knowing why it had come into my head. And when, where and how could Mr. Astley have been chosen by Polina to confide in? Though, of late, indeed, I had, to some extent, lost sight of Mr. Astley, and Polina was always an enigma to me, such an enigma that now, for instance, after launching into an account of my passion to Mr. Astley, I was suddenly struck while I was speaking by the fact that there was scarcely anything positive and definite I could say about our relations. Everything was, on the contrary, strange, unstable, and, in fact, quite unique.

"Oh, very well, very well. I am utterly perplexed and there is a great deal I can't understand at present," I answered, gasping as though I were breathless. "You are a good man, though. And now, another matter, and I ask not your advice, but your opinion."

After a brief pause I began.

"What do you think? why was the General so scared? Why did he make such a to-do over my stupid practical joke? Such a fuss that even De Grieux thought it necessary to interfere (and he interferes only in the most important matters); visited me (think of that!), begged and besought me—he, De Grieux —begged and besought me! Note, finally, he came at nine o'clock, and by that time Miss Polina's letter was in his hands. One wonders when it was written. Perhaps they waked Miss Polina up on purpose! Apart from what I see clearly from this, that Miss Polina is his slave (for she even begs my forgiveness!) —apart from that, how is she concerned in all this, she personally; why is she so much interested? Why are they frightened of some Baron? And what if the General is marrying Mlle. Blanche Cominges? They say that, owing to that circumstance, they must be *particular,* but you must admit that this is somewhat too particular! What do you think? I am sure from your eyes you know more about it than I do!"

Mr. Astley laughed and nodded.

"Certainly. I believe I know much more about it than you," he said. "Mlle. Blanche is the only person concerned, and I am sure that is the absolute truth."

"Well, what about Mlle. Blanche?" I cried impatiently. (I suddenly had a hope that something would be disclosed about Mlle. Polina.)

"I fancy that Mlle. Blanche has at the moment special reasons for avoiding a meeting with the Baron and Baroness, even more an unpleasant meeting, worse still, a scandalous one."

"Well, well . . ."

"Two years ago Mlle. Blanche was here af Roulettenburg in the season. I was here, too. Mlle. Blanche was not called Mlle. de Cominges then, and her mother, Madame la maman Cominges, was non-existent then. Anyway, she was never mentioned. De Grieux—De Grieux was not here either. I cherish the conviction that, far from being relations, they have only very recently become acquainted. He—De Grieux—has only become a marquis very recently, too—I am sure of that from one circumstance. One may assume, in fact, that his name has not been De Grieux very long either. I know a man here who has met him passing under another name."

"But he really has a very respectable circle of acquaintances."

"That may be. Even Mlle. Blanche may have. But two years ago, at the request of that very Baroness, Mlle. Blanche was invited by the police to leave the town, and she did leave it."

"How was that?"

"She made her appearance here first with an Italian, a prince of some sort, with an historical name—Barberini, or something like it—a man covered with rings and diamonds, not false ones either. They used to drive about in a magnificent carriage. Mlle. Blanche used to play *trente et quarante*, at first winning, though her luck changed later on, as far as I remember. I remember one evening she lost a considerable sum. But, worse still, *un beau matin* her prince vanished; the horses and the carriage vanished too, everything vanished. The bills owing at the hotels were immense. Mlle. Selma (she suddenly ceased to be Barberini, and became Mlle. Selma) was in the utmost despair. She was shrieking and wailing all over the hotel, and rent her clothes in her fury. There was a Polish count staying here at the hotel (all Polish travellers are counts), and Mlle. Selma, rending her garments and scratching her face like a cat with her beautiful perfumed fingers, made some impression on

47

him. They talked things over, and by dinner-time she was consoled. In the evening he made his appearance at the Casino with the lady on his arm. As usual, Mlle. Selma laughed very loudly, and her manner was somewhat more free and easy than before. She definitely showed that she belonged to the class of ladies who, when they go up to the roulette table, shoulder the other players aside to clear a space for themselves. That's particularly *chic* among such ladies. You must have noticed it?''

"Oh, yes."

"It's not worth noticing. To the annoyance of the decent public they are not moved on here—at least, not those of them who can change a thousand-rouble note every day, at the roulette table. As soon as they cease to produce a note to change they are asked to withdraw, however. Mlle. Selma still went on changing notes, but her play became more unlucky than ever. Note that such ladies are very often lucky in their play; they have a wonderful self-control. However, my story is finished. One day the Count vanished just as the Prince had done. However, Mlle. Selma made her appearance at the roulette table alone; this time no one came forward to offer her his arm. In two days she had lost everything. After laying down her last louis d'or and losing it, she looked round, and saw, close by her, Baron Burmerhelm, who was scrutinising her intently and with profound indignation. But Mlle. Selma, not noticing his indignation, accosted the Baron with that smile we all know so well, and asked him to put down ten louis d'or on the red for her. In consequence of a complaint from the Baroness she received that evening an invitation not to show herself at the Casino again. If you are surprised at my knowing all these petty and extremely improper details, it is because I have heard them from Mr. Fider, one of my relations, who carried off Mlle. Selma in his carriage from Roulettenburg to Spa that very evening. Now, remember, Mlle. Blanche wishes to become the General's wife; probably in order in future not to receive such invitations as that one from the police at the Casino, the year before last. Now she does not play; but that is because, as it seems, she has capital of her own which she lends out at a percentage to gamblers here. That's a much safer speculation. I even suspect that the luckless General is in debt to her. Perhaps De Grieux is, too. Perhaps De Grieux is associated with her. You will admit that, till the wedding, at any rate, she can hardly be anxious to attract the attention of the Baron and Baroness in any way. In short, in her position, nothing could be more disadvantageous than a scandal. You are connected with their party and your conduct might cause a scandal, especially as she appears in public every day either arm-in-arm with the General or in company with Miss Polina. Now do you understand?"

"No, I don't!" I cried, thumping the table so violently that the *garçon* ran up in alarm.

"Tell me, Mr. Astley," I said furiously. "If you knew all this story and, therefore, know positively what Mlle. Blanche de Cominges is, why didn't you warn me at least, the General, or, most of all, most of all, Miss Polina, who has shown herself here at the Casino in public, arm-in-arm with Mlle. Blanche? Can such a thing be allowed?"

"I had no reason to warn you, for you could have done nothing," Mr. Astley answered calmly. "Besides, warn them of what? The General knows about Mlle. Blanche perhaps more than I do, yet he still goes about with her and Miss Polina. The General is an unlucky man. I saw Mlle. Blanche yesterday, galloping on a splendid horse with M. de Grieux and that little Russian Prince, and the General was galloping after them on a chestnut. He told me in the morning that his legs ached, but he sat his horse well. And it struck me at that moment that he was an utterly ruined man. Besides, all this is no business of mine, and I have only lately had the honour of making Miss Polina's acquaintance. However" (Mr. Astley caught himself up), "I've told you already that I do not recognise your right to ask certain questions, though I have a genuine liking for you . . ."

"Enough," I said, getting up. "It is clear as daylight to me now that Miss Polina knows all about Mlle. Blanche, but that she cannot part from her Frenchman, and so she brings herself to going about with Mlle. Blanche. Believe me, no other influence would compel her to go about with Mlle. Blanche and to beg me in her letter not to interfere with the Baron! Damn it all, there's no understanding it!"

"You forget, in the first place, that this Mlle. de Cominges is the General's *fiancée,* and in the second place that Miss Polina is the General's stepdaughter, that she has a little brother and sister, the General's own children, who are utterly neglected by that insane man and have, I believe, been robbed by him."

"Yes, yes, that is so! To leave the children would mean abandoning them altogether; to remain means protecting their

49

interests and, perhaps, saving some fragments of their property. Yes, yes, all that is true. But still, still! . . . Ah now I understand why they are all so concerned about Granny!"

"About whom?" asked Mr. Astley.

"That old witch in Moscow who won't die, and about whom they are expecting a telegram that she is dying."

"Yes, of course, all interest is concentrated on her. Everything depends on what she leaves them! If he comes in for a fortune the General will marry, Miss Polina will be set free, and De Grieux . . ."

"Well, and De Grieux?"

"And De Grieux will be paid; that is all he is waiting for here."

"Is that all, do you think that is all he's waiting for?"

"I know nothing more." Mr. Astley was obstinately silent.

"But I do, I do!" I repeated fiercely. "He's waiting for the inheritance too, because Polina will get a dowry, and as soon as she gets the money will throw herself on his neck. All women are like that! Even the proudest of them turn into the meanest slaves! Polina is only capable of loving passionately: nothing else. That's my opinion of her! Look at her, particularly when she is sitting alone, thinking; it's something predestined, doomed, fated! She is capable of all the horrors of life, and passion . . . she . . . she . . . but who is that calling me?" I exclaimed suddenly. "Who is shouting? I heard someone shout in Russian: Alexey Ivanovitch! A woman's voice. Listen, listen!"

At this moment we were approaching the hotel. We had left the café long ago, almost without noticing it.

"I did hear a woman calling, but I don't know who was being called; it is Russian. Now I see where the shouts come from," said Mr. Astley. "It is that woman sitting in a big armchair who has just been carried up the steps by so many flunkeys. They are carrying trunks after her, so the train must have just come in."

"But why is she calling me? She is shouting again; look, she is waving to us."

"I see she is waving," said Mr. Astley.

"Alexey Ivanovitch! Alexey Ivanovitch! Mercy on us, what a dolt he is!" came desperate shouts from the hotel steps.

We almost ran to the entrance. I ran up the steps and . . . my hands dropped at my sides with amazement and my feet seemed rooted to the ground.

CHAPTER IX

AT the top of the broad steps at the hotel entrance, surrounded by footmen and maids and the many obsequious servants of the hotel, in the presence of the *ober-kellner* himself, eager to receive the exalted visitor, who had arrived with her own servants and with so many trunks and boxes, and had been carried up the steps in an invalid chair, was seated— *Granny!* Yes, it was she herself, the terrible old Moscow lady and wealthy landowner, Antonida Vassilyevna Tarasyevitchev, the *Granny* about whom telegrams had been sent and received, who had been dying and was not dead, and who had suddenly dropped upon us in person, like snow on our heads. Though she was seventy-five and had for the last five years lost the use of her legs and had to be carried about everywhere in a chair, yet she had arrived and was, as always, alert, captious, self-satisfied, sitting upright in her chair, shouting in a loud, peremptory voice and scolding everyone. In fact, she was exactly the same as she had been on the only two occasions that I had the honour of seeing her during the time I had been tutor in the General's family. Naturally I stood rooted to the spot with amazement. As she was being carried up the steps, she had detected me a hundred paces away, with her lynxlike eyes, had recognised me and called me by my name, which she had made a note of, once for all, as she always did. And this was the woman they had expected to be in her coffin, buried, and leaving them her property. That was the thought that flashed into my mind. "Why, she will outlive all of us and everyone in the hotel! But, my goodness! what will our friends do now, what will the General do? She will turn the whole hotel upside down!"

"Well, my good man, why are you standing with your eyes starting out of your head?" Granny went on shouting to me. "Can't you welcome me? Can't you say 'How do you do'? Or have you grown proud and won't? Or, perhaps, you don't recognise me? Potapitch, do you hear?" She turned to her butler, an old man with grey hair and a pink bald patch on his head, wearing a dress-coat and white tie. "Do you hear? he doesn't recognise me. They had buried me! They sent telegram upon telegram to ask whether I was dead or not! You see, I know all about it! Here, you see, I am quite alive."

"Upon my word, Antonida Vassilyevna, why should I wish you harm?" I answered gaily, recovering myself. "I was only surprised . . . And how could I help being surprised at such an unexpected . . ."

"What is there to surprise you? I just got into the train and came. The train was comfortable and not jolting. Have you been for a walk?"

"Yes, I've been a walk to the Casino."

"It's pleasant here," said Granny, looking about her. "It's warm and the trees are magnificent. I like that! Are the family at home? The General?"

"Oh, yes, at this time they are sure to be all at home."

"So they have fixed hours here, and everything in style? They set the tone. I am told they keep their carriage, *les seigneurs russes!* They spend all their money and then they go abroad. And is Praskovya with them?"

"Yes, Polina Alexandrovna, too."

"And the Frenchy? Oh, well, I shall see them all for myself. Alexey Ivanovitch, show me the way straight to him. Are you comfortable here?"

"Fairly so, Antonida Vassilyevna."

"Potapitch, tell that dolt, the *kellner,* to give me a nice convenient set of rooms, not too high up, and take my things there at once. Why are they all so eager to carry me? Why do they put themselves forward? Ech, the slavish creatures! Who is this with you?" she asked, addressing me again.

"This is Mr. Astley," I answered.

"What Mr. Astley?"

"A traveller, a good friend of mine; an acquaintance of the General's, too."

"An Englishman. To be sure, he stares at me and keeps his mouth shut. I like Englishmen, though. Well, carry me upstairs, straight to their rooms. Where are they?"

They carried Granny up; I walked up the broad staircase in front. Our procession was very striking. Everyone we met stopped and stared. Our hotel is considered the best, the most expensive, and the most aristocratic in the place. Magnificent ladies and dignified Englishmen were always to be met on the staircase and in the corridors. Many people were making inquiries below of the *ober-kellner,* who was greatly impressed. He answered, of course, that this was a distinguished foreign lady, *une russe, une comtesse, grande dame,* and that she was taking the very apartments that had been occupied the week before by *la grande duchesse de N.* Granny's commanding and authoritative appearance as she was carried up in the chair was chiefly responsible for the sensation she caused. Whenever she met anyone fresh she scrutinised him inquisitively and questioned me about him in a loud voice. Granny was powerfully built, and though she did not get up from her chair, it could be seen that she was very tall. Her back was as straight as a board and she did not lean back in her chair. Her big grey head with its large, bold features was held erect; she had a positively haughty and defiant expression; and it was evident that her air and gestures were perfectly natural. In spite of her seventy-five years there was still a certain vigour in her face: and even her teeth were almost perfect. She was wearing a black silk dress and a white cap.

"She interests me very much," Mr. Astley, who was going up beside me, whispered to me.

"She knows about the telegrams," I thought. "She knows about De Grieux, too, but I fancy she does not know much about Mlle. Blanche as yet." I communicated this thought to Mr. Astley.

Sinful man that I was, after the first surprise was over, I was immensely delighted at the thunderbolt that we were launching at the General. I was elated; and I walked in front feeling very gay.

Our apartments were on the third floor. Without announcing her arrival or even knocking at the door, I simply flung it wide open and Granny was carried in, in triumph. All of them were, as by design, assembled in the General's study. It was twelve o'clock and, I believe, some excursion was being planned for the whole party. Some were to drive, others were to ride on horseback, some acquaintances had been asked to join the party. Besides the General and Polina, with the children and their nurse, there were sitting in the study De Grieux, Mlle. Blanche, again wearing her riding-habit, her mother, the little Prince, and a learned German traveller whom I had not seen before.

Granny's chair was set down in the middle of the room, three paces from the General. My goodness! I shall never forget the sensation! As we went in the General was describing something, while De Grieux was correcting him. I must observe that Mlle. Blanche and De Grieux had for the last few days been particularly attentive to the little Prince, *à la barbe du pauvre général,* and the tone of the party was extremely gay

53

and genially intimate, though, perhaps, it was artificial. Seeing Granny, the General was struck dumb. His mouth dropped open and he broke off in the middle of a word. He gazed at her open-eyed, as though spellbound by the eye of a basilisk. Granny looked at him in silence, too, immovably, but what a triumphant, challenging and ironical look it was! They gazed at each other for ten full seconds in the midst of profound silence on the part of all around them. For the first moment De Grieux was petrified, but immediately afterwards a look of extreme uneasiness flitted over his face. Mlle. Blanche raised her eyebrows, opened her mouth and gazed wildly at Granny. The Prince and the learned German stared at the whole scene in great astonishment. Polina's eyes expressed the utmost wonder and perplexity, and she suddenly turned white as a handkerchief; a minute later the blood rushed rapidly into her face, flushing her cheeks. Yes, this was a catastrophe for all of them! I kept turning my eyes from Granny to all surrounding her and back again. Mr. Astley stood on one side, calm and polite as usual.

"Well, here I am! Instead of a telegram!" Granny broke the silence by going off into a peal of laughter. "Well, you didn't expect me?"

"Antonida Vassilyevna . . . Auntie . . . But how on earth . . ." muttered the unhappy General.

If Granny had remained silent for a few seconds longer, he would, perhaps, have had a stroke.

"How on earth what? I got into the train and came. What's the railway for? You all thought that I had been laid out, and had left you a fortune? You see, I know how you sent telegrams from here. What a lot of money you must have wasted on them! They cost a good bit from here. I simply threw my legs over my shoulders and came off here. Is this the Frenchman? M. de Grieux, I fancy?"

"*Oui, Madame,*" De Grieux responded; "*et croyez, je suis si enchanté . . . votre santé . . . c'est un miracle . . . vous voir ici . . . une surprise charmante. . . .*"

"*Charmante,* I daresay; I know you, you mummer. I haven't this much faith in you," and she pointed her little finger at him. "Who is this?" she asked, indicating Mlle. Blanche. The striking-looking Frenchwoman, in a riding-habit with a whip in her hand, evidently impressed her. "Someone living here?"

"This is Mlle. Blanche de Cominges, and this is her mamma,

Madame de Cominges; they are staying in this hotel," I explained.

"Is the daughter married?" Granny questioned me without ceremony.

"Mlle. de Cominges is an unmarried lady," I answered, purposely speaking in a low voice and as respectfully as possible.

"Lively?"

"I do not understand the question."

"You are not dull with her? Does she understand Russian? De Grieux picked it up in Moscow. He had a smattering of it."

I explained that Mlle. de Cominges had never been in Russia.

"*Bonjour,*" said Granny, turning abruptly to Mlle. Blanche.

"*Bonjour, madame.*" Mlle. Blanche made an elegant and ceremonious curtsey, hastening, under the cover of modesty and politeness, to express by her whole face and figure her extreme astonishment at such a strange question and manner of address.

"Oh, she casts down her eyes, she is giving herself airs and graces; you can see the sort she is at once; an actress of some kind. I'm stopping here below in the hotel," she said, turning suddenly to the General. "I shall be your neighbour. Are you glad or sorry?"

"Oh, Auntie! do believe in my sincere feelings . . . of pleasure," the General responded. He had by now recovered himself to some extent, and as, upon occasion, he could speak appropriately and with dignity, and even with some pretension to effectiveness, he began displaying his gifts now. "We have been so alarmed and upset by the news of your illness. . . . We received such despairing telegrams, and all at once . . ."

"Come, you are lying, you are lying," Granny interrupted at once.

"But how could you"—the General, too, made haste to interrupt, raising his voice and trying not to notice the word "lying"—"how could you bring yourself to undertake such a journey? You must admit that at your age and in your state of health . . . at any rate it is all so unexpected that our surprise is very natural. But I am so pleased . . . and we all" (he began smiling with an ingratiating and delighted air) "will try our utmost that you shall spend your season here as agreeably as possible . . ."

"Come, that's enough; that's idle chatter; you are talking nonsense, as usual. I can dispose of my time for myself.

Though I've nothing against you, I don't bear a grudge. You ask how I could come? What is there surprising about it? It was the simplest thing. And why are you so surprised? How are you, Praskovya? What do you do here?"

"How do you do, Granny?" said Polina, going up to her. "Have you been long on the journey?"

"Well, she's asked a sensible question—the others could say nothing but oh and ah! Why, you see, I lay in bed and lay in bed and was doctored and doctored, so I sent the doctors away and called in the sexton from St. Nicolas. He had cured a peasant woman of the same disease by means of hayseed. And he did me good, too. On the third day I was in a perspiration all day and I got up. Then my Germans gathered round again, put on their spectacles and began to argue. 'If you were to go abroad now,' said they, 'and take a course of the waters, all your symptoms would disappear.' And why shouldn't I? I thought. The fools of Zazhigins began sighing and moaning: 'Where are you off to?' they said. Well, so here I am! It took me a day to get ready, and the following week, on a Friday, I took a maid, and Potapitch, and the footman, Fyodor, but I sent Fyodor back from Berlin, because I saw he was not wanted, and I could have come quite alone. I took a special compartment and there are porters at all the stations, and for twenty kopecks they will carry you wherever you like. I say, what rooms he has taken!" she said in conclusion, looking about her. "How do you get the money, my good man? Why, everything you've got is mortgaged. What a lot of money you must owe to this Frenchman alone! I know all about it; you see, I know all about it!"

"Oh, Auntie. . . ." said the General, all confusion. "I am surprised, Auntie . . . I imagine that I am free to act . . . Besides, my expenses are not beyond my means, and we are here . . ."

"They are not? You say so! Then you must have robbed your children of their last farthing—you, their trustee!"

"After that, after such words," began the General, indignant, "I really don't know . . ."

"To be sure, you don't! I'll be bound you are always at roulette here? Have you whistled it all away?"

The General was so overwhelmed that he almost spluttered in the rush of his feelings.

"Roulette! I? In my position . . . I? Think what you are saying, Auntie; you must still be unwell . . ."

"Come, you are lying, you are lying. I'll be bound they can't tear you away; it's all lies! I'll have a look to-day what this roulette is like. You, Praskovya, tell me where to go and what to see, and Alexey Ivanovitch here will show me, and you, Potapitch, make a note of all the places to go to. What is there to see here?" she said, addressing Polina again.

"Close by are the ruins of the castle; then there is the Schlangenberg."

"What is it, the Schlangenberg? A wood or what?"

"No, not a wood, it's a mountain; there is a peak there . . ."

"What do you mean by a peak?"

"The very highest point on the mountain. It is an enclosed place—the view from it is unique."

"What about carrying my chair up the mountain? They wouldn't be able to drag it up, would they?"

"Oh, we can find porters," I answered.

At this moment, Fedosya, the nurse, came up to greet Granny and brought the General's children with her.

"Come, there's no need for kissing! I cannot bear kissing children, they always have dirty noses. Well, how do you get on here, Fedosya?"

"It's very, very nice here, Antonida Vassilyevna," answered Fedosya. "How have you been, ma'am? We've been so worried about you."

"I know, you are a good soul. Do you always have visitors?"—she turned to Polina again. "Who is that wretched little rascal in spectacles?"

"Prince Nilsky," Polina whispered.

"Ah, a Russian. And I thought he wouldn't understand! Perhaps he didn't hear. I have seen Mr. Astley already. Here he is again," said Granny, catching sight of him. "How do you do?"—she turned to him suddenly.

Mr. Astley bowed to her in silence.

"Have you no good news to tell me? Say something! Translate that to him, Polina."

Polina translated it.

"Yes. That with great pleasure and delight I am looking at you, and very glad that you are in good health," Mr. Astley answered seriously, but with perfect readiness. It was translated to Granny and it was evident she was pleased.

"How well Englishmen always answer," she observed. "That's why I always like Englishmen. There's no comparison between them and Frenchmen! Come and see me," she said,

57

addressing Mr. Astley again. "I'll try not to worry you too much. Translate that to him, and tell him that I am here below—here below—do you hear? Below, below," she repeated to Mr. Astley, pointing downwards.

Mr. Astley was extremely pleased at the invitation.

Granny looked Polina up and down attentively and with a satisfied air.

"I was fond of you, Praskovya," she said suddenly. "You're a fine wench, the best of the lot, and as for will—my goodness! Well, I have will too; turn round. That's not a false chignon, is it?"

"No, Granny, it's my own."

"To be sure. I don't care for the silly fashion of the day. You look very nice. I should fall in love with you if I were a young gentleman. Why don't you get married? But it is time for me to go. And I want to go out, for I've had nothing but the train and the train . . . Well, are you still cross?" she added, turning to the General.

"Upon my word, Auntie, what nonsense!" cried the General, delighted. "I understand at your age . . ."

"Cette vieille est tombée en enfance," De Grieux whispered to me.

"I want to see everything here. Will you let me have Alexey Ivanovitch?" Granny went on to the General.

"Oh, as much as you like, but I will myself . . . and Polina, M. de Grieux . . . we shall all think it a pleasure to accompany you."

"Mais, madame, cela sera un plaisir" . . . De Grieux addressed her with a bewitching smile.

"A *plaisir,* to be sure; you are absurd, my good sir. I am not going to give you any money, though," she added suddenly. "But now to my rooms; I must have a look at them, and then we'll go the round of everything. Come, lift me up." Granny was lifted up again and we all flocked downstairs behind her chair. The General walked as though stunned by a blow on the head. De Grieux was considering something. Mlle. Blanche seemed about to remain, but for some reason she made up her mind to come with the rest. The Prince followed her at once, and no one was left in the General's study but Madame de Cominges and the German.

CHAPTER X

AT watering-places and, I believe, in Europe generally, hotel-keepers and *ober-kellners,* in assigning rooms to their visitors, are guided not so much by the demands and desires of the latter as by their own personal opinion of them, and, one must add, they are rarely mistaken. But for some reason I cannot explain, they had assigned Granny such a splendid suite that they had quite overshot the mark. It consisted of four splendidly furnished rooms with a bathroom, quarters for the servants and a special room for the maid, and so on. Some *grande duchesse* really had been staying in those rooms the week before, a fact of which the new occupant was informed at once, in order to enhance the value of the apartments. Granny was carried, or rather wheeled, through all the rooms, and she looked at them attentively and severely. The *ober-kellner,* an elderly man with a bald head, followed her respectfully at this first survey.

I don't know what they all took Granny to be, but apparently for a very important and, above all, wealthy lady. They put down in the book at once: *"Madame la générale princesse de Tarasyevitchev,"* though Granny had never been a princess. Her servants, her special compartment in the train, the mass of useless bags, portmanteaux, and even chests that had come with Granny probably laid the foundation of her prestige; while her invalid-chair, her abrupt tone and voice, her eccentric questions, which were made with the most unconstrained air that would tolerate no contradiction—in short, Granny's whole figure, erect, brisk, imperious—increased the awe in which she was held by all. As she looked at the rooms, Granny sometimes told them to stop her chair, pointed to some object in the furniture and addressed unexpected questions to the *ober-kellner,* who still smiled respectfully, though he was beginning to feel nervous. Granny put her questions in French, which she spoke, however, rather badly, so that I usually translated. The *ober-kellner's* answers for the most part did not please her and seemed unsatisfactory. And, indeed, she kept asking about all sorts of things quite irrelevant. Suddenly, for instance, stopping before a picture, a rather feeble copy of some well-known picture of a mythological subject, she would ask:

"Whose portrait is that?"

The *ober-kellner* replied that no doubt it was some countess.

c

"How is it you don't know? You live here and don't know. Why is it here? Why is she squinting?"

The *ober-kellner* could not answer these questions satisfactorily, and positively lost his head.

"Oh, what a blockhead!" commented Granny, in Russian. She was wheeled on. The same performance was repeated with a Dresden statuette, which Granny looked at for a long time, and then ordered them to remove, no one knew why. Finally, she worried the *ober-kellner* about what the carpets in the bedroom cost, and where they had been woven! The *ober-kellner* promised to make inquiries.

"What asses," Granny grumbled, and concentrated her whole attention on the bed. "What a gorgeous canopy! Open the bed."

They opened the bed.

"More, more, turn it all over. Take off the pillows, the pillows, lift up the feather bed."

Everything was turned over. Granny examined it attentively.

"It's a good thing there are no bugs. Take away all the linen! Make it up with my linen and my pillows. But all this is too gorgeous. Such rooms are not for an old woman like me. I shall be dreary all alone. Alexey Ivanovitch, you must come and see me very often when your lessons with the children are over."

"I left the General's service yesterday," I answered, "and am living in the hotel quite independently."

"How is that?"

"A German of high rank, a Baron, with his Baroness, came here from Berlin the other day. I addressed him yesterday in German without keeping to the Berlin accent."

"Well, what then?"

"He thought it an impertinence and complained to the General, and yesterday the General discharged me."

"Why, did you swear at the Baron, or what? (though if you had it wouldn't have mattered!)"

"Oh, no. On the contrary, the Baron raised his stick to thrash me."

"And did you, sniveller, allow your tutor to be treated like that?" she said suddenly, addressing the General; "and turned him out of his place too! Noodles! you're all a set of noodles, as I see."

"Don't disturb yourself, Auntie," said the General, with a

shade of condescending familiarity; "I can manage my own business. Besides, Alexey Ivanovitch has not given you quite a correct account of it."

"And you just put up with it?"—she turned to me.

"I meant to challenge the Baron to a duel," I answered, as calmly and modestly as I could, "but the General opposed it."

"Why did you oppose it?"—Granny turned to the General again. ("And you can go, my good man; you can come when you are called," she said, addressing the *ober-kellner;* "no need to stand about gaping. I can't endure this Nürnberg rabble!")

The man bowed and went out, not, of course, understanding Granny's compliments.

"Upon my word, Auntie, surely a duel was out of the question."

"Why out of the question? Men are all cocks; so they should fight. You are all noodles, I see, you don't know how to stand up for your country. Come, take me up, Potapitch; see that there are always two porters: engage them. I don't want more than two. I shall only want them to carry me up and down stairs, and to wheel me on the levels in the street. Explain that to them; and pay them beforehand—they will be more respectful. You will always be with me yourself, and you, Alexey Ivanovitch, point out that Baron to me when we are out: that I may have a look at the von Baron. Well, where is the roulette?"

I explained that the roulette tables were in rooms in the Casino. Then followed questions: Were there many of them? Did many people play? Did they play all day long? How was it arranged? I answered at last that she had much better see all this with her own eyes, and that it was rather difficult to describe it.

"Well, then, take me straight there! You go first, Alexey Ivanovitch!"

"Why, Auntie, don't you really mean to rest after your journey?" the General asked anxiously. He seemed rather flurried, and, indeed, they all seemed embarrassed and were exchanging glances. Probably they all felt it rather risky and, indeed, humiliating to accompany Granny to the Casino, where, of course, she might do something eccentric, and in public; at the same time they all proposed to accompany her.

"Why should I rest? I am not tired and, besides, I've been sitting still for three days. And then we will go and see the

springs and medicinal waters; where are they? And then . . .
we'll go and see, what was it you said, Praskovya?—peak,
wasn't it?''

"Yes, Granny."

"Well, peak, then, if it is a peak. And what else is there
here?"

"There are a great many objects of interest, Granny," Polina
exerted herself to say.

"Why don't you know them! Marfa, you shall come with
me, too," she said, addressing her maid.

"But why should she come?" the General said fussily; "and
in fact it's out of the question, and I doubt whether Potapitch
will be admitted into the Casino."

"What nonsense! Am I to abandon her because she is a
servant? She's a human being, too; here we have been on our
travels for a week; she wants to have a look at things, too.
With whom could she go except me? She wouldn't dare show
her nose in the street by herself."

"But, Granny . . ."

"Why, are you ashamed to be with me? Then stay at home;
you are not asked. Why, what a General! I am a General's
widow myself. And why should you all come trailing after me?
I can look at it all with Alexey Ivanovitch."

But De Grieux insisted that we should all accompany her,
and launched out into the most polite phrases about the
pleasure of accompanying her, and so on. We all started.

"Elle est tombée en enfance," De Grieux repeated to the
General; *"seule, elle fera des bêtises . . ."* I heard nothing
more, but he evidently had some design, and, possibly, his
hopes had revived.

It was half a mile to the Casino. The way was through an
avenue of chestnuts to a square, going round which, they came
out straight on the Casino. The General was to some extent
reassured, for our procession, though somewhat eccentric, was,
nevertheless, decorous and presentable. And there was nothing
surprising in the fact of an invalid who could not walk putting
in an appearance at the Casino; but, anyway, the General was
afraid of the Casino; why should an invalid unable to walk, and
an old lady, too, go into the gambling saloon? Polina and Mlle.
Blanche walked on each side of the bath-chair. Mlle. Blanche
laughed, was modestly animated and even sometimes jested
very politely with Granny, so much so that the latter spoke of
her approvingly at last. Polina, on the other side, was obliged

to be continually answering Granny's innumerable questions, such as: "Who was that passed? Who was that woman driving past? Is it a big town? Is it a big garden? What are those trees? What's that hill? Do eagles fly here? What is that absurd-looking roof?" Mr. Astley walked beside me and whispered that he expected a great deal from that morning. Potapitch and Marfa walked in the background close behind the bath-chair, Potapitch in his swallow-tailed coat and white tie, but with a cap on his head, and Marfa (a red-faced maidservant, forty years old and beginning to turn grey) in a cap, cotton gown, and creaking goatskin slippers. Granny turned to them very often and addressed remarks to them. De Grieux was talking with an air of determination. Probably he was reassuring the General, evidently he was giving him some advice. But Granny had already pronounced the fatal phrase: "I am not going to give you money." Perhaps to De Grieux this announcement sounded incredible, but the General knew his aunt. I noticed that De Grieux and Mlle. Blanche were continually exchanging glances. I could distinguish the Prince and the German traveller at the farther end of the avenue; they had stopped, and were walking away from us.

Our visit to the Casino was a triumph. The porters and attendants displayed the same deference as in the hotel. They looked at us, however, with curiosity. Granny began by giving orders that she should be wheeled through all the rooms. Some she admired, others made no impression on her; she asked questions about them all. At last we came to the roulette room. The lackeys, who stood like sentinels at closed doors, flung the doors wide open as though they were impressed.

Granny's appearance at the roulette table made a profound impression on the public. At the roulette tables and at the other end of the room, where there was a table with *trente et quarante,* there was a crowd of a hundred and fifty or two hundred players, several rows deep. Those who had succeeded in squeezing their way right up to the table, held fast, as they always do, and would not give up their places to anyone until they had lost; for simple spectators were not allowed to stand at the tables and occupy the space. Though there were chairs set round the table, few of the players sat down, especially when there was a great crowd, because standing one could get closer and consequently pick out one's place and put down one's stake more conveniently. The second and the third rows pressed up upon the first, waiting and watching for their turn;

but sometimes a hand would be impatiently thrust forward through the first row to put down a stake. Even from the third row people managed to seize chances of poking forward their stakes; consequently every ten or even five minutes there was some "scene" over disputed stakes at one end of the hall or another. The police of the Casino were, however, fairly good. It was, of course, impossible to prevent crowding; on the contrary, the owners were glad of the rush of people because it was profitable, but eight croupiers sitting round the table kept a vigilant watch on the stakes: they even kept count of them, and when disputes arose they could settle them. In extreme cases they called in the police, and the trouble was over in an instant. There were police officers in plain clothes stationed here and there among the players, so that they could not be recognised. They were especially on the look-out for thieves and professional pickpockets, who are very numerous at the roulette tables, as it affords them excellent opportunity for exercising their skill. The fact is, elsewhere thieves must pick pockets or break locks, and such enterprises, when unsuccessful, have a very troublesome ending. But in this case the thief has only to go up to the roulette table, begin playing, and all at once, openly and publicly, take another person's winnings and put them in his pocket. If a dispute arises, the cheat insists loudly that the stake was his. If the trick is played cleverly and the witnesses hesitate, the thief may often succeed in carrying off the money, if the sum is not a very large one, of course. In that case the croupiers or some one of the other players are almost certain to have been keeping an eye on it. But if the sum is not a large one, the real owner sometimes actually declines to keep up the dispute, and goes away shrinking from the scandal. But if they succeed in detecting a thief, they turn him out at once with contumely.

All this Granny watched from a distance with wild curiosity. She was much delighted at a thief's being turned out. *Trente et quarante* did not interest her very much; she was more pleased at roulette and the rolling of the little ball. She evinced a desire at last to get a closer view of the game. I don't know how it happened, but the attendants and other officious persons (principally Poles who had lost, and who pressed their services on lucky players and foreigners of all sorts) at once, and in spite of the crowd, cleared a place for Granny in the very middle of the table beside the chief croupier, and wheeled her chair to it. A number of visitors who were not playing, but watching the play (chiefly Englishmen with their families), at once crowded round the table to watch Granny from behind the players. Numbers of lorgnettes were turned in her direction. The croupiers' expectations rose. Such an eccentric person certainly seemed to promise something out of the ordinary. An old woman of seventy, who could not walk, yet wished to play, was, of course, not a sight to be seen every day. I squeezed my way up to the table too, and took my stand beside Granny. Potapitch and Marfa were left somewhere in the distance among the crowd. The General, Polina, De Grieux, and Mlle. Blanche stood aside, too, among the spectators.

At first Granny began looking about at the players. She began in a half whisper asking me abrupt, jerky questions. Who was that man and who was this woman? She was particularly delighted by a young man at the end of the table who was playing for very high stakes, putting down thousands, and had, as people whispered around, already won as much as forty thousand francs, which lay before him in heaps of gold and banknotes. He was pale; his eyes glittered and his hands were shaking; he was staking now without counting, by handfuls, and yet he kept on winning and winning, kept raking in the money. The attendants hung about him solicitously, set a chair for him, cleared a place round him that he might have more room, that he might not be crowded—all this in expectation of a liberal tip. Some players, after they have won, tip the attendants without counting a handful of coins in their joy. A Pole had already established himself at his side, and was deferentially but continually whispering to him, probably telling him what to stake on, advising and directing his play—of course, he, too, expecting a tip later on! But the player scarcely looked at him. He staked at random and kept winning. He evidently did not know what he was doing.

Granny watched him for some minutes.

"Tell him," Granny said suddenly, growing excited and giving me a poke, "tell him to give it up, to take his money quickly and go away. He'll lose it all directly, he'll lose it all!" she urged, almost breathless with agitation. "Where's Potapitch? Send Potapitch to him. Come, tell him, tell him," she went on, poking me. "Where is Potapitch? *Sortez! Sortez!*" —she began herself shouting to the young man.

I bent down to her and whispered resolutely that she must not shout like this here, that even talking aloud was forbidden, because it hindered counting and that we should be turned out directly.

"How vexatious! The man's lost! I suppose it's his own doing. . . . I can't look at him, it quite upsets me. What a dolt!" and Granny made haste to turn in another direction.

On the left, on the other side of the table, there was conspicuous among the players a young lady, and beside her a sort of dwarf. Who this dwarf was, and whether he was a relation or brought by her for the sake of effect, I don't know. I had noticed the lady before; she made her appearance at the gambling table every day, at one o'clock in the afternoon, and went away exactly at two; she always played for an hour. She was already known, and a chair was set for her at once. She took out of her pocket some gold, some thousand-franc notes, and began staking quietly, coolly, prudently, making pencil notes on a bit of paper of the numbers about which the chances grouped themselves, and trying to work out a system. She staked considerable sums. She used to win every day—one, two, or at the most three thousand francs—not more, and instantly went away. Granny scrutinised her for a long time.

"Well, that one won't lose! That one there won't lose! Of what class is she? Do you know? Who is she?"

"She must be a Frenchwoman, of a certain class, you know," I whispered.

"Ah, one can tell the bird by its flight. One can see she has a sharp claw. Explain to me now what every turn means and how one has to bet!"

I explained as far as I could to Granny all the various points on which one could stake: *rouge et noir, pair et impair, manque et passe,* and finally the various subtleties in the system of the numbers. Granny listened attentively, remembered, asked questions, and began to master it. One could point to examples of every kind, so that she very quickly and readily picked up a great deal.

"But what about zéro?. You see that croupier, the curly-headed one, the chief one, showed zéro just now? And why did he scoop up everything that was on the table? Such a heap, he took it all for himself. What is the meaning of it?"

"Zéro, Granny, means that the bank wins all. If the little ball falls on zéro, everything on the table goes to the bank. It is true you can stake your money so as to keep it, but the bank pays nothing."

"You don't say so! And shall I get nothing?"

"No, Granny, if before this you had staked on zéro you would have got thirty-five times what you staked."

"What! thirty-five times, and does it often turn up? Why don't they stake on it, the fools."

"There are thirty-six chances against it, Granny."

"What nonsense. Potapitch! Potapitch! Stay, I've money with me—here." She took out of her pocket a tightly packed purse, and picked out of it a friedrich d'or. "Stake it on the zéro at once."

"Granny, zéro has only just turned up," I said; "so now it won't turn up for a long time. You will lose a great deal; wait a little, anyway."

"Oh, nonsense; put it down!"

"As you please, but it may not turn up again till the evening. You may go on staking thousands; it has happened."

"Oh, nonsense, nonsense. If you are afraid of the wolf you shouldn't go into the forest. What? Have I lost? Stake again!"

A second friedrich d'or was lost: she staked a third. Granny could scarcely sit still in her seat. She stared with feverish eyes at the little ball dancing on the spokes of the turning wheel. She lost a third, too. Granny was beside herself, she could not sit still, she even thumped on the table with her fist when the croupier announced "trente-six" instead of the zéro she was expecting.

"There, look at it," said Granny angrily; "isn't that cursed little zéro coming soon? As sure as I'm alive, I'll sit here till zéro does come! It's that cursed curly-headed croupier's doing; he'll never let it come! Alexey Ivanovitch, stake two gold pieces at once! Staking as much as you do, even if zéro does come you'll get nothing by it."

"Granny!"

"Stake, stake! it is not your money."

I staked two friedrichs d'or. The ball flew about the wheel for a long time, at last it began dancing about the spokes. Granny was numb with excitement, and squeezed my fingers, and all at once—

"Zéro!" boomed the croupier.

"You see, you see!"—Granny turned to me quickly, beaming and delighted. "I told you so. The Lord Himself put it into my head to stake those two gold pieces! Well, how much do I get now? Why don't they give it me? Potapitch, Marfa, where are they? Where have all our people got to? Potapitch, Potapitch!"

"Granny, afterwards," I whispered; "Potapitch is at the door, they won't let him in. Look, Granny, they are giving you the money, take it!" A heavy roll of printed blue notes, worth fifty friedrichs d'or, was thrust towards Granny and twenty friedrich d'or were counted out to her. I scooped it all up in a shovel and handed it to Granny.

"Faites le jeu, messieurs! Faites le jeu, messieurs! Rien ne va plus!" called the croupier, inviting the public to stake, and preparing to turn the wheel.

"Heavens! we are too late. They're just going to turn it. Put it down, put it down!" Granny urged me in a flurry. "Don't dawdle, make haste!" She was beside herself and poked me with all her might.

"What am I to stake it on, Granny?"

"On zéro, on zéro! On zéro again! Stake as much as possible! How much have we got altogether? Seventy friedrichs d'or. There's no need to spare it. Stake twenty friedrichs d'or at once."

"Think what you are doing, Granny! sometimes it does not turn up for two hundred times running! I assure you, you may go on staking your whole fortune."

"Oh, nonsense, nonsense! Put it down! How your tongue does wag! I know what I'm about." Granny was positively quivering with excitement.

"By the regulations it's not allowed to stake more than twelve roubles on zéro at once, Granny; here I have staked that."

"Why is it not allowed? Aren't you lying? Monsieur! Monsieur!"—she nudged the croupier, who was sitting near her on the left, and was about to set the wheel turning. *"Combien zéro? Douze? Douze?"*

I immediately interpreted the question in French.

"Oui, madame," the croupier confirmed politely; "as the winnings from no single stake must exceed four thousand florins by the regulations," he added in explanation.

"Well, there's no help for it, stake twelve."

"Le jeu est fait," cried the croupier. The wheel rotated, and thirty turned up. She had lost.

"Again, again, again! Stake again!" cried Granny. I no longer resisted, and, shrugging my shoulders, staked another twelve friedrichs d'or. The wheel turned a long time. Granny was simply quivering as she watched the wheel. "Can she really imagine that zéro will win again?" I thought, looking at

68

her with wonder. Her face was beaming with a firm conviction of winning, an unhesitating expectation that in another minute they would shout zéro. The ball jumped into the cage.

"Zéro!" cried the croupier.

"What!!!" Granny turned to me with intense triumph.

I was a gambler myself, I felt that at the moment my arms and legs were trembling, there was a throbbing in my head. Of course, this was a rare chance that zéro should have come up three times in some dozen turns; but there was nothing particularly wonderful about it. I had myself seen zéro turn up three times *running* two days before, and a gambler who had been zealously noting down the lucky numbers, observed aloud that, only the day before, zéro had turned up only once in twenty-four hours.

Granny's winnings were counted out to her with particular attention and deference as she had won such a large sum. She received four hundred and twenty friedrichs d'or, that is, four thousand florins and seventy friedrichs d'or. She was given twenty friedrichs d'or in gold, and four thousand florins in banknotes.

This time Granny did not call Potapitch; she had other preoccupations. She did not even babble or quiver outwardly! She was, if one may so express it, quivering inwardly. She was entirely concentrated on something, absorbed in one aim.

"Alexey Ivanovitch, he said that one could only stake four thousand florins at once, didn't he? Come, take it, stake the whole four thousand on the red," Granny commanded.

It was useless to protest; the wheel began rotating.

"*Rouge*," the croupier proclaimed.

Again she had won four thousand florins, making eight in all.

"Give me four, and stake four again on red," Granny commanded.

Again I staked four thousand.

"*Rouge*," the croupier pronounced again.

"Twelve thousand altogether! Give it me all here. Pour the gold here into the purse and put away the notes. That's enough! Home! Wheel my chair out."

CHAPTER XI

THE chair was wheeled to the door at the other end of the room. Granny was radiant. All our party immediately thronged round her with congratulations. However eccentric Granny's behaviour might be, her triumph covered a multitude of sins, and the General was no longer afraid of compromising himself in public by his relationship with such a strange woman. With a condescending and familiarly good-humoured smile, as though humouring a child, he congratulated Granny. He was, however, evidently impressed, like all the other spectators. People talked all round and pointed at Granny. Many passed by to get a closer view of her! Mr. Astley was talking of her aside, with two English acquaintances. Some majestic ladies gazed at her with majestic amazement, as though at a marvel . . . De Grieux positively showered congratulations and smiles upon her.

"*Quelle victoire!*" he said.

"*Mais, Madame, c'était du feu,*" Mlle. Blanche commented, with an ingratiating smile.

"Yes, I just went and won twelve thousand florins! Twelve, indeed; what about the gold? With the gold it makes almost thirteen. What is that in our money? Will it be six thousand?"

I explained that it made more than seven, and in the present state of exchange might even amount to eight.

"Well, that's something worth having, eight thousand! And you stay here, you noodles, and do nothing! Potapitch, Marfa, did you see?"

"My goodness! how did you do it, Ma'am? Eight thousand!" exclaimed Marfa, wriggling.

"There! there's five gold pieces for you, here!"

Potapitch and Marfa flew to kiss her hand.

"And give the porters, too, a friedrich d'or each. Give it them in gold, Alexey Ivanovitch. Why is that flunkey bowing and the other one too? Are they congratulating me? Give them a friedrich d'or too."

"*Madame la princesse . . . un pauvre expatrié . . . malheur continuel . . . les princes russes sont si généreux . . .*" A person with moustaches and an obsequious smile, in a threadbare coat and gay-coloured waistcoat, came cringing about Granny's chair, waving his hat in his hand.

"Give him a friedrich d'or too. . . . No, give him two; that's enough, or there will be no end to them. Lift me up and carry me out. Praskovya"—she turned to Polina Alexandrovna—"I'll buy you a dress to-morrow, and I'll buy Mlle. . . . what's her name, Mlle. Blanche, isn't it? I'll buy her a dress too. Translate that to her, Praskovya!"

"Merci, Madame." Mlle. Blanche made a grateful curtsey while she exchanged an ironical smile with De Grieux and the General. The General was rather embarrassed and was greatly relieved when we reached the avenue.

"Fedosya—won't Fedosya be surprised," said Granny, thinking of the General's nurse. "I must make her a present of a dress. Hey, Alexey Ivanovitch, Alexey Ivanovitch, give this to the poor man."

A man in rags, with bent back, passed us on the road, and looked at us.

"And perhaps he is not a poor man, but a rogue, Granny."

"Give him a gulden, give it him!"

I went up to the man and gave it him. He looked at me in wild amazement, but took the gulden, however. He smelt of spirits.

"And you, Alexey Ivanovitch. Have you not tried your luck yet?"

"No, Granny."

"But your eyes were burning, I saw them."

"I shall try, Granny, I certainly shall later."

"And stake on zéro straight away. You will see! How much have you in hand?"

"Only twenty friedrichs d'or, Granny."

"That's not much. I will give you fifty friedrichs d'or. I will lend it if you like. Here, take this roll—but don't you expect anything, all the same, my good man, I am not going to give you anything," she said, suddenly addressing the General.

The latter winced, but he said nothing. De Grieux frowned.

"Que diable, c'est une terrible vieille!" he muttered to the General through his teeth.

"A beggar, a beggar, another beggar!" cried Granny. "Give him a gulden, too, Alexey Ivanovitch."

This time it was a grey-headed old man with a wooden leg, in a long-skirted blue coat and with a long stick in his hand. He looked like an old soldier. But when I held out a gulden to him he stepped back and looked at me angrily.

"Was ist's der Teufel," he shouted, following up with a dozen oaths.

"Oh, he's a fool," cried Granny, dismissing him with a wave of her hand. "Go on! I'm hungry! Now we'll have dinner directly; then I'll rest a little, and back here again."

"You want to play again, Granny!" I cried.

"What do you expect? That you should all sit here and sulk while I watch you?"

"Mais, madame—" De Grieux drew near—*"les chances peuvent tourner, une seule mauvaise chance et vous perdrez tout . . . surtout avec votre jeu . . . C'est terrible!"*

"Vous perdrez absolument," chirped Mlle. Blanche.

"But what is it to do with all of you? I shouldn't lose your money, but my own! And where is that Mr. Astley?" she asked me.

"He stayed in the Casino, Granny."

"I'm sorry, he's such a nice man."

On reaching home Granny met the *ober-kellner* on the stairs, called him and began bragging of her winnings; then she sent for Fedosya, made her a present of three friedrichs d'or and ordered dinner to be served. Fedosya and Marfa hovered over her at dinner.

"I watched you, ma'am," Marfa cackled, "and said to Potapitch, 'What does our lady want to do?' And the money on the table—saints alive! the money! I haven't seen so much money in the whole of my life, and all round were gentlefolk—nothing but gentlefolk sitting. 'And wherever do all these gentlefolk come from, Potapitch?' said I. May our Lady Herself help her, I thought. I was praying for you, ma'am, and my heart was simply sinking, simply sinking; I was all of a tremble. Lord help her, I thought, and here the Lord has sent you luck. I've been trembling ever since, ma'am. I'm all of a tremble now."

"Alexey Ivanovitch, after dinner, at four o'clock, get ready and we'll go. Now good-bye for a time; don't forget to send for a doctor for me. I must drink the waters, too. Go, or maybe you'll forget."

As I left Granny I was in a sort of stupor. I tried to imagine what would happen now to all our people and what turn things would take. I saw clearly that they (especially the General) had not yet succeeded in recovering from the first shock. The fact of Granny's arrival instead of the telegram which they were expecting from hour to hour to announce her death (and consequently the inheritance of her fortune) had so completely shattered the whole fabric of their plans and intentions that

Granny's further exploits at roulette threw them into positive bewilderment and a sort of stupefaction seemed to have come over all of them.

Meanwhile this second fact was almost more important than the first; for though Granny had repeated twice that she would not give the General any money, yet, who knows?—there was no need to give up all hope yet. De Grieux, who was involved in all the General's affairs, had not lost hope. I am convinced that Mlle. Blanche, also much involved in the General's affairs (I should think so: to marry a General and with a considerable fortune!), would not have given up hope, and would have tried all her fascinating arts upon Granny—in contrast with the proud and incomprehensible Polina, who did not know how to curry favour with anyone. But now, now that Granny had had such success at roulette, now that Granny's personality had shown itself so clearly and so typically (a refractory and imperious old lady, *et tombée en enfance*), now, perhaps, all was lost. Why, she was as pleased as a child, so pleased that she would go on till she was ruined and had lost everything. Heavens! I thought (and, God forgive me, with a malignant laugh), why, every friedrich d'or Granny staked just now must have been a fresh sore in the General's heart, must have maddened De Grieux and infuriated Mlle. de Cominges, who saw the cup slipping from her lips. Another fact: even in her triumph and joy of winning, when Granny was giving money away to everyone, and taking every passer-by for a beggar, even then she had let fall to the General, "I'm not going to give you anything, though!" That meant that she had fastened upon that idea, was sticking to it, had made up her mind about it. There was danger! danger!

All these reflections were revolving in my mind as I mounted the front stairs from Granny's apartments to my garret in the very top storey. All this interested me strongly. Though, of course, I could before have divined the strongest leading motives prompting the actors before me, yet I did not know for certain all the mysteries and intrigues of the drama. Polina had never been fully open with me. Though it did happen at times that she revealed her feelings to me, yet I noticed that almost always after such confidences she would make fun of all she had said, or would try to obscure the matter and put it in a different light. Oh, she had hidden a great deal! In any case, I foresaw that the *dénouement* of this mysterious and constrained position was at hand. One more shock—and everything would be ended and revealed. About my fortunes, which were also involved in all this, I scarcely troubled. I was in a strange mood: I had only twenty friedrichs d'or in my pocket; I was in a foreign land without a job or means of livelihood, without hope, without prospects, and—I did not trouble my head about it! If it had not been for the thought of Polina, I should have abandoned myself to the comic interest of the approaching catastrophe, and would have been shouting with laughter. But I was troubled about Polina; her fate was being decided, I divined that; but I regret to say that it was not altogether her fate that troubled me. I wanted to fathom her secrets; I wanted her to come to me and say: "I love you," and if not that, if that was senseless insanity, then . . . well, what was there to care about? Did I know what I wanted? I was like one demented: all I wanted was to be near her, in the halo of her glory, in her radiance, always, for ever, all my life. I knew nothing more! And could I leave her?

In their passage on the third storey I felt as though something nudged me. I turned round and, twenty paces or more from me, I saw coming out of a door, Polina. She seemed waiting: and as soon as she saw me beckoned to me.

"Polina Alexandrovna . . ."

"Hush!" she said.

"Imagine," I whispered to her, "I felt as though someone had nudged me just now; I looked round—you! It seems as though there were a sort of electricity from you!"

"Take this letter," Polina articulated anxiously with a frown, probably not hearing what I had said, "and give it into Mr. Astley's own hands at once. Make haste, I beg you. There is no need of an answer. He will . . ."

She did not finish.

"Mr. Astley?" I repeated in surprise.

But Polina had already disappeared behind the door.

"Aha, so they are in correspondence!" I ran at once, of course, to Mr. Astley; first to his hotel, where I did not find him, then to the Casino, where I hurried through all the rooms: and at last, as I was returning home in vexation, almost in despair, I met him by chance, with a party of Englishmen and Englishwomen on horseback. I beckoned to him, stopped him and gave him the letter: we had not time even to exchange a glance. But I suspect that Mr. Astley purposely gave rein to his horse.

Was I tortured by jealousy? Anyway, I was in an utterly shattered condition. I did not even want to find out what they were writing to one another about. And so he was trusted by her! "Her friend, her friend," I thought, "and that is clear (and when has he had time to become her friend?), but is there love in the case? Of course not," common-sense whispered to me. But common-sense alone counts for little in such cases; anyway, this, too, had to be cleared up. Things were growing unpleasantly complicated.

Before I had time to go into the hotel, first the porter and then the *ober-kellner*, coming out of his room, informed me that I was wanted, that I had been asked for, three times they had sent to ask: where was I?—that I was asked to go as quickly as possible to the General's rooms. I was in the most disagreeable frame of mind. In the General's room I found, besides the General himself, De Grieux and Mlle. Blanche—alone, without her mother. The mother was evidently an official one, only used for show. But when it came to real *business* she acted for herself. And probably the woman knew little of her so-called daughter's affairs.

They were, however, consulting warmly about something, and the doors of the study were actually locked—which had never happened before. Coming to the door, I heard loud voices—De Grieux's insolent and malignant voice, Blanche's shrill fury, and the General's pitiful tones, evidently defending himself about something. Upon my entrance they all, as it were, pulled themselves up and restrained themselves. De Grieux smoothed his hair and forced a smile into his angry face—that horrid official French smile which I so detest. The crushed and desperate General tried to assume an air of dignity, but it was a mechanical effort. Only Mlle. Blanche's countenance, blazing with anger, scarcely changed. She only ceased speaking while she fixed her eyes upon me in impatient expectation. I may mention that hitherto she had treated me with extraordinary casualness, had even refused to respond to my bows, and had simply declined to see me.

"Alexey Ivanovitch," the General began in a soft and mollifying tone; "allow me to tell you that it is strange, exceedingly strange . . . in fact, your conduct in regard to me and my family . . . in fact, it is exceedingly strange . . ."

"*Eh! ce n'est pas ça,*" De Grieux interposed, with vexation and contempt. (There's no doubt he was the leading spirit.) "*Mon cher monsieur, notre cher général se trompe,* in taking up this tone" (I translate the rest of his speech in Russian), "but he meant to say . . . that is to warn you, or rather to beg

75

you most earnestly not to ruin him—yes, indeed, not to ruin him! I make use of that expression."

"But how, how?" I interrupted.

"Why, you are undertaking to be the guide (or how shall I express it?) of this old woman, *cette pauvre terrible vieille"*— De Grieux himself hesitated—"but you know she'll lose everything; she will gamble away her whole fortune! You know yourself, you have seen yourself, how she plays! If she begins to lose; she will never leave off, from obstinacy, from anger, and will lose everything, she will gamble away everything, and in such cases one can never regain one's losses and then . . . then . . ."

"And then," the General put in, "then you will ruin the whole family! I and my family are her heirs, she has no nearer relations. I tell you openly: my affairs are in a bad way, a very bad way. You know my position to some extent . . . If she loses a considerable sum or even (Lord help us!) her whole fortune, what will become of me, of my children!" (The General looked round at De Grieux.) "Of me." (He looked round at Mlle. Blanche, who turned away from him with contempt.) "Alexey Ivanovitch, save us, save us! . . ."

"But how, General, how, how can I? . . . What influence have I in the matter?"

"Refuse, refuse, give her up! . . ."

"Then someone else will turn up," I said.

"Ce n'est pas ça, ce n'est pas ça," De Grieux interrupted again, *"que diable!* No, don't desert her, but at least advise her, dissuade her, draw her away . . . don't let her play too much, distract her in some way."

"But how can I do that? If you would undertake the task yourself, M. de Grieux," I added, as naïvely as I could.

Here I caught a rapid, fiery, questioning glance from Mlle. Blanche at M. de Grieux. And in De Grieux's own face there was something peculiar, something he could not himself disguise.

"The point is, she won't accept me now!" De Grieux cried, with a wave of his hand. "If only . . . later on . . ."

De Grieux looked rapidly and meaningly at Mlle. Blanche.

"O, mon cher M. Alexis, soyez si bon." Mlle. Blanche herself took a step towards me with a most fascinating smile, she seized me by both hands and pressed them warmly. Damn it all! That diabolical face knew how to change completely in one moment. At that instant her face was so imploring, so sweet, it was such a child-like and even mischievous smile; at

the end of the phrase she gave me such a sly wink, unseen by all the rest; she meant to do for me completely, and it was successfully done; only it was horribly coarse.

Then the General leapt up, positively leapt up. "Alexey Ivanovitch, forgive me for beginning as I did just now. I did not mean that at all. . . . I beg you, I beseech you, I bow down before you in Russian style—you alone, you alone can save us. Mlle. de Cominges and I implore you—you understand, you understand, of course." He besought me, indicating Mlle. Blanche with his eyes. He was a very pitiful figure.

At that instant there came three subdued and respectful knocks at the door; it was opened—the corridor attendant was knocking and a few steps behind him stood Potapitch. They came with messages from Granny; they were charged to find and bring me at once. "She is angry," Potapitch informed me.

"But it is only half-past three."

"She could not get to sleep; she kept tossing about, and then at last she got up, sent for her chair and for you. She's at the front door now."

"*Quelle mégère*," cried De Grieux.

I did, in fact, find Granny on the steps, out of all patience at my not being there. She could not wait till four o'clock.

"Come," she cried, and we set off again to roulette.

CHAPTER XII

GRANNY was in an impatient and irritable mood; it was evident that roulette had made a deep impression on her mind. She took no notice of anything else and was altogether absent-minded. For instance, she asked me no questions on the road as she had done before. Seeing a luxurious carriage whirling by, she was on the point of raising her hand and asking: What is it? Whose is it?—but I believe she did not hear what I answered: her absorption was continually interrupted by abrupt and impatient gesticulations. When I pointed out to her Baron and Baroness Burmerhelm, who were approaching the Casino, she looked absent-mindedly at them and said, quite indifferently, "Ah!" and, turning round quickly to Potapitch and Marfa, who were walking behind her, snapped out to them—

"Why are you hanging upon us? We can't take you every

77

time! Go home! You and I are enough," she added, when they had hurriedly turned and gone home.

They were already expecting Granny at the Casino. They immediately made room for her in the same place, next to the croupier. I fancy that these croupiers, who are always so strictly decorous and appear to be ordinary officials who are absolutely indifferent as to whether the bank wins or loses, are by no means so unconcerned at the bank's losses and, of course, receive instructions for attracting players and for augmenting the profits—for which they doubtless receive prizes and bonuses. They looked upon Granny, anyway, as their prey.

Then just what we had expected happened.

This was how it was.

Granny pounced at once on zèro and immediately ordered me to stake twelve friedrichs d'or. She staked once, twice, three times—zéro never turned up.

"Put it down! Put it down!" Granny nudged me, impatiently. I obeyed.

"How many times have we staked?" she asked at last, grinding her teeth with impatience.

"I have staked twelve times, Granny. I have put down a hundred and forty-four friedrichs d'or. I tell you, Granny, very likely till evening . . ."

"Hold your tongue!" Granny interrupted. "Stake on zéro, and stake at once a thousand gulden on red. Here, take the note."

Red won, and zéro failed once more; a thousand gulden was gained.

"You see, you see!" whispered Granny, "we have gained almost all that we have lost. Stake again on zéro; we'll stake ten times more and then give it up."

But the fifth time Granny was thoroughly sick of it.

"The devil take that filthy zéro. Come, stake the whole four thousand gulden on the red," she commanded me.

"Granny! it will be so much; why, what if red does not turn up!" I besought her; but Granny almost beat me. (Indeed, she nudged me so violently that she might almost be said to have attacked me.) There was no help for it. I staked on red the whole four thousand won that morning. The wheel turned. Granny sat calmly and proudly erect, never doubting that she would certainly win.

"Zéro!" boomed the croupier.

At first Granny did not understand, but when she saw the

croupier scoop up her four thousand gulden, together with everything on the table, and learned that zéro, which had not turned up for so long and on which we had staked in vain almost two hundred friedrichs d'or, had, as though to spite her, turned up just as Granny was abusing it, she groaned and flung up her hands in view of the whole hall. People around actually laughed.

"Holy saints! The cursed thing has turned up!" Granny wailed, "the hateful, hateful thing! That's your doing! It's all your doing"—she pounced upon me furiously, pushing me.

"It was you persuaded me."

"Granny, I talked sense to you; how can I answer for chance?"

"I'll chance you," she whispered angrily. "Go away."

"Good-bye, Granny." I turned to go away.

"Alexey Ivanovitch, Alexey Ivanovitch! stop. Where are you off to? Come, what's the matter, what's the matter? Ach, he's in a rage! Stupid, come, stay, stay; come, don't be angry; I am a fool myself! Come, tell me what are we to do now!"

"I won't undertake to tell you, Granny, because you will blame me. Play for yourself, tell me and I'll put down the stakes."

"Well, well! Come, stake another four thousand gulden on red! Here, take my pocket-book." She took it out of her pocket and gave it me. "Come, make haste and take it, there's twenty thousand roubles sterling in it."

"Granny," I murmured, "such stakes . . ."

"As sure as I am alive, I'll win it back. . . . Stake."

We staked and lost.

"Stake, stake the whole eight!"

"You can't, Granny, four is the highest stake! . . ."

"Well, stake four!"

This time we won. Granny cheered up.

"You see, you see," she nudged me; "stake four again!"

She staked—she lost; then we lost again and again.

"Granny, the whole twelve thousand is gone," I told her.

"I see it's all gone," she answered with the calm of fury, if I may so express it. "I see, my good friend, I see," she muttered, with a fixed, as it were, absent-minded stare. "Ech, as sure I am alive, stake another four thousand gulden!"

"But there's no money, Granny; there are some of our Russian five per cents and some bills of exchange of some sort, but no money."

"And in the purse?"

"There's some small change, Granny."

"Are there any money-changers here? I was told one could change any of our notes," Granny inquired resolutely.

"Oh, as much as you like, but what you'll lose on the exchange . . . would horrify a Jew!"

"Nonsense! I'll win it all back. Take me! Call those blockheads!"

I wheeled away the chair; the porters appeared and we went out of the Casino.

"Make haste, make haste, make haste," Granny commanded. "Show us the way, Alexey Ivanovitch, and take us the nearest . . . Is it far?"

"Two steps, Granny."

But at the turning from the square into the avenue we were met by our whole party: the General, De Grieux, Mlle. Blanche and her mamma. Polina Alexandrovna was not with them, nor Mr. Astley either.

"Well! Don't stop us!" cried Granny. "Well, what do you want? I have no time to spare for you now!"

I walked behind; De Grieux ran up to me.

"She's lost all she gained this morning and twelve thousand gulden as well. We are going to change some five per cents," I whispered to him quickly.

De Grieux stamped and ran to tell the General. We went on wheeling Granny.

"Stop, stop!" the General whispered to me frantically.

"You try stopping her," I whispered.

"Auntie!" said the General, approaching, "Auntie . . . we are just . . . we are just . . ." his voice quivered and failed him, "hiring a horse and driving into the country . . . a most exquisite view . . . the peak . . . We were coming to invite you."

"Oh, bother you and your peak." Granny waved him off irritably.

"There are trees there . . . we will have tea . . ." the General went on, utterly desperate.

"*Nous boirons du lait, sur l'herbe fraîche,*" added De Grieux, with ferocious fury.

Du lait, de l'herbe fraîche, that is the Paris bourgeois notion of the ideally idyllic; that is, as we all know, his conception of *nature et la vérité!*

"Oh, go on with you and your milk! Lap it up yourself;

it gives me the bellyache. And why do you pester me?'' cried Granny. "I tell you I've no time to waste."

"It's here, Granny," I said; "it's here!"

We had reached the house where the bank was. I went in to change the notes; Granny was left waiting at the entrance; De Grieux, the General and Blanche stood apart waiting, not knowing what to do. Granny looked wrathfully at them, and they walked away in the direction of the Casino.

They offered me such ruinous terms that I did not accept them, and went back to Granny for instructions.

"Ah, the brigands!" she cried, flinging up her hands. "Well, never mind! Change it," she cried resolutely; "stay, call the banker out to me!"

"One of the clerks, Granny, do you mean?"

"Yes, a clerk, it's all the same. Ach, the brigands!"

The clerk consented to come when he learned that it was an invalid and aged countess, unable to come in, who was asking for him. Granny spent a long time loudly and angrily reproaching him for swindling her, and haggled with him in a mixture of Russian, French and German, while I came to the rescue in translating. The grave clerk listened to us in silence and shook his head. He looked at Granny with an intent stare that was hardly respectful; at last he began smiling.

"Well, get along with you," cried Granny. "Choke yourself with the money! Change it with him, Alexey Ivanovitch; there's no time to waste, or we would go elsewhere. . . ."

"The clerk says that other banks give even less."

I don't remember the sums exactly, but the banker's charges were terrible. I received close upon twelve thousand florins in gold and notes, took the account and carried it to Granny.

"Well, well, well, it's no use counting it," she said, with a wave of her hand. "Make haste, make haste, make haste!"

"I'll never stake again on that damned zéro nor on the red either," she pronounced, as she was wheeled up to the Casino.

This time I did my very utmost to impress upon her the necessity of staking smaller sums, trying to persuade her that with the change of luck she would always be able to increase her stake. But she was so impatient that, though she agreed at first, it was impossible to restrain her when the play had begun; as soon as she had won a stake of ten, of twenty friedrichs d'ors——

"There, you see, there, you see,' she would begin nudging

81

me; "there, you see, we've won; if only we had staked four thousand instead of ten, we should have won four thousand, but, as it is, what's the good? It's all your doing, all your doing!"

And, vexed as I felt, watching her play, I made up my mind at last to keep quiet and to give no more advice.

Suddenly De Grieux skipped up.

The other two were close by; I noticed Mlle. Blanche standing on one side with her mother, exchanging amenities with the Prince. The General was obviously out of favour, almost banished. Blanche would not even look at him, though he was doing his utmost to cajole her! The poor General! He flushed and grew pale by turns, trembled and could not even follow Granny's play. Blanche and the Prince finally went away; the General ran after them.

"Madame, madame," De Grieux whispered in a honeyed voice to Granny, squeezing his way close up to her ear. "Madame, such stakes do not answer. . . . No, no, it's impossible . . ." he said, in broken Russian. "No!"

"How, then? Come, show me!" said Granny, turning to him.

De Grieux babbled something rapidly in French, began excitedly advising, said she must wait for a chance, began reckoning some numbers. . . . Granny did not understand a word. He kept turning to me, for me to translate; tapped the table with his fingers, pointed; finally took a pencil and was about to reckon something on paper. At last Granny lost patience.

"Come, get away, get away! You keep talking nonsense! 'Madame, madame,' he doesn't understand it himself; go away."

"Mais, madame," De Grieux murmured, and he began once more showing and explaining.

"Well, stake once as he says," Granny said to me; "let us see: perhaps it really will answer."

All De Grieux wanted was to dissuade her from staking large sums; he suggested that she should stake on numbers, either individually or collectively. I staked as he directed, a friedrich d'or on each of the odd numbers in the first twelve and five friedrichs d'or respectively on the groups of numbers from twelve to eighteen and from eighteen to twenty-four, staking in all sixteen friedrichs d'or.

The wheel turned.

"Zéro," cried the croupier.

We had lost everything.

"You blockhead!" cried Granny, addressing De Grieux. "You scoundrelly Frenchman! So this is how he advises, the monster. Go away, go away! He knows nothing about it and comes fussing round!"

Fearfully offended, De Grieux shrugged his shoulders, looked contemptuously at Granny, and walked away. He felt ashamed of having interfered; he had been in too great a hurry.

An hour later, in spite of all our efforts, we had lost everything.

"Home," cried Granny.

She did not utter a single word till we got into the avenue. In the avenue and approaching the hotel she began to break into exclamations:

"What a fool! What a silly fool! You're an old fool, you are!"

As soon as we got to her apartments—

"Tea!" cried Granny. "And pack up at once! We are going!"

"Where does your honour mean to go?" Marfa was beginning.

"What has it to do with you? Mind your own business! Potapitch, pack up everything: all the luggage. We are going back to Moscow. I have thrown away fifteen thousand roubles!"

"Fifteen thousand, madame! My God!" Potapitch cried, flinging up his hands with deep feeling, probably meaning to humour her.

"Come, come, you fool! He is beginning to whimper! Hold your tongue! Pack up! The bill, make haste, make haste!"

"The next train goes at half-past nine, Granny," I said, to check her furore.

"And what is it now?"

"Half-past seven."

"How annoying! Well, it doesn't matter! Alexey Ivanovitch, I haven't a farthing. Here are two more notes. Run there and change these for me too. Or I have nothing for the journey."

I set off. Returning to the hotel half an hour later, I found our whole party at Granny's. Learning that Granny was going off to Moscow, they seemed to be even more upset than by her losses. Even though her going might save her property, what was to become of the General? Who would pay De Grieux? Mlle. Blanche would, of course, decline to wait for Granny to die and would certainly now make up to the Prince or to somebody else. They were all standing before Granny, trying to console her and persuade her. Again Polina was not there. Granny was shouting at them furiously.

"Let me alone, you devils! What business is it of yours? Why does that goat's-beard come forcing himself upon me?" she cried at De Grieux; "and you, my fine bird?" she cried, addressing Mlle. Blanche, "what are you after?"

"*Diantre!*" whispered Mlle. Blanche, with an angry flash of her eyes, but suddenly she burst out laughing and went out of the room.

"*Elle vivra cent ans!*" she called to the General, as she went out of the door.

"Ah, so you are reckoning on my death?" Granny yelled to the General. "Get away! Turn them all out, Alexey Ivanovitch! What business is it of yours? I've fooled away my own money, not yours!"

The General shrugged his shoulders, bowed and went out. De Grieux followed him.

"Call Praskovya," Granny told Marfa.

Five minutes later Marfa returned with Polina. All this time Polina had been sitting in her own room with the children, and I fancy had purposely made up her mind not to go out all day. Her face was serious, sad and anxious.

"Praskovya," began Granny, "is it true, as I learned by accident just now, that that fool, your stepfather, means to marry that silly feather-head of a Frenchwoman—an actress is she, or something worse? Tell me, is it true?"

"I don't know anything about it for certain, Granny," answered Polina, "but from the words of Mlle. Blanche herself, who does not feel it necessary to conceal anything, I conclude . . ."

"Enough," Granny broke in vigorously, "I understand! I always reckoned that he was capable of it and I have always thought him a most foolish and feather-headed man. He thinks no end of himself, because he is a General (he was promoted from a Colonel on retiring), and he gives himself airs. I know, my good girl, how you kept sending telegram after telegram to Moscow, to ask if your old Granny would soon be laid out. They were on the look-out for my money; without money that nasty hussy, what's her name—de Cominges—wouldn't take

84

him for her footman, especially with his false teeth. She has a lot of money herself, they say, lends at interest, has made a lot. I am not blaming you, Praskovya, it wasn't you who sent the telegrams; and I don't want to remember the past, either. I know you've got a bad temper—a wasp! You can sting to hurt; but I'm sorry for you because I was fond of your mother, Katerina. Well, you throw up everything here and come with me. You've nowhere to go, you know; and it's not fitting for you to be with them now. Stop!" cried Granny, as Polina was about to speak; "I've not finished. I ask nothing of you. As you know, I have in Moscow a palace; you can have a whole storey to yourself and not come and see me for weeks at a time if my temper does not suit you! Well, will you or not?"

"Let me ask you first: do you really mean to set off at once?"

"Do you suppose I'm joking, my good girl! I've said I'm going and I'm going. I've wasted fifteen thousand roubles to-day over your damned roulette. Five years ago I promised to rebuild a wooden church with stone on my estate near Moscow, and instead of that I've thrown away my money here. Now, my girl, I'm going home to build the church."

"And the waters, Granny? You came to drink the waters?"

"Bother you and the waters, too. Don't irritate me, Praskovya; are you doing it on purpose? Tell me, will you come or not?"

"I thank you very, very much," Polina began, with feeling, "for the home you offer me. You have guessed my position to some extent. I am so grateful to you that I shall perhaps come to you soon; but now there are reasons . . . important reasons . . . and I can't decide at once, on the spur of the moment. If you were staying only a fortnight . . ."

"You mean you won't?"

"I mean I can't. Besides, in any case I can't leave my brother and sister, as . . . as . . . as it may actually happen that they may be left abandoned, so . . . if you would take me with the children, Granny, I certainly would come, and, believe me, I would repay you for it!" she added warmly; "but without the children I can't come, Granny."

"Well, don't whimper" (Polina had no intention of whimpering—indeed, I had never seen her cry). "Some place will be found for the chickens, my henhouse is big enough. Besides, it is time they were at school. Well, so you are not coming now! Well, Praskovya, mind! I wished for your good, but

I know why you won't come! I know all about it, Praskovya. That Frenchman will bring you no good."

Polina flushed crimson. I positively shuddered. (Everyone knows all about it. I am the only one to know nothing!)

"Come, come, don't frown. I am not going to say anything more. Only take care no harm comes of it, understand. You are a clever wench; I shall be sorry for you. Well, that's enough. I should not like to look on you as on the others! Go along, good-bye!"

"I'll come to see you off," said Polina.

"There's no need, don't you interfere; I am sick of you all."

Polina was kissing Granny's hand, but the latter pulled it away and kissed her on the cheek.

As she passed me, Polina looked at me quickly and immediately turned away her eyes.

"Well, good-bye to you, too, Alexey Ivanovitch, there's only an hour before the train starts, and I think you must be tired out with me. Here, take these fifty pieces of gold."

"I thank you very much, Granny; I'm ashamed . . ."

"Come, come!" cried Granny, but so vigorously and angrily that I dared say no more and took it.

"When you are running about Moscow without a job come to me: I will give you some introductions. Now, get along with you!"

I went to my room and lay down on my bed. I lay there for half an hour on my back, with my hands clasped behind my head. The catastrophe had come at last, I had something to think about. I made up my mind to talk earnestly to Polina. The nasty Frenchman! So it was true then! But what could there be at the bottom of it? Polina and De Grieux! Heavens! what a pair!

It was all simply incredible. I suddenly jumped up, beside myself, to look for Mr. Astley, and at all costs to make him speak out. No doubt in this matter, too, he knew more than I did. Mr. Astley? He was another riddle to me!

But suddenly there was a tap at my door. I looked up. It was Potapitch.

"Alexey Ivanovitch, you are wanted to come to my lady!"

"What's the matter? Is she setting off? The train does not start for twenty minutes."

"She's uneasy, she can't sit still. 'Make haste, make haste!' she says, meaning to fetch you, sir. For Christ's sake, don't delay."

86

I ran downstairs at once. Granny was being wheeled out into the passage, her pocket-book was in her hand.

"Alexey Ivanovitch, go on ahead; we're coming."

"Where, Granny?"

"As sure as I'm alive, I'll win it back. Come, march, don't ask questions! Does the play go on there till midnight?"

I was thunderstruck. I thought a moment, but at once made up my mind.

"Do as you please, Antonida Vassilyevna, I'm not coming."

"What's that for? What now? Have you all eaten too many pancakes, or what?"

"Do as you please, I should blame myself for it afterwards; I won't. I won't take part in it or look on at it; spare me, Antonida Vassilyevna. Here are your fifty friedrichs d'or back; good-bye!" And, laying the fifty friedrichs d'or on the little table near which Granny's chair was standing, I bowed and went out.

"What nonsense!" Granny shouted after me. "Don't come if you don't want to, I can find the way by myself! Potapitch, come with me! Come, lift me up, carry me!"

I did not find Mr. Astley and returned home. It was late, after midnight, when I learned from Potapitch how Granny's day ended. She lost all that I had changed for her that evening —that is, in Russian money, another ten thousand roubles. The little Pole, to whom she had given two friedrichs d'or the day before, had attached himself to her and had directed her play the whole time. At first, before the Pole came, she had made Potapitch put down the stakes, but soon she dismissed him; it was at that moment the Pole turned up. As ill-luck would have it, he understood Russian and babbled away in a mixture of three languages, so that they understood each other after a fashion. Granny abused him mercilessly the whole time; and though he incessantly "laid himself at his lady's feet," "yet he couldn't be compared with you, Alexey Ivanovitch," said Potapitch. "She treated you *like a gentleman,* while the other—I saw it with my own eyes, God strike me dead—stole her money off the table. She caught him at it herself twice. She did give it to him with all sorts of names, sir, even pulled his hair once, upon my word she did, so that folks were laughing round about. She's lost everything, sir, everything, all you changed for her; we brought her back here—she only asked for a drink of water, crossed herself and went to bed. She's worn out, to be sure; she fell asleep at once. God send her heavenly dreams. Och! these foreign parts!" Potapitch wound up. "I said it would lead to no good. If only we could soon be back in Moscow! We'd everything we wanted at home in Moscow: a garden, flowers such as you don't have here, fragrance, the apples are swelling, plenty of room everywhere. No, we had to come abroad. Oh, oh, oh . . ."

CHAPTER XIII

NOW almost a whole month has passed since I touched these notes of mine, which were begun under the influence of confused but intense impressions. The catastrophe which I felt to be approaching has actually come, but in a form a hundred times more violent and startling than I had expected. It has all been something strange, grotesque and even tragic— at least for me. Several things have happened to me that were almost miraculous; that is, at least, how I look upon them to this day—though from another point of view, particularly in the whirl of events in which I was involved at that time, they were only somewhat out of the common. But what is most marvellous to me is my own attitude to all these events. To this day I cannot understand myself, and it has all floated by like a dream—even my passion—it was violent and sincere, but . . . what has become of it now? It is true that sometimes the thought flashes through my brain: "Wasn't I out of my mind then, and wasn't I all that time somewhere in a madhouse and perhaps I'm there now, so that was all my fancy and still is my fancy . . ." I put my notes together and read them over. (Who knows—perhaps to convince myself that I did not write them in a madhouse.) Now I am entirely alone. Autumn is coming on and the leaves are turning yellow. I'm still in this dismal little town (oh, how dismal the little German towns are!), and instead of considering what to do next, I go on living under the influence of the sensations I have just passed through, under the influence of memories still fresh, under the influence of the whirl of events which caught me up and flung me aside again. At times I fancy that I am still caught up in that whirlwind, that that storm is still raging, carrying me along with it, and again I lose sight of all order and measure and I whirl round and round again. . . .

88

However, I may, perhaps, leave off whirling and settle down in a way if, so far as I can, I put clearly before my mind all the incidents of the past month. I feel drawn to my pen again. Besides, I have sometimes nothing at all to do in the evenings. I am so hard up for something to do that, odd as it seems, I even take from the scurvy lending library here the novels of Paul de Kock (in a German translation), though I can't endure them; yet I read them and wonder at myself. It is as though I were afraid of breaking the spell of the recent past by a serious book or any serious occupation. It is as though that grotesque dream, with all the impressions left by it, was so precious to me that I am afraid to let anything new touch upon it for fear it should all vanish in smoke. Is it all so precious to me? Yes, of course it is precious. Perhaps I shall remember it for forty years . . .

And so I take up my writing again. I can give a brief account of it to some extent now: the impressions are not at all the same.

In the first place, to finish with Granny. The following day she lost everything. It was what was bound to happen. When once anyone is started upon that road, it is like a man in a sledge flying down a snow mountain more and more swiftly. She played all day till eight o'clock in the evening; I was not present and only know what happened from what I was told.

Potapitch was in attendance on her at the Casino all day. Several Poles in succession guided Granny's operations in the course of the day. She began by dismissing the Pole whose hair she had pulled the day before and taking on another, but he turned out almost worse. After dismissing the second, and accepting again the first, who had never left her side, but had been squeezing himself in behind her chair and continually poking his head in during the whole period of his disgrace, she sank at last into complete despair. The second Pole also refused to move away; one stationed himself on her right and the other on her left. They were abusing one another the whole time and quarrelling over the stakes and the game, calling each other *"laidak"* and other Polish civilities, making it up again, putting down money recklessly and playing at random. When they quarrelled they put the money down regardless of each other—one, for instance, on the red and the other on the black. It ended in their completely bewildering and overwhelming Granny, so that at last, almost in tears, she appealed to the old croupier, begging him to protect her and to send them away. They were, in fact, immediately turned out in spite of their outcries and protests; they both shouted out at once and tried to prove that Granny owed them something, that she had deceived them about something and had treated them basely and dishonourably. The luckless Potapitch told me all this the same evening almost with tears, and complained that they stuffed their pockets with money, that he himself had seen them shamelessly steal and continually thrust the money in their pockets. One, for instance, would beg five friedrichs d'or for his trouble and begin putting them down on the spot side by side with Granny's stakes. Granny won, but the man shouted that his stake was the winning one and that Granny's had lost. When they were dismissed Potapitch came forward and said that their pockets were full of gold. Granny at once bade the croupier to look into it and, in spite of the outcries of the Poles (they cackled like two cocks caught in the hand), the police came forward and their pockets were immediately emptied for Granny's benefit. Granny enjoyed unmistakable prestige among the croupiers and the whole staff of the Casino all that day, until she had lost everything. By degrees her fame spread all over the town. All the visitors at the watering-place, of all nations, small and great, streamed to look on at *"une vieille comtesse russe tombée en enfance"*, who had already lost "some millions".

But Granny gained very, very little by being rescued from the two Poles. They were at once replaced by a third, who spoke perfectly pure Russian and was dressed like a gentleman, though he did look like a flunkey with a huge moustache and a sense of his own importance. He, too, "laid himself at his lady's feet and kissed them," but behaved haughtily to those about him, was despotic over the play; in fact, immediately behaved like Granny's master rather than her servant. Every minute, at every turn in the game, he turned to her and swore with awful oaths that he was himself a *"pan* of good position", and that he wouldn't take a kopeck of Granny's money. He repeated this oath so many times that Granny was completely intimidated. But as this *pan* certainly seemed at first to improve her luck, Granny was not willing to abandon him on her own account. An hour later the two Poles who had been turned out of the Casino turned up behind Granny's chair again, and again proffered their services if only to run errands for her. Potapitch swore that the *"pan* of good position" winked at them and even put something in their hands. As Granny had no dinner and could not leave her chair, one of the Poles certainly was of use: he ran off at once to the dining-room of the Casino and brought her a cup of broth and afterwards some tea. They both ran about, however. But towards the end of the day, when it became evident to everyone that she would stake her last banknote, there were behind her chair as many as six Poles who had never been seen or heard of before. When Granny was playing her last coin, they not only ceased to obey her, but took no notice of her whatever, squeezed their way up to the table in front of her, snatched the money themselves, put down the stakes and made their own play, shouted and quarrelled, talked to the "*pan* of good position" as to one of themselves, while the "*pan* of good position" himself seemed almost oblivious of Granny's existence. Even when Granny, after losing everything, was returning after eight o'clock to the hotel, three or four Poles ran at the side of her bath-chair, still unable to bring themselves to leave her; they kept shouting at the top of their voices, declaring in a hurried gabble that Granny had cheated them in some way and must give them something. They followed her in this way right up to the hotel, from which they were at last driven away with blows.

By Potapitch's reckoning Granny had lost in all ninety thousand roubles that day, apart from what she had lost the day before. All her notes, her exchequer bonds, all the shares she had with her, she had changed, one after another. I marvelled how she could have stood those seven or eight hours sitting there in her chair and scarcely leaving the table, but Potapitch told me that three or four times she had begun winning considerably; and, carried on by fresh hope, she could not tear herself away. But gamblers know how a man can sit for almost twenty-four hours at cards, without looking to right or to left.

Meanwhile, very critical events were taking place all that day at the hotel. In the morning, before eleven o'clock, when Granny was still at home, our people—that is, the General and De Grieux—made up their minds to take the final step. Learning that Granny had given up all idea of setting off, but was going back to the Casino, they went in full conclave (all but Polina) to talk things over with her finally and even *openly*. The General, trembling and with a sinking heart in view of the awful possibilities for himself, overdid it. After spending half an hour in prayers and entreaties and making a clean breast of everything—that is, of all his debts and even his passion for Mlle. Blanche (he quite lost his head), the General suddenly adopted a menacing tone and even began shouting and stamping at Granny; cried that she was disgracing their name, had become a scandal to the whole town, and finally . . . finally: "You are shaming the Russian name," cried the General, and he told her that the police would be called in! Granny finally drove him from her with a stick (an actual stick). The General and De Grieux consulted once or twice that morning, and the question that agitated them was whether it were not possible in some way to bring in the police, on the plea that an unfortunate but venerable old lady, sinking into her dotage, was gambling away her whole fortune, and so on; whether, in fact, it would be possible to put her under any sort of supervision or restraint. . . . But De Grieux only shrugged his shoulders and laughed in the General's face, as the latter pranced up and down his study talking excitedly. Finally, De Grieux went off with a wave of his hand. In the evening we heard that he had left the hotel altogether, after having been in very earnest and mysterious confabulation with Mlle. Blanche. As for Mlle. Blanche, she had taken her measures early in the morning: she threw the General over completely and would not even admit him to her presence. When the General ran to the Casino in search of her and met her arm-in-arm with the Prince, neither she nor Madame de Cominges deigned to notice him. The Prince did not bow to him either. Mlle Blanche spent that whole day hard at work upon the Prince, trying to force from him a definite declaration. But alas! she was cruelly deceived in her reckoning! This little catastrophe took place in the evening. It suddenly came out that he was as poor as a church mouse, and, what is more, was himself reckoning on borrowing from her on an IOU to try his luck at roulette. Blanche turned him out indignantly and locked herself up in her room.

On the morning of that day I went to Mr. Astley—or, to be more exact, I went in search of Mr. Astley, but could find him nowhere. He was not at home, or in the park, or in the Casino. He was not dining at his hotel that day. It was past four o'clock when I suddenly saw him walking from the railway station towards the Hôtel d'Angleterre. He was in a hurry and was very much preoccupied, though it was hard to trace any anxiety or any perturbation whatever in his face. He held out his hand to me cordially, with his habitual exclamation:

"Ah!" but without stopping walked on with rather a rapid step. I attached myself to him, but he managed to answer me in such a way that I did not succeed in even asking him about anything. Moreover, I felt, for some reason, ashamed to begin speaking of Polina; he did not ask a word about her. I told him about Granny. He listened attentively and seriously and shrugged his shoulders.

"She will gamble away everything," I observed.

"Oh, yes," he answered; "she went in to play just as I was going away, and afterwards I learnt for a fact that she had lost everything. If there were time I would look in at the Casino, for it is curious."

"Where have you been?" I cried, wondering that I had not asked before.

"I've been in Frankfort."

"On business?"

"Yes, on business."

Well, what more was there for me to ask? I did, however, continue walking beside him, but he suddenly turned into the Hôtel des Quatre Saisons, nodded to me and vanished. As I walked home I gradually realised that if I had talked to him for a couple of hours I should have learnt absolutely nothing, because. . . I had nothing to ask him! Yes, that was so, of course! I could not possibly formulate my question.

All that day Polina spent walking with the children and their nurse in the park, or sitting at home. She had for a long time past avoided the General, and scarcely spoke to him about any-thing—about anything serious, at any rate. I had noticed that for a long time past. But knowing what a position the General was in to-day, I imagined that he could hardly pass her over—that is, there could not but be an important conversation about family affairs between them. When, however, I returned to the hotel, after my conversation with Mr. Astley, I met Polina with the children. There was an expression of the most un-ruffled calm on her face, as though she alone had remained untouched by the family tempest. She nodded in response to my bow. I returned home feeling quite malignant.

I had, of course, avoided seeing her and had seen nothing of her since the incident with the Burmerhelms. There was some affectation and pose in this; but as time went on, I felt more and more genuinely indignant. Even if she did not care for me in the least, she should not, I thought, have trampled on my feelings like that and have received my declarations so contemptuously. She knew that I really loved her; she admitted me, she allowed me to speak like that! It is true that it had begun rather strangely. Some time before, long ago, in fact, two months before, I began to notice that she wanted to make me her friend, her *confidant,* and indeed was in a way testing me. But somehow this did not come off then; instead of that there remained the strange relations that existed between us; that is how it was I began to speak to her like that. But if my love repelled her, why did she not directly forbid me to speak of it?

She did not forbid me; indeed she sometimes provoked me to talk of it and . . . and, of course, she did this for fun. I know for certain. I noticed it unmistakably—it was agreeable to her to listen and to work me up to a state of misery, to wound me by some display of the utmost contempt and disregard. And, of course, she knew that I could not exist without her. It was three days since the affair with the Baron and I could not endure our separation any longer. When I met her just now near the Casino, my heart throbbed so that I turned pale. But she could not get on without me, either! She needed me and— surely, surely not as a buffoon, a clown?

She had a secret—that was clear! Her conversation with Granny had stabbed my heart. Why, I had urged her a thousand times to be open with me, and she knew that I was ready to give my life for her. But she had always put me off, almost with contempt, or had asked of me, instead of the sacrifice of my life, such pranks as the one with the Baron!

Was not that enough to make one indignant? Could that Frenchman be all the world to her? And Mr. Astley? But at that point the position became utterly incomprehensible—and meanwhile, my God! what agonies I went through.

On getting home, in an access of fury I snatched up my pen and scribbled the following letter to her:

"Polina Alexandrovna, I see clearly that the *dénouement* is at hand which will affect you also. I repeat for the last time: do you need my life or not? If I can be of use in *any way whatever,* dispose of me as you think fit, and I will meanwhile remain in my room and not go out at all. If you need me, write to me or send for me."

I sealed up this note and sent it off by the corridor attendant, instructing him to give it into her hands. I expected no answer, but three minutes later the attendant returned with the message that "she sent her greetings".

It was past six when I was summoned to the General.

He was in his study, dressed as though he were on the point of going out. His hat and coat were lying on the sofa. It seemed to me as I went in that he was standing in the middle of the room with his legs wide apart and his head hanging, talking aloud to himself. But as soon as he saw me, he rushed at me almost crying out, so that I involuntarily stepped back and was almost running away, but he seized me by both hands and drew me to the sofa; sat down on the sofa himself, made me sit down in an armchair just opposite himself, and, keeping tight hold of my hand, with trembling lips and with tears suddenly glistening on his eyelashes, began speaking in an imploring voice.

"Alexey Ivanovitch, save, save me, spare me."

It was a long while before I could understand. He kept talking and talking and talking, continually repeating, "Spare me, spare me!" At last I guessed that he expected something in the way of advice from me; or rather, abandoned by all in his misery and anxiety, he had thought of me and had sent for me, simply to talk and talk and talk to me.

He was mad, or at any rate utterly distraught. He clasped his hands and was on the point of dropping on his knees before me to implore me (what do you suppose?) to go at once to Mlle. Blanche and to beseech, to urge her to return to him and marry him.

"Upon my word, General," I cried; "why, Mlle. Blanche is perhaps scarcely aware of my existence. What can I do?"

But it was vain to protest; he didn't understand what was said to him. He fell to talking about Granny, too, but with terrible incoherence; he was still harping on the idea of sending for the police.

"Among us, among us," he began, suddenly boiling over with indignation; "among us, in a well-ordered state, in fact, where there is a Government in control of things, such old women would have been put under guardianship at once! Yes, my dear sir, yes," he went on, suddenly dropping into a scolding tone, jumping up from his chair and pacing about the room; "you may not be aware of the fact, honoured sir," he said, addressing some imaginary "honoured sir" in the corner, "so let me tell you . . . yes . . . among us such old women

95

are kept in order, kept in order; yes, indeed. . . . Oh, damn it all!''

And he flung himself on the sofa again, and a minute later, almost sobbing, gasping for breath, hastened to tell me that Mlle. Blanche would not marry him because Granny had come instead of the telegram, and that now it was clear he would not come into the inheritance. He imagined that I knew nothing of this till then. I began to speak of De Grieux; he waved his hand: "He has gone away! Everything of mine he has in pawn; I'm stripped of everything! That money you brought . . . that money—I don't know how much there is, I think seven hundred francs are left and that's enough, that's all and what's to come—I don't know, I don't know! . . ."

"How will you pay your hotel bill?" I cried in alarm; "and . . . afterwards what will you do?"

He looked at me pensively, but I fancy he did not understand and perhaps did not hear what I said. I tried to speak of Polina Alexandrovna, of the children; he hurriedly answered: "Yes! yes!" but at once fell to talking of the Prince again, saying that Blanche would go away with him now and "then . . . then, what am I to do, Alexey Ivanovitch?" he asked, addressing me suddenly. "I vow, by God! I don't know what to do; tell me, isn't this ingratitude? Isn't this ingratitude?"

Finally he dissolved into floods of tears.

There was no doing anything with such a man; it would be dangerous to leave him alone, too—something might happen to him. I got rid of him somehow, but let nurse know she must look in upon him pretty frequently, and also spoke to the corridor attendant, a very sensible fellow; he, too, promised me to keep an eye on the General.

I had hardly left the General when Potapitch came to summon me to Granny. It was eight o'clock and she had only just come back from the Casino after losing everything. I went to her; the old lady was sitting in an armchair, utterly worn out and evidently ill. Marfa was giving her a cup of tea and almost forcing her to drink it. And Granny's tone and voice were utterly changed.

"Good-day, Alexey Ivanovitch, my good sir," she said, bending her head slowly, and with dignity; "excuse me for troubling you once more, you must excuse an old woman. I have left everything behind there, my friend, nearly a hundred thousand roubles. You did well not to come with me yesterday. Now I have no money, not a farthing. I don't want to delay a moment, at half-past nine I'm setting off. I have sent to that Englishman of yours—what's his name, Astley—I want to ask him to lend me three thousand francs for a week. So you must persuade him not to take it amiss and refuse. I am still fairly well off, my friend. I have still three villages and two houses. And there is still some money. I didn't bring it all with me. I tell you this that he may not feel any doubts . . . Ah, here he is! One can see he is a nice man."

Mr. Astley had hastened to come at Granny's first summons. With no hesitation and without wasting words he promptly counted out three thousand francs for an IOU which Granny signed. When this business was settled he made haste to take his leave and go away.

"And now you can go, too, Alexey Ivanovitch. I have only a little over an hour left. I want to lie down: my bones ache. Don't be hard on an old fool like me. Henceforward I won't blame young people for being flighty, and it would be a sin for me now to blame that luckless fellow, your General, either. I won't give him any money, though, as he wants me to, because —to my thinking he is utterly silly; only, old fool as I am, I've no more sense than he. Verily God seeks out and punishes pride, even in old age. Well, good-bye. Marfa, lift me up!"

I wanted to see Granny off, however. What's more, I was in a state of suspense; I kept expecting that in another minute something would happen. I could not sit quietly in my room. I went out into the corridor, even for a moment went for a saunter along the avenue. My letter to her had been clear and decisive and the present catastrophe was, of course, a final one. I heard in the hotel that De Grieux had left. If she rejected me as a friend, perhaps she would not reject me as a servant. I was necessary to her, I was of use to her, if only to run her errands, it was bound to be so!

When the train was due to start I ran to the station and saw Granny into the train. Her whole party were together, in a special reserved compartment. "Thank you, my good friend, for your disinterested sympathy," she said, at parting from me; "and tell Praskovya, in reference to what we were discussing yesterday, I shall expect her."

I went home. Passing the General's rooms I met the old nurse and inquired after the General. "Oh, he's all right, sir," she answered me dolefully. I went in, however, but stood still in positive amazement. Mlle. Blanche and the General were both laughing heartily. Madame de Cominges was sitting on

97

the sofa close by. The General was evidently beside himself
with delight. He was murmuring incoherently and going off
into prolonged fits of nervous laughter, during which his face
was puckered with innumerable wrinkles and his eyes disappeared from sight. Afterwards I learnt from Blanche herself
that, having dismissed the Prince and having heard how the
General was weeping, she had taken it into her head to comfort
him by going to see him for a minute. But the poor General
did not know that at that time his fate was decided, and that
Mlle. Blanche had already packed to set off for Paris by the
first train next morning.

Stopping in the doorway of the General's study, I changed
my mind and went away unnoticed. Going up to my own room
and opening the door, I suddenly noticed a figure in the half-
darkness sitting on a chair in the corner by the window. She
did not get up when I went in. I went up quickly, looked,
and—my heart stood still: it was Polina.

CHAPTER XIV

I POSITIVELY cried out aloud.
"What is it? What is it?" she asked me strangely. She
was pale and looked gloomy.

"You ask what is it? You? Here in my room!"

"If I come, then I come *altogether*. That's my way. You'll
see that directly; light the candle."

I lighted a candle. She got up, went up to the table, and put
before me an open letter.

"Read it," she ordered me.

"It's—it's De Grieux's handwriting," I cried, taking the
letter. My hands trembled and the lines danced before my eyes.
I have forgotten the exact wording of the letter, but here is
the main drift of it, if not the actual words.

"Mademoiselle," wrote De Grieux, "an unfortunate circumstance compels me to go away at once. You have, no doubt,
observed that I have purposely avoided a final explanation
with you until such time as the whole position might be cleared
up. The arrival of your old relation (*de la vieille dame*) and
her absurd behaviour have put an end to my doubts. The
unsettled state of my own affairs forbids me to cherish further

98

the sweet hopes which I permitted myself to indulge for some time. I regret the past, but I trust that you will not detect in my behaviour anything unworthy of a gentleman and an honest man (*gentilhomme et honnête homme*). Having lost almost all my money in loans to your stepfather, I find myself compelled to make the utmost use of what is left to me; I have already sent word to my friend in Petersburg to arrange at once for the sale of the estates he has mortgaged to me; knowing, however, that your frivolous stepfather has squandered your private fortune I have determined to forgive him fifty thousand francs, and I am returning him part of my claims on his property equivalent to that sum, so that you are now put in a position to regain all you have lost by demanding the property from him by legal process. I hope, Mademoiselle, that in the present position of affairs my action will be very advantageous to you. I hope, too, that by this action I am fully performing the duty of a man and a gentleman. Rest assured that your memory is imprinted upon my heart for ever."

"Well, that's all clear," I said, turning to Polina; "surely you could have expected nothing else," I added, with indignation.

"I expected nothing," she answered, with apparent composure, though there was a tremor in her voice; "I had made up my mind long ago; I read his mind and knew what he was thinking. He thought that I was trying—that I should insist . . ." (She broke off without finishing her sentence, bit her lips and was silent.) "I purposely doubled my scorn towards him," she began again. "I waited to see what was coming from him. If a telegram had come telling of the inheritance I'd have flung him the money borrowed from that idiot, my stepfather, and would have sent him about his business. He has been hateful to me for ages and ages. Oh! he was not the same man! a thousand times over, I tell you, he was different! but now, now . . . Oh, with what happiness I could fling that fifty thousand in his nasty face and spit and stamp . . ."

"But the security, the IOU for that fifty thousand, is in the General's hands. Take it and return it to De Grieux."

"Oh, that's not the same thing, that's not the same thing . . ."

"Yes, that's true, it's not the same thing. Besides, what is the General capable of now? And Granny!" I cried suddenly.

Polina looked at me, as it were absent-mindedly and impatiently.

"Why Granny?" asked Polina, with vexation. "I can't go to her . . . And I don't want to ask anyone's pardon," she added irritably.

"What's to be done!" I cried, "and how, oh, how could you love De Grieux! Oh, the scoundrel, the scoundrel! If you like I will kill him in a duel! Where is he now?"

"He's at Frankfurt, and will be there three days."

"One word from you and I'll set off to-morrow by the first train," I said, with stupid enthusiasm.

She laughed.

"Why, he'll say, maybe: 'Give me back the fifty thousand francs first.' Besides, what should you fight him for? . . . What nonsense it is!"

"But where, where is one to get that fifty thousand francs?" I repeated, grinding my teeth as though it had been possible to pick them up from the floor. "I say—Mr. Astley," I suggested, turning to her with a strange idea dawning upon me.

Her eyes flashed.

"What, do you mean to say *you yourself* want me to turn from you to that Englishman!" she said, looking in my face with a searching glance and smiling bitterly. For the first time in her life she addressed me in the second person singular.

I believe she was giddy with emotion at the moment, and all at once she sat down on the sofa as though she were exhausted.

It was as though I had been struck by a flash of lightning. I stood up and could not believe my eyes, could not believe my ears! Why, then she loved me! She had come to me and not to Mr. Astley!

She, she, a young girl, had come to my room in a hotel, so she had utterly compromised herself by her own act, and I, I was standing before her and still did not understand.

One wild idea flashed through my mind.

"Polina, give me only one hour. Stay here only one hour and . . . I'll come back. That's . . . that's essential! You shall see! Be here, be here!"

And I ran out of the room, not responding to her amazed and questioning look; she called something after me but I did not turn back.

Sometimes the wildest idea, the most apparently impossible thought, takes possession of one's mind so strongly that one accepts it at last as something substantial . . . more than that, if the idea is associated with a strong passionate desire, then sometimes one will accept it at last as something fated, inevitable, predestined—as something bound to be, and bound to happen. Perhaps there is something else in it, some combination of presentiments, some extraordinary effort of will, self-poisoning by one's own fancy—or something else—I don't know what, but on that evening (which I shall never in my life forget) something marvellous happened to me. Though it is quite justified by the laws of arithmetic, nevertheless it is a marvel to me to this day. And why, why had that conviction so long before taken such firm and deep root in my mind? I had certainly thought about it—I repeat—not as a chance among others which might or might not come to pass, but as something which was absolutely bound to happen!

It was a quarter-past ten. I went into the Casino with a confident expectation and at the same time with an excitement I had never experienced before. There were still a good many people in the gambling hall, though not half as many as in the morning.

Between ten and eleven there are still to be found in the gambling halls the genuine desperate gamblers for whom nothing exists at a spa but roulette, who have come for that alone, who scarcely notice what is going on around them and take no interest in anything during the whole season, but play from morning till night and would be ready perhaps to play all night till dawn, too, if it were possible. And they always disperse with annoyance when at twelve o'clock the roulette hall is closed. And when the senior croupier announces, just before midnight: *"Les trois derniers coups, messieurs,"* they are ready to stake on those last three strokes all they have in their pockets—and do, in fact, lose most at that time. I went up to the very table where Granny had sat that day. It was not crowded, and so I soon took my place at the table standing. Exactly before me was the word "Passe" scrawled on the green cloth.

"Passe" is the series of numbers from nineteen inclusive to thirty-six.

The first series of numbers from one to eighteen inclusive is called "Manque"; but what was that to me? I was not calculating, I had not even heard what had been the winning number last, and I did not ask about it when I began to play—as every player of any prudence would do. I pulled out all my twenty friedrichs d'or and staked them on "passe", the word which lay before me.

"Vingt deux," cried the croupier.

I had won and again staked all, including my winnings.

"Trente et un," cried the croupier.

I had won again. I had in all eighty friedrichs d'or. I staked the whole of that sum on the twelve middle numbers (my winnings would be three to one, but the chances were two to one against me.) The wheel rotated and stopped at twenty-four. I was passed three rolls each of fifty friedrichs d'or in paper and ten gold coins; I had now two hundred friedrichs d'or.

I was as though in delirium and I moved the whole heap of gold to red—and suddenly thought better of it. And for the only time that whole evening, all the time I was playing, I felt chilled with terror and a shudder made my arms and legs tremble. I felt with horror and instantly realised what losing would mean for me now! My whole life was at stake.

"Rouge," cried the croupier, and I drew a breath; fiery pins and needles were tingling all over my body. I was paid in bank-notes. It came to four thousand florins and eighty friedrichs d'or (I could still keep count at that stage).

Then, I remember, I staked two thousand florins on the twelve middle numbers, and lost: I staked my gold, the eighty friedrichs d'or, and lost. I was seized with fury: I snatched up the two thousand florins I had left and staked them on the first twelve numbers—haphazard, at random, without thinking! There was, however, an instant of suspense, like, perhaps, the feeling experienced by Madame Blanchard when she flew from a balloon in Paris to the earth.

"Quatre!" cried the croupier.

Now with my stake I had six thousand florins. I looked triumphant already. I was afraid of nothing—nothing, and staked four thousand florins on black. Nine people followed my example and staked on black. The croupiers exchanged glances and said something to one another. People were talking all round in suspense.

Black won. I don't remember my winnings after, nor what I staked on. I only remember as though in a dream that I won, I believe, sixteen thousand florins; suddenly three unlucky turns took twelve thousand from it; then I staked the last four thousand on "passe" (but I scarcely felt anything as I did so; I simply waited in a mechanical, senseless way)—and again I won; then I won four times running. I only remember that I gathered up money in thousands; I remember, too, that the middle twelve won most often and I kept to it. It turned up with a sort of regularity, certainly three or four times in succession, then it did not turn up twice running and then it followed three or four times in succession. Such astonishing regularity is sometimes met with in streaks, and that is what throws inveterate gamblers who calculate with a pencil in their hands out of their reckoning. And what horrible ironies of fate happen sometimes in such cases!

I believe not more than half an hour had passed since I came into the room, when suddenly the croupier informed me that I had won thirty thousand florins, and as the bank did not meet claims for a larger sum at one time the roulette would be closed till next morning. I snatched up all my gold, dropped it into my pockets, snatched up all my notes, and at once went into the other room where there was another roulette table; the whole crowd streamed after me; there at once a place was cleared for me and I fell to staking again haphazard without reckoning. I don't understand what saved me!

At times, however, a glimmer of prudence began to dawn upon my mind. I clung to certain numbers and combinations, but soon abandoned them and staked almost unconsciously. I must have been very absent-minded; I remember the croupiers several times corrected me. I made several gross mistakes. My temples were soaked with sweat and my hands were shaking. The Poles ran up, too, with offers of their services, but I listened to no one. My luck was unbroken! Suddenly there were sounds of loud talk and laughter, and everyone cried "Bravo, bravo!" some even clapped their hands. Here, too, I collected thirty thousand florins, and the bank closed till next day.

"Go away, go away," a voice whispered on my right.

It was a Frankfurt Jew; he was standing beside me all the time, and I believe sometimes helped me in my play.

"For goodness' sake go," another voice whispered in my left ear.

I took a hurried glance. It was a lady about thirty, very soberly and quietly dressed, with a tired, pale, sickly face which yet bore traces of having once been beautiful. At that moment I was stuffing my pockets with the notes, which I crumpled up anyhow, and gathering up the gold that lay on the table. Snatching up the last roll of notes, I succeeded in putting it into the pale lady's hands quite without attracting notice; I had an intense desire to do so at the time, and I remember her pale slim fingers pressed my hand warmly in token of gratitude. All that took place in one instant.

Having collected quickly all my winnings I went quickly to the trente et quarante.

Trente et quarante is frequented by the aristocratic public. Unlike roulette, it is a game of cards. Here the bank will pay up to a hundred thousand thalers at once. The largest stake is here also four thousand florins. I knew nothing of the game, and scarcely knew how to bet on it, except the red and the black, upon which one can bet in this game too. And I stuck to red and black. The whole Casino crowded round. I don't remember whether I once thought of Polina all this time. I was experiencing an overwhelming enjoyment in scooping up and taking away the notes which grew up in a heap before me.

It seemed as though fate were urging me on. This time, as luck would have it, a circumstance occurred which, however, is fairly frequent in the game. Chance favours red, for instance, ten or even fifteen times in succession. I had heard two days before that in the previous week red had turned up twenty-two times in succession; it was something which had never been remembered in roulette, and it was talked of with amazement. Everyone, of course, abandoned red at once, and after the tenth time, for instance, scarcely anyone dared to stake on it. But none of the experienced players staked on black either. The experienced gambler knows what is meant by this "freak of chance". It would mean that after red had won sixteen times, at the seventeenth time the luck would infallibly fall on black. Novices at play rush to this conclusion in crowds, double and treble their stakes, and lose terribly.

But, noticing that red had turned up seven times running, by strange perversity I staked on it. I am convinced that vanity was half responsible for it; I wanted to impress the spectators by taking a mad risk, and—oh, the strange sensation—I remember distinctly that, quite apart from the promptings of vanity, I was possessed by an intense craving for risk. Perhaps passing through so many sensations my soul was not satisfied but only irritated by them and craved still more sensation—and stronger and stronger ones—till utterly exhausted. And, truly I am not lying, if the regulations had allowed me to stake fifty thousand florins at once, I should certainly have staked them. People around shouted that it was madness— that red had won fourteen times already!

"*Monsieur a gagné déjá cent mille florins,*" I heard a voice say near me.

I suddenly came to myself. What? I had won during that evening a hundred thousand florins! And what more did I want? I fell on my banknotes, crumpled them up in my pockets without counting them, scooped up all my gold, all my rolls of notes, and ran out of the Casino. Everyone was laughing as I went through the room, looking at my bulging pockets and at the way I staggered under the weight of gold. I think it weighed over twenty pounds. Several hands were held out to me; I gave it away in handfuls as I snatched it up. Two Jews stopped me at the outer door.

"You are bold—you are very bold," they said to me, "but be sure to go away to-morrow as soon as possible, or else you will lose it all—you will lose it all . . ."

I didn't listen to them. The avenue was so dark that I could not see my hand before my face. It was half a mile to the hotel. I had never been afraid of thieves or robbers even as a small boy; I did not think of them now either. I don't remember what I thought of on the road; I had no thoughts. I was only aware of an immense enjoyment—success, victory, power— I don't know how to express it. Polina's image hovered before my mind too; I remembered her and was conscious I was going to her; I should be with her in a moment, should be telling her and showing her . . . But I hardly remembered what she had said to me earlier, and why I had gone, and all the sensations I had felt, not more than an hour and a half before, seemed to me something long past, transformed, grown old—something of which we should say no more because everything now would begin anew. Almost at the end of the avenue a sudden panic came upon me. What if I were robbed and murdered at this instant? At every step my panic grew greater. I almost ran. Suddenly, at the end of the avenue there was the glare of our hotel with its many windows lighted up— thank God, home!

I ran up to my storey and rapidly opened the door. Polina was there, sitting on the sofa with her arms crossed, with a lighted candle before her. She looked at me with amazement, and no doubt at that moment I must have looked rather strange. I stood before her and began flinging down all my piles of money on the table.

CHAPTER XV

I REMEMBER she fixed a very intent look on my face, but without even moving from her seat or changing her position.

"I've won two hundred thousand francs!" I cried, as I flung down the last roll of notes.

The huge bundles of notes and piles of gold filled up the whole table; I could not take my eyes off it. At moments I completely forgot Polina. At one moment I began arranging the heap of banknotes, folding them up together, at the next I began undoing the rolls of gold and heaping them up in one pile; then I abandoned it all and strode rapidly up and down the room, lost in thought, then went up to the table, counting the money again. Suddenly, as though coming to myself, I ran to the door and locked it with two turns of the key. Then I stood pondering before my little portmanteau.

"Shall I put it in the portmanteau till to-morrow?" I said, suddenly remembering Polina and turning towards her.

She was still sitting in the same place without stirring, but watching me attentively. Her expression was somehow strange; I did not like that expression. I am not mistaken if I say that there was hatred in it.

I went up to her quickly.

"Polina, here are twenty-five thousand florins—that's fifty thousand francs—more, in fact. Take it, throw it in his face to-morrow."

She did not answer me.

"If you like I will take you away early in the morning. Shall I?"

She suddenly burst out laughing. She laughed for a long time.

I looked at her with wonder and a mortified feeling. That laugh was very much like sarcastic laughter at my expense, which had always been so frequent at the times of my most passionate declarations.

At last she ceased laughing and frowned; she looked at me sternly from under her brows.

"I won't take your money," she declared contemptuously.

"How? What's this?" I cried. "Polina, why?"

"I won't take money for nothing."

"I offer it you as a friend; I offer you my life."

She looked at me with a long, penetrating look, as though she would pierce me through with it.

"You give too much," she said, with a laugh; "De Grieux's mistress is not worth fifty thousand francs."

"Polina, how can you talk to me like that!" I cried, reproachfully. "Am I a De Grieux?"

"I hate you! Yes . . . yes! . . . I love you no more than De Grieux," she cried, her eyes suddenly flashing.

Then she suddenly covered her face with her hands and went into hysterics. I rushed to her.

I realised that something had happened to her while I was away. She seemed quite out of her mind.

"Buy me! Do you want to? Do you want to? For fifty thousand francs, like De Grieux?" broke from her with convulsive sobs.

I held her in my arms, kissed her hands, her feet, fell on my knees before her.

Her hysterics passed off. She put both hands on my shoulders, and looked at me intently; she seemed trying to read something in my face. She listened to me, but evidently did not hear what I was saying to her. Some doubt and anxiety betrayed itself in her face. I was anxious about her; it seemed to me that her brain was giving way. Then she began softly drawing me to her; a trustful smile began straying over her face; but she suddenly pushed me away, and again fell to scanning me with a darkened look.

Suddenly she fell to embracing me.

"You love me, you love me, don't you?" she said. "Why, you . . . why, you . . . wanted to fight the Baron for my sake!"

And suddenly she burst out laughing—as though she had recalled something sweet and funny. She cried and laughed all at once. Well, what was I to do? I was in a fever myself. I remember she began saying something to me—but I could scarcely understand anything. It was a sort of delirium—a sort of babble—as though she wanted to tell me something as rapidly as possible—a delirium which was interrupted from time to time with the merriest laughter, which at last frightened me. "No, no; you are sweet, sweet," she repeated. "You are my faithful one!" And again she put her hand on my shoulders, again she looked at me and repeated, "You love me . . . love me . . . will love me?" I could not take my eyes off her; I had never seen her before in such a mood of love and

107

tenderness; it is true this, of course, was delirium, but . . . noticing my passionate expression, she suddenly began smiling slyly; apropos of nothing she began suddenly talking of Mr. Astley.

She talked incessantly of Mr. Astley, however (she talked of him particularly when she had been trying to tell me of something that evening), but what she meant exactly I could not quite grasp; she seemed to be actually laughing at him. She repeated continually that he was waiting and that, did I know, he was certainly standing under the window?

"Yes, yes, under the window; come, open it: look out: look out: he certainly is here!" She pushed me to the window, but as soon as I made a movement to go she went off into peals of laughter and I remained with her, and she fell to embracing me.

"Shall we go away? shall we go away to-morrow?" The question suddenly came into her mind uneasily. "Well . . ." (and she sank into thought). "Well, shall we overtake Granny; what do you think? I think we might overtake her at Berlin. What do you think she will say when she sees us? And Mr. Astley? . . . Well, he won't leap off the Schlangenberg—what do you think?" (She burst out laughing.) "Come, listen, do you know where he is going next summer? He wants to go to the North Pole for scientific investigations, and he has asked me to go with him, ha-ha-ha! He says that we Russians can do nothing without Europeans and are incapable of anything. . . . But he is good-natured, too! Do you know he makes excuses for the General? He says that Blanche . . . that passion—oh, I don't know, I don't know," she repeated, as though she didn't know what she was talking about. "They are poor—how sorry I am for them, and Granny . . . Come, listen, listen, how could you kill De Grieux? And did you really imagine you could kill him? Oh, silly fellow! Can you really think I would let you fight with De Grieux? Why, you did not even kill the Baron," she added, suddenly laughing. "Oh, how funny you were then with the Baron. I looked at you both from the seat; and how unwilling you were to go then, when I sent you. How I laughed then, how I laughed," she added, laughing.

And suddenly she kissed and embraced me again. Again she pressed her face to mine passionately and tenderly. I heard nothing and thought of nothing more. My head was in a whirl . . .

I think it was about seven o'clock in the morning when I woke up. The sun was shining into the room. Polina was sitting beside me and looking about her strangely, as though she were waking from some darkness and trying to collect her thoughts. She, too, had only just woken up and was gazing at the table and the money. My head ached and was heavy. I tried to take Polina by the hand: she pushed me away and jumped up from the sofa. The dawning day was overcast. Rain had fallen before sunrise. She went to the window, she opened it, put out her head and shoulders and with her face in her hands and her elbows on the window-sill, stayed for three minutes looking out without turning to me or hearing what I said to her. I wondered with dread what would happen now and how it would end. All at once she got up from the window, went up to the table and, looking at me with infinite hatred, with lips trembling with anger, she said to me:

"Well, give me my fifty thousand francs now!"

"Polina, again, again?" I was beginning.

"Or have you changed your mind? Ha-ha-ha! Perhaps you regret it now."

Twenty-five thousand florins, counted out the evening before, were lying on the table; I took the money and gave it to her.

"It's mine now, isn't it? That's so, isn't it? Isn't it?" she asked me, spitefully holding the money in her hand.

"Yes, it was always yours," I answered.

"Well, there are your fifty thousand francs for you!"

With a swing of her arm she flung the money at me. It hit me a stinging blow in the face and the coins flew all over the table. After doing this Polina ran out of the room.

I know that at that moment she was certainly not in her right mind, though I don't understand such temporary insanity. It is true that she is still ill, even now, a month later. What was the cause of her condition, and, above all, of this whim? Was it wounded pride? Despair at having brought herself to come to me? Had I shown any sign of priding myself on my happiness, and did I, like De Grieux, want to get rid of her by giving her fifty thousand francs? But that was not so; I know that, on my conscience. I believe that her vanity was partly responsible; her vanity prompted her to distrust and insult me, although all that, perhaps, was not clear, even to herself. In that case, of course, I was punished for De Grieux and was made responsible, though I was not much to blame. It is true that all this was almost only delirium; it is true, too, that I knew she was in delirium and . . . did not take that fact into consideration; perhaps she cannot forgive me for that now. Yes, but that is now; but then, then? Why, she was not in such a delirium and so ill then as to be utterly oblivious of what she was doing; when she came to me with De Grieux's letter she knew what she was doing.

I made haste to thrust all my notes and my heap of gold into the bed, covered it over and went out ten minutes after Polina. I made sure she would run home, and I thought I would slip into them on the sly, and in the hall ask the nurse how the young lady was. What was my astonishment when I learnt from nurse, whom I met on the stairs, that Polina had not yet returned home and that nurse was coming to me for her.

"She only just left my room about ten minutes ago; where can she have gone?"

Nurse looked at me reproachfully.

And meanwhile it had caused a regular scandal, which by now was all over the hotel. In the porter's room and at the *ober-kellner's* it was whispered that Fraülein had run out of the hotel in the rain at six o'clock in the morning in the direction of the Hôtel d'Angleterre. From what they said and hinted, I noticed that they all knew already that she had spent the night in my room. However, stories were being told of the whole family: it had become known all through the hotel that the General had gone out of his mind and was crying. The story was that Granny was his mother, who had come expressly from Russia to prevent her son's marriage with Mlle. de Cominges, and was going to cut him out of her will if he disobeyed her, and, as he certainly would disobey her, the Countess had purposely thrown away all her money at roulette before his eyes, so that he should get nothing. *"Diese Russen!"* repeated the *ober-kellner,* shaking his head indignantly. The others laughed. The *ober-kellner* was making out his bill. My winning was known about already. Karl, my corridor attendant, was the first to congratulate me. But I had no thought for any of them. I rushed to the Hôtel d'Angleterre.

It was early; Mr. Astley was seeing no one; learning that it was I, he came out into the corridor to me and stopped before me, turning his pewtery eyes upon me in silence, waiting to hear what I should say. I inquired about Polina.

"She is ill," answered Mr. Astley, looking at me as fixedly as before.

"Then she really is with you?"

"Yes, she is."

"Then, what do you . . . do you mean to keep her?"

"Yes."

"Mr. Astley, it will make a scandal; it's impossible. Besides, she is quite ill; perhaps you don't see it?"

"Oh, yes, I notice it, and I've just told you she is ill. If she had not been ill she would not have spent the night with you."

"Then you know that?"

"Yes, I know it. She came here yesterday and I would have taken her to a relation of mine, but as she was ill, she made a mistake and went to you."

"Fancy that! Well, I congratulate you, Mr. Astley. By the way, you've given me an idea: weren't you standing all night under our window? Miss Polina was making me open the window and look out all night to see whether you were standing under the window; she kept laughing about it."

"Really? No, I didn't stand under the window; but I was waiting in the corridor and walking round."

"But she must be looked after, Mr. Astley."

"Oh, yes, I've sent for the doctor, and, if she dies, you will answer to me for her death."

I was amazed.

"Upon my word, Mr. Astley, what do you want?"

"And is it true that you won two hundred thousand thalers yesterday?"

"Only a hundred thousand florins."

"Well, do you see, you had better go off to Paris this morning!"

"What for?"

"All Russians who have money go to Paris," Mr. Astley explained, in a tone of voice as though he had read this in a book.

"What could I do now in Paris, in the summer? I love her, Mr. Astley, you know it yourself."

"Really? I am convinced you don't. If you remain here you will certainly lose all you have won and you will have nothing left to go to Paris with. But, good-bye, I am perfectly certain you will go to Paris to-day."

"Very well, good-bye, only I shan't go to Paris. Think, Mr. Astley, what will be happening here? The General . . . and now this adventure with Miss Polina—why, that will be all over the town."

"Yes, all over the town; I believe the General is not thinking about that: he has no thoughts to spare for that. Besides, Miss Polina has a perfect right to live where she likes. In regard to that family, one may say quite correctly that the family no longer exists."

I walked away laughing at this Englishman's strange conviction that I was going to Paris. "He wants to shoot me in a duel, though," I thought, "if Mlle. Polina dies—what a complication!" I swear I was sorry for Polina, but, strange to say, from the very moment when I reached the gambling tables the previous evening and began winning a pile of money, my love had retreated, so to speak, into the background. I say this now; but at the time I did not realise all this clearly. Can I really be a gambler? Can I really . . . have loved Polina so strangely? No, I love her to this day. God is my witness! And then, when I left Mr. Astley and went home, I was genuinely miserable and blaming myself. But . . . at this point a very strange and silly thing happened to me.

I was hurrying to see the General, when suddenly, not far from his rooms, a door was opened and someone called me. It was Madame la veuve Cominges, and she called me at the bidding of Mlle. Blanche. I went in to see Mlle. Blanche.

They had a small suite of apartments, consisting of two rooms. I could hear Mlle. Blanche laugh and call out from the bedroom.

She was getting up.

"*A, c'est lui! Viens donc, bête!* Is it true, *que tu as gagné une montagne d'or et d'argent? J'aimerais mieux l'or.*"

"Yes, I did win," I answered, laughing.

"How much?"

"A hundred thousand florins."

"*Bibi, comme tu es bête.* Why, come in here. I can't hear anything. *Nous ferons bombance, n'est ce pas?*"

I went in to her. She was lying under a pink satin quilt, above which her robust, swarthy, wonderfully swarthy, shoulders were visible, shoulders such as one only sees in one's dreams, covered to some extent by a batiste nightgown bordered with white lace which was wonderfully becoming to her dark skin.

"*Mon fils, as-tu du cœur?*" she cried, seeing me, and burst out laughing. She laughed very good-humouredly, and sometimes quite genuinely.

"*Tout autre,*" I began, paraphrasing Corneille.

"Here you see, *vois-tu*," she began babbling; "to begin with, find my stockings, help me to put them on; and then, *si tu n'es pas trop bête, je te prends à Paris.* You know I am just going."

"Just going?"

"In half an hour."

All her things were indeed packed. All her portmanteaux and things were ready. Coffee had been served some time before.

"*Eh bien,* if you like, *tu verras Paris. Dis donc qu'est ce que c'est qu'un outchitel? Tu étais bien bête, quand tu étais outchitel.* Where are my stockings? Put them on for me!"

She thrust out some positively fascinating feet, little dark-skinned feet, not in the least misshapen, as feet that look so small in shoes always are. I laughed and began drawing her silk stockings on for her. Meanwhile Mlle. Blanche sat up in bed, prattling away.

"*Eh bien, que feras-tu, si je te prends avec?* To begin with, I want fifty thousand francs. You'll give them to me at Frankfurt. *Nous allons à Paris:* there we'll play together: *et je te ferai voir des étoiles en plein jour.* You will see women such as you have never seen before. Listen . . ."

"Wait a minute—if I give you fifty thousand francs, what will be left for me?"

"*Et cent cinquante mille francs,* you have forgotten: and what's more, I consent to live with you a month, two months: *que sais-je!* In those two months we shall certainly get through that hundred and fifty thousand francs, you see, *je suis bonne enfant,* and I tell you beforehand, *mais tu verras des étoiles.*"

"What! all in two months!"

"Why! does that horrify you? *Ah, vil esclave!* But, do you know? one month of such a life is worth your whole existence. One month—*et après le déluge! Mais tu ne peux comprendre; va!* Go along, go along, you are not worth it! *Aie, que fais tu?*"

At that moment I was putting a stocking on the other leg, but could not resist kissing it. She pulled it away and began hitting me on the head with the tip of her foot. At last, she turned me out altogether.

"*Et bien! mon outchitel, je t'attends, si tu veux;* I am starting in a quarter of an hour!" she called after me.

On returning home I felt as though my head were going round. Well, it was not my fault that Mlle. Polina had thrown the whole pile of money in my face, and had even yesterday preferred Mr. Astley to me. Some of the banknotes that had been scattered about were still lying on the floor; I picked them up. At that moment the door opened and the *ober-kellner* himself made his appearance (he had never deigned to look into my room before) with a suggestion that I might like to move downstairs to a magnificent suite of apartments which had just been vacated by Count V.

I stood still and thought a little.

"My bill—I am just leaving, in ten minutes," I cried. "If it's to be Paris, let it be Paris," I thought to myself; "it seems it was fated at my birth!"

A quarter of an hour later we were actually sitting in a reserved compartment, Mlle. Blanche, Madame la veuve Cominges and I. Mlle. Blanche, looking at me, laughed till she was almost hysterical. Madame de Cominges followed suit; I cannot say that I felt cheerful. My life had broken in two, but since the previous day I had grown used to staking everything on a card. Perhaps it is really the truth that my sudden wealth was too much for me and had turned my head. *Peut-être, je ne demandais pas mieux.* It seemed to me for a time—but only for a time, the scenes were shifted. "But in a month I shall be here, and then . . . and then we will try our strength, Mr. Astley!" No, as I recall it now, I was awfully sad then, though I did laugh as loudly as that idiot, Blanche.

"But what is the matter with you? How silly you are! Oh! how silly you are!" Blanche kept exclaiming, interrupting her laughter to scold me in earnest. "Oh well, oh well, we'll spend your two hundred thousand francs: but in exchange *mais tu seras heureux comme un petit roi;* I will tie your cravat myself and introduce you to Hortense. And when we have spent all our money, you will come back here and break the bank again. What did the Jews tell you? The great thing is— boldness, and you have it, and you will bring me money to Paris more than once again. *Quant à moi, je veux cinquante mille francs de rentes et alors . . ."*

"And the General?" I asked her.

"Why, the General, as you know, comes to see me every day with a bouquet. This time I purposely asked him to get me some very rare flowers. The poor fellow will come back and will find the bird has flown. He'll fly after us, you will see. Ha-ha-ha! I shall be awfully pleased to see him. He'll be of use to me in Paris; Mr. Astley will pay his bill here. . . ."

And so that was the way in which I went to Paris.

CHAPTER XVI

WHAT shall I say about Paris? It was madness, of course, and foolery. I only spent a little over three weeks in Paris, and by the end of that time my hundred thousand francs was finished. I speak only of a hundred thousand. The other hundred thousand I gave to Mlle. Blanche in hard cash—fifty thousand at Frankfurt and three days later in Paris I gave her an IOU for another fifty thousand francs, though a week later she exchanged this for cash from me. *"Et les cent mille francs, qui nous restent, tu les mangeras avec moi, mon outchitel."* She always called me an *outchitel*, i.e., a tutor. It is difficult to imagine anything in the world meaner, stingier and more niggardly than the class of creatures to which Mlle. Blanche belonged. But that was in the spending of her own money. As regards my hundred thousand francs, she openly informed me, later on, that she needed them to establish herself in Paris, "as now I am going to settle in decent style once for all, and now no one shall turn me aside for a long time; at least, that is my plan," she added. I hardly saw that hundred thousand, however; she kept the money the whole time, and in my purse, into which she looked every day, there was never more than a hundred francs, and always less and less.

"What do you want money for?" she would say, sometimes, in the simplest way, and I did not dispute with her. But she furnished and decorated her flat very nicely with that money, and afterwards, when she took me to her new abode, as she showed me the rooms, she said: "You see what care and taste can do even with the scantiest means." These "scanty means" amounted to fifty thousand francs, however. With the second fifty thousand she provided herself with a carriage and horses. Moreover, we gave two balls, that is, two evening parties at which were present Hortense, Lizette and Cléopatra, women remarkable in very many respects and even quite good-looking. At those two evenings I had to play the very foolish part of host, to receive and entertain the stupidest rich tradesmen, incredibly ignorant and shameless, various army lieutenants and miserable little authors and journalistic insects, who appeared in the most fashionable swallow-tails and straw-coloured gloves, and displayed a vanity and affectation whose proportions were beyond anything conceivable in Petersburg—and that is saying a great deal. Many of them thought fit to jeer at me; but I got drunk with champagne and lolled at full length in a back room. To me it was all loathsome to the last degree. *"C'est un outchitel,"* Blanche kept saying about me, *"il a gagné deux cent mille francs*. Without me he wouldn't have known how to spend it. And afterwards he will be an *outchitel* again; don't you know of a place for one? we ought to do something for him."

I had recourse to champagne very often, because I was often sad and dreadfully bored. I lived in the most bourgeois, in the most mercenary surroundings in which every *sou* was reckoned and accounted for. Blanche disliked me for the first fortnight: I noticed that; it is true, she dressed me like a dandy, and tied my cravat for me every day, but in her soul she genuinely despised me. I did not pay the slightest attention to that. Bored and dispirited, I used to go usually to the Château de Fleurs, where regularly every evening I got drunk and practised the *cancan* (which they dance so disgustingly there), and acquired in the end a kind of celebrity.

At last Blanche gauged my true character. She had for some reason conceived the idea that I should spend all the time we were together walking after her with a pencil and paper in my hand, and should always be reckoning how much she had spent, how much she had stolen, how much she would spend and how much more she would steal. And she was, of course, convinced that we should have a regular battle over every ten-franc piece. She had an answer in readiness for every attack that she anticipated from me; but when she found I did not attack her, she could not at first refrain from defending herself, unprovoked. Sometimes she would begin with great heat, but seeing that I remained silent as a rule, lying on a sofa gazing at the ceiling— at last, she was surprised. At first she thought I was simply stupid, *"un outchitel"*, and merely cut short her explanations, probably thinking to herself: "Why, he's a fool. There's no need to lay it on for him, since he doesn't understand." She would go away but come back again ten minutes later (this happened at a time when she was spending most ferociously, spending on a scale quite out of proportion to our means: she had, for instance, got rid of the horses first bought and bought another pair for sixteen thousand francs).

"Well, so you are not cross, bibi?" she said, coming up to me.

"N—n—n—no! You weary me!" I said, removing her

hands from me, but this seemed to her so curious that she immediately sat down beside me.

"You see, I only decided to pay so much because they could be sold later on if need be. They can be sold again for twenty thousand francs."

"No doubt, no doubt; they are splendid horses, and you have a fine turn-out now; it suits you; well, that's enough."

"Then you are not cross?"

"Why should I be? You are sensible to provide yourself with things that are necessary to you. All that will be of use to you afterwards. I see that it is quite necessary for you to establish yourself in such a style; otherwise you will never save up your million. Our hundred thousand francs is only a beginning; a drop in the ocean."

Blanche had expected from me anything but such reflections (instead of outcries and reproaches). She seemed to drop from the clouds.

"So that's what you are like! *Mais tu as l'esprit pour comprendre. Sais-tu, mon garçon,* though you are an *outchitel* you ought to have been born a prince. So you don't grudge the money's going so quickly?"

"Bother the money! the quicker the better!"

"*Mais sais-tu . . . mais dis donc,* are you rich? *Mais sais-tu,* you really despise money too much. *Qu'est ce que tu feras après, dis donc?*"

"*Après,* I shall go to Homburg and win another hundred thousand francs."

"*Oui, oui, c'est ça, c'est magnifique!* And I know you will certainly win it and bring it here. *Dis donc,* why you will make me really love you. *Eh bien,* I will love you all the time for being like that, and won't once be unfaithful to you. You see, I have not loved you all this time, *parceque je croyais que tu n'étais qu'un outchitel (quelque chose comme un laquais, n'est-ce pas?)*, but I have been faithful to you all the same, *parceque je suis bonne fille.*"

"Come, you are lying! How about Albert, that swarthy-faced little officer; do you suppose I didn't see last time?"

"*Oh, oh, mais tu es . . .*"

"Come, you are lying, you are lying; why, do you suppose I should be angry? Why, it's no matter; *il faut que la jeunesse se passe.* And there's no need for you to send him away if you had him before me and are fond of him. Only don't give him money, do you hear?"

117

"So you are not angry about it? *Mais tu es un vrai philosophe, sais-tu? Un vrai philosophe!*" she cried enthusiastically.

"*Eh bien! je t'aimerai, je t'aimerai—tu verras, tu seras content!*"

And from that time she really did seem to be attached to me, to be really affectionate; and so our last ten days passed. The "stars" promised me I did not see. But in some respects she really did keep her word. What is more, she introduced me to Hortense, who really was a remarkable woman in her own way, and in our circle was called *Thérèse philosophe* . . .

However, there is no need to enlarge upon that; all that might make a separate story, in a different tone, which I do not want to introduce into this story. The fact is, I longed above everything for this episode to be over. But our hundred thousand francs lasted, as I have mentioned already, almost a month—at which I was genuinely surprised; eighty thousand of that, at least, Blanche spent on things for herself, and we lived on no more than twenty thousand francs—and yet it was enough. Blanche, who was in the end almost open with me (or, at any rate, did not lie to me about some things), declared that, anyway, the debts she had been obliged to make would not fall upon me: "I have never given you bills or IOUs to sign," she said, "because I was sorry for you; but any other girl would have certainly done it and got you into prison. You see, you see how I loved you and how good I am! Think of what that devil of a wedding alone is going to cost me!"

We really were going to have a wedding. It took place at the very end of my month, and it may be assumed that the last remains of my hundred thousand francs went upon it; that was how the thing ended; that is, my month ended with that, and after it I received my formal dismissal.

This was how it happened: a week after our arrival in Paris the General suddenly turned up. He came straight to Blanche, and from his first call almost lived with us. He had a lodging of his own, it is true. Blanche received him joyfully, with shrieks of laughter, and even flew to embrace him; as things had turned out, she was unwilling to let him go: and he had to follow her about everywhere, on the boulevards, and to the theatres, and to call on her acquaintances, and to take her for drives. The General was still of use for such purposes; he was of rather imposing and decorous appearance—he was above the average in height, with dyed whiskers and moustaches (he had once served in the Cuirassiers); he was still presentable-looking, though his face was puffy. His manners were superb; he looked well in evening dress. In Paris he began wearing his decorations. The promenade on the boulevard with a man like this was not only possible, but *advantageous*. The good-natured and senseless General was immensely delighted with all this; he had not reckoned upon it at all when he came to see us on arriving in Paris. He had come, then, almost trembling with terror; he was afraid that Blanche would make an uproar and order him to be turned out; and so he was highly delighted at the changed aspect of the position, and spent the whole month in a sort of senseless rapture: and he was in the same state when I left him. I learnt that on the morning of our sudden departure from Roulettenburg he had some sort of a fit. He had fallen insensible, and had been all that week almost like a madman, talking incessantly. He was being nursed and doctored, but he suddenly threw up everything, got into the train and flew off to Paris. Of course, Blanche's reception was the best cure for him; but the traces of his illness remained long after, in spite of his joy and his enthusiastic condition. He was utterly incapable of reflection or even of carrying on a conversation on any serious subject; when any such topic was brought forward, he confined himself to nodding his head and ejaculating, "H'm!" at every word. He often laughed, but it was a nervous, sickly laugh, as though he were giggling; another time he would sit for hours looking as black as night, knitting his bushy brows. Of many things he had no recollection whatever; he had become absent-minded to an unseemly degree, and had acquired the habit of talking to himself. Blanche was the only person who could rouse him; and, indeed, his attacks of gloom and depression, when he hid himself in a corner, meant nothing but that he hadn't seen Blanche for a long time, or that Blanche had gone off somewhere without taking him, or had not been nice to him before going. At the same time he could not say what he wanted, and did not know why he was depressed and miserable. After sitting for two or three hours (I noticed this on two or three occasions when Blanche had gone out for the whole day, probably to see Albert), he would suddenly begin to look about him in a nervous fluster, to stare round, to recollect himself, and seem to be looking for something; but seeing no one and not remembering the question he meant to ask, he sank into forgetfulness again till Blanche reappeared, gay, frisky, gorgeously dressed, with her ringing laugh; she would run up to him, beging teasing him, and even kissing him—a favour which she did not often, however, bestow upon him. Once the General was so delighted to see her that he even burst into tears—I really marvelled at him.

From the very first, Blanche began to plead his cause before me. Indeed, she waxed eloquent in his behalf; reminded me that she had betrayed the General for my sake, that she was almost engaged to him, had given him her word; that he had abandoned his family on her account, and, lastly, that I had been in his service and ought to remember that, and that I ought to be ashamed . . . I said nothing while she rattled away at a terrific pace. At last I laughed: and with that the matter ended, that is, at first, she thought I was a fool: and at last came to the conclusion that I was a very nice and accommodating man. In fact, I had the good fortune to win in the end the complete approval of that excellent young woman. (Blanche really was, though, a very good-natured girl—in her own way, of course; I had not such a high opinion of her at first.) "You're a kind and clever man," she used to say to me towards the end, "and . . . and . . . it's only a pity you are such a fool! You never, never, save anything!"

"Un vrai russe, un calmouk!" Several times she sent me to take the General for a walk about the streets, exactly as she might send her lapdog out with her footman. I took him, however, to the theatre, and to the Bal-Mabille, and to the restaurants. Blanche gave me the money for this, though the General had some of his own, and he was very fond of taking out his pocket-book before people. But I had almost to use force to prevent him from buying a brooch for seven hundred francs, by which he was fascinated in the Palais Royal and of which he wanted, at all costs, to make Blanche a present. But what was a brooch of seven hundred francs to her? The General hadn't more than a thousand francs altogether. I could never find out where he had got that money from. I imagine it was from Mr. Astley, especially as the latter had paid their bill at the hotel. As for the General's attitude to me all this time, I believe that he did not even guess at my relations with Blanche. Though he had heard vaguely that I had won a fortune, yet he probably supposed that I was with Blanche in the capacity of a private secretary or even a servant. Anyway, he always, as before, spoke to be condescendingly, authoritatively, and even sometimes fell to scolding me. One morning he amused Blanche and me immensely at breakfast. He was not at all ready to take offence, but suddenly he was huffy with me—why?—I don't

know to this day. No doubt he did not know himself. In fact, he made a speech without a beginning or an end, *à bâtons-rompus*, shouted that I was an impudent boy, that he would give me a lesson . . . that he would let me know it . . . and so on. But no one could make out anything from it. Blanche went off into peals of laughter. At last he was somehow appeased and taken out for a walk. I noticed sometimes, however, that he grew sad, that he was regretting someone and something, he was missing something in spite of Blanche's presence. On two such occasions he began talking to me of himself, but could not express himself clearly, alluded to his times in the army, to his deceased wife, to his family affairs, to his property. He would stumble upon some phrase—and was delighted with it and would repeat it a hundred times a day, though perhaps it expressed neither his feelings nor his thoughts. I tried to talk to him about his children: but he turned off the subject with incoherent babble, and passed hurriedly to another topic: "Yes, yes, my children, you are right, my children!" Only once he grew sentimental—we were with him at the theatre: "Those unhappy children!" he began suddenly. "Yes, sir, those un—happy children!" And several times afterwards that evening he repeated the same words: "unhappy children!" Once, when I began to speak of Polina, he flew into a frenzy. "She's an ungrateful girl," he cried. "She's wicked and ungrateful! She has disgraced her family. If there were laws here I would make her mind her p's and q's. Yes, indeed, yes, indeed!" As for De Grieux, he could not bear even to hear his name: "He has been the ruin of me," he would say, "he has robbed me, he has destroyed me! He has been my nightmare for the last two years! He has haunted my dreams for whole months! It's, it's, it's . . . Oh, never speak to me of him!"

I saw there was an understanding between them, but, as usual, I said nothing. Blanche announced the news to me first—it was just a week before we parted: "*Il a du chance*," she babbled. "Granny really is ill this time, and certainly will die. Mr. Astley has sent a telegram. You must admit that the General is her heir, anyway, and even if he were not, he would not interfere with me in anything. In the first place, he has his pension, and in the second place, he will live in a back room and will be perfectly happy. I shall be 'Madame le Générale'. I shall get into a good set" (Blanche was continually dreaming of this), "in the end I shall be a Russian landowner, *j'aurai un château, des moujiks, et puis j'aurai toujours mon million*."

"Well, what if he begins to be jealous, begins to insist . . . on goodness knows what—do you understand?"

"Oh, no, *non, non, non!* How dare he! I have taken precautions, you needn't be afraid. I have even made him sign some IOUs for Albert. The least thing—and he will be arrested; and he won't dare!"

"Well, marry him . . ."

The marriage was celebrated without any great pomp; it was a quiet family affair. Albert was invited and a few other intimate friends. Hortense, Cléopatra and company were studiously excluded. The bridegroom was extremely interested in his position. Blanche herself tied his cravat with her own hands, and pomaded his head: and in his swallow-tailed coat with his white tie he looked *très comme il faut*.

"*Il est pourtant très comme il faut,*" Blanche herself observed to me, coming out of the General's room, as though the idea that the General was *très comme il faut* was a surprise even to her. Though I assisted at the whole affair as an idle spectator, yet I took so little interest in the details that I have to a great extent forgotten the course of events. I only remember that Blanche turned out not to be called "de Cominges", and her mamma not to be *la veuve* "Cominges", but "du Placet". Why they had been both "de Cominges" till then, I don't know. But the General remained very much pleased with that, and "du Placet" pleased him, in fact, better than "de Cominges". On the morning of the wedding, fully dressed for the part, he kept walking to and fro in the drawing-room, repeating to himself with a grave and important air, "Mlle. Blanche du Placet! Blanche du Placet, du Placet! . . . and his countenance beamed with a certain complacency. At church, before the *maire,* and at the wedding breakfast at home, he was not only joyful but proud. There was a change in both of them. Blanche, too, had an air of peculiar dignity.

"I shall have to behave myself quite differently now," she said to me, perfectly seriously: "*mais vois-tu,* I never thought of one very horrid thing: I even fancy, to this day, I can't learn my surname. Zagoryansky, Zagozyansky, Madame la Générale de Sago—Sago, *ces diables de noms russes, enfin madame la générale a quatorze consonnés! Comme c'est agréable, n'est-ce pas?*"

At last we parted, and Blanche, that silly Blanche, positively shed tears when she said good-bye to me. "*Tu étais bon enfant,*" she said, whimpering. "*Je te croyais bête et tu en avais l'air,*

122

but it suits you." And, pressing my hand at parting, she suddenly cried, "*Attends!*" rushed to her boudoir and, two minutes later, brought me a banknote for two thousand francs. That I should never have believed possible! "It may be of use to you. You may be a very learned *outchitel*, but you are an awfully stupid man. I am not going to give you more than two thousand, for you'll lose it gambling, anyway. Well, good-bye! *Nous serons toujours bon amis,* and if you win, be sure to come to me again, *et tu seras heureux!*"

I had five hundred francs left of my own. I had besides a splendid watch that cost a thousand francs, some diamond studs, and so on, so that I could go on a good time longer without anxiety. I am staying in this little town on purpose to collect myself, and, above all, I am waiting for Mr. Astley. I have learnt for a fact that he will pass through the town and stay here for twenty-four hours on business. I shall find out about everything: and then—then I shall go straight to Homburg. I am not going to Roulettenburg; not till next year anyway. They say it is a bad omen to try your luck twice running at the same tables; and Homburg is the real place for play.

CHAPTER XVII

IT is a year and eight months since I looked at these notes, and only now in sadness and dejection it has occurred to me to read them through. So I stopped then at my going to Homburg. My God! With what a light heart, comparatively speaking, I wrote those last lines! Though not with a light heart exactly, but with a sort of self-confidence, with undaunted hopes! Had I any doubt of myself? And now more than a year and a half has passed, and I am, to my own mind, far worse than a beggar! Yes, what is being a beggar? A beggar is nothing! I have simply ruined myself! However, there is nothing I can compare myself with, and there is no need to give myself a moral lecture! Nothing could be stupider than moral reflections at this date! Oh, self-satisfied people, with what proud satisfaction these prattlers prepare to deliver their lectures! If only they knew how thoroughly I understand the loathsomeness of my present position, they would not be able to bring their tongues to reprimand me. Why, what, what can they tell me that I do not

E

know? And is that the point? The point is that—one turn of the wheel, and all will be changed, and those very moralists will be the first (I am convinced of that) to come up to congratulate me with friendly jests. And they will not all turn away from me as they do now. But, hang them all! What am I now? Zero. What may I be to-morrow? To-morrow I may rise from the dead and begin to live again! There are still the makings of a man in me.

I did, in fact, go to Homburg then, but . . . afterwards I went to Roulettenburg again, and to Spa. I have even been in Baden, where I went as valet to the councillor Gintse, a scoundrel, who was my master here. Yes, I was a lackey for five whole months! I got a place immediately after coming out of prison. (I was sent to prison in Roulettenburg for a debt I made here.) Someone, I don't know who, paid my debt—who was it? Was it Mr. Astley? Polina? I don't know, but the debt was paid; two hundred thalers in all, and I was set free. What could I do? I entered the service of this Gintse. He is a young man and frivolous, he liked to be idle, and I could read and write in three languages. At first I went into his service as a sort of secretary at thirty guldens a month; but I ended by becoming a regular valet: he had not the means to keep a secretary; and he lowered my wages; I had nowhere to go, I remained—and in that way became a lackey by my own doing. I had not enough to eat or to drink in his service, but on the other hand, in five months I saved up seventy gulden. One evening in Baden, however, I announced to him that I intended parting from him; the same evening I went to roulette. Oh, how my heart beat! No, it was not money that I wanted. All that I wanted then was that next day all these Gintses, all these *ober-kellners,* all these magnificent Baden ladies—that they might be all talking about me, repeating my story, wondering at me, admiring me, praising me, and doing homage to my new success. All these are childish dreams and desires, but . . . who knows, perhaps I should meet Polina again, too, I should tell her, and she would see that I was above all these stupid ups and downs of fate. . . . Oh, it was not money that was dear to me! I knew I should fling it away to some Blanche again and should drive in Paris again for three weeks with a pair of my own horses, costing sixteen thousand francs. I know for certain that I am not mean; I believe that I am not even a spendthrift— and yet with what a tremor, with what a thrill at my heart, I hear the croupier's cry: *trente et un, rouge, impair et passe,* or: *quatre, noir, pair et manque!* With what avidity I look at the gambling table on which louis d'or, friedrichs d'or and thalers lie scattered: on the piles of gold when they are scattered from the croupier's shovel like glowing embers, or at the piles of silver a yard high that lie round the wheel. Even on my way to the gambling hall, as soon as I hear, two rooms away, the clink of the scattered money I almost go into convulsions.

Oh! that evening, when I took my seventy gulden to the gambling table, was remarkable too. I began with ten gulden, staking them again on *passe*. I have a prejudice in favour of *passe*. I lost. I had sixty gulden left in silver money; I thought a little and chose *zéro*. I began staking five gulden at a time on *zéro;* at the third turn the wheel stopped at *zéro;* I almost died of joy when I received one hundred and seventy-five gulden; I had not been so delighted when I won a hundred thousand gulden. I immediately staked a hundred gulden on *rouge*—it won; the two hundred on *rouge*—it won; the whole of the four hundred on *noir*—it won; the whole eight hundred on *manque*—it won; altogether with what I had before it made one thousand seven hundred gulden—and that in less than five minutes! Yes, at moments like that one forgets all one's former failures! Why, I had gained this by risking more than life itself, I dared to risk it, and—there I was again, a man among men.

I took a room at the hotel, locked myself in and sat till three o'clock counting over my money. In the morning I woke up, no longer a lackey. I determined the same day to go to Homburg: I had not been a lackey or been in prison there. Half an hour before my train left, I set off to stake on two hazards, no more, and lost fifteen hundred florins. Yet I went to Homburg all the same, and I have been here for a month. . . .

I am living, of course, in continual anxiety. I play for the tiniest stakes, and I keep waiting for something, calculating, standing for whole days at the gambling table and watching the play; I even dream of playing—but I feel that in all this, I have, as it were, grown stiff and wooden, as though I had sunk into a muddy swamp. I gather this from my feeling when I met Mr. Astley. We had not seen each other since that time, and we met by accident. This was how it happened: I was walking in the gardens and reckoning that now I was almost without money, but that I had fifty gulden—and that I had, moreover, three days before paid all I owed at the hotel. And so it was possible for me to go once more to roulette—if I were to win anything, I might be able to go on playing; if I lost I should have to get a lackey's place again, if I did not come across Russians in want of a tutor. Absorbed in these thoughts, I went my daily walk, across the park and the forest in the adjoining principality.

Sometimes I used to walk like this for four hours at a time, and go back to Homburg hungry and tired. I had scarcely gone out of the gardens in the park, when suddenly I saw on one of the seats Mr. Astley. He saw me before I saw him, and called to me. I sat down beside him. Detecting in him a certain dignity of manner, I instantly moderated my delight; though I was awfully delighted to see him.

"And so you are here! I thought I should meet you," he said to me. "Don't trouble yourself to tell me your story; I know, I know all about it; I know every detail of your life during this last year and eight months."

"Bah! What a watch you keep on your old friends!" I answered. "It is very creditable in you not to forget. . . . Stay, though, you have given me an idea. Wasn't it you bought me out of prison at Roulettenburg where I was imprisoned for debt for two hundred gulden? Some unknown person paid it for me."

"No, oh no; it was not I who bought you out when you were in prison at Roulettenburg for a debt of two hundred gulden. But I knew that you were imprisoned for a debt of two hundred gulden."

"Then you know who did pay my debt?"

"Oh, no, I can't say that I know who bought you out."

"Strange; I don't know any of our Russians; besides, the Russians here, I imagine, would not do it; at home in Russia the orthodox may buy out other orthodox Christians. I thought it must have been some eccentric Englishman who did it as a freak."

Mr. Astley listened to me with some surprise. I believe he had expected to find me dejected and crushed.

"I am very glad, however, to find that you have quite maintained your independence of spirit and even your cheerfulness," he pronounced, with a rather disagreeable air.

"That is, you are chafing inwardly with vexation at my not being crushed and humiliated," I said, laughing.

He did not at once understand, but when he understood, he smiled.

"I like your observations: I recognise in those words my clever, enthusiastic and, at the same time, cynical old friend; only Russians can combine in themselves so many opposites at the same time. It is true, a man likes to see even his best friend humiliated; a great part of friendship rests on humiliation. But in the present case I assure you that I am genuinely glad that you are not dejected. Tell me, do you intend to give up gambling?"

"Oh, damn! I shall give it up at once as soon as I . . ."

"As soon as you have won back what you have lost! Just what I thought; you needn't say any more—I know—you have spoken unawares, and so you have spoken the truth. Tell me, have you any occupation except gambling?"

"No, none. . . ."

He began cross-examining me. I knew nothing. I scarcely looked into the newspapers, and had literally not opened a single book all that time.

"You've grown rusty," he observed. "You have not only given up life, all your interests, private and public, the duties of a man and a citizen, your friends (and you really had friends) —you have not only given up your objects, such as they were, all but gambling—you have even given up your memories. I remember you at an intense and ardent moment of your life; but I am sure you have forgotten all the best feelings you had then; your dreams, your most genuine desires now do not rise above *pair, impair, rouge, noir,* the twelve middle numbers, and so on, I am sure!"

"Enough, Mr. Astley, please, please don't remind me," I cried with vexation, almost with anger, "let me tell you, I've forgotten absolutely nothing; but I've only for a time put everything out of my mind, even my memories, until I can make a radical improvement in my circumstances; then . . . then you will see, I shall rise again from the dead!"

"You will be here still in ten years' time," he said. "I bet you I shall remind you of this on this very seat, if I'm alive."

"Well, that's enough," I interrupted impatiently; "and to prove to you that I am not so forgetful of the past, let me ask: where is Miss Polina now? If it was not you who got me out of prison, it must have been her doing. I have had no news of her of any sort since that time."

"No, oh no, I don't believe she did buy you out. She's in Switzerland now, and you'll do me a great favour if you leave off asking about Miss Polina," he said resolutely, and even with some anger.

"That means that she has wounded you very much!" I laughed with displeasure.

"Miss Polina is of all people deserving of respect the very best, but I repeat—you will do me a great favour if you cease questioning me concerning Miss Polina. You never knew her: and her name on your lips I regard as an insult to my moral feelings."

"You don't say so! you are wrong, however; besides, what have I to talk to you about except that, tell me that? Why, all our memories really amount to that! Don't be uneasy, though; I don't want to know your private secret affairs. . . . I am only interested, so to say, in Miss Polina's external affairs. That you could tell me in a couple of words."

"Certainly, on condition that with those two words all is over. Miss Polina was ill for a long time; she's ill even now. For some time she stayed with my mother and sister in the north of England. Six months ago, her grandmother—you remember that madwoman?—died and left her, personally, a fortune of seven thousand pounds. At the present time Miss Polina is travelling with the family of my married sister. Her little brother and sister, too, were provided for by their grandmother's will, and are at school in London. The General, her stepfather, died a month ago in Paris of a stroke. Mlle. Blanche treated him well, but succeeded in getting possession of all he received from the grandmother. . . . I believe that's all."

"And De Grieux? Is not he travelling in Switzerland, too?"

"No, De Grieux is not travelling in Switzerland: and I don't know where De Grieux is; besides, once for all, I warn you to avoid such insinuations and ungentlemanly coupling of names, or you will certainly have to answer for it to me."

"What! in spite of our friendly relations in the past?"

"Yes, in spite of our friendly relations in the past."

"I beg a thousand pardons, Mr. Astley. But allow me, though: there is nothing insulting or ungentlemanly about it; I am not blaming Miss Polina for anything. Besides—a Frenchman and a Russian young lady, speaking generally—it's a combination, Mr. Astley, which is beyond your or my explaining or fully comprehending."

"If you will not mention the name of De Grieux in company with another name, I should like you to explain what you mean by the expression of 'the Frenchman and the Russian young lady'. What do you mean by that 'combination'? Why the Frenchman exactly and why the Russian young lady?"

"You see you are interested. But that's a long story, Mr. Astley. You need to understand many things first. But it is an important question, however absurd it may seem at first sight. The Frenchman, Mr. Astley, is the product of a finished beautiful tradition. You, as a Briton, may not agree with this; I, as a Russian, do not either, from envy maybe; but our young ladies may be of a different opinion. You may think Racine artificial, affected and perfumed; probably you won't even read him. I, too, think him artificial, affected and perfumed—from one point of view even absurd; but he is charming, Mr. Astley, and, what is more, he is a great poet, whether we like it or not. The national type of Frenchman, or, rather, of Parisian, had been moulded into elegant forms while we were still bears. The Revolution inherited the traditions of the aristocracy. Now even the vulgarest Frenchman has manners, modes of address, expressions and even thoughts, of perfectly elegant form, though his own initiative, his own soul and heart, have had no part in the creation of that form; it has all come to him through inheritance. Well, Mr. Astley, I must inform you now that there is not a creature on the earth more confiding, and more candid than a good, clean and not too sophisticated Russian girl. De Grieux, appearing in a peculiar rôle, masquerading, can conquer her heart with extraordinary ease; he has elegance of form, Mr. Astley, and the young lady takes this form for his individual soul, as the natural form of his soul and his heart, and not as an external garment, which has come to him by inheritance. Though it will greatly displease you, I must tell you that Englishmen are for the most part awkward and inelegant, and Russians are rather quick to detect beauty, and are eager for it. But to detect beauty of soul and originality of character needs incomparably more independence and freedom than is to be found in our women, above all in our young ladies—and of course ever so much more experience. Miss Polina—forgive me, the word is spoken and one can't take it back—needs a long, long time to bring herself to prefer you to the scoundrel De Grieux. She thinks highly of you, becomes your friend, opens all her heart to you; but yet the hateful scoundrel, the base and petty money-grubber, De Grieux, will still dominate her heart. Mere obstinacy and vanity, so to say, will maintain his supremacy, because at one time this De Grieux appeared to her with the halo of an elegant marquis, a disillusioned liberal, who is supposed to have ruined himself to help her family and her frivolous stepfather. All these shams have been discovered later on. But the fact that they have been discovered makes no difference: anyway, what she wants is the original De Grieux—that's what she wants! And the more she hates the present De Grieux the more she pines for the original one, though he existed only in her imagination. You are a sugar-boiler, Mr. Astley."

"Yes, I am a partner in the well-known firm, Lovel & Co."

"Well, you see, Mr. Astley, one one side—a sugar-boiler, and on the other—Apollo Belvedere; it is somewhat incongruous. And I am not even a sugar-boiler; I am simply a paltry gambler at roulette, and have even been a lackey, which I think Miss Polina knows very well, as I fancy she has good detectives."

"You are exasperated, and that is why you talk all this nonsense," Mr. Astley said coolly, after a moment's thought. "Besides, there is nothing original in what you say."

"I admit that! But the awful thing is, my noble friend, that however stale, however hackneyed, however farcical my statements may be—they are nevertheless true! Anyway, you and I have made no way at all!"

"That's disgusting nonsense . . . because, because . . . let me tell you!" Mr. Astley, with flashing eyes, pronounced in a quivering voice, "let me tell you, you ungrateful, unworthy, shallow and unhappy man, that I am come to Homburg expressly at her wish, to see you, to have a long and open conversation with you and to tell her everything—what you are feeling, thinking, hoping, and . . . what you remember!"

"Is it possible? Is it possible?" I cried, and tears rushed in streams from my eyes.

I could not restrain them. I believe it was the first time it happened in my life.

"Yes, unhappy man, she loved you, and I can tell you that, because you are—a lost man! What is more, if I were to tell you that she loves you to this day—you would stay here just the same! Yes, you have destroyed yourself. You had some abilities, a lively disposition, and were not a bad fellow; you might have even been of service to your country, which is in such need of men, but—you will remain here, and your life is over. I don't blame you. To my mind all Russians are like that, or disposed to be like that. If it is not roulette it is something similar. The exceptions are very rare. You are not the first who does not understand the meaning of work (I am not talking of your peasantry). Roulette is a game pre-eminently for the Russians. So far you've been honest and preferred serving as a lackey to stealing. . . . But I dread to think what may come in the future. Enough, good-bye! No doubt you are in want of money? Here are ten louis d'or from me. I won't give you more, for you'll gamble it away in any case. Take it and good-bye! Take it!"

"No, Mr. Astley, after all you have said."

"Ta—ake it!" he cried. "I believe that you are still an honourable man, and I give it as a true friend gives to another friend. If I were sure that you would throw up gambling, leave Homburg and would return to your own country, I would be ready to give you at once a thousand pounds to begin a new career. But I don't give you a thousand pounds: I give you only ten louis d'or just because a thousand pounds and ten louis d'or are just the same to you now; it's all the same—you'll gamble it away. Take it and good-bye."

"I will take it if you will let me embrace you at parting."

"Oh, with pleasure!"

We embraced with sincere feeling, and Mr. Astley went away.

No, he is wrong! If I was crude and silly about Polina and De Grieux, he was crude and hasty about Russians. I say nothing of myself. However . . . however, all that is not the point for the time: that is all words, words, and words; deeds are what are wanted! Switzerland is the great thing now! To-morrow . . . Oh, if only it were possible to set off to-morrow! To begin anew, to rise again. I must show them. . . . Let Polina know that I still can be a man. I have only to . . . But now it's too late—but to-morrow . . . oh, I have a presentiment and it cannot fail to be! I have now fifteen louis d'or, and I have begun with fifteen gulden! If one begins carefully . . . and can I, can I be such a baby! Can I fail to understand that I am a lost man, but—can I not rise again! Yes! I have only for once in my life to be prudent and patient and—that is all! I have only for once to show will power and in one hour I can transform my destiny! The great thing is will power. Only remember what happened to me seven months ago at Roulettenburg just before my final failure. Oh! it was a remarkable instance of determination: I had lost everything, then, everything. . . . I was going out of the Casino, I looked, there was still one gulden in my waistcoat pocket: "Then I shall have something for dinner," I thought. But after I had gone a hundred paces I changed my mind and went back. I staked that gulden on *manque* (that time it was on *manque*), and there really is something peculiar in the feeling when, alone in a strange land, far from home and from friends, not knowing whether you will have anything to eat that day—you stake your last gulden, your very last! I won, and twenty minutes later I went out of the Casino, having a hundred and seventy gulden in my pocket. That's a fact! That's what the last gulden can sometimes do! And what if I had lost heart then? What if I had not dared to risk it? . . .

To-morrow, to-morrow it will all be over!

POOR PEOPLE

A NOVEL

Ah, these story tellers! If only they would write anything useful, pleasant, soothing, but they will unearth all sorts of hidden things! . . . I would prohibit their writing! Why, it is beyond everything; you read . . . and you can't help thinking—and then all sorts of foolishness comes into your head; I would really prohibit their writing; I would simply prohibit it altogether.

PRINCE V. F. ODOEVSKY.

April 8.

MY PRECIOUS VARVARA ALEXYEVNA,

I was happy yesterday, immensely happy, impossibly happy! For once in your life, you obstinate person, you obeyed me. At eight o'clock in the evening I woke up (you know, little mother, that I love a little nap of an hour or two when my work is over). I got out a candle, I got paper ready, was mending a pen when suddenly I chanced to raise my eyes —upon my word it set my heart dancing! So you understood what I wanted, what was my heart's desire! I saw a tiny corner of your window-curtain twitched back and caught against the pot of balsams, just exactly as I hinted that day. Then I fancied I caught a glimpse of your little face at the window, that you were looking at me from your little room, that you were thinking of me. And how vexed I was, my darling, that I could not make out your charming little face distinctly! There was a time when we, too, could see clearly, dearie. It is poor fun being old, my own! Nowadays everything seems sort of spotty before my eyes; if one works a little in the evening, writes something, one's eyes are so red and tearful in the morning that one is really ashamed before strangers. In my imagination, though, your smile was beaming, my little angel, your kind friendly little smile; and I had just the same sensation in my heart as when I kissed you, Varinka, do you remember, little angel? Do you know, my darling, I even fancied that you shook your little finger at me? Did you, you naughty girl? You must be sure to describe all that fully in your letter.

Come, what do you think of our little plan about your curtain, Varinka? It is delightful, isn't it? Whether I am

133

sitting at work, or lying down for a nap, or waking up, I know that you are thinking about me over there, you are remembering me and that you are well and cheerful. You drop the curtain—it means "Good-bye, Makar Alexyevitch, it's bedtime!" You draw it up—"Good morning, Makar Alexyevitch, how have you slept or are you quite well, Makar Alexyevitch? As for me, thank God, I am well and all right!" You see, my darling, what a clever idea; there is no need of letters! It's cunning, isn't it? And you know it was my idea. What do you say to me now, Varvara Alevyevna?

I beg to inform you, Varvara Alexyevna, my dear, that I slept last night excellently, contrary to my expectations, at which I am very much pleased; though in new lodgings, after moving, it is always difficult to sleep; there is always some little thing amiss.

I got up this morning as gay as a lark! What a fine morning it was, my darling! Our window was opened; the sun shone so brightly; the birds were chirping; the air was full of the scents of spring and all nature seemed coming back to life—and everything else was to correspond; everything was right, to fit the spring. I even had rather pleasant dreams to-day, and my dreams were all of you, Varinka. I compared you with a bird of the air created for the delight of men and the adornment of nature. Then I thought, Varinka, that we men, living in care and anxiety, must envy the careless and innocent happiness of the birds of the air—and more of the same sort, like that; that is, I went on making such far-fetched comparisons. I have a book, Varinka, and there is the same thought in it, all very exactly described. I write this, my darling, because one has all sorts of dreams, you know. And now it's spring-time, so one's thoughts are always so pleasant; witty, amusing, and tender dreams visit one; everything is in a rosy light. That is why I have written all this; though, indeed, I took it all out of the book. The author there expresses the same desire in verse and writes:

"Why am I not a bird, a bird of prey!"

And so on, and so on. There are all sorts of thoughts in it, but never mind them now!

Oh, where were you going this morning, Varvara Alexyevna? Before I had begun to get ready for the office, you flew out of your room exactly like a bird of the air and crossed the yard, looking so gay. How glad it made me to look at you! Ah, Varinka, Varinka!—You must not be sad; tears are no help to sorrow; I know that, my dear, I know it from experience. Now you are so comfortable and you are getting a little stronger, too.

Well, how is your Fedora? Ah, what a good-natured woman she is! You must write and tell me, Varinka, how you get on with her now and whether you are satisfied with everything. Fedora is rather a grumbler; but you must not mind that, Varinka. God bless her! She has such a good heart. I have written to you already about Teresa here—she, too, is a good-natured and trustworthy woman. And how uneasy I was about our letters! How were they to be delivered? And behold the Lord sent us Teresa to make us happy. She is a good-natured woman, mild and long-suffering. But our landlady is simply merciless. She squeezes her at work like a rag.

Well, what a hole I have got into, Varvara Alexyevna! It is a lodging! I used to live like a bird in the woods, as you know yourself—it was so quiet and still that if a fly flew across the room you could hear it. Here it is all noise, shouting, uproar! But of course you don't know how it is all arranged here. Imagine a long passage, absolutely dark and very dirty. On the right hand there is a blank wall, and on the left, doors and doors, like the rooms in a hotel, in a long row. Well, these are lodgings and there is one room in each; there are people living by twos and by threes in one room. It is no use expecting order—it is a regular Noah's ark! They seem good sort of people, though, all so well educated and learned. One is in the service, a well-read man (he is somewhere in the literary department): he talks about Homer and Brambeus and authors of all sorts: he talks about everything; a very intelligent man! There are two officers who do nothing but play cards. There is a naval man; and an English teacher.

Wait a bit, I will divert you, my darling; I will describe them satirically in my next letter; that is, I will tell you what they are like in full detail. Our landlady is a very untidy little old woman, she goes about all day long in slippers and a dressing-gown, and all day long she is scolding at Teresa. I live in the kitchen, or rather, to be more accurate, there is a room near the kitchen (and our kitchen, I ought to tell you, is clean, light and very nice), a little room, a modest corner . . . or rather the kitchen is a big room of three windows so I have a partition running along the inside wall, so that it makes as it were another room, an extra lodging; it is roomy and comfortable, and there is a window and all—in fact, every convenience. Well, so that is my little corner. So don't you imagine, my darling, there is anything else about it, any mysterious significance in it; "here he is living in the kitchen!" you'll say. Well, if you like, I really am living in the kitchen, behind the partition, but that is nothing; I am quite private, apart from everyone, quiet and snug. I have put in a bed, a table, a chest of drawers and a couple of chairs, and I have hung up the ikon. It is true there are better lodgings—perhaps there may be much better, but convenience is the great thing; I have arranged it all for my own convenience, you know, and you must not imagine it is for anything else. Your little window is opposite, across the yard; and the yard is narrow, one catches glimpses of you passing—it is more cheerful for a poor, lonely fellow like me, and cheaper, too. The very cheapest room here with board costs thirty-five roubles in paper: beyond my means; but my lodging costs me seven roubles in paper and my board five in silver—that is, twenty-four and a half, and before I used to pay thirty and make it up by going without a great many things. I did not always have tea, but now I can spare enough for tea and sugar, too. And you know, my dear, one is ashamed as it were not to drink tea; here they are all well-to-do people so one feels ashamed. One drinks it, Varinka, for the sake of the other people, for the look of the thing; for myself I don't care, I am not particular. Think, too, of pocket-money—one must have a certain amount—then some sort of boots and clothes—is there much left? My salary is all I have. I am content and don't repine. It is sufficient. It has been sufficient for several years; there are extras, too.

Well, good-bye, my angel. I have bought a couple of pots of balsam and geranium—quite cheap—but perhaps you love mignonette? Well, there is mignonette, too, you write and tell me; be sure to write me everything as fully as possible, you know. Don't you imagine anything, though, or have any doubts about my having taken such a room, Varinka dear; no, it is my own convenience made me take it, and only the convenience of it tempted me. I am putting by money, you know, my darling, I am saving up: I have quite a lot of money. You must not think I am such a softy that a fly might knock me down with his wing. No, indeed, my own, I am not a fool, and I have as strong a will as a man of resolute and tranquil soul ought to have. Good-bye, my angel! I have scribbled you almost two sheets and I ought to have been at the office long ago. I kiss your fingers, my own, and remain

Your humble and faithful friend
MAKAR DYEVUSHKIN.

P.S.—One thing I beg you: answer me as fully as possible, my angel. I am sending you a pound of sweets with this, Varinka. You eat them up and may they do you good, and for God's sake do not worry about me and make a fuss. Well, good-bye then, my precious.

April 8.

DEAR SIR, MAKAR ALEXYEVITCH,

Do you know I shall have to quarrel with you outright at last. I swear to you, dear Makar Alexyevitch, that it really hurts me to take your presents. I know what they cost you, how you deny yourself, and deprive yourself of what is necessary. How many times have I told you that I need nothing, absolutely nothing; that I shall never be able to repay you for the kindnesses you have showered upon me? And why have you sent me these flowers? Well, the balsams I don't mind, but why the geranium? I have only to drop an incautious word, for instance, about that geranium, and you rush off and buy it. I am sure it must have been expensive? How charming the flowers are! Crimson, in little crosses. Where did you get such a pretty geranium? I have put it in the middle of the window in the most conspicuous place; I am putting a bench on the floor and arranging the rest of the flowers on the bench; you just wait until I get rich myself! Fedora is overjoyed; it's like paradise now, in our room—so clean, so bright!

Now, why those sweets? Upon my word, I guessed at once from your letter that there was something amiss with you—nature and spring and the sweet scents and the birds chirping. "What's this," I thought, "isn't it poetry?" Yes, indeed, your letter ought to have been in verse, that was all that was wanting, Makar Alexyevitch! There are the tender sentiments and dreams in roseate hues—everything in it! As for the curtain, I never thought of it; I suppose it got hitched up of itself when I moved the flower-pots, so there!

Ah, Makar Alexyevitch! Whatever you may say, however you may reckon over your income to deceive me, to prove that your money is all spent on yourself, you won't take me in and

137

you won't hide anything from me. It is clear that you are depriving yourself of necessities for my sake. What possessed you, for instance, to take such a lodging? Why, you will be disturbed and worried; you are cramped for room, uncomfortable. You love solitude, and here, goodness knows what you have all about you! You might live a great deal better, judging from your salary. Fedora says you used to live ever so much better than you do now. Can you have spent all your life like this in solitude, in privation, without pleasure, without a friendly affectionate word, a lodger among strangers? Ah, dear friend, how sorry I am for you! Take care of your health, anyway, Makar Alexyevitch! You say your eyes are weak; so you must not write by candlelight; why write? Your devotion to your work must be known to your superiors without that.

Once more I entreat you not to spend so much money on me. I know that you love me, but you are not well off yourself. . . . I got up this morning feeling gay, too. I was so happy; Fedora had been at work a long time and had got work for me, too. I was so delighted; I only went out to buy silk and then I set to work. The whole morning I felt so lighthearted, I was so gay! But now it is all black thoughts and sadness again; my heart keeps aching.

Ah, what will become of me, what will be my fate! What is painful is that I am in such uncertainty, that I have no future to look forward to, that I cannot even guess what will become of me. It is dreadful to look back, too. There is such sorrow in the past, and my heart is torn in two at the very memory of it. All my life I shall be in suffering, thanks to the wicked people who have ruined me.

It is getting dark. Time for work. I should have liked to have written to you of lots of things but I have not the time, I must get to work. I must make haste. Of course letters are a good thing; they make it more cheerful, anyway. But why do you never come to see us yourself? Why is that, Makar Alexyevitch? Now we are so near, you know, and sometimes you surely can make time. Please do come! I have seen your Teresa. She looks such a sickly creature; I felt sorry for her and gave her twenty kopecks. Yes! I was almost forgetting: you must write to me all about your life and your surroundings as fully as possible. What sort of people are they about you and do you get on with them? I am longing to know all that. Mind you write to me! To-day I will hitch up the curtain on purpose. You should go to bed earlier; last night I saw your light till midnight. Well, good-bye. To-day I am miserable and bored and sad! It seems it is an unlucky day! Good-bye.

Yours,

VARVARA DOBROSELOV.

April 8.

DEAR MADAM, VARVARA ALEXYEVNA,

Yes, dear friend, yes, my own, it seems it was a bad day for poor luckless me! Yes; you mocked at an old man like me, Varvara Alexyevna! It was my fault, though, entirely my fault! I ought not in my old age, with scarcely any hair on my head, to have launched out into lyrical nonsense and fine phrases. . . . And I will say more, my dear: man is sometimes a strange creature, very strange. My goodness! he begins talking of something and is carried away directly! And what comes of it, what does it lead to? Why, absolutely nothing comes of it, and it leads to such nonsense that—Lord preserve me! I am not angry, Varinka dear, only I am very much vexed to remember it all, vexed that I wrote to you in such a foolish, high-flown way. And I went to the office to-day so cock-a-hoop; there was such radiance in my heart. For no rhyme or reason there was a regular holiday in my soul; I felt so gay. I took up my papers eagerly—but what did it all amount to! As soon as I looked about me, everything was as before, grey and dingy. Still the same ink-spots, the same tables and papers, and I, too, was just the same; as I always have been, so I was still—so what reason was there to mount upon Pegasus? And what was it all due to? The sun peeping out and the sky growing blue! Was that it? And how could I talk of the scents of spring? when you never know what there may be in our yard under the windows! I suppose I fancied all that in my foolishness. You know a man does sometimes make such mistakes in his own feelings and writes nonsense. That is due to nothing but foolish, excessive warmth of heart.

I did not walk but crawled home. For no particular reason my head had begun to ache; well that, to be sure, was one thing on the top of another. (I suppose I got a chill to my spine.) I was so delighted with the spring, like a fool, that I went out in a thin greatcoat. And you were mistaken in my feelings, my dear!

You took my outpouring of them quite in the wrong way. I was inspired by fatherly affection—nothing but a pure fatherly

139

affection, Varvara Alexyevna. For I take the place of a father to you, in your sad fatherless and motherless state; I say this from my soul, from a pure heart, as a relation. After all, though, I am but a distant relation, as the proverb says "only the seventh water on the jelly," still I am a relation and now your nearest relation and protector; seeing that where you had most right to look for protection and support you have met with insult and treachery. As for verses, let me tell you, my love, it would not be seemly for me in my old age to be making verses. Poetry is nonsense! Why, boys are thrashed at school nowadays for making poetry . . . so that is how it is, my dear. . . .

⸙What are you writing to me, Varvara Alexyevna, about comfort, about quiet and all sorts of things? I am not particular, my dear soul, I am not exacting. I have never lived better than I am doing now; so why should I be hard to please in my old age? I am well fed and clothed and shod; and it is not for us to indulge our whims! We are not royalties! My father was not of noble rank and his income was less than mine for his whole family. I have not lived in the lap of luxury! However, if I must tell the truth, everything was a good deal better in my old lodging; it was more roomy and convenient, dear friend. Of course my present lodging is nice, even in some respects more cheerful, and more varied if you like; I have nothing to say against that but yet I regret the old one. We old, that is elderly people, get used to old things as though to something akin to us. The room was a little one, you know; the walls were . . . there, what is the use of talking! . . . the walls were like all other walls, they don't matter, and yet remembering all my past makes me depressed . . . it's a strange thing: it's painful, yet the memories are, as it were, pleasant. Even what was nasty, what I was vexed with at the time, is, as it were, purified from nastiness in my memory and presents itself in an attractive shape to my imagination. We lived peacefully, Varinka, I and my old landlady who is dead. I remember my old landlady with a sad feeling now. She was a good woman and did not charge me much for my lodging. She used to knit all sorts of rugs out of rags on needles a yard long. She used to do nothing else. We used to share light and fuel, so we worked at one table. She had a grand-daughter, Masha—I remember her quite a little thing. Now she must be a girl of thirteen. She was such a mischievous little thing—very merry, always kept us amused, and we lived together, the three of us. Sometimes in the long winter evenings we would sit down to the round table, drink a cup of tea and then set to work. And to keep Masha amused and out of mischief the old lady used to begin to tell tales. And what tales they were! A sensible intelligent man would listen to them with pleasure, let alone a child. Why, I used to light my pipe and be so interested that I forgot my work. And the child, our little mischief, would be so grave, she would lean her rosy cheek on her little hand, open her pretty little mouth and, if the story were the least bit terrible, she would huddle up to the old woman. And we liked to look at her; and did not notice how the candle wanted snuffing nor hear the wind roaring and the storm raging outside.

We had a happy life, Varinka, and we lived together for almost twenty years.

But how I have been prattling on! Perhaps you don't care for such a subject, and it is not very cheering for me to remember it, especially just now in the twilight. Teresa's busy about something, my head aches and my back aches a little, too. And my thoughts are so queer, they seem to be aching as well. I am sad to-day, Varinka!

What's this you write, my dear? How can I come and see you? My darling, what would people say? Why, I should have to cross the yard, our folks would notice it, would begin asking questions—there would be gossip, there would be scandal, they would put a wrong construction on it. No, my angel, I had better see you to-morrow at the evening service, that will be more sensible and more prudent for both of us. And don't be vexed with me, my precious, for writing you such a letter; reading it over I see it is all so incoherent. I am an old man, Varinka, and not well-educated; I had no education in my youth and now I could get nothing into my head if I began studying over again. I am aware, Varinka, that I am no hand at writing, and I know without anyone else pointing it out and laughing at me that if I were to try to write something more amusing I should only write nonsense.

I saw you at your window to-day, I saw you let down your blind. Good-bye, good-bye, God keep you! Good-bye, Varvara Alexyevna.

Your disinterested friend,
MAKAR DYEVUSHKIN.

P.S.—I can't write satirical accounts of anyone now, my

dear. I am too old, Varvara Alexyevna, to be facetious, and I should make myself a laughing-stock; as the proverb has it: "those who live in glass houses should not throw stones."

April 9.

Dear Sir, Makar Alexyevitch,

Come, are not you ashamed, Makar Alexyevitch, my friend and benefactor, to be so depressed and naughty? Surely you are not offended! Oh, I am often too hasty, but I never thought that you would take my words for a biting jest. Believe me, I could never dare to jest at your age and your character. It has all happened through my thoughtlessness, or rather from my being horribly dull, and dullness may drive one to anything! I thought that you meant to make fun yourself in your letter. I felt dreadfully sad when I saw that you were displeased with me. No, my dear friend and benefactor, you are wrong if you ever suspect me of being unfriendly and ungrateful. In my heart I know how to appreciate all you have done for me, defending me from wicked people, from their persecution and hatred. I shall pray for you always, and if my prayer rises to God and heaven accepts it you will be happy.

I feel very unwell to-day. I am feverish and shivering by turns. Fedora is very anxious about me. There is no need for you to be ashamed to come and see us, Makar Alexyevitch; what business is it of other people's! We are acquaintances, and that is all about it. . . .

Good-bye, Makar Alexyevitch. I have nothing more to write now, and indeed I can't write; I am horribly unwell. I beg you once more not to be angry with me and to rest assured of the invariable respect and devotion,

With which I have the honour to remain,
Your most devoted and obedient servant,
Varvara Dobroselov.

April 12.

Dear Madam, Varvara Alexyevna,

Oh, my honey, what is the matter with you! This is how you frighten me every time. I write to you in every letter to take care of yourself, to wrap yourself up, not to go out in bad weather, to be cautious in every way—and, my angel, you don't heed me. Ah, my darling, you are just like some child! Why, you are frail, frail as a little straw, I know that. If there is the least little wind, you fall ill. So you must be careful, look after yourself, avoid risks and not reduce your friends to grief and distress.

You express the desire, dear Varinka, to have a full account of my daily life and all my surroundings. I gladly hasten to carry out your wish, my dear. I will begin from the beginning, my love: it will be more orderly.

To begin with, the staircases to the front entrance are very passable in our house; especially the main staircase—it is clean, light, wide, all cast-iron and mahogany, but don't ask about the backstairs: winding like a screw, damp, dirty, with steps broken and the walls so greasy that your hand sticks when you lean against them. On every landing there are boxes, broken chairs and cupboards, rags hung out, windows broken, tubs stand about full of all sorts of dirt and litter, eggshells and the refuse of fish; there is a horrid smell . . . in fact it is not nice.

I have already described the arrangement of the rooms; it is convenient, there is no denying; that is true, but it is rather stuffy in them. I don't mean that there is a bad smell, but, if I may so express it, a rather decaying, acrid, sweetish smell. At first it makes an unfavourable impression, but that is of no consequence; one has only to be a couple of minutes among us and it passes off and you don't notice how it passes off for you begin to smell bad yourself, your clothes smell, your hands smell and everything smells—well, you get used to it. Siskins simply die with us. The naval man is just buying the fifth— they can't live in our air and that is the long and short of it. Our kitchen is big, roomy and light. In the mornings, it is true, it is rather stifling when they are cooking fish or meat and splashing and slopping water everywhere, but in the evening it is paradise. In our kitchen there is always old linen hanging on a line; and as my room is not far off, that is, is almost part of the kitchen, the smell of it does worry me a little; but no matter, in time one gets used to anything.

Very early in the morning the hubbub begins, people moving about, walking, knocking—everyone who has to is getting up, some to go to the office, others about their own business; they all begin drinking tea. The samovars for the most part belong to the landlady; there are few of them, so we all use them in turn, and if anyone goes with his teapot out of his turn, he catches it.

I, for instance, the first time made that mistake, and . . .

143

but why describe it? I made the acquaintance of everyone
at once. The naval man was the first I got to know; he is
such an open fellow, told me everything: about his father and
mother, about his sister married to an assessor in Tula, and
about the town of Kronstadt. He promised to protect me and
at once invited me to tea with him. I found him in the room
where they usually play cards. There they gave me tea and
were very insistent that I should play a game of chance with
them. Whether they were laughing at me or not I don't know,
but they were losing the whole night and they were still playing
when I went away. Chalk, cards—and the room so full of
smoke that it made my eyes smart. I did not play and they at
once observed that I was talking of philosophy. After that no
one said another word to me the whole time; but to tell the
truth I was glad of it. I am not going to see them now; it's
gambling with them, pure gambling. The clerk in the literary
department has little gatherings in the evening, too. Well,
there it is nice, quiet, harmless and delicate; everything is on a
refined footing.

Well, Varinka, I will remark in passing that our landlady is
a very horrid woman and a regular old hag. You've seen
Teresa. You know what she is like, as thin as a plucked, dried-
up chicken. There are two of them in the house, Teresa and
Faldoni. I don't know whether he has any other name, he
always answers to that one and everyone calls him that. He is
a red-haired, foul-tongued Finn, with only one eye and a snub
nose: he is always swearing at Teresa, they almost fight.

On the whole life here is not exactly perfect at all times. . . .
If only all would go to sleep at once at night and be quiet—
that never happens. They are for ever sitting somewhere playing, and sometimes things go on that one would be ashamed
to describe. By now I have grown accustomed to it; but I
wonder how people with families get along in such a Bedlam.
There is a whole family of poor creatures living in one of our
landlady's rooms, not in the same row with the other lodgings
but on the other side, in a corner apart. They are quiet people!
No one hears anything of them. They live in one little room
dividing it with a screen. He is a clerk out of work, discharged
from the service seven years ago for something. His name is
Gorshkov—such a grey little man; he goes about in such
greasy, such threadbare clothes that it is sad to see him; ever
so much worse than mine. He is a pitiful, decrepit figure (we
sometimes meet in the passage); his knees shake, his hands

shake, his head shakes, from some illness I suppose, poor fellow. He is timid, afraid of everyone and sidles along edgeways; I am shy at times, but he is a great deal worse. His family consists of a wife and three children. The eldest, a boy, is just like his father, just as frail. The wife was once very good-looking, even now one can see it; she, poor thing, goes about in pitiful tatters. They are in debt to the landlady, I have heard, she is none too gracious to them. I have heard, too, that there is some unpleasant business hanging over Gorshkov in connection with which he lost his place. . . . Whether it is a lawsuit—whether he is to be tried, or prosecuted, or what, I can't tell you for certain. Poor they are, mercy on us! It is always still and quiet in their room as if no one were living there. There is no sound even of the children. And it never happens that the children frolic about and play, and that is a bad sign. One evening I happened to pass their door; it was unusually quiet in the house at the time; I heard a sobbing, then a whisper, then sobbing again as though they were crying but so quietly, so pitifully that it was heart-rending, and the thought of those poor creatures haunted me all night so that I could not get to sleep properly.

Well, good-bye, my precious little friend, Varinka. I have described everything to the best of my abilities. I have been thinking of nothing but you all day. My heart aches over you, my dear. I know, my love, you have no warm cloak. Ah! these Petersburg springs, these winds and rain mixed with snow—they'll be the death of me, Varinka! Such salubrious airs, Lord preserve us!

Don't scorn my description, my love. I have no style, Varinka, no style whatever. I only wish I had. I write just what comes into my head only to cheer you up with something. If only I had had some education it would have been a different matter, but how much education have I had? Not a ha'porth.

Always your faithful friend,
MAKAR DYEVUSHKIN.

April 25.

HONOURED SIR, MAKAR ALEXYEVITCH,
I met my cousin Sasha to-day! It is horrible! She will be ruined too, poor thing! I heard, too, from other sources that Anna Fyodorovna is still making inquiries about me. It seems as though she will never leave off persecuting me. She says that she wants to *forgive me*, to forget all the past and

that she must come and see me. She says that you are no
relation to me at all, that she is a nearer relation, that you
have no right to meddle in our family affairs and that it is
shameful and shocking to live on your charity and at your
expense. . . . She says that I have forgotten her hospitality,
that she saved mother and me from starving to death, perhaps,
that she gave us food and drink, and for more than a year
and a half was put to expense on our account, and that besides
all that she forgave us a debt. Even mother she will not spare!
and if only poor mother knew how they have treated me! God
sees it! . . . Anna Fyodorovna says that I was so silly that I
did not know how to take advantage of my luck, that she put
me in the way of good luck, that she is not to blame for anything else, and that I myself was not able or perhaps was not
anxious to defend my own honour. Who was to blame in that,
great God! She says that Mr. Bykov was perfectly right and
that he would not marry just anybody who . . . but why
write it!

It is cruel to hear such falsehoods, Makar Alexyevitch! I
can't tell you what a state I am in now. I am trembling,
crying, sobbing. I have been two hours over writing this letter
to you. I thought that at least she recognised how wrongly she
had treated me; and you see what she is now!

For God's sake don't be alarmed, my friend, the one friend
who wishes me well! Fedora exaggerates everything, I am not
ill. I only caught cold a little yesterday when I went to the
requiem service for mother at Volkovo. Why did you not come
with me? I begged you so much to do so. Ah, my poor, poor
mother, if she could rise from the grave, if she could see how
they have treated me!   V. D.

May 20.

MY DARLING VARINKA,

    I send you a few grapes, my love; I am told they are good
for a convalescent and the doctor recommends them for quench-
ing the thirst—simply for thirst. You were longing the other
day for a few roses, my darling, so I am sending you some
now. Have you any appetite, my love?—that is the most
important thing.

    Thank God, though, that it is all over and done with, and
that our troubles, too, will be soon at an end. We must give
thanks to haven!

    As for books, I cannot get hold of them anywhere for the

moment. I am told there is a good book here written in very fine language; they say it is good, I have not read it myself, but it is very much praised here. I have asked for it and they have promised to lend it me, only will you read it? You are so hard to please in that line; it is difficult to satisfy your taste, I know that already, my darling. No doubt you want poetry, inspiration, lyrics—well, I will get poems too, I will get anything; there is a manuscript book full of extracts here.

'I am getting on very well. Please don't be uneasy about me, my dearie. What Fedora told you about me is all nonsense; you tell her that she told a lie, be sure to tell her so, the wicked gossip! . . . I have not sold my new uniform. And why should I . . . judge for yourself, why should I sell it? Here, I am told, I have forty roubles bonus coming to me, so why should I sell it? Don't you worry, my precious; she's suspicious, your Fedora, she's suspicious. We shall get on splendidly, my darling! Only you get well, my angel, for God's sake, get well. Don't grieve your old friend. Who told you I had grown thin? It is slander, slander again! I am well and hearty and getting so fat that I am quite ashamed. I am well fed and well content: the only thing is for you to get strong again!

Come, good-bye, my angel; I kiss your little fingers,
And remain, always,
Your faithful friend,
Makar Dyevushkin.

P.S.—Ah, my love, what do you mean by writing like that again? . . . What nonsense you talk! Why, how can I come and see you so often, my precious? I ask you how can I? Perhaps snatching a chance after dark; but there, there's scarcely any night at all now, at this season. As it was, my angel, I scarcely left you at all while you were ill, while you were unconscious; but really I don't know how I managed it all; and afterwards I gave up going to you for people had begun to be inquisitive and to ask questions. There had been gossip going about here, even apart from that. I rely upon Teresa; she is not one to talk; but think for yourself, my darling, what a to-do there will be when they find out everything about us. They will imagine something and what will they say then? So you must keep a brave heart, my darling, and wait until you are quite strong again; and then we will arrange a *rendezvous* somewhere out of doors.

MY DEAR MAKAR ALEXYEVITCH,

I so long to do something nice that will please you in
return for all the care and trouble you have taken about me,
and all your love for me, that at last I have overcome my dis-
inclination to rummage in my chest and find my diary, which
I am sending to you now. I began it in the happy time of my
life. You used often to question me with curiosity about my
manner of life in the past, my mother, Pokrovskoe, my time
with Anna Fyodorovna and my troubles in the recent past, and
you were so impatiently anxious to read the manuscript in
which I took the fancy, God knows why, to record some
moments of my life that I have no doubt the parcel I am sending will be a pleasure to you. It made me sad to read it
over. I feel that I am twice as old as when I wrote the last line
in that diary. It was all written at different dates. Good-bye,
Makar Alexyevitch! I feel horribly depressed now and often
I am troubled with sleeplessness. Convalescence is a very
dreary business!   V. D.

I

I was only fourteen when my father died. My childhood was
the happiest time of my life. It began not here but far away
in a province in the wilds. My father was the steward of Prince
P.'s huge estate in the province of T——. We lived in one of
the Prince's villages and led a quiet, obscure, happy life. . . .
I was a playful little thing; I used to do nothing but run about
the fields, the copses and the gardens, and no one troubled about
me. My father was constantly busy about his work, my mother
looked after the house; no one taught me anything, for which
I was very glad. Sometimes at daybreak I would run away
either to the pond or to the copse or to the hayfield or to the
reapers—and it did not matter that the sun was baking, that I
was running, I did not know where, away from the village,
that I was scratched by the bushes, that I tore my dress. . . .
I should be scolded afterwards at home, but I did not care for
that.

And it seems to me that I should have been so happy if it
had been my lot to have spent all my life in one place and never
to have left the country. But I had to leave my native place
while I was still a child. I was only twelve when we moved

to Petersburg. Ah, how well I remember our sorrowful preparations! How I cried when I said good-bye to everything that was so dear to me. I remember that I threw myself on father's neck and besought him with tears to remain a little longer in the country. Father scolded me, mother wept; she said that we had to go, that we could not help it. Old Prince P—— was dead. His heirs had discharged father from his post. Father had some money in the hands of private persons in Petersburg. Hoping to improve his position he thought his presence here in person essential. All this I learnt from mother. We settled here on the Petersburg Side and lived in the same spot up to the time of father's death.

How hard it was for me to get used to our new life! We moved to Petersburg in the autumn. When we left the country it was a clear, warm, brilliant day; the work of the fields was over; huge stacks of wheat were piled up on the threshing-floors and flocks of birds were calling about the fields; everything was so bright and gay: here as we came into the town we found rain, damp autumn chilliness, muggy greyness, sleet and a crowd of new, unknown faces, unwelcoming, ill-humoured, angry! We settled in somehow. I remember we were all in such a fuss, so troubled and busy in arranging our new life. Father was never at home, mother had not a quiet minute—I was forgotten altogether. I felt sad getting up in the morning after the first night in our new abode—our windows looked out on a yellow fence. The street was always covered with mud. The passers-by were few and they were all muffled up, they were all so cold. And for whole days together it was terribly miserable and dreary at home. We had scarcely a relation or intimate acquaintance. Father was not on friendly terms with Anna Fyodorovna. (He was in her debt.) People came on business to us pretty often. Usually they quarrelled, shouted and made an uproar. After every visit father was ill-humoured and cross; he would walk up and down the room by the hour together, frowning and not saying a word to anyone. Mother was silent then and did not dare to speak to him. I used to sit in a corner over a book, still and quiet, not daring to stir.

Three months after we came to Petersburg I was sent to boarding-school. How sad I was at first with strangers! Everything was so cold, so unfriendly! The teachers had such loud voices, the girls laughed at me so and I was such a wild creature. It was so stern and exacting! The fixed hours for everything, the meals in common, the tedious teachers—all that at first fretted and harassed me. I could not even sleep there. I used to cry the whole night, the long, dreary, cold night. Sometimes when they were all repeating or learning their lessons in the evening I would sit over my French translation or vocabularies, not daring to move and dreaming all the while of our little home, of father, of mother, of our old nurse, of nurse's stories. . . . Oh, how I used to grieve! The most trifling thing in the house I would recall with pleasure. I would keep dreaming how nice it would be now at home! I should be sitting in our little room by the samovar with my own people; it would be so warm, so nice, so familiar. How, I used to think, I would hug mother now, how tightly, how warmly! One would think and think and begin crying softly from misery, choking back one's tears, and the vocabularies would never get into one's head. I could not learn my lessons for next day; all night I would dream of the teacher, the mistress, the girls; all night I would be repeating my lessons in my sleep and would not know them next day. They would make me kneel down and give me only one dish for dinner. I was so depressed and dejected. At first all the girls laughed at me and teased me and tried to confuse me when I was saying my lessons, pinched me when in rows we walked into dinner or tea, made complaints against me to the teacher for next to nothing. But how heavenly it was when nurse used to come for me on Saturday evening. I used to hug the old darling in a frenzy of joy. She would put on my things, and wrap me up, and could not keep pace with me, while I would chatter and chatter and tell her everything. I would arrive home gay and happy, would hug everyone as though I had been away for ten years. There would be explanations, talks; descriptions would begin. I would greet everyone, laugh, giggle, skip and run about. Then there would be serious conversations with father about our studies, our teachers, French, Lomond's grammar, and we were all so pleased and happy. It makes me happy even now to remember those minutes. I tried my very utmost to learn and please father. I saw he was spending his last farthing on me and God knows what straits he was in. Every day he grew more gloomy, more ill-humoured, more angry. His character was quite changed, his business was unsuccessful, he had a mass of debts. Mother was sometimes afraid to cry, afraid to say a word for fear of making father angry. She was getting quite ill, was getting thinner and thinner and had begun to have a bad cough.

When I came back from school I used to find such sad faces, mother weeping stealthily, father angry. Then there would be scolding and upbraiding. Father would begin saying that I was no joy, no comfort to them; that they were depriving themselves of everything for my sake and I could not speak French yet; in fact all his failures, all his misfortunes were vented on me and mother. And how could he worry poor mother! It was heartrending to look at her; her cheeks were hollow, her eyes were sunken, there was a hectic flush in her face.

I used to come in for more scolding than anyone. It always began with trifles, and goodness knows what it went on to. Often I did not understand what it was about. Everything was a subject of complaint! . . . French and my being a great dunce and that the mistress of our school was a careless, stupid woman; that she paid no attention to our morals, that father was still unable to find a job, that Lomond's was a very poor grammar and that Zapolsky's was very much better, that a lot of money had been thrown away on me, that I was an unfeeling, stony-hearted girl—in fact, though I, poor thing, was striving my utmost, repeating conversations and vocabularies, I was to blame for everything, I was responsible for everything! And this was not because father did not love me; he was devoted to mother and me, but it was just his character.

Anxieties, disappointments, failures worried my poor father to distraction; he became suspicious, bitter; often he was close upon despair, he began to neglect his health, caught cold and all at once fell ill. He did not suffer long, but died so suddenly, so unexpectedly that we were all beside ourselves with the shock for some days. Mother seemed stunned; I actually feared for her reason.

As soon as father was dead creditors seemed to spring up from everywhere and rushed upon us like a torrent. Everything we had we gave them. Our little house on Petersburg Side, which father had bought six months after moving to Petersburg, was sold too. I don't know how they settled the rest, but we were left without refuge, without sustenance Mother was suffering from a wasting disease, we could not earn our bread, we had nothing to live on, ruin stared us in the face. I was then only just fourteen. It was at this point that Anna Fyodorovna visited us. She always said that she owned landed estates and that she was some sort of relation of ours. Mother said, too, that she was a relation, only a very distant one.

While father was alive she never came to see us. She made her appearance now with tears in her eyes and said she felt great sympathy for us; she condoled with us on our loss and our poverty-stricken condition; added that it was father's own fault; that he had lived beyond his means, had borrowed right and left and that he had been too self-confident. She expressed a desire to be on more friendly terms with us, said we must let by-gones be by-gones; when mother declared she had never felt any hostility towards her, she shed tears, took mother to church and ordered a requiem service for the "dear man". (That was how she referred to father.) After that she was solemnly reconciled to mother.

After leading up to the subject in many lengthy preambles, Anna Fyodorovna first depicted in glaring colours our poverty-stricken and forlorn position, our helplessness and hopelessness, and then invited us, as she expressed it, to take refuge with her. Mother thanked her, but for a long time could not make up her mind to accept; but seeing that there was nothing else she could do and no help for it, she told Anna Fyodorovna at last that we would accept her offer with gratitude.

I remember as though it were to-day the morning on which we moved from the Petersburg Side to Vassilyevsky Ostrov. It was a clear, dry, frosty autumn morning. Mother was crying. I felt horribly sad; my heart was torn and ached with a terrible inexplicable misery . . . it was a terrible time. . . .

II

At first till we—that is mother and I—had grown used to our new home we both felt strange and miserable at Anna Fyodorovna's. Anna Fyodorovna lived in a house of her own in Sixth Row. There were only five living-rooms in the house. In three of them lived Anna Fyodorovna and my cousin Sasha, a child who was being brought up by her, an orphan, fatherless and motherless. Then we lived in one room, and in the last room, next to ours, there was a poor student called Pokrovsky who was lodging in the house.

Anna Fyodorovna lived very well, in a more wealthy style than one could have expected; but her fortune was mysterious and so were her pursuits. She was always in a bustle, was always full of business, she drove out and came back several times a day; but what she was doing, what she was in a fuss about and with what object she was busy I could never make out. She had a large and varied circle of acquaintances. Visitors were always calling upon her, and the queerest people, always on business of some sort and to see her for a minute. Mother always carried me off to my room as soon as the bell rang. Anna Fyodorovna was horribly vexed with mother for this and was continually repeating that we were too proud, that we were proud beyond our means, that we had nothing to be proud about, and she would go on like that for hours together. I did not understand these reproaches at the time and, in fact, it is only now that I have found out, or rather that I guess why mother could not make up her mind to live with Anna Fyodorovna. Anna Fyodorovna was a spiteful woman, she was continually tormenting us. To this day it is a mystery to me why it was she invited us to live with her. At first she was fairly nice to us, but afterwards she began to show her real character as soon as she saw we were utterly helpless and had nowhere else to go. Later on she became very affectionate to me, even rather coarsely affectionate and flattering, but at first I suffered in the same way as mother. Every minute she was upbraiding us, she did nothing but talk of her charitable deeds. She introduced us to outsiders as her poor relations—a helpless widow and orphan to whom in the kindness of her heart, out of Christian charity, she had given a home. At meals she watched every morsel we took, while if we did not eat, there would be a fuss again; she would say we were fastidious, that we should not be over-nice, that we should be thankful for what we had; that she doubted if we had had anything better in our own home. She was continually abusing father, saying that he wanted to be better than other people and much good that had done him; that he had left his wife and daughter penniless and that if they had not had a benevolent relation, a Christian soul with a feeling heart, then, God knows, they might have been rotting in the street and dying of hunger. What did she not say! It was not so much painful as disgusting to hear her.

Mother was continually crying; her health grew worse from day to day. She was visibly wasting, yet she and I worked from morning till night, taking in sewing, which Anna Fyodorovna very much disliked, she was continually saying that she was not going to have her house turned into a dressmaker's shop. But we had to have clothes; we had to lay by for unforeseen expenses; it was absolutely necessary to have money of our own. We saved on the off-chance, hoping we might be able in time to move elsewhere. But mother lost what little health was left her over work; she grew weaker every day. The disease sucked the life out of her like a worm and hurried her to the grave. I saw it all, I felt it all, I realised it all and suffered; it all went on before my eyes

The days passed and each day was like the one before. We lived as quietly as if we were not in a town. Anna Fyodorovna calmed down by degrees as she began fully to recognise her power. Though, indeed, no one ever thought of contradicting her. We were separated from her rooms by the corridor, and Pokrovsky's room was, as I have mentioned before, next to ours. He used to teach Sasha French and German, history, geography—all the sciences, as Anna Fyodorovna said, and for this he had his board and lodging from her. Sasha was a very intelligent child, though playful and mischievous; she was thirteen. Anna Fyodorovna observed to mother that it would not be amiss if I were to have lessons, since my education had not been finished at the boarding-school, and for a whole year I shared Sasha's lessons with Pokrovsky. Pokrovsky was poor, very poor. His health had prevented him from continuing his studies and it was only from habit that he was called a student. He was so retiring, so quiet and so still that we heard no sound of him from our room. He was very queer-looking; he walked so awkwardly, bowed so awkwardly and spoke so queerly that at first I could not look at him without laughing. Sasha was continually mocking at him, especially when he was giving us our lessons. He was of an irritable temper, too, was constantly getting cross, was beside himself about every trifle, scolded us, complained of us, and often went off into his own room in anger without finishing the lesson. He used to sit for days together over his books. He had a great many books, and such rare and expensive books. He gave other lessons, too, for which he was paid, and as soon as ever he had money he would go and buy books.

In time I got to know him better and more intimately. He was a very kind and good young man, the best person it has been my lot to meet. Mother had a great respect for him. Afterwards he became the best of my friends—next to mother, of course.

At first, though I was such a big girl, I was as mischievous as Sasha. We used to rack our brains for hours together to find ways to tease him and exhaust his patience. His anger was extremely funny, and we used to find it awfully amusing. (I am ashamed even to think of it now.) Once we teased him almost to the point of tears and I distinctly heard him whisper, "Spiteful children." I was suddenly overcome with confusion; I felt ashamed and miserable and sorry for him. I remember that I blushed up to my ears and almost with tears in my eyes began begging him not to mind and not to be offended at our stupid mischief. But he closed the book and without finishing the lesson went off to his own room. I was torn with penitence all day long. The thought that we children had reduced him to tears by our cruelty was insufferable. So we had waited for his tears. So we had wanted them; so we had succeeded in driving him out of all patience; so we had forced him, a poor unfortunate man, to realise his hard lot.

I could not sleep all night for vexation, sorrow, repentance. They say repentance relieves the soul—on the contrary. There was an element of vanity mixed, I don't know how, with my sadness. I did not want him to look upon me as a child, I was fifteen then.

From that day I began worrying my imagination, creating thousands of plans to make Pokrovsky change his opinion about me. But I had become all of a sudden timid and shy; in my real position I could venture upon nothing and confined myself to dreams (and God knows what dreams!). I left off joining in Sasha's pranks; he left off being angry with us; but for my vanity that was little comfort.

Now I will say a few words about the strangest, most curious and most pathetic figure I have ever chanced to meet. I speak of him now, at this passage in my diary, because until that period I had hardly paid any attention to him. But now everything that concerned Pokrovsky had suddenly become interesting to me.

There used sometimes to come to the house a little old man, grey-headed, grubby, badly-dressed, clumsy, awkward, incredibly queer in fact. At the first glance at him one might imagine that he was, as it were, abashed by something—as it were, ashamed of himself. That is why he always seemed to be shrinking into himself, to be, as it were, cowering; he had such queer tricks and ways that one might almost have concluded he was not in his right mind. He would come to the house and stand at the glass door in the entry without daring to come in. If one of us passed by—Sasha or I or any one of the servants he knew to be rather kind to him—he would begin waving at once, beckoning, making gesticulations, and only when one nodded and called to him—a sign agreed upon that there was no outsider in the house and that he might come in when he liked—only then the old man stealthily opened the door with a smile of glee, and rubbing his hands with satisfaction, walked on tiptoe straight to Pokrovsky's room. This was Pokrovsky's father.

Later on, I learnt the whole story of this poor old man. He had once been in the service, was entirely without ability, and filled the very lowest and most insignificant post. When his first wife (our Pokrovsky's mother) died he took it into his head to marry a second time and married a girl of the working-class. Everything was turned topsy-turvy under the rule of his new wife. She let no one live in peace, she domineered over everyone. Our Pokrovsky was still a child, ten years old. His stepmother hated him, but fate was kind to the boy. A country gentleman called Bykov, who had known the elder Pokrovsky and at one time been his patron, took the child under his protection and sent him to school. He was interested in him because he had known his mother, who had been a protégée of Anna Fyodorovna's and had by her been married to Pokrovsky. Mr. Bykov, a very intimate friend of Anna Fyodorovna's, had generously given the girl a dowry of five thousand roubles on her marriage. Where that money went to I don't know.

That was the story Anna Fyodorovna told me; young Pokrovsky never liked speaking of his family circumstances. They say his mother was very pretty, and it seems strange to me that she should have been so unfortunately married to such an insignificant man. He was quite young when she died four years after their marriage.

From boarding-school young Pokrovsky went on to a high school and then to the university. Mr. Bykov, who very often came to Petersburg, did not confine his protection to that. Owing to the breakdown of his health Pokrovsky could not continue his studies at the university. Mr. Bykov introduced him to Anna Fyodorovna, commended him to her good offices and so young Pokrovsky was taken into the house and was given his board on condition of teaching Sasha everything that was necessary. Old Pokrovsky was driven by grief at his wife's cruelty to the worst of vices and was scarcely ever sober. His wife used to beat him, make him live in the kitchen, and brought things at last to such a pass that he was quite accustomed to being beaten and ill-treated and did not complain of it. He was not a very old man, but his mind had almost given way owing to his bad habits. The one sign he showed of generous and humane feeling was his boundless love for his son. It was said that young Pokrovsky was as like his dead mother as one drop of water is like another. Maybe it was the memory of his first good wife that stirred in the ruined old man's heart this infinite love for his son. The old man could speak of nothing but his son and always visited him twice a week. He did not dare to come oftener, for young Pokrovsky could not endure his father's visits. Of all his failings, undoubtedly the greatest and foremost was his disrespect to his father. The old man certainly was at times the most insufferable creature in the world. In the first place he was horribly inquisitive, secondly, by remarks and questions of the most trivial and senseless kind he interrupted his son's work every minute, and, lastly, he would sometimes come under the influence of drink. The son gradually trained the old man to overcome his vices, his curiosity and incessant chatter, and at last had brought things to such a point that the old man obeyed him in everything like an oracle and did not dare open his mouth without permission.

The poor old man could not sufficiently admire and marvel at his Petinka (as he called his son). When he came to see him he almost always had a timid, careworn air, most likely from uncertainty as to the reception his son would give him. He was usually a long time making up his mind to come in, and if I happened to be there he would spend twenty minutes questioning me: "How was Petinka? Was he quite well? What sort of mood was he in, and was he busy over anything important? What was he doing? Was he writing, or absorbed in reflection?" When I had sufficiently cheered and reassured him, the old man at last ventured to come in, and very, very quietly, very, very cautiously opened the door, first poked in his head, and if his son nodded to him and the old man saw he was not angry, he moved stealthily into the room, took off his overcoat and his hat, which was always crushed, full of holes and with a broken brim, hung them on a hook, did everything quietly, noiselessly; then cautiously sat down on a chair, never taking his eyes off his son, watching every movement and trying to guess what mood his "Petinka" was in. If his son seemed ever so little out of humour and the old man noticed it, he got up from his seat at once and explained, "I just looked in, Petinka, only for a minute. I have been a long walk, I was passing and came in for a rest." And then, dumbly, submissively he would take his coat, his wretched hat, again he would stealthily open the door and go away, keeping a forced smile on his face to check the rush of disappointment in his heart and to hide it from his son.

But when the son made the father welcome, the old man was beside himself with joy. His face, his gestures, his movements all betrayed his pleasure. If his son began talking to him, the old man always rose a little from the chair and answered softly, deferentially, almost with reverence, always trying to use the choicest, that is, the most absurd expressions. But he was not blessed with the gift of words; he was always nervous and confused, so that he did not know what to do with his hands, what to do with himself, and kept whispering the answer to himself long afterwards as though trying to correct himself. If he did succeed in giving a good answer, the old man smoothed himself down, straightened his waistcoat, his tie, his coat and assumed an air of dignity. Sometimes he plucked up so much courage and grew so bold that he stealthily got up from his chair, went up to the bookshelf, took down some book and even began reading something on the spot, whatever the book might be. All this he did with an air of assumed unconcern and coolness, as though he could always do what he liked with his son's books, as though his son's graciousness was nothing out of the way.

But I once happened to see how frightened the poor fellow was when Pokrovsky asked him not to touch the books. He grew nervous and confused, put the book back upside down, then tried to right it, turned it round and put it in with the edges outside; smiled, flushed and did not know how to efface his crime. Pokrovsky by his persuasions did succeed in turning the old man a little from his evil propensities, and whenever the son saw his father sober three times running he would give him twenty-five kopecks, fifty kopecks, or more at parting. Sometimes he would buy his father a pair of boots, a tie or a waistcoat; then the old man was as proud as a cock in his new clothes.

Sometimes he used to come to us. He used to bring Sasha and me gingerbread cocks and apples and always talked to us of Petinka. He used to beg us to be attentive and obedient at lessons, used to tell us that Petinka was a good son, an exemplary son and, what was more, a learned son. Meanwhile he would wink at us so funnily with his left eye and make such amusing grimaces that we could not help smiling, and went into peals of laughter at him. Mother was very fond of him. But the old man hated Anna Fyodorovna, though he was stiller than water, humbler than grass in her presence.

Soon I left off having lessons with Pokrovsky. As before, he looked upon me as a child, a mischievous little girl on a level with Sasha. This hurt me very much, for I was trying my utmost to efface the impression of my behaviour in the past, but I was not noticed. That irritated me more and more. I scarcely ever spoke to Pokrovsky except at our lessons, and indeed I could not speak. I blushed and was confused, and afterwards shed tears of vexation in some corner.

I do not know how all this would have ended if a strange circumstance had not helped to bring us together. One evening when mother was sitting with Anna Fyodorovna I went stealthily into Pokrovsky's room. I knew he was not at home, and I really don't know what put it into my head to go into his room. Until that moment I had never peeped into it, though we had lived next door for over a year. This time my heart throbbed violently, so violently that it seemed it would leap out of my bosom. I looked around with peculiar curiosity. Pokrovsky's room was very poorly furnished: it was untidy. Papers were lying on the table and the chairs. Books and papers! A strange thought came to me, and at the same time an unpleasant feeling of vexation took possession of me. It seemed to me that my affection, my loving heart were little to him. He was learned while I was stupid, and knew nothing, had read nothing, not a single book . . . at that point I looked enviously at the long shelves which were almost breaking down under the weight of the books. I was overcome by anger, misery, a sort of fury. I longed and at once determined to read his books, every one of them, and as quickly as possible. I don't know, perhaps I thought that when I learned all he knew I should be more worthy of his friendship. I rushed to the first shelf; without stopping to think I seized the first dusty old volume; flushing and turning pale by turns, trembling with excitement and dread, I carried off the stolen book, resolved to read it at night—by the night-light while mother was asleep.

But what was my vexation when, returning to our room, I hurriedly opened the book and saw it was some old work in Latin. It was half decayed and worm-eaten. I went back without loss of time. Just as I was trying to put the book back in the shelf I heard a noise in the passage and approaching footsteps. I tried with nervous haste to be quick, but the insufferable book had been so tightly wedged in the shelf that when I took it out all the others had shifted and packed closer of themselves, so now there was no room for their former companion. I had not the strength to force the book in. I pushed the books with all my might, however. The rusty nail which supported the shelf, and which seemed to be waiting for that moment to break, broke. One end of the shelf fell down. The books dropped noisily on the floor in all directions. The door opened and Pokrovsky walked into the room.

I must observe that he could not bear anyone to meddle in his domain. Woe to anyone who touched his books! Imagine my horror when the books, little and big, of all sizes and shapes dashed off the shelf, flew dancing under the table, under the chairs, all over the room! I would have run, but it was too late. It is all over, I thought, it is all over. I am lost, I am done for! I am naughty and mischievous like a child of ten, I am a silly chit of a girl! I am a great fool!

Pokrovsky was dreadfully angry.

"Well, this is the last straw!" he shouted. "Are not you ashamed to be so mischievous? . . . Will you ever learn sense?" and he rushed to collect the books. "Don't, don't!" he shouted. "You would do better not to come where you are not invited."

A little softened, however, by my humble movement, he went on more quietly, in his usual lecturing tone, speaking as though he were still my teacher:

"Why, when will you learn to behave properly and begin to be sensible? You should look at yourself. You are not a little child. You are not a little girl. Why, you are fifteen!"

And at that point, probably to satisfy himself that I was not a little girl, he glanced at me and blushed up to his ears. I did not understand. I stood before him staring in amazement. He got up, came towards me with an embarrassed air, was horribly confused, said something, seemed to be apologising for something, perhaps for having only just noticed that I was such a big girl. At last I understood. I don't remember what happened to me then; I was overcome with confusion, lost my head, blushed even more crimson than Pokrovsky, hid my face in my hands and ran out of the room.

I did not know what to do, where to hide myself for shame.

The mere fact that he had found me in his room was enough! For three whole days I could not look at him: I blushed until the tears came into my eyes. The most absurd ideas whirled through my brain. One of them—the maddest—was a plan to go to him, explain myself to him, confess everything to him, tell him all openly and assure him I had not behaved like a silly little girl but had acted with good intentions. I quite resolved to go but, thank God, my courage failed me. I can imagine what a mess I should have made of it! Even now I am ashamed to remember it all.

A few days later mother suddenly became dangerously ill. After two days in bed, on the third night, she was feverish and delirious. I did not sleep all one night, looking after mother, sitting by her bedside, bringing her drink and giving her medicine at certain hours. The second night I was utterly exhausted. At times I was overcome with sleep, my head went round and everything was green before my eyes. I was ready any minute to drop with fatigue, but mother's weak moans roused me, I started up, waked for an instant and then was overwhelmed with drowsiness again. I was in torment. I don't know, I cannot remember, but some horrible dream, some awful apparition haunted my over-wrought brain at the agonising moment of struggling between sleeping and waking. I woke up in terror. The room was dark; the night-light had burned out. Streaks of light suddenly filled the whole room, gleamed over the wall and disappeared. I was frightened, a sort of panic came over me. My imagination had been upset by a horrible dream, my heart was oppressed with misery. . . . I leapt up from my chair and unconsciously shrieked from an agonising, horribly oppressive feeling. At that moment the door opened and Pokrovsky walked into our room.

All I remember is that I came to myself in his arms. He carefully put me in a low chair, gave me a glass of water and showered questions on me. I don't remember what I answered. "You are ill, you are very ill yourself," he said, taking my hand. "You are feverish, you will kill yourself. You do not think of your health; calm yourself, lie down, go to sleep. I will wake you in two hours time. Rest a little . . . lie down, lie down!" not letting me utter a word in objection. I was too tired to object; my eyes were closing with weakness. I lay down in a low chair, resolved to sleep only half an hour, and slept till morning. Pokrovsky only waked me when the time came to give mother her medicine.

The next evening when, after a brief rest in the daytime, I made ready to sit up by mother's bedside again, firmly resolved not to fall asleep this time, Pokrovsky at eleven o'clock knocked at our door. I opened it.

"It is dull for you, sitting alone," he said to me. "Here is a book; take it, it won't be so dull, anyway."

I took it; I don't remember what the book was like; I hardly glanced into it, though I did not sleep all night. A strange inward excitement would not let me sleep; I could not remain sitting still; several times I got up from the chair and walked about the room. A sort of inward content was suffused through my whole being. I was so glad of Pokrovsky's attention. I was proud of his anxiety and uneasiness about me. I spent the whole night, musing and dreaming. Pokrovsky did not come in again, and I knew he would not come, and I wondered about the following evening.

The next evening, when everyone in the house had gone to bed, Pokrovsky opened his door and began talking to me, standing in the doorway of his room. I do not remember now a single word of what we said to one another; I only remember that I was shy, confused, vexed with myself and looked forward impatiently to the end of the conversation, though I had been desiring it intensely, dreaming of it all day, and making up my questions and answers. . . . The first stage of our friendship began from that evening. All through mother's illness we spent several hours together every night. I got over my shyness by degrees, though after every conversation I found something in it to be vexed with myself about. Yet with secret joy and proud satisfaction I saw that for my sake he was beginning to forget his insufferable books.

By chance the conversation once turned in jest on his books having fallen off the shelf. It was a strange moment. I was, as it were, *too* open and candid. I was carried away by excitement and a strange enthusiasm, and I confessed everything to him. . . . Confessed that I longed to study, to know something, that it vexed me to be considered a little girl. . . . I repeat that I was in a very strange mood; my heart was soft, there were tears in my eyes—I concealed nothing and told him everything—everything—my affection for him, my desire to love him, to live with him, to comfort him, to console him. He looked at me somewhat strangely, with hesitation and perplexity, and did not say one word. I felt all at once horribly sore and miserable. It seemed to me that he did not understand me, that perhaps he was laughing at me. I suddenly burst out crying like a child, I could not restrain myself, and sobbed as though I were in a sort of fit. He took my hands, kissed them and pressed them to his heart; talked to me, comforted me; he was much touched. I do not remember what he said to me, only I kept on crying and laughing and crying again, blushing, and so joyful that I could not utter a word. In spite of my emotion, I noticed, however, that Pokrovsky still showed traces of embarrassment and constraint. It seemed as though he were overwhelmed with wonder at my enthusiasm, my delight, my sudden warm, ardent affection. Perhaps it only seemed strange to him at first; later on his hesitation vanished and he accepted my devotion to him, my friendly words, my attentions, with the same simple, direct feeling that I showed, and responded to it all with the same attentiveness, as affectionately and warmly as a sincere friend, a true brother. My heart felt so warm, so happy. . . . I was not reserved, I concealed nothing from him, he saw it all and grew every day more and more attached to me.

And really I do not remember what we used to talk about in those tormenting, and at the same time happy, hours when we met at night by the flickering light of a little lamp, and almost by my poor mother's bedside. . . . We talked of everything that came into our minds, that broke from our hearts, that craved expression, and we were almost happy. . . . Oh, it was a sad and joyful time, both at once. . . . And it makes me both sad and joyful now to think of him. Memories are always tormenting, whether they are glad or bitter; it is so with me, anyway; but even the torment is sweet. And when the heart grows heavy, sick, weary and sad, then memories refresh and revive it, as the drops of dew on a moist evening after a hot day refresh and revive a poor sickly flower, parched by the midday heat.

Mother began to get better, but I still sat up by her bedside at night. Pokrovsky used to give me books; at first I read them to keep myself awake; then more attentively, and afterwards with eagerness. They opened all at once before me much that was new, unknown and unfamiliar. New thoughts, new impressions rushed in a perfect flood into my heart. And the more emotion, the more perplexity and effort it cost me to assimilate those new impressions, the dearer they were to me and the more sweetly they thrilled my soul. They crowded upon my heart all at once, giving it no rest. A strange chaos began to trouble my whole being. But that spiritual commotion could not upset my balance altogether. I was too dreamy and that saved me.

When mother's illness was over, our long talks and evening interviews were at an end; we succeeded sometimes in exchanging words, often trivial and of little consequence, but I was fond of giving everything its significance, its peculiar underlying value. My life was full, I was happy, calmly, quietly happy. So passed several weeks. . . .

One day old Pokrovsky came to see us. He talked to us for a long time, was exceptionally gay, cheerful and communicative, he laughed, made jokes after his fashion, and at last explained the mystery of his ecstatic condition, and told us that that day week would be Petinka's birthday and that for the occasion he should come and see his son; that he should put on a new waistcoat and that his wife had promised to buy him new boots. In fact, the old man was completely happy and chatted away of everything in his mind. His birthday! That birthday gave me no rest day or night. I made up my mind to give Pokrovsky something as a sign of my affection. But what? At last I thought of giving him books. I knew he wanted to have Pushkin's works in the latest, complete edition, and I decided to buy Pushkin. I had thirty roubles of my own money earned by needlework. The money had been saved up to buy me a dress. I promptly sent old Matrona, our cook, to find out what the whole of Pushkin cost. Alas! The price of the eleven volumes, including the cost of binding, was at least sixty roubles. Where could I get the money? I thought and thought and did not know what to decide upon. I did not want to ask mother. Of course mother would have certainly helped me; but then everyone in the house would have known of our present; besides, the present would have become a token of gratitude in repayment for all that Pokrovsky had done for us during the past year. I wanted to give it alone and no one else to know of it. And for what he had done for me I wanted to be indebted to him for ever without any sort of repayment except my affection.

At last I found a way out of my difficulty.

I knew at the second-hand shops in the Gostiny Dvor one could sometimes, with a little bargaining, buy at half-price a book hardly the worse for wear and almost completely new. I resolved to visit the Gostiny Dvor. As it happened, next day some things had to be bought for us and also for Anna Fyodorovna. Mother was not very well, and Anna Fyodorovna, very luckily, was lazy, so that it fell to me to make these purchases and I set off with Matrona.

I was so fortunate as to find a Pushkin very quickly and one in a very fine binding. I began bargaining. At first they demanded a price higher than that in the bookseller's shops; but in the end, though not without trouble, and walking away several times, I brought the shopman to knocking down the price and asking no more than ten roubles in silver. How I enjoyed bargaining! . . . Poor Matrona could not make out what was the matter with me and what possessed me to buy so many books. But, oh, horror! My whole capital consisted of thirty roubles in paper, and the shopman would not consent to let the books go cheaper. At last I began beseeching him, begged and begged him and at last persuaded him. He gave way but only took off two and a half roubles and swore he only made that concession for my sake because I was such a nice young lady and he would not have done it for anyone else. I still had not enough by two and a half roubles. I was ready to cry with vexation. But the most unexpected circumstance came to my assistance in my distress.

Not far off at another bookstall I saw old Pokrovsky. Four or five second-hand dealers were clustering about him; they were bewildering him completely and he was at his wits' end. Each of them was proffering his wares and there was no end to the books they offered and he longed to buy. The poor old man stood in the midst of them, looking a disconsolate figure and did not know what to choose from what was offered him. I went up and asked him what he was doing here. The old man was delighted to see me; he was extremely fond of me, hardly less than of his Petinka, perhaps.

"Why, I'm buying books, Varvara Alexyevna," he answered. "I am buying books for Petinka. Here it will soon be his birthday and he is fond of books, so, you see, I am going to buy them for him. . . ."

The old man always expressed himself in a very funny way and now he was in the utmost confusion besides. Whatever he asked the price of, it was always a silver rouble, or two or three silver roubles; he had by now given up inquiring about the bigger books and only looked covetously at them, turning over the leaves, weighing them in his hands and putting them back again in their places.

"No, no, that's dear," he would say in an undertone, "but maybe there'll be something here."

And then he would begin turning over thin pamphlets, song-books, almanacs; these were all very cheap.

"But why do you want to buy those?" I asked him. "They are all awful rubbish."

"Oh, no," he answered. "No, you only look what good little books there are here. They are very, very good little books!"

And the last words he brought out in such a plaintive sing-song that I fancied he was ready to cry with vexation at the good books being so dear, and in another moment a tear would drop from his pale cheeks on his red nose. I asked him whether he had plenty of money.

"Why, here," the poor fellow pulled out at once all his money wrapped up in a piece of greasy newspaper. "Here there's half a rouble, a twenty-kopeck piece and twenty kopecks in copper."

I carried him off at once to my second-hand bookseller.

"Here, these eleven volumes cost only thirty-two roubles and a half; I have thirty; put your two and a half to it and we will buy all these books and give them to him together."

The old man was beside himself with delight, he shook out all his money, and the bookseller piled all our purchased volumes upon him. The old man stuffed volumes in all his pockets, carried them in both hands and under his arms and bore them all off to his home, giving me his word to bring them all to me in secret next day.

Next day the old man came to see his son, spent about an hour with him as usual, then came in to us and sat down beside me with a very comical mysterious air. Rubbing his hands in proud delight at being in possession of a secret, he began with a smile by telling me that all the books had been conveyed here unnoticed and were standing in a corner in the kitchen under Matrona's protection. Then the conversation naturally passed to the day we were looking forward to; the old man talked at length of how we would give our present, and the more absorbed he became in the subject the more apparent it was to me that he had something in his heart of which he could not, dared not, speak, which, in fact, he was afraid to put into words. I waited and said nothing. The secret joy, the secret satisfaction which I had readily discerned at first in his strange gestures and grimaces and the winking of his left eye, disappeared. Every moment he grew more uneasy and disconsolate; at last he could not contain himself.

"Listen," he began timidly in an undertone.

"Listen, Varvara Alexyevna . . . do you know what, Varvara Alexyevna . . . ?" The old man was in terrible confusion. "When the day of his birthday comes, you know, you take ten books and give them yourself, that is from yourself, on your own account; I'll take only the eleventh, and I, too, will give it from myself, that is, apart, on my own account. So then, do you see—you will have something to give, and I shall have something to give; we shall both have something to give."

At this point the old man was overcome with confusion and relapsed into silence. I glanced at him; he was waiting for my verdict with timid expectation.

"But why do you want us not to give them together, Zahar Petrovitch?"

"Why, you see, Varvara Alexyevna, it's just . . . it's only, you know . . ."

In short, the old man faltered, flushed, got stuck in his sentence and could not proceed.

"You see," he explained at last, "Varvara Alexyevna, I indulge at times . . . that is, I want to tell you that I am almost always indulging, constantly indulging . . . I have a habit which is very bad . . . that is, you know, it's apt to be so cold outdoors and at times there are unpleasantnesses of all sorts, or something makes one sad, or something happens amiss and then I give way at once and begin to indulge and sometimes drink too much. Petrusha dislikes that very much. He gets angry with me, do you see, Varvara Alexyevna, scolds me and gives me lectures, so that I should have liked now to show him by my present that I am reforming and beginning to behave properly, that here I've saved up to buy the book, saved up for ever so long, for I scarcely ever have any money except it may happen Petrusha gives me something. He knows that. So here he will see how I have used my money and will know that I have done all that only for him."

I felt dreadfully sorry for the old man. I thought for a moment. The old man looked at me uneasily.

"Listen, Zahar Petrovitch," I said; "you give him them all."

"How all? Do you mean all the books?"

"Why, yes, all the books."

"And from myself?"

"Yes, from yourself."

"From myself alone? Do you mean on my own account?"

"Why yes, on your own account."

I believe I made my meaning very clear, but it was a long time before the old man could understand me.

"Why yes," he said, after pondering. "Yes! That would be very nice, but how about you, Varvara Alexyevna?"

"Oh, well, I shall give nothing."

"What!" cried the old man, almost alarmed. "So you don't want to give Petinka anything?"

The old man was dismayed; at that moment he was ready, I believe, to give up his project in order that I might be able to give his son something. He was a kind-hearted old fellow! I assured him that I should have been glad to give something, but did not want to deprive him of the pleasure.

"If your son is satisfied and you are glad," I added, "then I shall be glad, for I shall feel secretly in my heart as though I were really giving it myself."

With that the old man was completely satisfied. He spent another two hours with us, but could not sit still in his place and was continually getting up, fussing noisily about, playing with Sasha, stealthily kissing me, pinching my hand and making faces at Anna Fyodorovna on the sly. Anna Fyodorovna turned him out of the house at last. The old man was, in fact, in his delight, more excited than he had perhaps ever been before.

On the festive day he appeared exactly at eleven o'clock, coming straight from mass in a decently mended swallow-tail coat and actually wearing a new waistcoat and new boots. He had a bundle of books in each hand. We were all sitting drinking coffee in Anna Fyodorovna's drawing-room at the time (it was Sunday). The old man began by saying, I believe, that Pushkin was a very fine poet; then, with much hesitation and confusion, he passed suddenly to the necessity of one's behaving oneself properly, and that if a man does not behave properly then he will indulge; that bad habits are the ruin and destruction of a man; he even enumerated several fatal instances of intemperance, and wound up by saying that for some time past he had been completely reformed and his behaviour now was excellent and exemplary; that he had even, in the past, felt the justice of his son's exhortations, that he felt it all long ago and laid it to heart, but now he had begun to control himself in practice, too. In proof of which he presented him with the books bought with money which he had saved up during a long period of time.

I could not help laughing and crying as I listened to the poor old man; so he knew how to lie on occasion! The books were carried into Pokrovsky's room and arranged on the shelves. Pokrovsky at once guessed the truth. The old man was invited to dinner. We were all so merry that day; after dinner we played forfeits and cards; Sasha was in wild spirits and I was hardly less so. Pokrovsky was attentive to me and kept seeking an opportunity to speak to me alone, but I would not let him. It was the happiest day of all those four years of my life.

And now come sad, bitter memories, and I begin the story of my gloomy days. That is why, perhaps, my pen moves more slowly and seems to refuse to write more. That is why, perhaps, I have dwelt in memory with such eagerness and such love on the smallest details of my trivial existence in my happy days. Those days were so brief; they were followed by grief, black grief, and God only knows when it will end.

My troubles began with the illness and death of Pokrovsky. He fell ill about two months after the last incidents I have described here. He spent those two months in unceasing efforts to secure some means of subsistence, for he still had no settled position. Like all consumptives he clung up to the very last moment to the hope of a very long life. A post as a teacher turned up for him, but he had a great distaste for that calling. He could not take a place in a government office on account of his health. Besides, he would have had to wait a long time for the first instalment of his salary. In short, Pokrovsky met with nothing but disappointment on all sides and this tried his temper. His health was suffering, but he paid no attention to it. Autumn was coming on, every day he went out in his thin little overcoat to try and get work, to beg and implore for a place, which was inwardly an agony to him; he used to get his feet wet and to be soaked through with the rain, and at last he took to his bed and never got up from it again. . . . He died in the middle of autumn at the end of October.

I scarcely left his room during the whole time of his illness, I nursed him and looked after him. Often I did not sleep for nights together. He was frequently delirious and rarely quite himself; he talked of goodness knows what, of his post, of his books, of me, of his father . . . and it was then I heard a great deal about his circumstances of which I had not known or even guessed before. When first he was ill, all of them looked at me somehow strangely; Anna Fyodorovna shook her head. But I looked them all straight in the face and they did not blame me any more for my sympathy for Pokrovsky—at least my mother did not.

Sometimes Pokrovsky knew me, but this was seldom. He was almost all the time unconscious. Sometimes for whole nights together he would carry on long, long conversations with someone in obscure, indistinct words and his hoarse voice resounded with a hollow echo in his narrow room as in a coffin; I used to feel terrified then. Especially on the last night he seemed in a frenzy; he suffered terribly, was in anguish; his moans wrung my heart. Everyone in the house was in alarm. Anna Fyodorovna kept praying that God would take him more quickly. They sent for the doctor. The doctor said that the patient would certainly die by the morning.

Old Pokrovsky spent the whole night in the passage at the door of his son's room; a rug of some sort was put down there for him. He kept coming into the room, it was dreadful to look at him. He was so crushed by sorrow that he seemed utterly senseless and without feeling. His head was shaking with terror. He was trembling all over and kept whispering something, talking about something to himself. It seemed to me he was going out of his mind.

Just before dawn the old man, worn out with mental suffering, fell asleep on his mat and slept like the dead. Between seven and eight his son began to die. I waked the father. Pokrovsky was fully conscious and said good-bye to us all. Strange! I could not cry, but my heart was torn to pieces.

But his last moments distressed and tortured me more than all. He kept asking for something at great length with his halting tongue and I could make out nothing from his words. My heart was lacerated! For a whole hour he was uneasy, kept grieving over something, trying to make some sign with his chill hands and then beginning pitifully to entreat me in his hoarse hollow voice; but his words were disconnected sounds and again I could make nothing of them. I brought everyone of the household to him, I gave him drink, but still he shook his head mournfully. At last I guessed what he wanted. He was begging me to draw up the window curtain and open the shutters. No doubt he wanted to look for the last time at the day, at God's light, at the sunshine. I drew back the curtain, but the dawning day was sad and melancholy as the poor failing life of the dying man. There was no sun. The clouds covered the sky with a shroud of mist; it was rainy, overcast, mournful. A fine rain was pattering on the window-panes and washing them with little rivulets of cold dirty water; it was dark and dingy. The pale daylight scarcely penetrated into the room and hardly rivalled the flickering flame of the little lamp lighted before the ikon. The dying man glanced at me mournfully, mournfully and shook his head; a minute later he died.

Anna Fyodorovna herself made the arrangements for the funeral. A coffin of the cheapest kind was bought and a carter was hired. To defray these expenses Anna Fyodorovna seized all Pokrovsky's books and other belongings. The old man argued with her, made a noise, took away all the books he could from her, stuffed his pockets full of them, put them in his hat, wherever he could, went about with them all those three days, and did not part with them even when he had to go to church. During those three days he seemed as it were, stupefied, as though he did not know what he was doing, and he kept fussing about the coffin with a strange solicitude; at one moment he set straight the wreath on his dead son and at the next he lighted and took away candles. It was evident that his thoughts could not rest on anything. Neither mother nor Anna Fyodorovna was at the funeral service at the church. Mother was ill; Anna Fyodorovna had got ready to go, but she quarrelled with old Pokrovsky and stayed behind. I went alone with the old man. During the service a terror came upon me—as though a foreboding of the future. I could scarcely stand up in church.

At last the coffin was closed, nailed up, put in the cart and taken away. I followed it only to the end of the street. The man drove at a trot. The old man ran after him, weeping loudly, his lamentations quivering and broken by his haste. The poor old man lost his hat and did not stop to pick it up. His head was drenched by the rain and the wind was rising; the sleet lashed and stung his face. The old man seemed not to feel the cold and wet and ran wailing from one side of the cart to the other, the skirts of his old coat fluttering in the wind like wings. Books were sticking out from all his pockets; in his hands was a huge volume which he held tightly. The passers-by took off their caps and crossed themselves. Some stopped and stood gazing in wonder at the poor old man. The books kept falling out of his pockets into the mud. People stopped him and pointed to what he had lost, he picked them up and fell to racing after the coffin again. At the corner of the street an old beggar woman joined him to follow the coffin with him. The cart turned the corner at last and disappeared from my sight. I went home. I threw myself on mother's bosom in terrible distress. I pressed her tightly in my arms, I kissed her and burst into floods of tears, huddling up to her fearfully as though trying to keep in my arms my last friend and not to give her up to death . . . but death was already hovering over poor mother. . . .

June 11.

How grateful I am to you for our walk yesterday to the Island, Makar Alexyevitch! How fresh and lovely it is there, how leafy and green! It's so long since I saw green leaves— when I was ill I kept fancying that I had to die and that I certainly should die—judge what must have been my sensations yesterday, how I must have felt . . .

You must not be angry with me for having been so sad yesterday; I was very happy, very content, but in my very best moments I am always for some reason sad. As for my crying, that means nothing. I don't know myself why I am always crying. I feel ill and irritable; my sensations are due to illness. The pale cloudless sky, the sunset, the evening stillness—all that—I don't know—but I was somehow in the mood yesterday to take a dreary and miserable view of everything, so that my heart was too full and needed the relief of tears. But why am I writing all this to you? It is hard to make all that clear to one's own heart and still harder to convey it to another. But you, perhaps, will understand me. Sadness and laughter both at once! How kind you are really, Makar Alexyevitch! You looked into my eyes yesterday as though to read in them what I was feeling and were delighted with my rapture. Whether it was a bush, an avenue, a piece of water— you were there standing before me showing its beauties and peeping into my eyes as though you were displaying your possessions to me. That proves that you have a kind heart, Makar Alexyevitch. It's for that that I love you. Well, good-bye. I'm ill again to-day; I got my feet wet yesterday and have caught cold. Fedora is ailing, too, so now we are both on the sick list. Don't forget me. Come as often as you can.

Your V. D.

My darling Varvara Alexyevna,

Well, I had expected, my dear soul, that you would write me a description of our yesterday's expedition in a regular poem, and you have turned out nothing but one simple sheet. I say this because, though you wrote me so little in your sheet, yet you did describe it extraordinarily well and sweetly. The charms of nature, and the various rural scenes and all the rest about your feeling—in short, you described it all very well. Now I have no talent for it. If I smudge a dozen papers there's nothing to show for it; I can't describe anything. I have tried.

You write to me, my own, that I am a kind-hearted, good-natured man, incapable of injuring my neighbour, and able to understand the blessings of the Lord made manifest in nature, and you bestow various praises on me, in fact. All that is true, my darling, all that is perfectly true; I really am all that you say and I know it myself; but when one reads what you write one's heart is touched in spite of oneself and then all sorts of painful reflections come to one. Well, listen to me, Varinka dear, I will tell you something, my own.

I will begin with when I was only seventeen and went into the service, and soon the thirtieth year of my career there will be here. Well, I needn't say I have worn out many a uniform; I grew to manhood and to good sense and saw something of the world; I have lived, I may say, I have lived in the world so that on one occasion they even wanted to send up my name to receive a cross. Maybe you will not believe me, but I am really not lying. But there, my darling, in spite of everything, I have been badly treated by malicious people! I tell you, my own, that though I am an obscure person, a stupid person, perhaps, yet I have my feelings like anyone else. Do you know, Varinka, what a spiteful man did to me? I am ashamed to say what he has done to me; you will ask why did he do it? Why, because I am meek, because I am quiet, because I am good-natured! I did not suit their taste, so that's what brought it upon me. At first it began with, "You are this and that, Makar Alexyevitch," and then it came to saying, "It's no good asking Makar Alexyevitch!" And then it ended by, "Of course, that is Makar Alexyevitch!" You see, my precious, what a pass it came to; always Makar Alexyevitch to blame for everything; they managed to make Makar Alexyevitch a by-word all over the department, and it was not enough that they made me a by-word and almost a term of abuse, they attacked my boots, my uniform, my hair, my figure; nothing was to their taste, everything ought to be different! And all this has been repeated every blessed day from time immemorial. I am used to it, for I grow used to anything, because I am a meek man; but what is it all for? What harm do I do to anyone? Have I stolen promotion from anyone, or what? Have I blackened anyone's reputation with his superiors? Have I asked for anything extra out of turn? Have I got up some intrigue? Why, it's a sin for you to imagine such a thing, my dear soul! As though I could do anything of that sort! You've only to look at me, my own. Have I sufficient ability for intrigue and ambition? Then why have such misfortunes come upon me? God forgive me, Here you consider me a decent man, and you are ever so much better than any of them, my darling. Why, what is the greatest virtue in a citizen? A day or two ago, in private conversation, Yevstafy Ivanovitch said that the most important virtue in a citizen was to earn money. He said in jest (I know it was in jest) that morality consists in not being a burden to anyone. Well, I'm not a burden to anyone. My crust of bread is my own; it is true it is a plain crust of bread, at times a dry one; but there it is, earned by my toil and put to lawful and irreproachable use. Why, what can one do? I know very well, of course, that I don't do much by copying; but all the same I am proud of working and earning my bread in the sweat of my brow. Why, what if I am a copying clerk, after all? What harm is there in copying, after all? "He's a copying clerk," they say, but what is there discreditable in that? My handwriting is good, distinct and pleasant to the eye, and his Excellency is satisfied with it. I have no gift of language, of course, I know myself that I haven't the confounded thing; that's why I have not got on in the service, and why even now, my own, I am writing to you simply, artlessly, just as the thought comes into my heart. . . . I know all that; but there, if everyone became an author, who would do the copying? I ask you that question and I beg you to answer it, Varinka dear. So I see now that I am necessary, that I am indispensable, and that it's no use to worry a man with nonsense. Well, let me be a rat if you like, since they see a resemblance! But the rat is necessary, but the rat is of service, but the rat is depended upon, but the rat is given a reward, so that's the sort of rat he is!

Enough about that subject though, my own! I did not

intend to talk about that at all, but I got a little heated. Besides, it's pleasant from time to time to do oneself justice. Good-bye, my own, my darling, my kind comforter! I will come, I will certainly come to see you, my dearie, and meanwhile, don't be dull, I will bring you a book. Well, good-bye, then, Varinka.

Your devoted well-wisher,

MAKAR DYEVUSHKIN.

June 20.

DEAR SIR, MAKAR ALEXYEVITCH,

I write a hurried line, I am in haste, I have to finish my work up to time. You see, this is how it is: you can make a good bargain. Fedora says that a friend of hers has a uniform, quite new, underclothes, a waistcoat and cap, and all very cheap, they say; so you ought to buy them. You see, you are not badly off now, you say you have money; you say so yourself. Give over being so stingy, please. You know all those things are necessary. Just look at yourself, what old clothes you go about in. It's a disgrace! You're all in patches. You have no new clothes; I know that, though you declare that you have. God knows how you have managed to dispose of them. So do as I tell you, please buy these things. Do it for my sake; if you love me, do it.

You sent me some linen as a present; but upon my word, Makar Alexyevitch, you are ruining yourself. It's no joke what you've spent on me, it's awful to think how much money! How fond you are of throwing away your money! I don't want it; it's all absolutely unnecessary. I know—I am convinced—that you love me. It is really unnecessary to remind me of it with presents; and it worries me taking them from you; I know what they cost you. Once for all, leave off, do you hear? I beg you, I beseech you. You ask me, Makar Alexyevitch, to send you the continuation of my diary, you want me to finish it. I don't know how what I have written came to be written! But I haven't the strength now to talk of my past; I don't even want to think of it; I feel frightened of those memories. To talk of my poor mother leaving her poor child to those monsters, too, is more painful than anything. My heart throbs at the very thought of it: it is all still so fresh: I have not had time to think things over, still less to regain my calm, though it is all more than a year ago, now. But you know all that.

I've told you what Anna Fyodorovna thinks now; she blames me for ingratitude and repudiates all blame for her association

with Mr. Bykov! She invites me to stay with her; she says
that I am living on charity, that I am going to the bad. She
says that if I go back to her she will undertake to set right
everything with Mr. Bykov and compel him to make up for his
behaviour to me. She says Mr. Bykov wants to give me a
dowry. Bother them! I am happy here with you close by,
with my kind Fedora whose devotion reminds me of my old
nurse. Though you are only a distant relation you will protect me with your name. I don't know them. I shall forget
them if I can. What more do they want of me? Fedora says
that it is all talk, that they will leave me alone at last. God
grant they may!

V. D.

June 21.

MY DARLING VARINKA,

I want to write, but I don't know how to begin. How
strange it is, my precious, how we are living now. I say this
because I have never spent my days in such joyfulness. Why,
it is as though God had blessed me with a home and family of
my own, my child, my pretty! But why are you making such a
fuss about the four chemises I sent you? You needed them,
you know—I found that out from Fedora. And it's a special
happiness for me to satisfy your needs, Varinka, dear; it's my
pleasure. You let me alone, my dear soul. Don't interfere
with me and don't contradict me. I've never known anything
like it, my darling. I've taken to going into society now. In
the first place my life is twice as full; because you are living
very near me and are a great comfort to me; and secondly,
I have been invited to tea to-day by a lodger, a neighbour of
mine, that clerk, Ratazyaev, who has the literary evenings.
We meet this evening, we are going to read literature. So you
see how we are getting on now, Varinka—you see! Well,
good-bye. I've written all this for no apparent reason, simply
to let you know of the affection I feel for you. You told Teresa
to tell me, my love, that you want some silk for coloured
embroidery. I will get you it, my darling, I will get the silk,
I will get it. To-morrow I shall have the pleasure of satisfying
you. I know where to buy it, too. And now I remain,

Your sincere friend,
MAKAR DYEVUSHKIN.

176

Dear Madam, Varvara Alexyevna,

I must tell you, my own, that a very pitiful thing has happened in our flat, truly, truly, deserving of pity! Between four and five this morning Gorshkov's little boy died. I don't know what he died of. It seemed to be a sort of scarlatina, God only knows! I went to see these Gorshkovs. Oh, my dear soul, how poor they are! And what disorder! And no wonder; the whole family lives in one room, only divided by a screen for decency. There was a little coffin standing in the room already—a simple little coffin, but rather pretty; they bought it ready-made; the boy was nine years old, he was a promising boy, they say. But it was pitiful to look at them, Varinka! The mother did not cry, but she was so sad, so poor. And perhaps it will make it easier for them to have got one off their shoulders; but there are still two left, a baby, and a little girl, not much more than six. There's not much comfort really in seeing a child suffer, especially one's own little child, and having no means of helping him! The father was sitting in a greasy old dress suit on a broken chair. The tears were flowing from his eyes, but perhaps not from grief, but just the usual thing—his eyes are inflamed. He's such a strange fellow! He always turns red when you speak to him, gets confused and does not know what to answer. The little girl, their daughter, stood leaning against the coffin, such a poor little, sad, brooding child! And Varinka, my darling, I don't like it when children brood; it's painful to see! A doll made of rags was lying on the floor beside her; she did not play with it, she held her finger on her lips; she stood, without stirring. The landlady gave her a sweetmeat; she took it but did not eat it.

It was sad, Varinka, wasn't it?

MAKAR DYEVUSHKIN.

Dear Makar Alexyevitch,

I am sending you back your book. A wretched, worthless little book not fit to touch! Where did you ferret out such a treasure? Joking apart, can you really like such a book, Makar Alexyevitch? I was promised the other day something to read. I will share it with you, if you like. And now goodbye. I really have not time to write more.

V. D.

DEAR VARINKA,

The fact is that I really had not read that horrid book, my dear girl. It is true, I looked through it and saw it was nonsense, just written to be funny, to make people laugh; well, I thought, it really is amusing; maybe Varinka will like it, so I sent it you.

Now, Ratazyaev has promised to give me some real literature to read, so you will have some books, my darling. Ratazyaev knows, he's a connoisseur; he writes himself, ough, how he writes! His pen is so bold and he has a wonderful style, that is, there is no end to what there is in every word— in the most foolish ordinary vulgar word such as I might say sometimes to Faldoni or Teresa, even in such he has style. I go to his evenings. We smoke and he reads to us, he reads five hours at a stretch and we listen all the time. It's a perfect feast. Such charm, such flowers, simply flowers, you can gather a bouquet from each page! He is so affable, so kindly and friendly. Why, what am I beside him? What am I? Nothing. He is a man with a reputation, and what am I? I simply don't exist, yet he is cordial even to me. I am copying something for him. Only don't you imagine, Varinka, that there is something amiss in that, that he is friendly to me just because I am copying for him; don't you believe tittle-tattle, my dear girl, don't you believe worthless tittle-tattle. No, I am doing it of myself, of my own accord for his pleasure. I understand refinement of manners, my love; he is a kind, very kind man, and an incomparable writer.

Literature is a fine thing, Varinka, a very fine thing. I learnt that from them the day before yesterday. A profound thing, strengthening men's hearts, instructing them; there are all sorts of things written about that in their book. Very well written! Literature is a picture, that is, in a certain sense, a picture and a mirror: it's the passions, the expression, the subtlest criticism, edifying instruction and a document. I gathered all that from them. I tell you frankly, my darling, that one sits with them, one listens (one smokes a pipe like them, too, if you please), and when they begin to discuss and dispute about all sorts of matters, then I simply sit dumb; then, my dear soul, you and I can do nothing else but sit dumb. I am simply a blockhead, it seems. I am ashamed of myself, so that I try all the evening how to put in half a word in the general conversation, but there, as ill-luck would have it, I can't find that half word! And one is sorry for oneself, Varinka, that one is not this thing, nor that thing, that, as the saying is, "A man one is grown, but no mind of one's own." Why, what do I do in my free time now? I sleep like a fool! While instead of useless sleep I might have been busy in useful occupation; I might have sat down and written something that would have been of use to oneself and pleasant to others. Why, my dearie, you should only see what they get for it, God forgive them! Take Ratazyaev, for instance, what he gets. What is it for him to write a chapter? Why, sometimes he writes five in a day and he gets three hundred roubles a chapter. Some little anecdote, something curious—five hundred! take it or leave it, give it or be damned! Or another time, we'll put a thousand in our pocket! What do you say to that, Varvara Alexyevna? Why, he's got a little book of poems—such short poems—he's asking seven thousand, my dear girl, he's asking seven thousand; think of it! Why, it's real estate, it's house property! He says that they will give him five thousand, but he won't take it. I reasoned with him. I said, "Take five thousand for them, sir, and don't mind them. Why, five thousand's money!" "No,' said he, "they'll give me seven, the swindlers!" He's a cunning fellow, really.

Well, my love, since we are talking of it I will copy a passage from the *Italian Passions* for you. That's the name of his book. Here, read it, Varinka, and judge for yourself. . . .

"Vladimir shuddered and his passion gurgled up furiously within him and his blood boiled. . . .

" 'Countess,' he cried. 'Countess! Do you know how awful is this passion, how boundless this madness? No, my dreams did not deceive me! I love, I love ecstatically, furiously, madly! All your husband's blood would not quench the frantic surging ecstasy of my soul! A trivial obstacle cannot check the all-destroying, hellish fire that harrows my exhausted breast. Oh, Zinaida, Zinaida!' . . .

" 'Vladimir,' whispered the countess, beside herself, leaning on his shoulder. . . .

" 'Zinaida!' cried the enraptured Smyelsky.

"His bosom exhaled a sigh. The fire flamed brightly on the altar of love and consumed the heart of the unhappy victims.

" 'Vladimir,' the countess whispered, intoxicated. Her bosom heaved, her cheeks glowed crimson, her eyes glowed. . . .

"A new, terrible union was accomplished!

"Half an hour later the old count went into his wife's boudoir.

" 'Well, my love, should we not order the samovar for our welcome guest?' he said, patting his wife on the cheek."

Well, I ask you, my dear soul, what do you think of it after that? It's true, it's a little free, there's no disputing that, but still it is fine. What is fine is fine! And now, if you will allow me, I will copy you another little bit from the novel *Yermak and Zuleika*.

You must imagine, my precious, that the Cossack, Yermak, the fierce and savage conqueror of Siberia, is in love with the daughter of Kutchum, the Tsar of Siberia, the Princess Zuleika, who has been taken captive by him. An episode straight from the times of Ivan the Terrible, as you see. Here is the conversation of Yermak and Zuleika.

" 'You love me, Zuleika! Oh, repeat it, repeat it!' . . .

" 'I love you, Yermak,' whispered Zuleika.

" 'Heaven and earth, I thank you! I am happy! . . . You have given me everything, everything, for which my turbulent soul has striven from my boyhood's years. So it was to this thou hast led me, my guiding star, so it was for this thou hast led me here, beyond the Belt of Stone! I will show to all the world my Zuleika, and men, the frantic monsters, will not dare to blame me! Ah, if they could understand the secret sufferings of her tender soul, if they could see a whole poem in a tear of my Zuleika! Oh, let me dry that tear with kisses, let me drink it up, that heavenly tear . . . unearthly one!'

" 'Yermak,' said Zuleika, 'the world is wicked, men are unjust! They will persecute us, they will condemn us, my sweet Yermak! What is the poor maiden, nurtured amid the snows of Siberia in her father's *yurta* to do in your cold, icy, soulless, selfish world? People will not understand me, my desired one, my beloved one.'

" 'Then will the Cossack's sabre rise up hissing about them.' "

And now, what do you say to Yermak, Varinka, when he finds out that his Zuleika has been murdered? . . . The blind old man, Kutchum, under cover of night steals into Yermak's tent in his absence and slays Zuleika, intending to deal a mortal blow at Yermak, who has robbed him of his sceptre and his crown.

" 'Sweet is it to me to rasp the iron against the stone,'

shouted Yermak in wild frenzy, whetting his knife of Damascus steel upon the magic stone; 'I'll have their blood, their blood! I will hack them! hack them! hack them to pieces!!!' "

And, after all that, Yermak, unable to survive his Zuleika, throws himself into the Irtish, and so it all ends.

And this, for instance, a tiny fragment written in a jocose style, simply to make one laugh.

"Do you know Ivan Prokofyevitch Yellow-paunch? Why, the man who bit Prokofy Ivanovitch's leg. Ivan Prokofyevitch is a man of hasty temper, but, on the other hand, of rare virtues; Prokofy Ivanovitch, on the other hand, is extremely fond of a rarebit on toast. Why, when Pelagea Antonovna used to know him . . . Do you know Pelagea Antonovna? the woman who always wears her petticoat inside out."

That's humour, you know, Varinka, simply humour. He rocked with laughter when he read us that. He *is* a fellow, God forgive him! But though it's rather jocose and very playful, Varinka dear, it is quite innocent, without the slightest trace of free-thinking or liberal ideas. I must observe, my love, that Ratazyaev is a very well-behaved man and so an excellent author, not like other authors.

And, after all, an idea sometimes comes into one's head, you know. . . . What if I were to write something, what would happen then? Suppose that, for instance, apropos of nothing, there came into the world a book with the title—*Poems by Makar Dyevushkin?* What would my little angel say then? How does that strike you? What do you think of it? And I can tell you, my darling, that as soon as my book came out, I certainly should not dare to show myself in the Nevsky Prospect. Why, how should I feel when everyone would be saying, Here comes the author and poet, Dyevushkin? There's Dyevushkin himself, they would say! What should I do with my boots then? They are, I may mention in passing, my dear girl, almost always covered with patches, and the soles too, to tell the truth, sometimes break away in a very unseemly fashion. What should we do when everyone knew that the author Dyevushkin had patches on his boots! Some countess or duchess would hear of it, and what would she say, the darling? Perhaps she would not notice it; for I imagine countesses don't trouble themselves about boots, especially clerks' boots (for you know there are boots and boots), but they would tell her all about it, her friends would give me away. Ratazyaev, for instance, would be the first to give me

away; he visits the Countess V.; he says that he goes to all
her receptions, and he's quite at home there. He says she is
such a darling, such a literary lady, he says. He's a rogue, that
Ratazyaev!

But enough of that subject; I write all this for fun, my little
angel, to amuse you. Good-bye, my darling, I have scribbled
you a lot of nonsense, but that is just because I am in a very
good humour to-day. We all dined together to-day at
Ratazyaev's (they are rogues, Varinka dear), and brought out
such a cordial. . . .

But there, why write to you about that! Only mind you
don't imagine anything about me, Varinka. I don't mean anything by it. I will send you the books, I will certainly send
them. . . . One of Paul de Kock's novels is being passed
round from one to another, but Paul de Kock will not do for
you, my precious. . . . No, no! Paul de Kock won't do for
you. They say of him, Varinka dear, that he rouses all the
Petersburg critics to righteous indignation. I send you a pound
of sweetmeats—I bought them on purpose for you. Do you
hear, darling? think of me at every sweetmeat. Only don't
nibble up the sugar-candy but only suck it, or you will get
toothache. And perhaps you like candied peel?——write and
tell me. Well, good-bye, good-bye. Christ be with you, my
darling!

I remain ever,
Your most faithful friend,
MAKAR DYEVUSHKIN.

June 27.

DEAR SIR, MAKAR ALEXYEVITCH,

Fedora tells me that, if I like, certain people will be pleased
to interest themselves in my position, and will get me a very
good position as a governess in a family. What do you think
about it, my friend—shall I go, or shall I not? Of course I
should not then be a burden upon you, and the situation seems
a good one; but, on the other hand, I feel somehow frightened
at going into a strange house. They are people with an estate
in the country. When they want to know all about me, when
they begin asking questions, making inquiries—why, what
should I say then?—besides, I am so shy and unsociable, I like
to go on living in the corner I am used to. It's better somehow
where one is used to being; even though one spends half one's

time grieving, still it is better. Besides, it means leaving Petersburg; and God knows what my duties will be, either; perhaps they will simply make me look after the children, like a nurse. And they are such queer people, too; they've had three governesses already in two years. Do advise me, Makar Alexyevitch, whether to go or not. And why do you never come and see me? You hardly ever show your face, we scarcely ever meet except on Sundays at mass. What an unsociable person you are! You are as bad as I am! And you know I am almost a relation. You don't love me, Makar Alexyevitch, and I am sometimes very sad all alone. Sometimes, especially when it is getting dark, one sits all alone. Fedora goes off somewhere, one sits and sits and thinks—one remembers all the past, joyful and sad alike—it all passes before one's eyes, it all rises up as though out of a mist. Familiar faces appear (I am almost beginning to see them in reality)—I see mother most often of all . . . And what dreams I have! I feel that I am not at all well, I am so weak; to-day, for instance, when I got out of bed this morning, I turned giddy; and I have such a horrid cough, too! I feel, I know, that I shall soon die. Who will bury me? Who will follow my coffin! Who will grieve for me! . . . And perhaps I may have to die in a strange place, in a strange house! . . . My goodness! how sad life is, Makar Alexyevitch. Why do you keep feeding me on sweetmeats? I really don't know where you get so much money from? Ah, my friend, take care of your money, for God's sake, take care of it. Fedora is selling the cloth rug I have embroidered; she is getting fifty paper roubles for it. That's very good, I thought it would be less. I shall give Fedora three silver roubles, and shall get a new dress for myself, a plain one but warm. I shall make you a waistcoat, I shall make it myself, and I shall choose a good material.

Fedora got me a book, *Byelkin's Stories*, which I will send you, if you care to read it. Only don't please keep it, or make it dirty, it belongs to someone else—it's one of Pushkin's works. Two years ago I read these stories with my mother. And it was so sad for me now to read them over again. If you have any books send them to me—only not if you get them from Ratazyaev. He will certainly lend you his books if he has ever published anything. How do you like his works, Makar Alexyevitch? Such nonsense . . . Well, good-bye! How I have been chattering! When I am sad I am glad to chatter about anything. It does me good; at once one feels better, especially if one expresses all that lies in one's heart. Good-bye. Good-bye, my friend!

Your

V. D.

June 28.

MY PRECIOUS VARVARA ALEXYEVNA,

Leave off worrying yourself, I wonder you are not ashamed. Come, give over, my angel! How is it such thoughts come into your mind? You are not ill, my love, you are not ill at all; you are blooming, you are really blooming; a little pale, but still blooming. And what do you mean by these dreams, these visions? For shame, my darling, give over; you must simply laugh at them. Why do I sleep well? Why is nothing wrong with me? You should look at me, my dear soul. I get along all right, I sleep quietly, I am as healthy and hearty as can be, a treat to look at. Give over, give over, darling, for shame. You must reform. I know your little ways, my dearie; as soon as any trouble comes, you begin fancying things and worrying about something. For my sake give over, my darling. Go into a family?—Never! No, no, no, and what notion is this of yours? What is this idea that has come over you? And to leave Petersburg too. No, my darling, I won't allow it. I will use every means in my power to oppose such a plan. I'll sell my old coat and walk about the street in my shirt before you shall want for anything. No, Varinka, no, I know you! It's folly, pure folly. And there is no doubt that it is all Fedora's fault: she's evidently a stupid woman, she puts all these ideas into your head. Don't you trust her, my dear girl. You probably don't know everything yet, my love. . . . She's a silly woman, discontented and nonsensical; she worried her husband out of his life. Or perhaps she has vexed you in some way? No, no, my precious, not for anything! And what would become of me then, what would there be left for me to do? No, Varinka darling, you put that out of your little head. What is there wanting in your life with us? We can never rejoice enough over you, you love us, so do go on living here quietly. Sew or read, or don't sew if you like—it does not matter—only go on living with us or, only think yourself, why, what would it be like without you? . . . .

Here, I will get you some books and then maybe we'll go for a walk somewhere again. Only you must give over, my dearie, you must give over. Pull yourself together and don't be foolish

184

over trifles! I'll come and see you and very soon too. Only accept what I tell you plainly and candidly about it; you are wrong, my darling, very wrong. Of course, I am an ignorant man and I know myself that I am ignorant, that I have hardly a ha'porth of education. But that's not what I am talking about, and I'm not what matters, but I will stand up for Ratazyaev, say what you like. He writes well, very, very well, and I say it again, he writes very well. I don't agree with you and I never can agree with you. It's written in a flowery abrupt style, with figures of speech. There are ideas of all sorts in it, it is very good! Perhaps you read it without feeling, Varinka; you were out of humour when you read it, vexed with Fedora, or something had gone wrong. No, you read it with feeling; best when you are pleased and happy and in a pleasant humour, when, for instance, you have got a sweetmeat in your mouth, that's when you must read it. I don't dispute (who denies it?) that there are better writers than Ratazyaev, and very much better in fact, but they are good and Ratazyaev is good too. He writes in his own special way, and does very well to write. Well, good-bye, my precious, I can't write more; I must make haste, I have work to do. Mind now, my love, my precious little dearie; calm yourself, and God will be with you, and I remain your faithful friend,

MAKAR DYEVUSHKIN.

P.S.—Thanks for the book, my own; we will read Pushkin too, and this evening I shall be sure to come and see you.

My DEAR MAKAR ALEXYEVITCH,

No, my friend, no, I ought not to go on living among you. On second thoughts I consider that I am doing very wrong to refuse such a good situation. I shall have at least my daily bread secure; I will do my best, I will win the affection of the strangers, I will even try to overcome my defects, if necessary. Of course it is painful and irksome to live with strangers, to try and win their good-will, to hide one's feelings, and suppress oneself, but God will help me. I mustn't be a recluse all my life. I have had experiences like it before. I remember when I was a little thing and used to go to school. I used to be frolicking and skipping about all Sundays at home; sometimes mother would scold me—but nothing mattered, my heart was light and my soul was full of joy all the while. As evening approached an immense sadness would come over me—at nine o'clock I had to go back to school, and there it was all cold, strange, severe, the teachers were so cross on Mondays, one had such a pain at one's heart, one wanted to cry; one would go into a corner and cry all alone, hiding one's tears—they would say one was lazy; and I wasn't crying in the least because I had to do my lessons.

But, after all, I got used to it, and when I had to leave school I cried also when I said good-bye to my schoolfellows. And I am not doing right to go on being a burden to both of you. That thought is a torment to me. I tell you all this openly because I am accustomed to be open with you. Do you suppose I don't see how early Fedora gets up in the morning, and sets to work at her washing and works till late at night?— and old bones want rest. Do you suppose I don't see how you are ruining yourself over me, and spending every halfpenny? You are not a man of property, my friend! You tell me that you will sell your last rag before I shall want for anything. I believe you, my friend, I trust your kind heart, but you say that now. Now you have money you did not expect, you've received something extra, but later on? You know yourself, I am always ill; and I can't work like you, though I should be heartily glad to, and one does not always get work. What is left for me? To break my heart with grief looking at you two dear ones. In what way can I be of the slightest use to you? And why am I so necessary to you, my friend? What good have I done you? I am only devoted to you with my whole soul, I love you warmly, intensely, with my whole heart, but— my fate is a bitter one! I know how to love and I can love, but I can do nothing to repay you for your kindness. Don't dissuade me any more, think it over and tell me your final opinion. Meanwhile I remain your loving,

V. D.

July 1.

Nonsense, nonsense, Varinka, simply nonsense! Let you alone and there's no knowing what notion you will take into your little head. And I see now that it is all nonsense. And what more do you want, my dear girl? just tell me that! We love you, you love us, we're all contented and happy—what more do you want? And what will you do among strangers? I expect you don't know yet what strangers are like . . . You had better ask me and I will tell you what strangers are like. I know them, my darling, I know them very well, I've had to eat their bread. They are spiteful, Varinka, spiteful; so spiteful that you would have no heart left, they would torment it so with reproach, upbraiding and ill looks. You are snug and happy among us as though you were in a little nest; besides, we shall feel as though we had lost our head when you are gone; why, what can we do without you; what is an old man like me to do then? You are no use to us? No good to us? How no good? Come, my love, think yourself how much good you are! You are a great deal of good to me, Varinka. You have such a good influence . . . Here I am thinking about you now and I am happy . . . Sometimes I write you a letter and put all my feelings into it and get a full answer to everything back from you. I bought you a little wardrobe, got you a hat; some commission comes from you; I carry out the commission . . . How can you say, you are no use to me? And what should I be good for in my old age? Perhaps you have not thought of that, Varinka; that's just what you had better think about, 'what will he be good for without me?' I am used to you, my darling. Or else what will come of it? I shall go straight to the Neva, and that will be the end of it. Yes, really, Varinka, that will be the only thing left for me to do when you are gone. Ah, Varinka, my darling. It seems you want me to be taken to Volkovo Cemetery in a common cart; with only an old draggletail beggar-woman to follow me to the grave; you want them to throw the earth upon me and go away and leave me alone. It's too bad, too bad, my dear! It's sinful really, upon my word it's a sin! I send you back your book, Varinka, my darling, and if you ask my opinion about your book, dear, I must say that never in my life have I read such a splendid book. I wonder now, my darling, how I can have lived till now such an ignoramus, God forgive me! What have I been doing? What backwoods have I been brought up in? Why, I know nothing, my dear girl; why, I know absolutely nothing. I know nothing at all. I tell you, Varinka, plainly—I'm a man of no education: I have read little hitherto —very little, scarcely anything: I have read *The Picture of Man*, a clever work; I have read *The boy who played funny tunes on the bells* and *The Cranes of Ibicus;* that's all, and I never read anything else. Now I have read *The Stationmaster* in your book; let me tell you, my darling, it happens that one goes on living, and one does not know that there is a book there at one's side where one's whole life is set forth, as though

G

it were reckoned upon one's fingers. And what one never so much as guessed before, when one begins reading such a book one remembers little by little and guesses and discovers. And this is another reason why I like your book: one sometimes reads a book, whatever it may be, and you can't for the life of you understand it, it's so deep. I, for instance, am stupid, I'm stupid by nature, so I can't read very serious books; but I read this as though I had written it myself, as though I had taken my own heart, just as it is, and turned it inside out before people and described it in detail, that's what it is like. And it's a simple subject, my goodness, yet what a thing it is! Really it is just as I should have described it; why not describe it? You know I feel exactly the same as in the book, and I have been at times in exactly the same positions as, for instance, that Samson Vyrin, poor fellow. And how many Samson Vyrins are going about amongst us, poor dears! And how clearly it is all described! Tears almost started into my eyes when I read that the poor sinner took to drink, became such a drunkard that he lost his senses and slept the whole day under a sheepskin coat and drowned his grief in punch, and wept piteously, wiping his eyes with the dirty skirt of his coat when he thought of his lost lamb, his daughter Dunyasha. Yes, it's natural. You should read it, it's natural. It's living! I've seen it myself; it's all about me; take Teresa, for instance— but why go so far? Take our poor clerk, for instance—Why, he is perhaps just a Samson Vyrin, only he has another surname, Gorshkov. It's the general lot, Varinka dear, it might happen to you or to me. And the count who lives on the Nevsky on the riverside, he would be just the same, it would only seem different because everything there is done in their own way, in style, yet he would be just the same, anything may happen, and the same thing may happen to me. That's the truth of the matter, my darling, and yet you want to go away from us; it's a sin, Varinka, it may be the end of me. You may be the ruin of yourself and me too, my own. Oh, my little dearie, for God's sake put out of your little head all these wilful ideas and don't torment me for nothing. How can you keep yourself, my weak little unfledged bird? How can you save yourself from ruin, protect yourself from villains? Give over, Varinka, think better of it; don't listen to non-sensical advice and persuasion, and read your book again, read it with attention; that will do you good.

I talked of *The Stationmaster* to Ratazyaev. He told me

that that was all old-fashioned and that now books with pictures and descriptions have all come in; I really did not quite understand what he said about it. He ended by saying that Pushkin is fine and that he is a glory to holy Russia, and he said a great deal more to me about him. Yes, it's good, Varinka, very good; read it again with attention; follow my advice, and make an old man happy by your obedience. Then God Himself will reward you, my own, He will certainly reward you.

Your sincere friend,
MAKAR DYEVUSHKIN.

DEAR SIR, MAKAR DYEVUSHKIN,

Fedora brought me fifteen silver roubles to-day. How pleased she was, poor thing, when I gave her three! I write to you in haste. I am now cutting you out a waistcoat—it's charming material—yellow with flowers on it. I send you a book: there are all sorts of stories in it; I have read some of them, read the one called *The Cloak*. You persuade me to go to the theatre with you; wouldn't it be expensive? Perhaps we could go to the gallery somewhere. It's a long while since I've been to the theatre, in fact I can't remember when I went. Only I'm afraid whether such a treat would not cost too much? Fedora simply shakes her head. She says that you have begun to live beyond your means and I see how much you spend, on me alone! Mind, my friend, that you don't get into difficulties. Fedora tells me of rumours—that you have had a quarrel with your landlady for not paying your rent; I am very anxious about you. Well, good-bye, I'm in a hurry. It's a trifling matter, I'm altering a ribbon on a hat.

P.S.—You know, if we go to the theatre, I shall wear my new hat and my black mantle. Will that be all right?

July 7.

DEAR MADAM, VARVARA ALEXYEVNA,

. . . So I keep thinking about yesterday. Yes, my dear girl, even we have had our follies in the past. I fell in love with that actress, I fell head over ears in love with her, but that was nothing. The strangest thing was that I had scarcely seen her at all, and had only been at the theatre once, and yet for all that I fell in love. There lived next door to me five noisy young fellows. I got to know them, I could not help getting to know them, though I always kept at a respectable distance from

them. But not to be behind them I agreed with them in everything. They talked to me about this actress. Every evening as
soon as the theatre was opened, the whole company—they
never had a halfpenny for necessities—the whole party set off
to the theatre to the gallery and kept clapping and clapping,
and calling, calling for that actress—they were simply frantic!
And after that they would not let one sleep; they would talk
about her all night without ceasing, everyone called her his
Glasha, everyone of them was in love with her, they all had
the same canary in their hearts. They worked me up: I was a
helpless youngster then. I don't know how I came to go, but
one evening I found myself in the fourth gallery with them.
As for seeing, I could see nothing more than the corner of the
curtain, but I heard everything. The actress certainly had a
pretty voice—a musical voice like a nightingale, as sweet as
honey; we all clapped our hands and shouted and shouted, we
almost got into trouble, one was actually turned out. I went
home. I walked along as though I were drunk! I had nothing
left in my pocket but one silver rouble, and it was a good ten
days before I could get my salary. And what do you think, my
love? Next day before going to the office I went to a French
perfumer's and spent my whole fortune on perfume and scented
soap—I really don't know why I bought all that. And I did
not dine at home but spent the whole time walking up and
down outside her window. She lived in Nevsky Prospect on
the fourth storey. I went home for an hour or so, rested, and
out into the Nevsky again, simply to pass by her windows. For
six weeks I used to walk to and fro like that and hang about
her; I was constantly hiring smart sledges and kept driving
about so as to pass her window: I ruined myself completely,
ran into debt, and then got over my passion, I got tired of it.
So you see, my precious, what an actress can make of a respectable man! I was a youngster though , I was a youngster
then! . . .

M. D.

July 8.

DEAR MADAM, VARVARA ALEXYEVNA,
      I hasten to return you the book you lent me on the
sixth of this month, and therewith I hasten to discuss the
matter with you. It's wrong of you, my dear girl, it's wrong of
you to put me to the necessity of it. Allow me to tell you, my
good friend, every position in the lot of man is ordained by

the Almighty. One man is ordained to wear the epaulettes of a general, while it is another's lot to serve as a titular councillor; it is for one to give commands, for another to obey without repining, in fear and humility. It is in accordance with man's capacities; one is fit for one thing and one for another, and their capacities are ordained by God himself. I have been nearly thirty years in the service; my record is irreproachable; I have been sober in my behaviour, and I have never had any irregularity put down to me. As a citizen I look upon myself in my own mind as having my faults, but my virtues, too. I am respected by my superiors, and His Excellency himself is satisfied with me; and though he has not so far shown me any special marks of favour, yet I know that he is satisfied. My handwriting is fairly legible and good, not too big and not too small, rather in the style of italics, but in any case satisfactory; there is no one among us except, perhaps, Ivan Prokofyevitch who writes as well. I am old and my hair is grey; that's the only fault I know of in me. Of course, there is no one without his little failings. We're all sinners, even you are a sinner, my dear! But no serious offence, no impudence has ever been recorded against me, such as anything against the regulations, or any disturbance of public tranquillity; I have never been noticed for anything like that, such a thing has never happened —in fact, I almost got a decoration, but what's the use of talking! You ought to have known all that, my dear, and he ought to have known; if a man undertakes to write he ought to know all about it. No, I did not expect this from you, my dear girl, no, Varinka! You are the last person from whom I should have expected it.

What! So now you can't live quietly in your own little corner—whatever it may be like—not stirring up any mud, as the saying is, interfering with no one, knowing yourself, and fearing God, without people's interfering with you, without their prying into your little den and trying to see what sort of life you lead at home, whether for instance you have a good waistcoat, whether you have all you ought to have in the way of underclothes, whether you have boots and what they are lined with; what you eat, what you drink, what you write? And what even if I do sometimes walk on tiptoe to save my boots where the pavement's bad? Why write of another man that he sometimes goes short, that he has no tea to drink, as though everyone is always bound to drink tea—do I look into another man's mouth to see how he chews his crust, have I ever insulted anyone in that way? No, my dear, why insult people, when they are not interfering with you! Look here, Varvara Alexyevna, this is what it comes to: you work, and work regularly and devotedly; and your superiors respect you (however things may be, they do respect you), and here under your very nose, for no apparent reason, neither with your leave nor by your leave, somebody makes a caricature of you. Of course one does sometimes get something new—and is so pleased that one lies awake thinking about it, one is so pleased, one puts on new boots for instance, with such enjoyment; that is true: I have felt it because it is pleasant to see one's foot in a fine smart boot—that's truly described! But I am really surprised that Fyodor Fyodorovitch should have let such a book pass without notice and without defending himself. It is true that, though he is a high official, he is young and likes at times to make his voice heard. Why shouldn't he make his voice heard, why not give us a scolding if we need it? Scold to keep up the tone of the office, for instance—well, he must, to keep up the tone; you must teach men, you must give them a good talking to; for, between ourselves, Varinka, we clerks do nothing without a good talking to. Everyone is only on the look-out to get off somewhere, so as to say, I was sent here or there, and to avoid work and edge out of it. And as there are various grades in the service and as each grade requires a special sort of reprimand corresponding to the grade, it's natural that the tone of the reprimand should differ in the various grades—that's in the order of things—why, the whole world rests on that, my dear soul, on our all keeping up our authority with one another, on each one of us scolding the other. Without that precaution, the world could not go on and there would be no sort of order. I am really surprised that Fyodor Fyodorovitch let such an insult pass without attention. And why write such things? And what's the use of it? Why, will someone who reads it order me a cloak because of it; will he buy me new boots? No, Varinka, he will read it and ask for a contribution. One hides oneself sometimes, one hides oneself, one tries to conceal one's weak points, one's afraid to show one's nose at times anywhere because one is afraid of tittle-tattle, because they can work up a tale against you about anything in the world—anything. And here now all one's private and public life is being dragged into literature, it is all printed, read, laughed and gossiped about! Why, it will be impossible to show oneself in the street. It's all so plainly told, you know, that one might be recognised in one's walk. To be sure, it's as well that he does make up for it a little at the end, that he does soften it a bit, that after that passage when they throw the papers at his head, it does put in, for instance, that for all that he was a conscientious man, a good citizen, that he did not deserve such treatment from his fellow-clerks, that he respected his elders (his example might be followed, perhaps, in that), had no ill-will against anyone, believed in God and died (if he will have it that he died) regretted. But it would have been better not to let him die, poor fellow, but to make the coat be found, to make Fyodor Fyodorovitch—what am I saying? I mean, make that general, finding out his good qualities, question him in his office, promote him in his office, and give him a good increase in his salary, for then, you see, wickedness would have been punished, and virtue would have been triumphant, and his fellow-clerks would have got nothing by it. I should have done that, for instance, but as it is, what is there special about it, what is there good in it? It's just an insignificant example from vulgar, everyday life. And what induced you to send me such a book, my own? Why, it's a book of an evil tendency, Varinka, it's untrue to life, for there cannot have been such a clerk. No, I must make a complaint, Varinka. I must make a formal complaint.

Your very humble servant,

MAKAR DYEVUSHKIN.

July 27.

DEAR SIR, MAKAR ALEXYEVITCH,

Your latest doings and letters have frightened, shocked, and amazed me, and what Fedora tells me has explained it all. But what reason had you to be so desperate and to sink to such a depth as you have sunk to, Makar Alexyevitch? Your explanation has not satisfied me at all. Isn't it clear that I was right in trying to insist on taking the situation that was offered me? Besides, my last adventure has thoroughly frightened me. You say that it's your love for me that makes you keep in hiding from me. I saw that I was deeply indebted to you while you persuaded me that you were only spending your savings on me, which you said you had lying by in the bank in case of need. Now, when I learn that you had no such money at all, but, hearing by chance of my straitened position, and touched by it, you actually spent your salary, getting it in advance, and even sold your clothes when I was ill—now that

I have discovered all this I am put in such an agonising position that I still don't know how to take it, and what to think about it. Oh, Makar Alexyevitch! You ought to have confined yourself to that first kind help inspired by sympathy and the feeling of kinship and not have wasted money afterwards on luxuries. You have been false to our friendship, Makar Alexyevitch, for you weren't open with me. And now, when I see that you were spending your last penny on finery, on sweetmeats, on excursions, on the theatre and on books—now I am paying dearly for all that in regret for my frivolity (for I took it all from you without troubling myself about you); and everything with which you tried to give me pleasure is now turned to grief for me, and has left nothing but useless regret. I have noticed your depression of late, and, although I was nervously apprehensive of some trouble, what has happened never entered my head. What! Could you lose heart so completely, Makar Alexyevitch! Why, what am I to think of you now, what will everyone who knows you say of you now? You, whom I always respected for your good heart, your discretion, and your good sense. You have suddenly given way to such a revolting vice, of which one saw no sign in you before. What were my feelings when Fedora told me you were found in the street in a state of inebriety, and were brought home to your lodgings by the police! I was petrified with amazement, though I did expect something extraordinary, as there had been no sign of you for four days. Have you thought, Makar Alexyevitch, what your chiefs at the office will say when they learn the true cause of your absence? You say that everyone laughs at you, that they all know of our friendship, and that your neighbours speak of me in their jokes, too. Don't pay any attention to that, Makar Alexyevitch, and for goodness' sake, calm yourself. I am alarmed about your affair with those officers, too; I have heard a vague account of it. Do explain what it all means. You write that you were afraid to tell me, that you were afraid to lose my affection by your confession, that you were in despair, not knowing how to help me in my illness, that you sold everything to keep me and prevent my going to hospital, that you got into debt as far as you possibly could, and have unpleasant scenes every day with your landlady—but you made a mistake in concealing all this from me. Now I know it all, however. You were reluctant to make me realise that I was the cause of your unhappy position, and now you have caused me twice as much grief by your behaviour.

All this has shocked me, Makar Alexyevitch. Oh, my dear friend! misfortune is an infectious disease, the poor and unfortunate ought to avoid one another, for fear of making each other worse. I have brought you trouble such as you knew nothing of in your old humble and solitary existence. All this is distressing and killing me.

Write me now openly all that happened to you and how you came to behave like that. Set my mind at rest if possible. It isn't selfishness makes me write to you about my peace of mind, but my affection and love for you, which nothing will ever efface from my heart. Good-bye. I await your answer with impatience. You had a very poor idea of me, Makar Alexyevitch.

Your loving
VARVARA DOBROSELOV.

July 28.

MY PRECIOUS VARVARA ALEXYEVNA—

Well, as now everything is over and, little by little, things are beginning to be as they used to be, again let me tell you one thing, my good friend: you are worried by what people will think about me, to which I hasten to assure you, Varvara Alexyevna, that my reputation is dearer to me than anything. For which reason and with reference to my misfortunes and all those disorderly proceedings I beg to inform you that no one of the authorities at the office know anything about it or will know anything about it. So that they will all feel the same respect for me as before. The one thing I'm afraid of is gossip. At home our landlady did nothing but shout, and now that with the help of your ten roubles I have paid part of what I owe her she does nothing more than grumble; as for other people, they don't matter, one mustn't borrow money of them, that's all, and to conclude my explanations I tell you, Varvara Alexyevna, that your respect for me I esteem more highly than anything on earth, and I am comforted by it now in my temporary troubles. Thank God that the first blow and the first shock are over and that you have taken it as you have, and don't look on me as a false friend, or an egoist for keeping you here and deceiving you because I love you as my angel and could not bring myself to part from you. I've set to work again assiduously and have begun performing my duties well. Yevstafy Ivanovitch did just say a word when I passed him by yesterday. I will not conceal from you, Varinka, that I am overwhelmed by my debts and the awful condition of my wardrobe, but that again does not matter, and about that too, I entreat you, do not despair, my dear. Send me another half rouble. Varinka, that half rouble rends my heart too. So that's what it has come to now, that is how it is, old fool that I am; it's not I helping you, my angel, but you, my poor little orphan, helping me. Fedora did well to get the money. - For the time I have no hopes of getting any, but if there should be any prospects I will write to you fully about it all. But gossip, gossip is what I am most uneasy about. I kiss your little hand and implore you to get well. I don't write more fully because I am in haste to get to the office. For I want by industry and assiduity to atone for all my shortcomings in the way of negligence in the office; a further account of all that happened and my adventures with the officers I put off till this evening.

Your respectful and loving
MAKAR DYEVUSHKIN.

July 28.

MY PRECIOUS VARINKA—

Ach, Varinka, Varinka! This time the sin is on your side and your conscience. You completely upset and perplexed me by your letter, and only now, when at my leisure I looked into the inmost recesses of my heart, I saw that I was right, perfectly right. I am not talking of my drinking (that's enough of it, my dear soul, that's enough) but about my loving you and that I was not at all unreasonable in loving you, not at all unreasonable. You know nothing about it, my darling; why, if only you knew why it all was, why I was bound to love you, you wouldn't talk like that. All your reasoning about it is only talk, and I am sure that in your heart you feel quite differently.

My precious, I don't even know myself and don't remember what happened between me and the officers. I must tell you, my angel, that up to that time I was in the most terrible perturbation. Only imagine! for a whole month I had been clinging to one thread, so to say. My position was most awful. I was concealing it from you, and concealing it at home too. But my landlady made a fuss and a clamour. I should not have minded that. The wretched woman might have clamoured but, for one thing, it was the disgrace and, for another, she had found out about our friendship—God knows how—and was making such talk about it all over the house that I was numb with horror and put wool in my ears, but the worst of it is that other people did not put wool in theirs, but pricked them up, on the contrary. Even now I don't know where to hide myself. . . .

Well, my angel, all this accumulation of misfortunes of all sorts overwhelmed me utterly. Suddenly I heard a strange thing from Fedora: that a worthless profligate had called upon you and had insulted you by dishonourable proposals; that he did insult you, insult you deeply, I can judge from myself, my darling, for I was deeply insulted myself. That crushed me, my angel, that overwhelmed me and made me lose my head completely. I ran out, Varinka dear, in unutterable fury. I wanted to go straight to him, the reprobate. I did not know what I meant to do. I won't have you insulted, my angel! Well, I was sad! And at that time it was raining, sleet was falling, it was horribly wretched! . . . I meant to turn back. . . . Then came my downfall. I met Emelyan Ilyitch—he is a clerk, that is, was a clerk, but he is not a clerk now because he was turned out of our office. I don't know what he does now, he just hangs about there. Well, I went with him. Then —but there, Varinka, will it amuse you to read about your friend's misfortunes, his troubles, and the story of the trials he has endured? Three days later that Emelyan egged me on and I went to see him, that officer. I got his address from our porter. Since we are talking about it, my dear, I noticed that young gallant long ago: I kept an eye upon him when he lodged in our buildings. I see now that what I did was unseemly, because I was not myself when I was shown up to him. Truly, Varinka, I don't remember anything about it, all I remember is that there were a great many officers with him, else I was seeing double—goodness knows. I don't remember what I said either, I only know that I said a great deal in my honest indignation. But then they turned me out, then they threw me downstairs—that is, not really threw me downstairs, but turned me out. You know already, Varinka, how I returned: that's the whole story. Of course I lowered myself and my reputation has suffered, but, after all, no one knows of it but you, no outsider knows of it, and so it is all as though it had never happened. Perhaps that is so, Varinka, what do you think? The only thing is, I know for a fact that last year Aksenty Osipovitch in the same way assaulted Pyotr Petrovitch but in secret, he did it in secret. He called him into the porter's room—I saw it all through the crack in the door—and there he settled the matter, as was fitting, but in a gentlemanly way, for no one saw it except me, and I did not matter—that is, I did not tell anyone. Well, after that Pyotr Petrovitch and Aksenty Osipovitch were all right together. Pyotr Petrovitch, you know, is a man with self-respect, so he told no one, so that now they even bow and shake hands. I don't dispute, Varinka, I don't venture to dispute with you that I have degraded myself terribly, and, what is worst of all, I have lowered myself in my own opinion, but no doubt it was destined from my birth, no doubt it was my fate, and there's no escaping one's fate, you know.

Well, that is an exact account of my troubles and misfortunes, Varinka, all of them, things such that reading of them is unprofitable. I am very far from well, Varinka, and have lost all the playfulness of my feelings. Herewith I beg to testify to my devotion, love and respect. I remain, dear madam, Varvara Alexyevna,

Your humble servant,
MAKAR DYEVUSHKIN.

July 29.

MY DEAR MAKAR ALEXYEVITCH!

I have read your two letters, and positively groaned! Listen, my dear; you are either concealing something from me and have written to me only part of all your troubles, or . . . really, Makar Alexyevitch, there is a touch of incoherency about your letters still. . . . Come and see me, for goodness' sake, come to-day; and listen, come straight to dinner, you know I don't know how you are living, or how you have managed about your landlady. You write nothing about all that, and your silence seems intentional. So, good-bye, my friend; be sure and come to us to-day; and you would do better to come to us for dinner every day. Fedora cooks very nicely. Good-bye.

Your
VARVARA DOBROSELOV.

August 1.

MY DEAR VARVARA ALEXYEVNA—

You are glad, my dear girl, that God has sent you a chance to do one good turn for another and show your gratitude to me. I believe that, Varinka, and I believe in the goodness of your angelic heart, and I am not saying it to reproach you—only do not upbraid me for being a spendthrift in my old age. Well, if I have done wrong, there's no help for it; only to hear it from you, my dearie, is very bitter! Don't be angry with me for saying so, my heart's all one ache. Poor people are touchy—that's in the nature of things. I felt that even in the past. The poor man is exacting; he takes a different view of God's world, and looks askance at every passer-by and turns a troubled gaze about him and looks to every word, wondering whether people are not talking about him, whether they are saying that he is so ugly, speculating about what he would feel exactly, what he would be on this side and what he would be on that side, and everyone knows, Varinka, that a poor man is worse than a rag and can get no respect from anyone; whatever they may write, those scribblers, it will always be the same with the poor man as it has been. And why will it always be as it has been? Because to their thinking the poor man must be turned inside out, he must have no privacy, no pride whatever! Emelyan told me the other day that they got up a subscription for him and made a sort of official inspection over every sixpence; they thought that they were giving him his sixpences for nothing, but they were not; they were paid for them by showing him he was a poor man. Nowadays, my dear soul, benevolence is practised in a very queer way . . . and perhaps it always has been so, who knows! Either people don't know how to do it or they are first-rate hands at it—one of the two. Perhaps you did not know it, so there it is for you. On anything else we can say nothing, but on this subject we are authorities! And how is it a poor man knows all this and thinks of it all like this? Why?—from experience! Because he knows for instance, that there is a gentleman at his side, who is going somewhere to a restaurant and saying to himself, "What's this beggarly clerk going to eat to-day? I'm going to eat *sauté papillotte* while he is going to eat porridge without butter, maybe." And what business is it to him that I am going to eat porridge without butter? There are men, Varinka, there are men who think of nothing else. And they go about, the indecent caricaturists, and look whether one puts one's whole foot down on the pavement or walks on tiptoe; they notice that such a clerk, of such a department, a titular councillor, has his bare toes sticking out of his boot, that he has holes in his elbow— and then they sit down at home and describe it all and publish such rubbish . . . and what business is it of yours, sir, if my elbows are in holes? Yes, if you will excuse me the coarse expression, Varinka, I will tell you that the poor man has the same sort of modesty on that score as you, for instance, have maidenly modesty. Why, you wouldn't divest yourself of your clothing before everyone—forgive my coarse comparison. So, in the same way, the poor man does not like people to peep into his poor hole and wonder about his domestic arrangements. So what need was there to join in insulting me, Varinka, with the enemies who are attacking an honest man's honour and reputation?

And in the office to-day I sat like a hen, like a plucked sparrow, so that I almost turned with shame at myself. I was ashamed, Varinka! And one is naturally timid, when one's elbows are seeing daylight through one's sleeves, and one's buttons are hanging on threads. And, as ill-luck would have it, all my things were in such disorder! You can't help losing heart. Why! . . . Stepan Karlovitch himself began speaking to me about my work to-day, he talked and talked away and added, as though unawares, "Well, really, Makar Alexyevitch!" and did not say what was in his mind, only I understood what it was for myself, and blushed so that even the bald patch on my head was crimson. It was really only a trifle, but still it made me uneasy, and aroused bitter reflections. If only they have heard nothing! Ah, God forbid that they should hear about anything! I confess I do suspect one man. I suspect him very much. Why, these villains stick at nothing, they will betray me, they will give away one's whole private life for a halfpenny—nothing is sacred to them.

I know now whose doing it is; it is Ratazyaev's doing. He knows someone in our office, and most likely in the course of conversation has told them the whole story with additions; or maybe he has told the story in his own office, and it has crept out and crept into our office. In our lodging, they all know it down to the lowest, and point at your window; I know that they do point. And when I went to dinner with you yesterday, they all poked their heads out of window and the landlady said: "Look," said she, "the devil has made friends with the baby." And then she called you an unseemly name. But all that's nothing beside Ratazyaev's disgusting design to put you and me into his writing and to describe us in a cunning satire; he spoke of this himself, and friendly fellow-lodgers have repeated it to me. I can think of nothing else, my darling, and don't know what to decide to do. There is no concealing the fact, we have provoked the wrath of God, little angel. You meant to send me a book, my good friend, to relieve my dullness; what is the use of a book, my love, what's the good of it? It's arrant nonsense! The story is nonsense and it is written as nonsense, just for idle people to read; trust me, my dear soul, trust the experience of my age. And what if they talk to you of some Shakespeare, saying, "You see that Shakespeare wrote literature," well, then, Shakespeare is nonsense; it's all arrant nonsense and only written to jeer at folk!

Yours,
MAKAR DYEVUSHKIN.

August 2.

DEAR MAKAR ALEXYEVITCH!

Don't worry about anything; please God it will all be set right. Fedora has got a lot of work both for herself and for me, and we have set to work very happily; perhaps we shall save the situation. She suspects that Anna Fyodorovna had some hand in this last unpleasant business; but now I don't care. I feel somehow particularly cheerful to-day. You want to borrow money—God forbid! You'll get into trouble afterwards when you need to pay it back. We had much better live more frugally; come to us more often, and don't take any notice of your landlady. As for your other enemies and ill-wishers, I am sure you are worrying yourself with needless suspicions, Makar Alexyevitch! Mind, I told you last time that your language was very exaggerated. Well, good-bye till we meet. I expect you without fail.

Your
V. D.

August 3.

MY ANGEL, VARVARA ALEXYEVNA,

I hasten to tell you, my little life, I have fresh hopes of something. But excuse me, my little daughter, you write, my angel, that I am not to borrow money. My darling, it is impossible to avoid it; here I am in a bad way, and what if anything were suddenly amiss with you! You are frail, you know; so that's why I say we must borrow. Well, so I will continue.

I beg to inform you, Varvara Alexyevna, that in the office I am sitting next to Emelyan Ivanovitch. That's not the Emelyan Ilyitch whom you know. He is, like me, a titular councillor, and he and I are almost the oldest veterans in the office. He is a good-natured soul, an unworldly soul; he's not given to talking and always sits like a regular bear. But he is a good clerk and has a good English handwriting and, to tell the whole truth, he writes as well as I do—he's a worthy man! I never was very intimate with him, but only just say good-morning and good-evening; or if I wanted the pen-knife, I would say, "Give me the pen-knife, Emelyan Ivanovitch"; in short, our intercourse was confined to our common necessities. Well so, he says to me to-day, "Makar Alexyevitch, why are you so thoughtful?" I see the man wishes me kindly, so I told him— I said, "This is how it is, Emelyan Ivanovitch"—that is, I did not tell him everything, and indeed, God forbid! I never will tell the story because I haven't the heart to, but just told him something, that I was in straits for money, and so on. "You should borrow, my good soul," said Emelyan Ivanovitch: "you should borrow; from Pyotr Petrovitch you might borrow, he lends money at interest; I have borrowed and he asks a decent rate of interest, not exorbitant.' Well, Varinka, my heart gave a leap. I thought and thought maybe the Lord will put it into the heart of Pyotr Petrovitch and in his benevolence he will lend me the money. Already I was reckoning to myself that I could pay the landlady and help you, and clear myself all round. Whereas now it is such a disgrace, one is afraid to be in one's own place, let alone the jeers of our grinning jackanapes. Bother them! And besides, his Excellency sometimes passes by our table: why, God forbid! he may cast a glance in my direction and notice I'm not decently dressed! And he makes a great point of neatness and tidiness. Maybe he would say nothing, but I should die of shame—that's how it would be. In consequence I screwed myself up and, putting my pride in my ragged pocket, I went up to Pyotr Petrovitch full of hope and at the same time more dead than alive with suspense. But, after all, Varinka, it all ended in foolishness! He was busy with something, talking with Fedosey Ivanovitch. I went up to him sideways and pulled him by the sleeve, saying, "Pyotr Petrovitch, I say, Pyotr Petrovitch!" He looked round, and I went on: saying, "this is how it is, thirty roubles,'" and so on. At first he did not understand me, and when I explained it all to him, he laughed, and said nothing. I said the same thing again. And he said to me, "Have you got a pledge?" And he buried himself in his writing and did not even glance at me. I was a little flustered. "No," I said, Pyotr Petrovitch, I've no pledge," and I explained to him that when I got my salary I would pay him, would be sure to pay him, I should consider it my first duty. Then somebody called him. I waited for him, he came back and began mending a pen and did not seem to notice me, and I kept on with "Pyotr Petrovitch, can't you manage it somehow?" He said nothing and seemed not to hear me. I kept on standing there. Well, I thought I would try for the last time, and pulled him by the sleeve. He just muttered something, cleaned his pen, and began writing. I walked away. You see, my dear girl, they may be excellent people, but proud, very proud—but I don't mind! We are not fit company for them, Varinka! That is why I have written all this to you. Emelyan Ivanovitch laughed, too, and shook his head, but he cheered me up, the dear fellow —Emelyan Ivanovitch is a worthy man. He promised to introduce me to a man who lives in the Vybord Side, Varinka, and lends money at interest too; he is some sort of clerk of the fourteenth class. Emelyan Ivanovitch says he will be sure to lend it. Shall I go to him to-morrow, my angel, eh? What do you think? It is awful if I don't. My landlady is almost turning me out and won't consent to give me my dinner; besides, my boots are in a dreadful state, my dear; I've no buttons either and nothing else besides. And what if anyone in authority at the office notices such unseemliness; it will be awful, Varinka, simply awful!

MAKAR DYEVUSHKIN.

August 4.

DEAR MAKAR ALEXYEVITCH,

For God's sake, Makar Alexyevitch, borrow some money as soon as possible! I would not for anything have asked you for help as things are at present, but if you only knew what a position I am in. It's utterly impossible for us to remain in this lodging. A horribly unpleasant thing has happened here, and if only you knew how upset and agitated I am! Only imagine, my friend; this morning a stranger came into our lodging, an elderly, almost old man, wearing orders. I was amazed, not knowing what he wanted with us. Fedora had gone out to a shop at the time. He began asking me how I lived and what I did, and without waiting for an answer, told me that he was the uncle of that officer; that he was very angry with his nephew for his disgraceful behaviour, and for having given us a bad name all over the buildings; said that his nephew was a featherheaded scamp, and that he was ready to take me under his protection; advised me not to listen to young men, added that he sympathised with me like a father, that he felt a father's feeling for me and was ready to help me in any way. I blushed all over, not knowing what to think, but was in no haste to thank him. He took my hand by force, patted me on the cheek, told me I was very pretty and that he was delighted to find I had dimples in my cheeks (goodness knows what he said!) and at last tried to kiss me, saying that he was an old man (he was so loathsome). At that point Fedora came in. He was a little disconcerted and began saying again that he felt respect for me, for my discretion and good principles, and that he was very anxious that I should not treat him as a stranger. Then he drew Fedora aside and on some strange pretext wanted to give her a lot of money. Fedora, of course, would not take it. At last he got up to go, he repeated once more all his assurances, said that he would come and see me again and bring me some ear-rings (I believe he, too, was very much embarrassed); he advised me to change my lodgings and recommended me a very nice lodging which he had his eye on, and which would cost me nothing; he said that he liked me very much for being an honest and sensible girl, advised me to beware of profligate men, and finally told us that he knew Anna Fyodorovna and that Anna Fyodorovna had commissioned him to tell me that she would come and see me herself. Then I understood it all. I don't know what came over me; it was the first time in my life I had had such an experience; I flew into a fury, I put him to shame completely. Fedora helped me, and we almost turned him out of the flat. We've come to the conclusion that it is all Anna Fyodorovna's doing; how else could he have heard of us?

Now I appeal to you, Makar Alexyevitch, and entreat you to help us. For God's sake, don't desert me in this awful position. Please borrow, get hold of some money anyway; we've no money to move with and we mustn't stay here any longer; that's Fedora's advice. We need at least thirty-five roubles; I'll pay you back the money; I'll earn it. Fedora will get me some more work in a day or two, so that if they ask a high interest, never mind it, but agree to anything. I'll pay it all back, only for God's sake, don't abandon me. I can't bear worrying you now when you are in such circumstances . . . Good-bye, Makar Alexyevitch; think of me, and God grant you are successful.

Yours,

V. D.

My darling Varvara Alexyevna!

All these unexpected blows positively shatter me! Such terrible calamities destroy my spirit! These scoundrelly libertines and rascally old men will not only bring you, my angel, to a bed of sickness, they mean to be the death of me, too. And they will be, too, I swear they will. You know I am ready to die sooner than not help you! If I don't help you it will be the death of me, Varinka, the actual literal death of me, and if I do help you, you'll fly away from me like a bird out of its nest, to escape these owls, these birds of prey that were trying to peck her. That's what tortures me, my precious. And you too, Varinka, you are so cruel! How can you do it? You are tormented, you are insulted, you, my little bird, are in distress, and then you regret that you must worry me and promise to repay the debt, which means, to tell the truth, that with your delicate health you will kill yourself, in order to get the money for me in time. Why, only think, Varinka, what you are talking about. Why should you sew? Why should you work, worry your poor little head with anxiety, spoil your pretty eyes and destroy your health? Ah, Varinka, Varinka! You see, my darling, I am good for nothing, I know myself that I am good for nothing, but I'll manage to be good for something! I will overcome all obstacles. I will get outside work, I will copy all sorts of manuscripts for all sorts of literary men. I will go to them, I won't wait to be asked, I'll force them to give me work, for you know, my darling, they are on the look-out for good copyists, I know they look out for them, but I won't let you wear yourself out; I won't let you carry out such a disastrous intention. I will certainly borrow it, my angel, I'd sooner die than not borrow it. You write, my darling, that I am not to be afraid of a high rate of interest—and I won't be afraid of it, my dear soul, I won't be frightened. I won't be frightened of anything now. I will ask for forty roubles in paper, my dear; that's not much, you know, Varinka, what do you think? Will they trust me with forty roubles at the first word? That is, I mean to say, do you consider me capable of inspiring trust and confidence at first sight. Can they form a favourable impression of me from my physiognomy at first sight? Recall my appearance, my angel; am I capable of inspiring confidence? What do you think yourself? You know I feel such terror; it makes me quite ill, to tell the truth, quite ill. Of the forty roubles I set aside twenty-five for you, Varinka, two silver roubles will be for the landlady, and the rest I design for my own expenses. You see I ought to give the landlady more, I must, in fact; but if you think it all over, my dear girl, and reckon out all I need, then you'll see that it is impossible to give her more, consequently there's no use talking about it and no need to refer to it. For a silver rouble I shall buy a pair of boots—I really don't know whether I shall be able to appear at the office in the old ones; a new necktie would have been necessary, too, for I have had the old one a year, but since you've promised to make me, not only a tie, but a shirtfront cut out of your old apron, I shall think no more of a tie. So there we have boots and a tie. Now for buttons, my dear. You will agree, my darling, that I can't go on without buttons and almost half have dropped off. I tremble when I think that his Excellency may notice such untidiness and say something, and what he would say! I shouldn't hear what he would say, my darling, for I should die, die, die on the spot, simply go and die of shame at the very thought!—Ah, Varinka!—Well, after all these necessities, there will be three roubles left, so that would do to live on and get half a pound of tobacco, for I can't live without tobacco, my little angel, and this is the ninth day since I had my pipe in my mouth. To tell the truth, I should have bought it and said nothing to you, but I was ashamed. You are there in trouble depriving yourself of everything, and here am I enjoying luxuries of all sorts; so that's why I tell you about it to escape the stings of conscience. I frankly confess, Varinka, I am now in an extremely straitened position, that is, nothing like it has ever happened before. My landlady despises me, I get no sort of respect from anyone; my terrible lapses, my debts; and at the office, where I had anything but a good time, in the old days, at the hands of my fellow clerks—now, Varinka, it is beyond words. I hide everything, I carefully hide everything from everyone, and I edge into the office sideways, I hold aloof from all. It's only to you that I have the heart to confess it. . . . And what if they won't give me the money! No, we had better not think about that, Varinka, not depress our spirits beforehand with such thoughts. That's why I am writing this, to warn you not to think about it, and not to worry yourself with evil imaginations. Ah! my God! what will happen to you then! It's true that then you will not move from that lodging and I shall be with you then. But, no, I should not come back then, I should simply perish somewhere and be lost. Here I have been writing away to you and I ought to have been shaving; it makes one more presentable, and to be presentable always counts for something. Well, God help us, I will say my prayers, and then set off.

M. DYEVUSHKIN.

August 5.

MY DEAR MAKAR ALEXYEVITCH,

You really mustn't give way to despair. There's trouble enough without that.

I send you thirty kopecks in silver, I cannot manage more. Buy yourself what you need most, so as to get along somehow, until to-morrow. We have scarcely anything left ourselves, and I don't know what will happen to-morrow. It's sad, Makar Alexyevitch! Don't be sad, though, if you've not succeeded, there's no help for it. Fedora says that there is no harm done so far, that we can stay for the time in this lodging, that if we did move we shouldn't gain much by it, and that they can find us anywhere if they want to. Though I don't feel comfortable at staying here now. If it were not so sad I would have written you an account of something.

What a strange character you have, Makar Alexyevitch; you take everything too much to heart and so you will be always a very unhappy man. I read all your letters attentively and I see in every letter you are anxious and worried about me as you never are about yourself. Everyone says, of course, that you have a good heart, but I say that it is too good. I will give you some friendly advice, Makar Alexyevitch. I am grateful to you, very grateful for all that you have done for me, I feel it very much; so judge what it must be for me to see that even now, after all your misfortunes of which I have been the unconscious cause—that even now you are only living in my life, my joys, my sorrows, my feelings! If one takes all another person's troubles so to heart and sympathises so intensely with everything it is bound to make one very unhappy. To-day, when you came in to see me from the office I was frightened at the sight of you. You were so pale, so despairing, so frightened-looking; you did not look like yourself—and all because you were afraid to tell me of your failure, afraid of disappointing me, of frightening me, and when you saw I nearly laughed your heart was almost at ease. Makar Alexyevitch, don't grieve, don't despair, be more sensible, I beg you, I implore you. Come, you will see that everything will be all right. Everything will take a better turn: why, life will be a misery to you, for ever grieving and being miserable over other people's troubles. Good-bye, my dear friend. I beseech you not to think too much about it.

V. D.

August 5.

MY DARLING VARINKA,

Very well, my angel, very well! You have made up your mind that it is no harm so far that I have not got the money. Well, very good, I feel reassured, I am happy as regards you. I am delighted, in fact, that you are not going to leave me in my old age but are going to stay in your lodging. In fact, to tell you everything, my heart was brimming over with joy when I saw that you wrote so nicely about me in your letter and gave due credit to my feelings. I don't say this from pride, but because I see how you love me when you are so anxious about my heart. Well, what's the use of talking about my heart! The heart goes its own way, but you hint, my precious, that I mustn't be downhearted. Yes, my angel, maybe, and I say myself it is of no use being downhearted! but for all that, you tell me, my dear girl, what boots I am to go to the office in to-morrow! That's the trouble, Varinka; and you know such a thought destroys a man, destroys him utterly. And the worst of it is, my own, that it is not for myself I am troubled, it is not for myself I am distressed; as far as I am concerned I don't mind going about without an overcoat and without boots in the hardest frost; I don't care: I can stand anything, and put up with anything. I am a humble man of no importance,—but what will people say? My enemies with their spiteful tongues, what will they say, when one goes about without an overcoat? You know it is for the sake of other people one wears an overcoat, yes, and boots, too, you put on, perhaps, on their account. Boots, in such cases, Varinka darling, are necessary to keep up one's dignity and good name: in boots with holes in them, both dignity and good name are lost; trust the experience of my years, my dear child, listen to an old man like me who knows the world and what people are, and not to any scurrilous scribblers and satirists.

I have not yet told you in detail, my darling, how it all happened to-day. I suffered so much, I endured in one morning more mental anguish than many a man endures in a year. This is how it was: first, I set off very early in the morning, so as to find him and be in time for the office afterwards. There was such a rain, such a sleet falling this morning! I wrapped myself up in my overcoat, my little dearie. I walked on and on and I kept thinking: "Oh, Lord, forgive my transgressions and grant the fulfilment of my desires!" Passing St. X's Church, I crossed myself, repented of all my sins, and thought that it was wrong of me to bargain with the Almighty. I was lost in my thoughts and did not feel like looking at anything; so I walked without picking my way. The streets were empty, and the few I met all seemed anxious and preoccupied, and no wonder: who would go out at such an early hour and in such weather! A gang of workmen, grinning all over, met me, the rough fellows shoved against me! A feeling of dread came over me, I felt panic-stricken, to tell the truth I didn't like even to think about the money—I felt I must just take my chance! Just at Voskressensky Bridge the sole came off my boot, so I really don't know what I walked upon. And then I met our office attendant, Yermolaev. He drew himself up at attention and stood looking after me as though he would ask for a drink. "Ech, a drink, brother," I thought; "not much chance of a drink!" I was awfully tired. I stood still, rested a bit and pushed on farther; I looked about on purpose for something to fasten my attention on, to distract my mind, to cheer me up, but no, I couldn't fix one thought on anything and, besides, I was so muddy that I felt ashamed of myself. At last I saw in the distance a yellow wooden house with an upper storey in the style of a belvedere. "Well," thought I, "so that's it, that's how Emelyan Ivanovitch described it— Markov's house." (It is this Markov himself, Varinka, who lends money.) I scarcely knew what I was doing, and I knew, of course, that it was Markov's house, but I asked a policeman. "Whose house is that, brother?" said I. The policeman was a surly fellow, seemed loth to speak and cross with someone; he filtered his words through his teeth, but he did say it was Markov's house. These policemen are always so unfeeling, but what did the policeman matter?—well, it all made a bad and unpleasant impression, in short, there was one thing on the top of another; one finds in everything something akin to one's own position, and it is always so. I took three turns past the house, along the street, and the further I went, the worse I felt. "No," I thought, "he won't give it me, nothing will induce him to give it me. I am a stranger and it's a ticklish business, and I am not an attractive figure. Well," I thought, "leave it to

Fate, if only I do not regret it afterwards; they won't devour me for making the attempt," and I softly opened the gate, and then another misfortune happened. A wretched, stupid yard dog fastened upon me. It was beside itself and barked its loudest!—and it's just such wretched, trivial incidents that always madden a man, Varinka, and make him nervous and destroy all the determination he has been fortifying himself with beforehand; so that I went into the house more dead than alive and walked straight into trouble again. Without seeing what was below me straight in the doorway, I went in, stumbled over a woman who was busy straining some milk from a pail into a jug, and spilt all the milk. The silly woman shrieked and made an outcry, saying, "Where are you shoving to, my man?" and made a deuce of a row. I may say, Varinka, it is always like this with me in such cases; it seems it is my fate, I always get mixed up in something. An old hag, the Finnish landlady, poked her head out at the noise. I went straight up to her. "Does Markov live here?" said I. "No," said she. She stood still and took a good look at me. "And what do you want with him?" I explained to her that Emelyan had told me this and that, and all the rest of it—said it was a matter of business. The old woman called her daughter, a barelegged girl in her teens. "Call your father; he's upstairs at the lodger's, most likely."

I went in. The room was all right, there were pictures on the wall—all portraits of generals, a sofa, round table, mignonette, and balsam—I wondered whether I had not better clear out and take myself off for good and all. And, oh dear, I did want to run away, Varinka. "I had better come to-morrow," I thought, "and the weather will be better and I will wait a little —to-day the milk's been spilt and the generals look so cross . . ." I was already at the door—but he came in—a greyheaded man with thievish eyes, in a greasy dressing-gown with a cord round his waist. He enquired how and why, and I told him that Emelyan Ivanovitch had told me this and that— "Forty roubles," I said, "is what I've come about"—and I couldn't finish. I saw from his eyes that the game was lost. "No," says he; "the fact is, I've no money; and have you brought anything to pledge as security?"

I began explaining that I had brought nothing to pledge, but that Emelyan Ivanovitch—I explained in fact, what was wanted. He heard it all. "No," said he; "what is Emelyan Ivanovitch! I've no money."

Well, I thought, "There it is, I knew—I had a foreboding of it." Well, Varinka, it would have been better really if the earth had opened under me. I felt chill all over, my feet went numb and a shiver ran down my back. I looked at him and he looked at me and almost said, Come, run along, brother, it is no use your staying here—so that if such a thing had happened in other circumstances, I should have been quite ashamed. "And what do you want money for?"—(do you know, he asked that, Varinka). I opened my mouth, if only not to stand there doing nothing, but he wouldn't listen. "No," he said, "I have no money, I would have lent it with pleasure," said he. Then I pressed him, telling him I only wanted a little, saying I would pay him back on the day fixed, that I would pay him back before the day fixed, that he could ask any interest he liked and that, by God! I would pay him back. At that instant, my darling, I thought of you, I thought of all your troubles and privations, I thought of your poor little half-rouble. "But no," says he, "the interest is no matter; if there had been a pledge now! Besides, I have no money. I have none, by God! or I'd oblige you with pleasure," —he took God's name, too, the villain!

Well, I don't remember, my own, how I went out, how I walked along Vyborgsky Street; how I got to Voskressensky Bridge. I was fearfully tired, shivering, wet through, and only succeeded in reaching the office at ten o'clock. I wanted to brush the mud off, but Snyegirev, the porter, said I mustn't, I should spoil the brush, and "the brush is government property," said he. That's how they all go on now, my dear, these gentry treat me no better than a rag to wipe their boots on. Do you know what is killing me, Varinka? it's not the money that's killing me, but all these little daily cares, these whispers, smiles and jokes. His Excellency may by chance have to refer to me. Oh, my darling, my golden days are over. I read over all your letters to-day; it's sad, Varinka! Good-bye, my own! The Lord keep you.

M. DYEVUSHKIN.

P.S.—I meant to describe my troubles half in joke, Varinka, only it seems that it does not come off with me, joking. I wanted to satisfy you. I am coming to see you, my dear girl, I will be sure to come.

VARVARA ALEXYEVNA, MY DARLING,

I am lost, we are both lost, both together irretrievably lost. My reputation, my dignity—all is destroyed! I am ruined and you are ruined, my darling. You are hopelessly ruined with me! It's my doing, I have brought you to ruin! I am persecuted, Varinka, I am despised, turned into a laughing-stock, and the landlady has simply begun to abuse me; she shouted and shouted at me, to-day; she rated and rated at me and treated me as though I were dirt. And in the evening, at Ratazyaev's, one of them began reading aloud the rough copy of a letter to you which I had accidentally dropped out of my pocket. My precious, what a joke they made of it! They called us all sorts of flattering names and roared with laughter, the traitors! I went to them and taxed Ratazyaev with his perfidy, told him he was a traitor! And Ratazyaev answered that I was a traitor myself, that I amused myself with making conquests among the fair sex. He said, "You take good care to keep it from us; you're a Lovelace," he said; and now they all call me Lovelace and I have no other name! Do you hear, my little angel, do you hear?— they know it all now, they know all about it, and they know about you, my own, and whatever you have, they know about it all! And that's not all. Even Faldoni is in it, he's following their lead; I sent him to-day to the sausage-shop to get me something; he wouldn't go. "I am busy," that was all he said! "But you know it's your duty," I said. "No, indeed," he said, "it's not my duty. Here, you don't pay my mistress her money, so I have no duty to you." I could not stand this insult from him, an illiterate peasant, and I said, "You fool," and he answered back, "Fool yourself." I thought he must have had a drop too much to be so rude, and I said: "You are drunk, you peasant!" and he answered: "Well, not at your expense, anyway, you've nothing to get drunk on yourself; you are begging for twenty kopecks from somebody yourself," and he even added: "Ugh! and a gentleman too!" There, my dear girl, that's what it has come to! One's ashamed to be alive, Varinka! As though one were some sort of outcast, worse than a tramp without a passport. An awful calamity! I am ruined, simply ruined! I am irretrievably ruined!

M. D.

MY DEAR MAKAR ALEXYEVITCH,

It's nothing but one trouble after another upon us. I don't know myself what to do! What will happen to you now?—and I have very little to hope for either; I burnt my left hand this morning with an iron; I dropped it accidentally and bruised myself and burnt my hand at the same time. I can't work at all, and Fedora has been poorly for the last three days. I am in painful anxiety. I send you thirty kopecks in silver; it is almost all we have left, and God knows how I should have liked to help you in your need. I am so vexed I could cry. Good-bye, my friend! You would comfort me very much if you would come and see us to-day.

V. D.

MAKAR ALEXYEVITCH

What is the matter with you? It seems you have no fear of God! You are simply driving me out of my mind. Aren't you ashamed? You will be your own ruin; you should at least think of your good name! You're a man of honour, of gentlemanly feelings, of self-respect; well, when everyone finds out about you! Why, you will simply die of shame! Have you no pity for your grey hairs? Have you no fear of God? Fedora says she won't help you again, and I won't give you money either. What have you brought me to, Makar Alexyevitch? I suppose you think that it is nothing to me, your behaving so badly? You don't know what I have to put up with on your account! I can't even go down our staircase; everyone looks at me and points at me, and says such awful things; they say plainly that I have *taken up with a drunkard*. Think what it is to hear that! When you are brought in all the lodgers point at you with contempt: "Look," they say, "they've brought that clerk in." And I'm ready to faint with shame over you. I swear I shall move from here. I shall go somewhere as a housemaid or a laundrymaid, I shan't stay here. I wrote to you to come and see me here but you did not come. So are my tears and entreaties nothing to you, Makar Alexyevitch? And where do you get the money? For God's sake, do be careful. Why, you are ruining yourself, ruining yourself for nothing! And it's a shame and a disgrace! The landlady would not let you in last night, you spent the night in the porch. I know all about it. If only you knew how miserable I was when I knew all about it. Come to see me; you will be happy with us; we will read together, we will recall the past. Fedora will tell us about her wanderings as a pilgrim. For my sake, don't destroy yourself and me. Why, I only live for you, for your sake I am staying with you. And this is how you are behaving now! Be a fine man, steadfast in misfortune, remember that poverty is not a vice. And why despair? It is all temporary! Please God, it will all be set right, only you must restrain yourself now. I send you twenty kopecks. Buy yourself tobacco or anything you want, only for God's sake don't spend it on what's harmful. Come and see us, be sure to come. Perhaps you will be ashamed as you were before, but don't be ashamed; it's false shame. If only you would show genuine penitence. Trust in God. He will do all things for the best.

V. D.

August 19.

VARVARA ALEXYEVNA, DARLING,

I am ashamed, little dearie, Varvara Alexyevna; I am quite ashamed. But, after all, what is there so particular about it, my dear? Why not rejoice the heart a little? Then I don't think about my sole, for one's sole is nonsense, and will always remain a simple, nasty, muddy sole. Yes, and boots are nonsense, too! The Greek sages used to go about without boots, so why should people like us pamper ourselves with such unworthy objects? Oh! my dearie, my dearie, you have found something to write about! You tell Fedora that she is a nonsensical, fidgety, fussy woman, and, what's more, she's a silly one, too, unutterably silly! As for my grey hairs, you are quite mistaken about that, my own, for I am by no means so old as you think. Emelyan sends you his regards. You write that you have been breaking your heart and crying; and I write to you that I am breaking my heart, too, and crying. In conclusion I wish you the best of health and prosperity, and as for me I am in the best of health and prosperity, too, and I remain, my angel, your friend,

MAKAR DYEVUSHKIN.

August 21.

HONOURED MADAM AND DEAR FRIEND, VARVARA ALEXYEVNA,

I feel that I am to blame, I feel that I have wronged you, and to my mind there's no benefit at all, dear friend, in my feeling it, whatever you may say. I felt all that even before my misconduct, but I lost heart and fell, knowing I was doing wrong. My dear, I am not a bad man and not cruel-hearted, and to torture your little heart, my little darling, one must be, more or less, like a bloodthirsty tiger. Well, I have the heart of a lamb and, as you know, have no inclination towards bloodthirstiness; consequently, my angel, I am not altogether to blame in my misconduct, since neither my feelings nor my thoughts were to blame; and in fact, I don't know what was to blame; it's all so incomprehensible, my darling! you sent me thirty kopecks in silver, and then you sent me twenty kopecks. My heart ached looking at your poor little coins. You had burnt your hand, you would soon be going hungry yourself, and you write that I am to buy tobacco. Well, how could I behave in such a position? Was I without a pang of conscience to begin plundering you, poor little orphan, like a robber! Then I lost heart altogether, my darling—that is, at first I could not help feeling that I was good for nothing and that I was hardly better than the sole of my boot. And so I felt it was unseemly to consider myself of any consequence, and began to look upon myself as something unseemly and somewhat indecent. Well, and when I lost my self-respect and denied my good qualities and my dignity, then it was all up with me, it meant degradation, inevitable degradation! That is ordained by destiny and I'm not to blame for it.

I went out at first to get a little air, then it was one thing after another; nature was so tearful, the weather was cold and it was raining. Well, Emelyan turned up. He had pawned everything he had, Varinka, everything he had is gone: and when I met him he had not put a drop of the rosy to his lips for two whole days and nights, so that he was ready to pawn what you can't pawn, because such things are never taken in pawn. Well, Varinka, I gave way more from a feeling of humanity than my own inclination, that's how the sin came to pass, my dear! How we wept together! We spoke of you. He's very good-natured, he's a very good-natured fellow and a very feeling man. I feel all that myself, my dear girl, that is just why it all happens to me, that I feel it all very much. I know how much I owe to you, my darling. Getting to know you, I came first to know myself better and to love you; and before I knew you, my angel, I was solitary and as it were asleep, and scarcely alive. They said, the spiteful creatures, that even my appearance was unseemly and they were disgusted with me, and so I began to be disgusted with myself; they said I was stupid and I really thought that I was stupid. When you came to me, you lighted up my dark life, so that my heart and my soul were filled with light and I gained peace at heart, and knew that I was no worse than others; that the only thing is that I am not brilliant in any way, that I have no polish or style about me, but I am still a man, in heart and mind a man. Well now, feeling that I was persecuted and humiliated by destiny, I lost all faith in my own good qualities, and, shattered by calamities, I lost all heart. And now since you know all about it, my dear, I beg you with tears not to question me further about that matter, for my heart is breaking and it is very bitter for me and hard to bear.

Assuring you of my respect, I remain, your faithful

MAKAR DYEVUSHKIN.

September 3.

I did not finish my last letter, Makar Alexyevitch, because it was difficult for me to write. Sometimes I have moments when I am glad to be alone, to mourn, with none to share my grief, and such moments are becoming more and more frequent with me. In my recollections there is something inexplicable to me, which attacks me unaccountably and so intensely that for hours at a stretch I am insensible to all surrounding me and I forget everything—all the present. And there is no impression of my present life, whether pleasant or painful and sad, which would not remind me of something similar in my past, and most often in my childhood, my golden childhood! But I always feel oppressed after such moments. I am somehow weakened by them; my dreaminess exhausts me, and apart from that my health grows worse and worse. But to-day the fresh bright sunny morning, such as are rare in autumn here, revived me and I welcomed it joyfully. And so autumn is with us already! How I used to love the autumn in the country! I was a child then, but I had already felt a great deal. I loved the autumn evening better than the morning. I remember that there was a lake at the bottom of the hill a few yards from our house. That lake—I feel as though I could see it now—that lake was so broad, so smooth, as bright and clear as crystal! At times, if it were a still evening, the lake was calm; not a leaf would stir on the trees that grew on the bank, and the water would be as motionless as a mirror. It was so fresh, so cool! The dew would be falling on the grass, the lights begin twinkling in the cottages on the bank, and they would be driving the cattle home. Then I could creep out to look at my lake, and I would forget everything, looking at it. At the water's edge, the fishermen would have a faggot burning and the light would be reflected far, far, over the water. The sky was so cold and blue, with streaks of fiery red along the horizon, and the streaks kept growing paler and paler; the moon would rise; the air so resonant that if a frightened bird fluttered, or a reed stirred in the faint breeze, or a fish splashed in the water, everything could be heard. A white steam, thin and transparent, rises up over the blue water: the distance darkens; everything seems drowned in the mist, while close by it all stands out so sharply, as though cut by a chisel, the boat, the banks, the islands; the tub thrown away and forgotten floats in the water close to the bank, the willow branch hangs with its yellow leaves tangled in the reeds, a belated gull flies up, then dives into the cold water, flies up again and is lost in the mist—while I gaze and listen. How lovely, how marvellous it was to me! and I was a child, almost a baby. . . .

I was so fond of the autumn, the late autumn when they were carrying the harvest, finishing all the labours of the year, when the peasants began gathering together in their cottages in the evening, when they were all expecting winter. Then it kept growing darker. The yellow leaves strewed the paths at the edges of the bare forest while the forest grew bluer and darker—especially at evening when a damp mist fell and the trees glimmered in the mist like giants, like terrible misshapen phantoms. If one were late out for a walk, dropped behind the others, how one hurried on alone—it was dreadful! One trembled like a leaf and kept thinking that in another minute someone terrible would peep out from behind that hollow tree; meanwhile the wind would rush through the woods, roaring and whistling, howling so plaintively, tearing a crowd of leaves from a withered twig, whirling them in the air, and with wild, shrill cries the birds would fly after them in a great, noisy flock, so that the sky would be all covered and darkened with them. One feels frightened, and then, just as though one heard someone speaking—some voice—as though someone whispered: "Run, run, child, don't be late; it will be dreadful here soon; run, child!"—with a thrill of horror at one's heart one would run till one was out of breath. One would reach home, breathless; there it was all noise and gaiety; all of us children had

217

some work given to us to do, shelling peas or shaking out poppy seeds. The damp wood crackles in the stove. Cheerfully mother looks after our cheerful work; our old nurse, Ulyana, tells us stories about old times or terrible tales of wizards and dead bodies. We children squeeze up to one another with smiles on our lips. Then suddenly we are all silent . . . Oh! a noise as though someone were knocking— it was nothing; it was old Frolovna's spindle; how we laughed! Then at night we would lie awake for hours, we had such fearful dreams. One would wake and not dare to stir, and lie shivering under the quilt till daybreak. In the morning one would get up, fresh as a flower. One would look out of the window; all the country would be covered with frost, the thin hoarfrost of autumn would be hanging on the bare boughs, the lake would be covered with ice, thin as a leaf, a white mist would be rising over it, the birds would be calling merrily, the sun would light up everything with its brilliant rays and break the thin ice like glass. It was so bright, so shining, so gay, the fire would be crackling in the stove again, we would sit down round the samovar while our black dog, Polkan, numb with cold from the night, would peep in at the window with a friendly wag of his tail. A peasant would ride by the window on his good horse to fetch wood from the forest. Everyone was so gay, so happy! . . . There were masses and masses of corn stored up in the threshing-barns; the huge, huge stacks covered with straw shone golden in the sun, a comforting sight! And all are calm and joyful. God has blessed us all with the harvest; they all know they will have bread for the winter; the peasant knows that his wife and children will have food to eat; and so there is no end to the singing of the girls and their dances and games in the evening, and on the Saints' days! All pray in the house of God with grateful tears! Oh! what a golden, golden age was my childhood! . . .

Here I am crying like a child, carried away by my reminiscences. I remembered it all so vividly, so vividly, all the past stood out so brightly before me, and the present is so dim, so dark! . . . How will it end, how will it all end? Do you know I have a sort of conviction, a feeling of certainty, that I shall die this autumn. I am very, very ill. I often think about dying, but still I don't want to die like this, to lie in the earth here. Perhaps I shall be laid up as I was in the spring; I've not fully recovered from that illness yet. I am feeling very dreary just now. Fedora has gone off somewhere for the whole day and I am sitting alone. And for some time now I've been afraid of being left alone; I always feel as though there were someone else in the room, that someone is talking to me; especially when I begin dreaming about something and suddenly wake up from my brooding, then I feel frightened. That is why I've written you such a long letter; it goes off when I write. Good-bye; I finish my letter because I have neither time nor paper for more. Of the money from pawning my dress and my hat I have only one rouble in silver left. You have given the landlady two roubles in silver; that's very good. She will keep quiet now for a time.

You must improve your clothes somehow. Good-bye, I'm so tired; I don't know why I am growing so feeble. The least work exhausts me. If I do get work, how am I to work? It is that thought that's killing me.

V. D.

September 5.

MY DARLING VARINKA,

I have received a great number of impressions this morning, my angel. To begin with I had a headache all day. To freshen myself up a bit I went for a walk along Fontanka. It was such a damp, dark evening. By six o'clock it was getting dusk—that is what we are coming to now. It was not raining but there was mist equal to a good rain. There were broad, long stretches of storm-cloud across the sky. There were masses of people walking along the canal bank, and, as ill-luck would have it, the people had such horrible depressing faces, drunken peasants, snub-nosed Finnish women, in high boots with nothing on their heads, workmen, cab-drivers, people like me out on some errand, boys, a carpenter's apprentice in a striped dressing-gown, thin and wasted-looking, with his face bathed in smutty oil, and a lock in his hand; a discharged soldier seven feet high waiting for somebody to buy a pen-knife or a bronze ring from him. That was the sort of crowd. It seems it was an hour when no other sort of people could be about. Fontanka is a canal for traffic! Such a mass of barges that one wonders how there can be room for them all! On the bridges there are women sitting with wet gingerbread and rotten apples, and they all of them looked so muddy, so drenched. It's dreary walking along Fontanka! The wet granite under one's feet, with tall, black, sooty houses on both sides. Fog underfoot and fog overhead. How dark and melancholy it was this evening!

When I went back to Gorohovoy Street it was already getting dark and they had begun lighting the gas. I have not been in Gorohovoy Street for quite a long while, I haven't happened to go there. It's a noisy street! What shops, what magnificent establishments; everything is simply shining and resplendent; materials, flowers under glass, hats of all sorts with ribbons. One would fancy they were all displayed as a show—but no: you know there are people who buy all those things and present them to their wives. It's a wealthy street! There are a great many German bakers in Gorohovoy Street, so they must be a very prosperous set of people, too. What numbers of carriages roll by every minute; I wonder the paving is not worn out! Such gorgeous equipages, windows shining like mirrors, silk and velvet inside, and aristocratic footmen wearing epaulettes and carrying a sword; I glanced into all the carriages, there were always ladies in them dressed up to the nines, perhaps countesses and princesses. No doubt it was the hour when they were all hastening to balls and assemblies. It would be interesting to get a closer view of princesses and ladies of rank in general; it must be very nice; I have never seen them; except just as to-day, a passing glance at their carriages. I thought of you then. Ah, my darling, my own! When I think of you my heart begins aching! Why are you so unlucky, my Varinka? You are every bit as good as any of them. You are good, lovely, well-educated—why has such a cruel fortune fallen to your lot? Why does it happen that a good man is left forlorn and forsaken, while happiness seems thrust upon another? I know, I know, my dear, that it's wrong to think that, that it is free-thinking; but to speak honestly, to speak the whole truth, why is it fate, like a raven, croaks good fortune for one still unborn, while another begins life in the orphan asylum? And you know it often happens that Ivan the fool is favoured by fortune. "You, Ivan the fool, rummage in the family money bags, eat, drink and be merry, while you, So-and-so, can lick your lips. That's all you are fit for, you, brother So-and-so!" It's a sin, my darling, it's a sin to think like that, but sometimes one cannot help sin creeping into one's heart. You ought to be driving in such a carriage, my own little dearie. Generals should be craving the favour of a glance from you—not the likes of us; you ought to be dressed in silk and gold, instead of a little old linen gown. You would not

220

be a thin, delicate little thing, as you are now, but like a little sugar figure, fresh, plump and rosy. And then, I should be happy simply to look in at you from the street through the brightly lighted windows; simply to see your shadow. The thought that you were happy and gay, my pretty little bird, would be enough to make me gay, too. But as it is, it is not enough that spiteful people have ruined you, a worthless profligate wretch goes and insults you. Because his coat hangs smartly on him, because he stares at you from a golden eye-glass, the shameless fellow, he can do what he likes, and one must listen to what he says indulgently, however unseemly it is! Wait a bit—is it really so, my pretty gentlemen? And why is all this? Because you are an orphan, because you are defenceless, because you have no powerful friend to help and protect you. And what can one call people who are ready to insult an orphan? They are worthless beasts, not men; simply trash. They are mere ciphers and have no real existence, of that I am convinced. That's what they are like, these people! And to my thinking, my own, the hurdy-gurdy man I met to-day in Gorohovoy Street is more worthy of respect than they are. He goes about the whole day long, hoping to get some wretched spare farthing for food, but he is his own master, he does earn his own living. He won't ask for charity; but he works like a machine wound up to give pleasure. "Here," he says, "I do what I can to give pleasure." He's a beggar, he's a beggar, it is true, he's a beggar all the same, but he's an honourable beggar; he is cold and weary, but still he works; though it's in his own way, still he works. And there are many honest men, my darling, who, though they earn very little in proportion to the amount and usefulness of their work, yet they bow down to no one and buy their bread of no one. Here I am just like that hurdy-gurdy man—that is, not at all like him. But in my own sense, in an honourable and aristocratic sense, just as he does, to the best of my abilities, I work as I can. That's enough about me, it's neither here nor there.

I speak of that hurdy-gurdy, my darling, because it has happened that I have felt my poverty twice as much to-day. I stopped to look at the hurdy-gurdy man. I was in such a mood that I stopped to distract my thoughts. I was standing there, and also two cab-drivers, a woman of some sort, and a little girl, such a grubby little thing. The hurdy-gurdy man stopped before the windows of a house. I noticed a little boy about ten years old; he would have been pretty, but he looked so ill, so frail, with hardly anything but his shirt on and almost barefoot, with his mouth open; he was listening to the music—like a child! He watched the German's dolls dancing, while his own hands and feet were numb with cold; he shivered and nibbled the edge of his sleeve. I noticed that he had a bit of paper of some sort in his hands. A gentleman passed and flung the hurdy-gurdy man some small coin, which fell straight into the box in a little garden in which the toy Frenchman was dancing with the ladies. At the clink of the coin the boy started, looked round and evidently thought that I had given the money. He ran up to me, his little hands trembling, his little voice trembling, he held the paper out to me and said, "A letter." I opened the letter; well, it was the usual thing, saying: "Kind gentleman, a mother's dying with three children hungry, so help us now, and as I am dying I will pray for you, my benefactor, in the next world for not forgetting my babes now." Well, what of it?—one could see what it meant, an everyday matter, but what could I give him? Well, I gave him nothing, and how sorry I was! The boy was poor, blue with cold, perhaps hungry, too, and not lying, surely he was not lying, I know that for certain. But what is wrong is that these horrid mothers don't take care of their children and send them out half naked in the cold to beg. Maybe she's a weak-willed, silly woman; and there's no one, maybe, to do anything for her, so she simply sits with her legs tucked under her, maybe she's really ill. Well, anyway, she should apply in the proper quarter. Though, maybe, she's a cheat and sends a hungry, delicate child out on purpose to deceive people, and makes him ill. And what sort of training is it for a poor boy? It simply hardens his heart, he runs about begging, people pass and have no time for him. Their hearts are stony, their words are cruel. "Get away, go along, you are naughty!" that is what he hears from everyone, and the child's heart grows hard, and in vain the poor little frightened boy shivers with cold like a fledgling fallen out of a broken nest. His hands and feet are frozen, he gasps for breath. The next thing he is coughing, before long disease, like an unclean reptile, creeps into his bosom and death is standing over him in some dark corner, no help, no escape, and that's his life! That is what life is like sometimes! Oh, Varinka, it's wretched to hear "for Christ's sake," and to pass by and give nothing, telling him "God will provide." Sometimes "for Christ's sake" is all right (it's not always the same, you know, Varinka), sometimes it's a long, drawling, habitual, practised, regular beggar's whine; it's not so painful to refuse one like that; he's an old hand, a beggar by profession. He's accustomed to it, one thinks; he can cope with it and knows how to cope with it. Sometimes "for Christ's sake" sounds unaccustomed, rude, terrible—as to-day, when I was taking the letter from the boy, a man standing close to the fence, not begging from everyone, said to me: "Give us a halfpenny, sir, for Christ's sake," and in such a harsh, jerky voice that I started with a horrible feeling and did not give him a halfpenny, I hadn't one. Rich people don't like the poor to complain aloud of their harsh lot, they say they disturb them, they are troublesome! Yes, indeed, poverty is always troublesome; maybe their hungry groans hinder the rich from sleeping!

To make a confession, my own, I began to describe all this to you partly to relieve my heart but chiefly to give you an example of the fine style of my composition, for you have no doubt noticed yourself, my dear girl, that of late my style has been forming, but such a depression came over me that I began to pity my feelings to the depth of my soul, and though I know, my dear, that one gets no good by self-pity, yet one must do oneself justice in some way, and often, my own, for no reason whatever, one literally annihilates oneself, makes oneself of no account, and not worth a straw. And perhaps that is why it happens that I am panic-stricken and persecuted like that poor boy who asked me for alms. Now I will tell you, by way of instance and illustration, Varinka; listen: hurrying to the office early in the morning, my own, I sometimes look at the town, how it wakes, gets up, begins smoking, hurrying with life, resounding—sometimes you feel so small before such a sight that it is as though someone had given you a flip on your intrusive nose and you creep along your way noiseless as water, and humble as grass, and hold your peace! Now just look into it and see what is going on in those great, black, smutty buildings. Get to the bottom of that and then judge whether one was right to abuse oneself for no reason and to be reduced to undignified mortification. Note, Varinka, that I am speaking figuratively, not in a literal sense. But let us look what is going on in those houses. There, in some smoky corner, in some damp hole, which, through poverty, passes as a lodging, some workman wakes up from his sleep; and all night he has been dreaming of boots, for instance,

223

which he had accidentally slit the day before, as though a man ought to dream of such nonsense! But he's an artisan, he's a shoemaker; it's excusable for him to think of nothing but his own subject. His children are crying and his wife is hungry; and it's not only shoemakers who get up in the morning like that, my own—that would not matter, and would not be worth writing about, but this is the point, Varinka: close by in the same house, in a storey higher or lower, a wealthy man in his gilded apartments dreams at night, it may be, of those same boots, that is, boots in a different manner, in a different sense, but still boots, for in the sense I am using the word, Varinka, everyone of us is a bit of a shoemaker, my darling; and that would not matter, only it's a pity there is no one at that wealthy person's side, no man who could whisper in his ear: "Come, give over thinking of such things, thinking of nothing but yourself, living for nothing but yourself; your children are healthy, your wife is not begging for food. Look about you, can't you see some object more noble to worry about than your boots?" That's what I wanted to say to you in a figurative way, Varinka. Perhaps it's too free a thought, my own, but sometimes one has that thought, sometimes it comes to one and one cannot help its bursting out from one's heart in warm language. And so it seems there was no reason to make oneself so cheap, and to be scared by mere noise and uproar. I will conclude by saying, Varinka, that perhaps you think what I am saying is unjust, or that I'm suffering from a fit of the spleen, or that I have copied this out of some book. No, my dear girl, you must dismiss that idea, it is not that; I abominate injustice, I am not suffering from spleen, and I've not copied anything out of a book—so there.

I went home in a melancholy frame of mind; I sat down to the table and heated my teapot to have a glass of two of tea. Suddenly I saw coming towards me Gorshkov, our poor lodger. I had noticed in the morning that he kept hanging about round the other lodgers, and trying to approach me. And I may say, in passing, Varinka, that they live ever so much worse than I do. Yes, indeed, he has a wife and children! So that if I were in his place I don't know what I should do. Well, my Gorshkov comes up to me, bows to me, a running tear as always on his eyelashes, he scrapes with his foot and can't utter a word. I made him sit down on a chair—it was a broken one, it is true, but there was no other. I offered him some tea. He refused from politeness, refused for a long time, but at last he took a glass. He would have drunk it without sugar, began apologising again, when I tried to persuade him that he must have sugar; he argued for a long time, kept refusing, but at last put the very smallest lump of sugar in his glass, and began declaring that his tea was extremely sweet. Oh, to what degradation poverty does reduce people! "Well, my good friend, what is it?" I said. "Well, it is like this, Makar Alexyevitch, my benefactor," he said, "show the mercy of the Lord, come to the help of my unhappy family; my wife and children have nothing to eat; think what it is for me, their father," said he. I tried to speak, but he interrupted me. "I am afraid of everyone here, Makar Alexyevitch—that is, not exactly afraid but as it were ashamed with them; they are all proud and haughty people. I would not have troubled you, my benefactor, I know that you have been in difficulties yourself, I know you can't give me much, but do lend me a trifle, and I make bold to ask you," said he, "because I know your kind heart. I know that you are in need yourself, that you know what trouble is now, and so your heart feels compassion." He ended by saying, "Forgive my boldness and unmannerliness, Makar Alexyevitch." I answered him that I should be heartily glad, but that I had nothing, absolutely nothing. "Makar Alexyevitch, sir," said he, "I am not asking for much, but you see it is like this— (then he flushed crimson)—my wife, my children, hungry—if only a ten-kopeck piece." Well, it sent a twinge to my heart. Why, I thought, they are worse off than I, even. Twenty kopecks was all I had left, and I was reckoning on it. I meant to spend it next day on my most pressing needs.

"No, my dear fellow, I can't, it is like this," I said.

"Makar Alexyevitch, my dear soul, what you like," he said, "if it is only ten kopecks."

Well, I took my twenty kopecks out of my box, Varinka, and gave it him; it's a good deed anyway! Ah! poverty! I had a good talk with him: "Why, how is it, my good soul," I said, "that you are in such want and yet you rent a room for five silver roubles?" He explained to me that he had taken it six months before and paid for it six months in advance; and since then circumstances had been such that the poor fellow does not know which way to turn. He expected his case would be over by this time. It's an unpleasant business. You see, Varinka, he has to answer for something before the court, he is mixed up in a case with a merchant who swindled the government over a contract; the cheat was discovered and the

225

merchant was arrested and he's managed to implicate Gorshkov, who had something to do with it, too. But in reality Gorshkov was only guilty of negligence, of injudiciousness and unpardonable disregard of the interests of government. The case has been going on for some years. Gorshkov has had to face all sorts of difficulties.

"I'm not guilty, not in the least guilty of the dishonesty attributed to me," said Gorshkov; "I am not guilty of swindling and robbery."

This case has thrown a slur on his character; he has been turned out of the service, and though he has not been found guilty of any legal crime, yet, till he has completely cleared himself he cannot recover from the merchant a considerable sum of money due to him which is now the subject of dispute before the courts. I believe him, but the court won't take his word for it; the case is all in such a coil and a tangle that it would take a hundred years to unravel it. As soon as they untie one knot the merchant brings forward another and then another. I feel the deepest sympathy for Gorshkov, my own, I am very sorry for him. The man's out of work, he won't be taken anywhere without a character; all they had saved has been spent on food, the case is complicated and, meanwhile, they have had to live, and meanwhile, apropos of nothing and most inappropriately, a baby has been born, and that is an expense; his son fell ill—expense; died—expense; his wife is ill; he's afflicted with some disease of long standing—in fact, he has suffered, he has suffered to the utmost; he says, however, that he is expecting a favourable conclusion to his business in a day or two and that there is no doubt of it now. I am sorry for him, I am sorry for him; I am very sorry for him, Varinka. I was kind to him, he's a poor lost, scared creature; he needs a friend so I was kind to him. Well, good-bye, my dear one, Christ be with you, keep well. My darling! when I think of you it's like laying a salve on my sore heart. And though I suffer for you, yet it eases my heart to suffer for you.

Your true friend,
MAKAR DYEVUSHKIN.

September 9.

MY DARLING, VARVARA ALEXYEVNA,
I am writing to you almost beside myself. I have been thoroughly upset by a terrible incident. My head is going

round. Ah, my own, what a thing I have to tell you now! This we did not foresee. No, I don't believe that I did not foresee it; I did foresee it all. I had a presentiment of it in my heart. I even dreamed of something of the kind a day or two ago.

This is what happened! I will write to you regardless of style, just as God puts it into my heart. I went to the office to-day. I went in, I sat down, I began writing. And you must know, Varinka, that I was writing yesterday too. Well, this is how it was: Timofey Ivanovitch came up to me and was pleased to explain to me in person, "The document is wanted in a hurry," said he. "Copy it very clearly as quickly as possible and carefully, Makar Alexyevitch," he said; "it goes to be signed to-day." I must observe, my angel, that I was not myself yesterday, I could not bear the sight of anything; such a mood of sadness and depression had come over me! It was cold in my heart and dark in my soul, you were in my mind all the while, my little dearie. But I set to work to copy it; I copied it clearly, legibly, only—I really don't know how to explain it—whether the devil himself muddled me, or whether it was ordained by some secret decree of destiny, or simply it had to be—but I left out a whole line, goodness knows what sense it made, it simply made none at all. They were late with the document yesterday and only took it to his Excellency to be signed to-day. I turned up this morning at the usual hour as though nothing had happened and settled myself beside Emelyan Ivanovitch. I must observe, my own, that of late I have been more abashed and ill at ease than ever. Of late I have given up looking at anyone. If I hear so much as a chair creak I feel more dead than alive. That is just how it was to-day, I sat down like a hedgehog crouched up and shrinking into myself, so that Efim Akimovitch (there never was such a fellow for teasing) said in the hearing of all: "Why are you sitting like a picture of misery, Makar Alexyevitch?" And he made such a grimace that everyone sitting near him and me went off into roars of laughter, and at my expense of course. And they went on and on. I put my hands over my ears, and screwed up my eyes, I sat without stirring. That's what I always do; they leave off the sooner. Suddenly I heard a noise, a fuss and a bustle; I heard —did not my ears deceive me?—they were mentioning me, asking for me, calling Dyevushkin. My heart began shuddering within me, and I don't know myself why I was so

227

frightened; I only know I was panic-stricken as I had never been before in my life. I sat rooted to my chair—as though there were nothing the matter, as though it were not I. But they began getting nearer and nearer. And at last, close to my ear, they were calling, "Dyevushkin, Dyevushkin! Where is Dyevushkin?" I raised my eyes: Yevstafy Ivanovitch stood before me; he said: "Makar Alexyevitch, make haste to his Excellency! You've made a mistake in that document!" That was all he said, but it was enough; enough had been said, hadn't it, Varinka? Half dead, frozen with terror, not knowing what I was doing, I went—why, I was more dead than alive. I was led through one room, through a second, through a third, to his Excellency's study. I was in his presence! I can give you no exact account of what my thoughts were then. I saw his Excellency standing up, they were all standing round him. I believe I did not bow, I forgot. I was so flustered that my lips were trembling, my legs were trembling. And I had reason to be, my dear girl! To begin with, I was ashamed; I glanced into the looking-glass on the right hand and what I saw there was enough to send one out of one's mind. And in the second place, I had always tried to behave as if there were no such person in the world. So that his Excellency could hardly have been aware of my existence. Perhaps he may have heard casually that there was a clerk called Dyevushkin in the office, but he had never gone into the matter more closely.

He began, angrily: "What were you about, sir? Where were your eyes? The copy was wanted; it was wanted in a hurry, and you spoil it."

At this point, his Excellency turned to Yevstafy Ivanovitch. I could only catch a word here and there: "Negligence! Carelessness! You will get us into difficulties!" I would have opened my mouth to say something. I wanted to beg for forgiveness, but I could not; I wanted to run away, but dared not attempt it, and then . . . then, Varinka, something happened so awful that I can hardly hold my pen, for shame, even now. A button—the devil take the button—which was hanging by a thread on my uniform—suddenly flew off, bounced on the floor (I must have caught hold of it accidentally) with a jingle, the damned thing, and rolled straight to his Excellency's feet, and that in the midst of a profound silence! And that was my only justification, my sole apology, my only answer, all that I had to say to his

Excellency! What followed was awful. His Excellency's attention was at once turned to my appearance and my attire. I remembered what I had seen in the looking-glass; I flew to catch the button! Some idiocy possessed me! I bent down, I tried to pick up the button—it twirled and rolled, I couldn't pick it up—in fact, I distinguished myself by my agility. Then I felt that my last faculties were deserting me, that everything, everything was lost, my whole reputation was lost, my dignity as a man was lost, and then, apropos of nothing, I had the voices of Teresa and Faldoni ringing in my ears. At last I picked up the button, stood up and drew myself erect, and if I were a fool I might at least have stood quietly with my hands at my sides! But not a bit of it. I began fitting the button to the torn threads as though it might hang on, and I actually smiled, actually smiled. His Excellency turned away at first, then he glanced at me again—I heard him say to Yevstafy Ivanovitch: "How is this? . . . Look at him! . . . What is he? . . . What sort of man? . . ." Ah, my own, think of that! "What is he?" and, "what sort of man?" I had distinguished myself! I heard Yevstafy Ivanovitch say: "No note against him, no note against him for anything, behaviour excellent, salary in accordance with his grade . . ." "Well, assist him in some way, let him have something in advance," says his Excellency. . . . "But he has had an advance," he said; "he has had his salary in advance for such and such a time. He is apparently in difficulties, but his conduct is good, and there is no note, there never has been a note against him."

My angel, I was burning, burning in the fires of hell! I was dying. . . .

"Well," said his Excellency, "make haste and copy it again; Dyevushkin, come here, copy it over again without a mistake; and listen . . ." Here his Excellency turned to the others, gave them various instructions and they all went away. As soon as they had gone, his Excellency hurriedly took out his notebook and from it took a hundred-rouble note. "Here," said he, "take it as you like, so far as I can help you, take it . . ." and he thrust it into my hand. I trembled, my angel, my whole soul was quivering; I don't know what happened to me, I tried to seize his hand to kiss it, but he flushed crimson, my darling, and—here I am not departing one hair's breadth from the truth, my own—he took my unworthy hand and shook it, just took it and shook it, as though I had been his equal, as though I had been just such a General as himself. "You can go," he said; "whatever I can do for you . . . don't make mistakes, but there, no great harm done this time."

Now Varinka, this is what I have decided. I beg you and Fedora, and if I had any children I should bid them, to pray every day and all our lives for his Excellency as they would not pray for their own father! I will say more, my dear, and I say it solemnly—pay attention, Varinka—I swear that however cast down I was and afflicted in the bitterest days of our misfortunes, looking at you, at your poverty, and at myself, my degradation and my uselessness, in spite of all that, I swear that the hundred roubles is not as much to me as that his Excellency deigned to shake hands with me, a straw, a worthless drunkard! By that he has restored me to myself, by that action he has lifted up my spirit, has made my life sweeter for ever, and I am firmly persuaded that, however sinful I may be before the Almighty, yet my prayers for the happiness and prosperity of his Excellency will reach His Throne! . . .

My darling! I am dreadfully upset, dreadfully excited now, my heart is beating as though it would burst out of my breast, and I feel, as it were, weak all over.

I am sending you forty-five roubles; I am giving the landlady twenty and leaving thirty-five for myself. For twenty I can put my wardrobe in order, and I shall have fifteen left to go on with. But just now all the impressions of the morning have shaken my whole being, I am going to lie down. I am at peace, quite at peace, though; only there is an ache in my heart and deep down within me I feel my soul quivering, trembling, stirring.

I am coming to see you: but now I am simply drunk with all these sensations. . . . . God sees all, my Varinka, my priceless darling!

Your worthy friend,
Makar Dyevushkin.

September 10.

My dear Makar Alexyevitch,

I am unutterably delighted at your happiness and fully appreciate the goodness of your chief, my friend. So now you will have a little respite from trouble! But, for God's sake, don't waste your money again. Live quietly and as frugally as possible, and from to-day begin to put by a little that misfortune may not find you unprepared again. For goodness' sake don't worry about us. Fedora and I will get along somehow. Why have you sent us so much money, Makar Alexye-vitch? We don't need it at all. We are satisfied with what we have. It is true we shall soon want money for moving from this lodging, but Fedora is hoping to be repaid an old debt that has been owing for years. I will keep twenty roubles, however, in case of extreme necessity. The rest I send you back. Please take care of your money, Makar Alexyevitch. Good-bye. Be at peace now, keep well and happy. I would write more to you, but I feel dreadfully tired; yesterday I did not get up all day. You do well to promise to come. Do come and see me, please, Makar Alexyevitch.

V. D.

September 11.

My dear Varvara Alexyevna,

I beseech you, my own, not to part from me now, now when I am quite happy and contented with everything. My darling! Don't listen to Fedora and I will do anything you like; I shall behave well if only from respect to his Excellency. I will behave well and carefully; we will write to each other happy letters again, we will confide in each other our thoughts, our joys, our cares, if we have any cares; we will live together in happiness and concord. We'll study literature . . . My angel! My whole fate has changed and everything has changed for the better. The landlady has become more amenable. Teresa is more sensible, even Faldoni has become prompter. I have made it up with Ratazyaev. In my joy I went to him of myself. He's really a good fellow, Varinka, and all the harm that was said of him was nonsense. I have discovered that it was all an abominable slander. He had no idea whatever of describing us. He read me a new work of his. And as for his calling me a Lovelace, that was not an insulting or abusive name; he explained it to me. The word is taken straight from a foreign source and means *a clever fellow,* and to express it more elegantly, in a literary fashion, it means a young man you must be on the lookout with, you see, and nothing of that sort. It was an innocent jest, my angel! I'm an ignoramus and in my foolishness I was offended. In fact, it is I who apologised to him now. . . . And the weather is so wonderful to-day, Varinka, so fine. It is true there was a slight frost this morning, as though it had been sifted through a sieve. It was nothing. It only made the air a little fresher. I went to buy some boots, and I bought some wonderful boots. I walked

231

along the Nevsky. I read the *Bee*. Why! I am forgetting to tell you the principal thing.

It was this, do you see.

This morning I talked to Emelyan Ivanovitch and to Axentey Mihalovitch about his Excellency. Yes, Varinka, I'm not the only one he has treated so graciously. I am not the only one he has befriended, and he is known to all the world for the goodness of his heart. His praises are sung in very many quarters, and tears of gratitude are shed. An orphan girl was brought up in his house. He gave her a dowry and married her to a man in a good position, to a clerk on special commissions, who was in attendance on his Excellency. He installed a son of a widow in some office, and has done a great many other acts of kindness. I thought it my duty at that point to add my mite and described his Excellency's action in the hearing of all; I told them all and concealed nothing. I put my pride in my pocket, as though pride or dignity mattered in a case like that. So I told it aloud—to do glory to the good deeds of his Excellency! I spoke enthusiastically, I spoke with warmth, I did not blush, on the contrary, I was proud that I had such a story to tell. I told them about everything (only I was judiciously silent about you, Varinka), about my landlady, about Faldoni, about Ratazyaev, about my boots and about Markov—I told them everything. Some of them laughed a little, in fact, they all laughed a little. Probably they found something funny in my appearance, or it may have been about my boots—yes, it must have been about my boots. They could not have done it with any bad intention. It was nothing, just youthfulness, or perhaps because they are well-to-do people, but they could not jeer at what I said with any bad, evil intention. That is, what I said about his Excellency—that they could not do. Could they, Varinka?

I still can't get over it, my darling. The whole incident has so overwhelmed me! Have you got any firewood? Don't catch cold, Varinka; you can so easily catch cold. Ah, my own precious, you crush me with your sad thoughts. I pray to God, how I pray to Him for you, my dearie! For instance, have you got woollen stockings, and other warm underclothing? Mind, my darling, if you need anything, for God's sake don't wound your old friend, come straight to me. Now our bad times are over. Don't be anxious about me. Everything is so bright, so happy in the future!

It was a sad time, Varinka! But there, no matter, it's past!

Years will pass and we shall sigh for that time. I remember my young days. Why, I often hadn't a farthing! I was cold and hungry, but light-hearted, that was all. In the morning I would walk along the Nevsky, see a pretty little face and be happy all day. It was a splendid, splendid time, my darling! It is nice to be alive, Varinka! Especially in Petersburg. I repented with tears in my eyes yesterday, and prayed to the Lord God to forgive me all my sins in that sad time: my repining, my liberal ideas, my drinking and despair. I remembered you with emotion in my prayers. You were my only support, Varinka, you were my only comfort, you cheered me on my way with counsel and good advice. I can never forget that, dear one. I have kissed all your letters to-day, my darling! Well, good-bye, my precious. They say that somewhere near here there is a sale of clothing. So I will make inquiries a little. Good-bye, my angel. Good-bye!

Your deeply devoted,
MAKAR DYEVUSHKIN.

September 15.

DEAR MAKAR ALEXYEVITCH,

I feel dreadfully upset. Listen what has happened here. I foresee something momentous. Judge yourself, my precious friend; Mr. Bykov is in Petersburg, Fedora met him. He was driving, he ordered the cab to stop, went up to Fedora himself and began asking where she was living. At first she would not tell him. Then he said, laughing, that he knew who was living with her. (Evidently Anna Fyodorovna had told him all about it.) Then Fedora could not contain herself and began upbraiding him on the spot, in the street, reproaching him, telling him he was an immoral man and the cause of all my troubles. He answered, that one who has not a halfpenny is bound to have misfortunes. Fedora answered that I might have been able to earn my own living, that I might have been married or else have had some situation, but that now my happiness was wrecked for ever and that I was ill besides, and would not live long. To this he answered that I was still young, that I had still a lot of nonsense in my head and that my virtues were getting a little tarnished (his words). Fedora and I thought he did not know our lodging when suddenly, yesterday, just after I had gone out to buy some things in the Gostiny Dvor he walked into our room. I believe he did not want to find me at home. He questioned Fedora at length concerning our manner of life, examined everything we had; he looked at my work; at last asked, "Who is this clerk you have made friends with?" At that moment you walked across the yard; Fedora pointed to you; he glanced and laughed; Fedora begged him to go away, told him that I was unwell, as it was, from grieving, and that to see him in our room would be very distasteful to me. He was silent for a while; said that he had just looked in with no object and tried to give Fedora twenty-five roubles; she, of course, did not take it.

What can it mean? What has he come to see us for? I cannot understand where he has found out all about us! I am lost in conjecture. Fedora says that Axinya, her sister-in-law, who comes to see us, is friendly with Nastasya the laundress, and Nastasya's cousin is a porter in the office in which a friend of Anna Fyodorovna's nephew is serving. So has not, perhaps, some ill-natured gossip crept round? But it is very possible that Fedora is mistaken; we don't know what to think Is it possible he will come to us again! The mere thought of it terrifies me! When Fedora told me all about it yesterday, I was so frightened that I almost fainted with terror! What more does he want? I don't want to know him now! What does he want with me, poor me? Oh! I am in such terror now, I keep expecting Bykov to walk in every minute. What will happen to me, what more has fate in store for me? For Christ's sake, come and see me now, Makar Alexyevitch. Do come, for God's sake, come.

September 18.

MY DARLING VARVARA ALEXYEVNA!

To-day an unutterably sad, quite unaccountable and unexpected event has occurred here. Our poor Gorshkov (I must tell you, Varinka) has had his character completely cleared. The case was concluded some time ago and to-day he went to hear the final judgment. The case ended very happily for him. He was fully exonerated of any blame for negligence and carelessness. The merchant was condemned to pay him a considerable sum of money, so that his financial position was vastly improved and no stain left on his honour and things were better all round—in fact, he won everything he could have desired.

He came home at three o'clock this afternoon. He did not look like himself, his face was white as a sheet, his lips quivered and he kept smiling—he embraced his wife and children. We all flocked to congratulate him. He was greatly touched by our action, he bowed in all directions, shook hands with all of us several times. It even seemed to me as though he were taller and more erect, and no longer had that running tear in his eye. He was in such excitement, poor fellow. He could not stand still for two minutes: he picked up anything he came across, then dropped it again; and kept continually smiling and bowing, sitting down, getting up and sitting down again. Goodness knows what he said: "My honour, my honour, my good name, my children," and that was how he kept talking! He even shed tears. Most of us were moved to tears, too; Ratazyaev clearly wanted to cheer him up, and said, "What is honour, old man, when one has nothing to eat? The money, the money's the thing, old man, thank God for that!" and thereupon he slapped him on the shoulder. It seemed to me that Gorshkov was offended—not that he openly showed dissatisfaction, but he looked rather strangely at Ratazyaev and took his hand off his shoulder. And that had never happened before, Varinka! But characters differ. Now I, for instance, should not have stood on my dignity, at a time of such joy; why, my own, sometimes one is too liberal with one's bows and almost cringing from nothing but excess of good-nature and soft-heartedness. . . . However, no matter about me!

"Yes," he said, "the money is a good thing too, thank God, thank God!" And then all the time we were with him he kept repeating, "Thank God, thank God."

His wife ordered a rather nicer and more ample dinner. Our landlady cooked for them herself. Our landlady is a good-natured woman in a way. And until dinner-time Gorshkov could not sit still in his seat. He went into the lodgers' rooms, without waiting to be invited. He just went in, smiled, sat down on the edge of a chair, said a word or two, or even said nothing, and went away again. At the naval man's he even took a hand at cards; they made up a game with him as fourth. He played a little, made a muddle of it, played three or four rounds and threw down the cards. "No," he said, "you see, I just looked in, I just looked in," and he went away from them. He met me in the passage, took both my hands, looked me straight in the face, but so strangely; then shook hands with me and walked away, and kept smiling, but with a strange, painful smile like a dead man. His wife was crying with joy; everything was cheerful as though it were a holiday. They soon had dinner. After dinner he said to his wife: "I tell you what,

235

my love, I'll lie down a little," and he went to his bed. He called his little girl, put his hand on her head, and for a long time he was stroking the child's head. Then he turned to his wife again, "And what of Petinka? our Petya!" he said. "Petinka?" . . . His wife crossed herself and answered that he was dead. "Yes, yes, I know all about it. Petinka is now in the Kingdom of Heaven." His wife saw that he was not himself, that what had happened had completely upset him, and she said to him, "You ought to have a nap, my love." "Yes, very well, I will directly . . . just a little," then he turned away, lay still for a bit, then turned round, tried to say something. His wife could not make out what he said, and asked him, "What it is, my dear?" and he did not answer. She waited a little, "Well, he's asleep," she thought, and went into the landlady's for an hour. An hour later she came back, she saw her husband had not woken up and was not stirring. She thought he was asleep, and she sat down and began working at something. She said that for half an hour she was so lost in musing that she did not know what she was thinking about, all she can say is that she did not think of her husband. But suddenly she was roused by the feeling of uneasiness, and what struck her first of all was the death-like silence in the room. . . . She looked at the bed and saw that her husband was lying in the same position. She went up to him, pulled down the quilt and looked at him—and he was already cold—he was dead, my darling. Gorshkov was dead, he had died suddenly, as though he had been killed by a thunder-bolt. And why he died, God only knows. It was such a shock to me, Varinka, that I can't get over it now. One can't believe that a man could die so easily. He was such a poor, unlucky fellow, that Gorshkov! And what a fate, what a fate! His wife was in tears and panic-stricken. The little girl crept away into a corner. There is such a hubbub going on, they will hold a post-mortem and inquest . . . I can't tell you just what. But the pity of it, oh, the pity of it! It's sad to think that in reality one does not know the day or the hour . . . One dies so easily for no reason. . . .

Your
MAKAR DYEVUSHKIN.

DEAR VARVARA ALEXYEVNA,

I hasten to inform you, my dear, that Ratazyaev has found me work with a writer. Someone came to him, and brought him such a fat manuscript—thank God, a lot of work. But it's so illegibly written that I don't know how to set to work on it: they want it in a hurry. It's all written in such a way that one does not understand it. . . . They have agreed to pay forty kopecks the sixteen pages. I write you all this, my own, because now I shall have extra money. And now, good-bye, my darling, I have come straight from work.

Your faithful friend,

MAKAR DYEVUSHKIN.

September 23.

MY DEAR FRIEND, MAKAR ALEXYEVITCH,

For three days I have not written you a word, and I have had a great many anxieties and worries.

The day before yesterday Bykov was here. I was alone, Fedora had gone off somewhere. I opened the door to him, and was so frightened when I saw him that I could not move. I felt that I turned pale. He walked in as he always does, with a loud laugh, took a chair and sat down. For a long while I could not recover myself. At last I sat down in the corner to my work. He even left off laughing. I believe my appearance impressed him. I have grown so thin of late, my eyes and my cheeks are hollow, I was as white as a sheet . . . it would really be hard for anyone to recognise me who had known me a year ago. He looked long and intently at me; then at last he began to be lively again, said something or other; I don't know what I answered, and he laughed again. He stayed a whole hour with me; talked to me a long time; asked me some questions. At last just before leaving, he took me by the hand and said (I write you it word for word): "Varvara Alexyevitch, between ourselves, be it said, your relation and my intimate friend, Anna Fyodorovna, is a very nasty woman" (then he used an unseemly word about her). "She led your cousin astray, and ruined you. I behaved like a rascal in that case, too; but after all, it's a thing that happens every day." Then he laughed heartily. Then he observed that he was not great at fine speeches, and that most of what he had to explain, about which the obligations of gentlemanly feeling forebade him to be silent, he had told me already, and that in brief words he would come to the rest. Then he told me he was asking my hand in marriage, that he thought it his duty to restore my good name, that he was rich, that after the wedding he would take me away to his estates in the steppes, that he wanted to go coursing hares there; that he would never come back to Petersburg again, because it was horrid in Petersburg; that he had here in Petersburg—as he expressed it—a good-for-nothing nephew whom he had sworn to deprive of the estate, and it was just for that reason in the hope of having legitimate heirs that he sought my hand, that it was the chief cause of his courtship. Then he observed that I was living in a very poor way: and it was no wonder I was ill living in such a slum; predicted that I should certainly die if I stayed there another month; said that lodgings in Petersburg were horrid, and finally asked me if I wanted anything.

I was so overcome at his offer that, I don't know why, I began crying. He took my tears for gratitude and told me he had always been sure I was a good, feeling, and educated girl, but that he had not been able to make up his mind to take this step till he had found out about my present behaviour in full detail. Then he asked me about you, said that he had heard all about it, that you were a man of good principles, that he did not want to be indebted to you and asked whether five hundred roubles would be enough for all that you had done for me. When I explained to him that what you had done for me no money could repay, he said that it was all nonsense, that that was all romantic stuff out of novels, that I was young and read poetry, that novels were the ruin of young girls, that books were destructive of morality and that he could not bear books of any sort, he advised me to wait till I was his age and then talk about people. "Then," he added, "you will know what men are like." Then he said I was to think over his offer thoroughly, that he would very much dislike it if I were to take such an important step thoughtlessly; he added that thoughtlessness and impulsiveness were the ruin of inexperienced youth, but that he quite hoped for a favourable answer from me, but that in the opposite event, he should be forced to marry some Moscow shopkeeper's daughter, "because," he said, "I have sworn that good-for-nothing nephew shall not have the estate."

He forced five hundred roubles into my hands, as he said, 'to buy sweetmeats". He said that in the country I should grow as round as a bun, that with him I should be living on the fat of the land, that he had a terrible number of things to see to now, that he was dragging about all day on business, and that he had just slipped in to see me between his engagements. Then he went away.

I thought for a long time, I pondered many things, I wore myself out thinking, my friend; at last I made up my mind. My friend, I shall marry him. I ought to accept his offer. If anyone can rescue me from my shame, restore my good name, and ward off poverty, privation and misfortune from me in the future, it is he and no one else. What more can one expect from the future, what more can one expect from fate? Fedora says I must not throw away my good fortune; she says, if this isn't good fortune, what is? Anyway, I can find no other course for me, my precious friend. What am I to do? I have ruined my health with work as it is; I can't go on working continually. Go into a family? I should pine away with depression, besides I should be of no use to anyone. I am of a sickly constitution, and so I shall always be a burden on other people. Of course I am not going into a paradise, but what am I to do, my friend, what am I to do? What choice have I?

I have not asked your advice. I wanted to think it over alone. The decision you have just read is unalterable, and I shall immediately inform Bykov of it, he is pressing me to answer quickly. He said that his business would not wait, that he must be off, and that he couldn't put it off for nonsense. God knows whether I shall be happy, my fate is in His holy, inscrutable power, but I have made up my mind. They say Bykov is a kind-hearted man: he will respect me; perhaps I, too, shall respect him. What more can one expect from such a marriage?

I will let you know about everything, Makar Alexyevitch. I am sure you will understand all my wretchedness. Do not try to dissuade me from my intention. Your efforts will be in vain. Weigh in your own mind all that has forced me to this step. I was very much distressed at first, but now I am calmer. What is before me, I don't know. What will be, will be; as God wills! . . .

Bykov has come, I leave this letter unfinished. I wanted to tell you a great deal more. Bykov is here already!

September 23.

MY DARLING VARVARA ALEXYEVNA,

I hasten to answer you, my dear; I hasten to tell you, my precious, that I am dumbfounded. It all seems so . . .

239

Yesterday we buried Gorshkov. Yes, that is so, Varinka, that is so; Bykov has behaved honourably; only, you see, my own . . . so you have consented. Of course, everything is according to God's will; that is so, that certainly must be so—that is, it certainly must be God's will in this; and the providence of the Heavenly Creator is blessed, of course, and inscrutable, and it is fate too, and they are the same. Fedora sympathises with you too. Of course you will be happy now, my precious, you will live in comfort, my darling, my little dearie, little angel and light of my eyes—only Varinka, how can it be so soon? . . . Yes, business. . . . Mr. Bykov has business—of course, everyone has business, and he may have it too. . . . I saw him as he came out from you. He's a good-looking man, good-looking; a very good-looking man, in fact. Only there is something queer about it, the point is not whether he is a good-looking man. Indeed, I am not myself at all. Why, how are we to go on writing to one another? I . . . I shall be left alone. I am weighing everything, my angel, I am weighing everything as you write to me, I am weighing it all in my heart, the reasons. I had just finished copying the twentieth quire, and meanwhile these events have come upon us! Here you are going a journey, my darling, you will have to buy all sorts of things, shoes of all kinds, a dress, and I know just the shop in Gorohovoy Street; do you remember how I described it to you? But no! How can you, Varinka? what are you about? You can't go away now, it's quite impossible, utterly impossible. Why, you will have to buy a great many things and get a carriage. Besides, the weather is so awful now; look, the rain is coming down in bucketfuls, and such soaking rain, too, and what's more . . . what's more, you will be cold, my angel; your little heart will be cold! Why, you are afraid of anyone strange, and yet you go. And to whom am I left, all alone here? Yes! Here, Fedora says that there is great happiness in store for you . . . but you know she's a headstrong woman, she wants to be the death of me. Are you going to the evening service to-night, Varinka? I would go to have a look at you. It's true, perfectly true, my darling, that you are a well-educated, virtuous and feeling girl, only he had much better marry the shopkeeper's daughter! Don't you think so, my precious? He had better marry the shopkeeper's daughter! I will come to see you, Varinka, as soon as it gets dark, I shall just run in for an hour. It will get dark early to-day, then I shall run in. I shall certainly come to you for an hour this evening, my darling. Now you are expecting Bykov, but when he goes, then . . . Wait a bit, Varinka, I shall run across . . .

MAKAR DYEVUSHKIN.

September 27.

MY DEAR FRIEND, MAKAR ALEXYEVITCH,

Mr. Bykov says I must have three dozen linen chemises. So I must make haste and find seamstresses to make two dozen, and we have very little time. Mr. Bykov is angry and says there is a great deal of bother over these rags. Our wedding is to be in five days, and we are to set off the day after the wedding. Mr. Bykov is in a hurry, he says we must not waste much time over nonsense. I am worn out with all this fuss and can hardly stand on my feet. There is a terrible lot to do, and perhaps it would have been better if all this had not happened. Another thing: we have not enough net or lace, so we ought to buy some more, for Mr. Bykov says he does not want his wife to go about like a cook, and that I simply must "wipe all the country ladies' noses for them". That was his own expression. So, Makar Alexyevitch, please apply to Madame Chiffon in Gorohovoy Street, and ask her first to send us some seamstresses, and secondly, to be so good as to come herself. I am ill to-day. It's so cold in our new lodging and the disorder is terrible. Mr. Bykov's aunt can scarcely breathe, she is so old. I am afraid she may die before we set off, but Mr. Bykov says that it is nothing, she'll wake up. Everything in the house is in the most awful confusion. Mr. Bykov is not living with us, so the servants are racing about in all directions, goodness knows where. Sometimes Fedora is the only one to wait on us, and Mr. Bykov's valet, who looks after everything, has disappeared no one knows where for the last three days. Mr. Bykov comes to see us every morning, and yesterday he beat the superintendent of the house, for which he got into trouble with the police. I have not even had anyone to take my letters to you. I am writing by post. Yes! I had almost forgotten the most important point. Tell Madame Chiffon to be sure and change the net, matching it with the pattern she had yesterday, and to come to me herself to show the new, and tell her, too, that I have changed my mind about the embroidery, that it must be done in crochet; and another thing, that the letters for the monogram on the handkerchiefs must be done in tambour stitch, do you hear? Tambour stitch and not satin stitch. Mind you don't forget that it is to be tambour stitch! Some-

241

thing else I had almost forgotten! For God's sake tell her also that the leaves on the pelerine are to be raised and that the tendrils and thorns are to be in appliqué; and, then, the collar is to be edged with lace, or a deep frill. Please tell her, Makar Alexyevitch.

Your
V. D.

P.S.—I am so ashamed of worrying you with all my errands. The day before yesterday you were running about all the morning. But what can I do! There's no sort of order in the house here, and I am not well. So don't be vexed with me, Makar Alexyevitch. I'm so miserable. Oh, how will it end, my friend, my dear, my kind Makar Alexyevitch? I'm afraid to look into my future. I have a presentiment of something and am living in a sort of delirium.

P.P.S.—For God's sake, my friend, don't forget anything of what I have told you. I am so afraid you will make a mistake. Remember tambour, not satin stitch.

V. D.

September 27.

DEAR VARVARA ALEXYEVNA,

I have carried out all your commissions carefully. Madame Chiffon says that she had thought herself of doing them in tambour stitch; that it is more correct, or something, I don't know, I didn't take it in properly. And you wrote about a frill, too, and she talked about the frill. Only I have forgotten, my darling, what she told me about the frill. All I remember is, that she said a great deal; such a horrid woman! What on earth was it? But she will tell you about it herself. I have become quite dissipated, Varinka, I have not even been to the office to-day. But there's no need for you to be in despair about that, my own. I am ready to go the round of all the shops for your peace of mind. You say you are afraid to look into the future. But at seven o'clock this evening you will know all about it. Madame Chiffon is coming to see you herself. So don't be in despair; you must hope for the best, everything will turn out for the best—so there. Well, now, I keep thinking about that cursed frill—ugh! bother that frill! I should have run round to you, my angel, I should have looked in, I should certainly have looked in; I have been to the gates of your house,

242

once or twice. But Bykov—that is, I mean, Mr. Bykov—is always so cross, you see it doesn't . . . Well, what of it!
MAKAR DYEVUSHKIN.

September 28.

MY DEAR MAKAR ALEXYEVITCH,

For God's sake, run at once to the jeweller's: tell him that he must not make the pearl and emerald ear-rings. Mr. Bykov says that it is too gorgeous, that it's too expensive. He is angry; he says, that as it is, it is costing him a pretty penny, and we are robbing him, and yesterday he said that if he had known beforehand and had any notion of the expense he would not have bound himself. He says that as soon as we are married we will set off at once, that we shall have no visitors and that I needn't hope for dancing and flirtation, and that the holidays are a long way off. That's how he talks. And, God knows, I don't want anything of that sort! Mr. Bykov ordered everything himself. I don't dare to answer him: he is so hasty. What will become of me?

V. D.

September 28.

MY DARLING VARVARA ALEXYEVNA,

I—that is, the jeweller said—very good; and I meant to say at first that I have been taken ill and cannot get up. Here now, at such an urgent, busy time I have caught a cold, the devil take it! I must tell you, to complete my misfortunes, his Excellency was pleased to be stern and was very angry with Emelyan Ivanovitch and scolded him, and he was quite worn out at last, poor man. You see, I tell you about everything. I wanted to write to you about something else, but I am afraid to trouble you. You see, I am a foolish, simple man, Varinka, I just write what comes, so that, maybe, you may—— But there, never mind!

Your
MAKAR DYEVUSHKIN.

September 29.

VARVARA ALEXYEVITCH, MY OWN,

I saw Fedora to-day, my darling, she says that you are to be married to-morrow, and that the day after you are setting off, and that Mr. Bykov is engaging horses already. I have told you about his Excellency already, my darling. Another

243

thing—I have checked the bills from the shop in Gorohovoy; it is all correct, only the things are very dear. But why is Mr. Bykov angry with you? Well, may you be happy, Varinka! I am glad, yes, I shall be glad if you are happy. I should come to the church, my dear, but I've got lumbago. So I keep on about our letters; who will carry them for us, my precious? Yes! You have been a good friend to Fedora, my own! You have done a good deed, my dear, you have done quite right. It's a good deed! And God will bless you for every good deed. Good deeds never go unrewarded, and virtue will sooner or later be rewarded by the eternal justice of God. Varinka! I wanted to write to you a great deal; I could go on writing and writing every minute, every hour! I have one of your books still, *Byelkin's Stories*. I tell you what, Varinka, don't take it away, make me a present of it, my darling. It is not so much that I want to read it. But you know yourself, my darling, winter is coming on: the evenings will be long; it will be sad, and then I could read. I shall move from my lodgings, Varinka, into your old room and lodge with Fedora. I would not part from that honest woman for anything now; besides, she is such a hard-working woman. I looked at your empty room carefully yesterday. Your embroidery frame has remained untouched, just as it was with embroidery on it. I examined your needlework; there were all sorts of little scraps left there, you had begun winding thread on one of my letters. On the little table I found a piece of paper with the words "Dear Makar Alexyevitch, I hasten—" and that was all. Someone must have interrupted you at the most interesting place. In the corner behind the screen stands your little bed. . . . Oh, my darling!!! Well, good-bye, good-bye, send me some answer to this letter quickly.

MAKAR DYEVUSHKIN.

September 30.

MY PRECIOUS FRIEND, MAKAR ALEXYEVITCH,

Everything is over! My lot is cast; I don't know what it will be, but I am resigned to God's will. To-morrow we set off. I say good-bye to you for the last time, my precious one, my friend, my benefactor, my own! Don't grieve for me, live happily, think of me, and may God's blessing descend on us! I shall often remember you in my thoughts, in my prayers. So this time is over! I bring to my new life little consolation from the memories of the past; the more precious will be my memory of you, the more precious will your memory be to my heart. You are my one friend; you are the only one there who loved me. You know I have seen it all, I know how you love me! You were happy in a smile from me and a few words from my pen. Now you will have to get used to being without me. How will you do, left alone here? To whom am I leaving you my kind, precious, only friend! I leave you the book, the embroidery frame, the unfinished letter; when you look at those first words, you must read in your thoughts all that you would like to hear or read from me, all that I should have written to you; and what I could not write now! Think of your poor Varinka who loves you so truly. All your letters are at Fedora's in the top drawer of a chest. You write that you are ill and Mr. Bykov will not let me go out anywhere to-day. I will write to you, my friend, I promise; but, God alone knows what may happen. And so we are saying good-bye now for ever, my friend, my darling, my own, for ever. . . . Oh, if only I could embrace you now! Good-bye, my dear; good-bye, good-bye. Live happily, keep well. My prayers will be always for you. Oh! how sad I am, how weighed down in my heart. Mr. Bykov is calling me.

Your ever loving

V.

P.S.—My soul is so full, so full of tears now . . . tears are choking me, rending my heart. Good-bye. Oh, God, how sad I am!

Remember me, remember your poor Varinka.

VARINKA, MY DARLING, MY PRECIOUS,

You are being carried off, you are going. They had better have torn the heart out of my breast than take you from me! How could you do it? Here you are weeping and going away! Here I have just had a letter from you, all smudged with tears. So you don't want to go; so you are being taken away by force; so you are sorry for me; so you love me! And with whom will you be now? Your little heart will be sad, sick and cold out there. It will be sapped by misery, torn by grief. You will die out there, they will put you in the damp earth; there will be no one to weep for you there! Mr. Bykov will be always coursing hares. Oh, my darling, my darling! What have you brought yourself to? How could you make up your mind to such a step? What have you done, what have you

245

done, what have you done to yourself? They'll drive you to your grave out there; they will be the death of you, my angel. You know you are as weak as a little feather, my own! And where was I, old fool, where were my eyes! I saw the child did not know what she was doing, the child was simply in a fever! I ought simply—— But no, fool, fool, I thought nothing and saw nothing, as though that were the right thing, as though it had nothing to do with me; and went running after frills and flounces too. . . . No, Varinka, I shall get up; to-morrow, maybe, I shall be better and then I shall get up! . . . I'll throw myself under the wheels, my precious, I won't let you go away! Oh, no, how can it be? By what right is all this done? I will go with you; I will run after your carriage if you won't take me, and will run my hardest as long as there is a breath left in my body. And do you know what it is like where you are going, my darling? Maybe you don't know—if so, ask me! There it is, the steppe, my own, the steppe, the bare steppe; why, it is as bare as my hand; there, there are hard-hearted peasant women and uneducated drunken peasants. There the leaves are falling off the trees now, there it is cold and rainy—and you are going there! Well, Mr. Bykov has something to do there: he will be with his hares; but what about you? Do you want to be a grand country lady, Varinka? But, my little cherub! you should just look at yourself. Do you look like a grand country lady? . . . Why, how can such a thing be, Varinka? To whom am I going to write letters, my darling? Yes! You must take that into consideration, my darling—you must ask yourself, to whom is he going to write letters? Whom am I to call my darling; whom am I to call by that loving name, where am I to find you afterwards, my angel? I shall die, Varinka, I shall certainly die; my heart will never survive such a calamity! I loved you like God's sunshine, I loved you like my own daughter, I loved everything in you, my darling, my own! And I lived only for you! I worked and copied papers, and walked and went about and put my thoughts down on paper, in friendly letters, all because you, my precious, were living here opposite, close by; perhaps you did not know it, but that was how it was. Yes, listen, Varinka; you only think, my sweet darling, how is it possible that you should go away from us? You can't go away, my own, it is impossible; it's simply utterly impossible! Why, it's raining, you are delicate, you will catch cold. Your carriage will be wet through; it will certainly get wet through. It won't get beyond the city gates before it will break down; it will break down on purpose. They make these carriages in Petersburg so badly: I know all those carriage makers; they are only fit to turn out a little model, a plaything, not anything solid. I'll take my oath they won't build it solid. I'll throw myself on my knees before Mr. Bykov: I will explain to him, I will explain everything, and you, my precious, explain to him, make him see reason! Tell him that you will stay and that you cannot go away! . . . Ah, why didn't he marry a shopkeeper's daughter in Moscow? He might just as well have married her! The shopkeeper's daughter would have suited him much better, she would have suited him much better. I know why! And I should have kept you here. What is he to you, my darling, what is Bykov? How has he suddenly become so dear to you? Perhaps it's because he is always buying you frills and flounces. But what are frills and flounces? What good are frills and flounces? Why, it is nonsense, Varinka! Here it is a question of a man's life: and you know a frill's a rag; it's a rag, Varinka, a frill is; why, I shall buy you frills myself, that's all the reward I get; I shall buy them for you, my darling, I know a shop, that's all the reward you let me hope for, my cherub, Varinka. Oh Lord! Lord! So, you are really going to the steppes with Mr. Bykov, going away never to return! Ah, my darling! . . . No, you must write to me again, you must write another letter about everything, and when you go away you must write to me from there, or else, my heavenly angel, this will be the last letter and you know that this cannot be, this cannot be the last letter! Why, how can it be, so suddenly, actually the last? Oh no, I shall write and you will write. . . . Besides, I am acquiring a literary style. . . . Oh, my own, what does style matter, now? I don't know, now, what I am writing, I don't know at all, I don't know and I don't read it over and I don't improve the style. I write only to write, only to go on writing to you . . . my darling, my own, my Varinka. . . .

THE LANDLADY

A STORY

PART I

CHAPTER I

ORDYNOV had made up his mind at last to change his
lodgings. The landlady with whom he lodged, the poor
and elderly widow of a petty functionary, was leaving Petersburg, for some reason or other, and setting off to a remote
province to live with relations, before the first of the month
when his time at the lodging was up. Staying on till his time
was up the young man thought regretfully of his old quarters
and felt vexed at having to leave them; he was poor and
lodgings were dear. The day after his landlady went away,
he took his cap and went out to wander about the back streets
of Petersburg, looking at all the bills stuck up on the gates of
the houses, and choosing by preference the dingiest and most
populous blocks of buildings, where there was always more
chance of finding a corner in some poor tenant's flat.

He had been looking for a long time, very carefully, but soon
he was visited by new, almost unknown, sensations. He looked
about him at first carelessly and absent-mindedly, then with
attention, and finally with intense curiosity. The crowd and
bustle of the street, the noise, the movement, the novelty of
objects and the novelty of his position, all the paltry, everyday triviality of town life so wearisome to a busy Petersburger
spending his whole life in the fruitless effort to gain by toil,
by sweat and by various other means a snug little home, in
which to rest in peace and quiet—all this vulgar prose and
dreariness aroused in Ordynov, on the contrary, a sensation of
gentle gladness and serenity. His pale cheeks began to be
suffused with a faint flush, his eyes began to shine as though
with new hope, and he drew deep and eager breaths of the
cold fresh air. He felt unusually lighthearted.

He always led a quiet and absolutely solitary life. Three
years before, after taking his degree and becoming to a great
extent his own master, he went to see an old man whom he had
known only at second-hand, and was kept waiting a long while
before the liveried servants consented to take his name in a

248

second time. Then he walked into a dark, lofty, and deserted room, one of those dreary-looking rooms still to be found in old-fashioned family mansions that have been spared by time, and saw in it a grey-headed old man, hung with orders of distinction, who had been the friend and colleague of his father, and was his guardian. The old man handed him a tiny screw of notes. It turned out to be a very small sum: it was all that was left of his ancestral estates, which had been sold by auction to pay the family debts. Ordynov accepted his inheritance unconcernedly, took leave for ever of his guardian, and went out into the street. It was a cold, gloomy, autumn evening; the young man was dreamy and his heart was torn with a sort of unconscious sadness. There was a glow of fire in his eyes; he felt feverish, and was hot and chilly by turns. He calculated on the way that on his money he could live for two or three years, or even on half rations for four years. It grew dusk and began to drizzle with rain. He had taken the first corner he came across, and within an hour had moved into it. There he shut himself up as though he were in a monastery, as though he had renounced the world. Within two years he had become a complete recluse.

He had grown shy and unsociable without being aware of the fact; meanwhile, it never occurred to him that there was another sort of life—full of noise and uproar, of continual excitement, of continual variety, which was inviting him and was sooner or later inevitable. It is true that he could not avoid hearing of it, but he had never known it or sought to know it: from childhood his life had been exceptional; and now it was more exceptional than ever. He was devoured by the deepest and most insatiable passion, which absorbs a man's whole life and does not, for beings like Ordynov, provide any niche in the domain of practical daily activity. This passion was science. Meanwhile it was consuming his youth, marring his rest at nights with its slow, intoxicating poison, robbing him of wholesome food and of fresh air which never penetrated to his stifling corner. Yet, intoxicated by his passion, Ordynov refused to notice it. He was young and, so far, asked for nothing more. His passion made him a babe as regards external existence and totally incapable of forcing other people to stand aside when needful to make some sort of place for himself among them. Some clever people's science is a capital in their hands; for Ordynov it was a weapon turned against himself.

He was prompted rather by an instinctive impulse than by a logical, clearly defined motive for studying and knowing, and it was the same in every other work he had done hitherto, even the most trivial.[6] Even as a child he had been thought queer and unlike his schoolfellows. He had never known his parents; he had to put up with coarse and brutal treatment from his schoolfellows, provoked by his odd and unsociable disposition, and that made him really unsociable and morose, and little by little he grew more and more secluded in his habits. But there never had been and was not even now any order and system in his solitary studies; even now he had only the first ecstasy, the first fever, the first delirium of the artist. He was creating a system for himself, it was being evolved in him by the years; and the dim, vague, but marvellously soothing image of an idea, embodied in a new, clarified form, was gradually emerging in his soul. And this form craved expression, fretting his soul; he was still timidly aware of its originality, its truth, its independence : creative genius was already showing, it was gathering strength and taking shape. But the moment of embodiment and creation was still far off, perhaps very far off, perhaps altogether impossible!

Now he walked about the streets like a recluse, like a hermit who has suddenly come from his dumb wilderness into the noisy, roaring city. Everything seemed to him new and strange. But he was so remote from all the world that was surging and clattering around him that he did not wonder at his own strange sensation. He seemed unconscious of his own aloofness; on the contrary, there was springing up in his heart a joyful feeling, a sort of intoxication, like the ecstasy of a hungry man who has meat and drink set before him after a long fast; though, of course, it was strange that such a trivial novelty as a change of lodgings could excite and thrill any inhabitant of Petersburg, even Ordynov; but the truth is that it had scarcely ever happened to him to go out with a practical object.

He enjoyed wandering about the streets more and more. He stared about at everything like a *flâneur*.

But, even now, inconsequent as ever, he was reading significance in the picture that lay so brightly before him, as though between the lines of a book. Everything struck him; he did not miss a single impression, and looked with thoughtful eyes into the faces of passing people, watched the characteristic aspect of everything around him and listened lovingly to the speech of the people as though verifying in everything the conclusions that had been formed in the stillness of solitary nights. Often some trifle impressed him, gave rise to an idea, and for the first time he felt vexed that he had so buried himself alive in his cell. Here everything moved more swiftly, his pulse was full and rapid, his mind, which had been oppressed by solitude and had been stirred and uplifted only by strained, exalted activity, worked now swiftly, calmly and boldly. Moreover, he had an unconscious longing to squeeze himself somehow into this life which was so strange to him, of which he had hitherto known—or rather correctly divined—only by the instinct of the artist. His heart began instinctively throbbing with a yearning for love and sympathy. He looked more attentively at the people who passed by him; but they were strangers, preoccupied and absorbed in thought, and by degrees Ordynov's careless lightheartedness began unconsciously to pass away; reality began to weigh upon him, and to inspire in him a sort of unconscious dread and awe. He began to be weary from the surfeit of new impressions, like an invalid who for the first time joyfully gets up from his sick bed, and sinks down giddy and stupefied by the movement and exhausted by the light, the glare, the whirl of life, the noise and medley of colours in the crowd that flutters by him. He began to feel dejected and miserable, he began to be full of dread for his whole life, for his work, and even for the future. A new idea destroyed his peace. A thought suddenly occurred to him that all his life he had been solitary and no one had loved him—and, indeed, he had succeeded in loving no one either. Some of the passers-by, with whom he had chanced to enter into conversation at the beginning of his walk, had looked at him rudely and strangely. He saw that they took him for a madman or a very original, eccentric fellow, which was, indeed, perfectly correct. He remembered that everyone was always somewhat ill at ease in his presence, that even in his childhood everyone had avoided him on account of his dreamy, obstinate character, that sympathy for people had always been difficult and oppressive to him, and had been unnoticed by others, for though it existed in him there was no moral equality perceptible in it, a fact which had worried him even as a child, when he was utterly unlike other children of his own age. Now he remembered and reflected that always, at all times, he had been left out and passed over by everyone.

I

Without noticing it, he had come into an end of Petersburg remote from the centre of the town. Dining after a fashion in a solitary restaurant, he went out to wander about again. Again he passed through many streets and squares. After them stretched long fences, grey and yellow; he began to come across quite dilapidated little cottages, instead of wealthy houses, and mingled with them colossal factories, monstrous, soot-begrimed, red buildings, with long chimneys. All round it was deserted and desolate, everything looked grim and forbidding, so at least it seemed to Ordynov. It was by now evening. He came out of a long side-street into a square where there stood a parish church.

He went into it without thinking. The service was just over, the church was almost empty, only two old women were kneeling near the entrance. The verger, a grey-headed old man, was putting out the candles. The rays of the setting sun were streaming down from above through a narrow window in the cupola and flooding one of the chapels with a sea of brilliant light, but it grew fainter and fainter, and the blacker the darkness that gathered under the vaulted roof, the more brilliantly glittered in places the gilt ikons, reflecting the flickering glow of the lamps and the lights. In an access of profound depression and some stifled feeling Ordynov leaned against the wall in the darkest corner of the church, and for an instant sank into forgetfulness. He came to himself when the even, hollow sound of the footsteps of two persons resounded in the building. He raised his eyes and an indescribable curiosity took possession of him at the sight of the two advancing figures. They were an old man and a young woman. The old man was tall, still upright and hale-looking, but thin and of a sickly pallor. From his appearance he might have been taken for a merchant from some distant province. He was wearing a long black full-skirted coat trimmed with fur, evidently a holiday dress, and he wore it unbuttoned; under it could be seen some other long-skirted Russian garment, buttoned closely from top to bottom. His bare neck was covered with a bright red handkerchief carelessly knotted; in his hands he held a fur cap. His thin, long, grizzled beard fell down to his chest, and fiery, feverishly glowing eyes flashed a haughty, prolonged stare from under his frowning, overhanging brows. The woman was about twenty and wonderfully beautiful. She wore a splendid blue, fur-trimmed jacket, and her head was covered with a white satin kerchief tied under her chin. She walked with her eyes cast down, and a sort of melancholy dignity pervaded her whole figure and was vividly and mournfully reflected in the sweet contours of the childishly soft, mild lines of her face. There was something strange in this surprising couple.

The old man stood still in the middle of the church, and bowed to all the four points of the compass, though the church was quite empty; his companion did the same. Then he took her by the hand and led her up to the big ikon of the Virgin, to whom the church was dedicated. It was shining on the altar, with the dazzling light of the candles reflected on the gold and precious stones of the setting. The church verger, the last one remaining in the church, bowed respectfully to the old man; the latter nodded to him. The woman fell on her face, before the ikon. The old man took the hem of the veil that hung at the pedestal of the ikon and covered her head. A muffled sob echoed through the church.

Ordynov was impressed by the solemnity of this scene and waited in impatience for its conclusion. Two minutes later the woman raised her head and again the bright light of the lamp fell on her charming face. Ordynov started and took a step forward. She had aready given her hand to the old man and they both walked quietly out of the church. Tears were welling up from her dark blue eyes under the long eyelashes that glistened against the milky pallor of her face, and were rolling down her pale cheeks. There was a glimpse of a smile on her lips; but there were traces in her face of some childlike fear and mysterious horror. She pressed timidly close to the old man and it could be seen that she was trembling from emotion.

Overwhelmed, tormented by a sweet and persistent feeling that was novel to him, Ordynov followed them quickly and overtook them in the church porch. The old man looked at him with unfriendly churlishness; she glanced at him, too, but absent-mindedly, without curiosity, as though her mind were absorbed by some far-away thought. Ordynov followed them without understanding his own action. By now it had grown quite dark; he followed at a little distance. The old man and the young woman turned into a long, wide, dirty street full of hucksters' booths, corn chandlers' shops and taverns, leading straight to the city gates, and turned from it into a long narrow lane, with long fences on each side of it, running alongside the huge, blackened wall of a four-storeyed block of buildings, by the gates of which one could pass into another street also big and crowded. They were approaching the house; suddenly the old man turned round and looked with impatience at Ordynov. The young man stood still as though he had been shot; he felt himself how strange his impulsive conduct was. The old man looked round once more, as though he wanted to assure himself that his menacing gaze had produced its effect, and then the two of them, he and the young woman, went in at the narrow gate of the courtyard. Ordynov turned back.

He was in the most discontented humour and was vexed with himself, reflecting that he had wasted his day, that he had tired himself for nothing, and had ended foolishly by magnifying into an adventure an incident that was absolutely ordinary.

However severe he had been with himself in the morning for his recluse habits, yet it was instinctive with him to shun anything that might distract him, impress and shock him in his external, not in his internal, artistic world. Now he thought mournfully and regretfully of his sheltered corner; then he was overcome by depression and anxiety about his unsettled position and the exertions before him. At last, exhausted and incapable of putting two ideas together, he made his way late at night to his lodging and realised with amazement that he had been about to pass the house in which he lived. Dumbfoundered, he shook his head, and put down his absentmindedness to fatigue and, going up the stairs, at last reached his garret under the roof. There he lighted a candle—and a minute later the image of the weeping woman rose vividly before his imagination. So glowing, so intense was the impression, so longingly did his heart reproduce those mild, gentle features, quivering with mysterious emotion and horror, and bathed in tears of ecstasy or childish penitence, that there was a mist before his eyes and a thrill of fire seemed to run through all his limbs. But the vision did not last long. After enthusiasm, after ecstasy came reflection, then vexation, then impotent anger; without undressing he threw himself on his hard bed . . .

Ordynov woke up rather late in the morning, in a nervous, timid and oppressed state of mind. He hurriedly got ready, almost forcing himself to concentrate his mind on the practical problems before him, and set off in the opposite direction from that he had taken on his pilgrimage the day before. At last he found a lodging, a little room in the flat of a poor German called Schpies, who lived alone with a daughter called Tinchen. On receiving a deposit Schpies instantly took down the notice that was nailed on the gate to attract lodgers, complimented Ordynov on his devotion to science, and promised to work with him zealously himself. Ordynov said that he would move in in the evening. From there he was going home, but changed his mind and turned off in the other direction; his self-confidence had returned and he smiled at his own curiosity. In his impatience the way seemed very long to him. At last he reached the church in which he had been the evening before. Evening service was going on. He chose a place from which he could see almost all the congregation; but the figures he was looking for were not there. After waiting a long time he went away, blushing. Resolutely suppressing in himself an involuntary feeling, he tried obstinately to force himself, to change the current of his thoughts. Reflecting on everyday practical matters, he remembered he had not had dinner and, feeling that he was hungry, he went into the same tavern in which he had dined the day before. Unconsciously he sauntered a long time about the streets, through crowded and deserted alleys, and at last came out into a desolate region where the town ended in a vista of fields that were turning yellow; he came to himself when the deathlike silence struck him by its strangeness and unfamiliarity. It was a dry and frosty day such as are frequent in Petersburg in October. Not far away was a cottage; and near it stood two haystacks; a little horse with prominent ribs was standing unharnessed, with drooping head and lip thrust out, beside a little two-wheeled gig, and seemed to be pondering over something. A watch-dog, growling, gnawed a bone beside a broken wheel, and a child of three who, with nothing on but his shirt, was engaged in combing his shaggy white head, stared in wonder at the solitary stranger from the town. Behind the cottage there was a stretch of field and cottage garden. There was a dark patch of forest against the blue sky on the horizon, and on the opposite side were thick snow-clouds, which seemed chasing before them a flock of flying birds moving noiselessly one after another across the sky. All was still and, as it were, solemnly melancholy, full of a palpitating, hidden suspense . . . Ordynov was walking on farther and farther, but the desolation weighed upon him. He turned back to the town, from which there suddenly floated the deep clamour of bells, ringing for evening service; he redoubled his pace and within a short time he was again entering

255

the church that had been so familiar to him since the day before.

The unknown woman was there already. She was kneeling at the very entrance, among the crowd of worshippers. Ordynov forced his way through the dense mass of beggars, old women in rags, sick people and cripples, who were waiting for alms at the church door, and knelt down beside the stranger. His clothes touched her clothes and he heard the breath that came irregularly from her lips as she whispered a fervent prayer. As before, her features were quivering with a feeling of boundless devotion, and tears again were falling and drying on her burning cheeks, as though washing away some fearful crime. It was quite dark in the place where they were both kneeling, and only from time to time the dim flame of the lamp, flickering in the draught from the narrow open window pane, threw a quivering glimmer on her face, every feature of which printed itself on the young man's memory, making his eyes swim, and rending his heart with a vague, insufferable pain. But this torment had a peculiar, intense ecstasy of its own. At last he could not endure it; his breast began shuddering and aching all in one instant with a sweet and unfamiliar yearning, and, bursting into sobs, he bowed down with his feverish head to the cold pavement of the church. He saw nothing and felt nothing but the ache in his heart, which thrilled with sweet anguish.

This extreme impressionability, sensitiveness, and lack of resisting power may have been developed by solitude, or this impulsiveness of heart may have been evolved in the exhausting, suffocating and hopeless silence of long, sleepless nights, in the midst of unconscious yearnings and impatient stirrings of spirit, till it was ready at last to explode and find an outlet, or it may have been simply that the time for that solemn moment had suddenly arrived and it was as inevitable as when on a sullen, stifling day the whole sky grows suddenly black and a storm pours rain and fire on the parched earth, hangs pearly drops on the emerald twigs, beats down the grass, the crops, crushes to the earth the tender cups of the flowers, in order that afterwards, at the first rays of the sun, everything, reviving again, may shine and rise to meet it, and triumphantly lift to the sky its sweet, luxuriant incense, glad and rejoicing in its new life . . .

But Ordynov could not think now what was the matter with him. He was scarcely conscious.

256

He hardly noticed how the service ended, and only recovered his senses as he threaded his way after his unknown lady through the crowd that thronged the entrance. At times he met her clear and wondering eyes. Stopped every minute by the people passing out, she turned round to him more than once; he could see that her surprise grew greater and greater, and all at once she flushed a fiery red. At that minute the same old man came forward again out of the crowd and took her by the arm. Ordynov met his morose and sarcastic stare again, and a strange anger suddenly gripped his heart. At last he lost sight of them in the darkness; then, with a superhuman effort, he pushed forward and got out of the church. But the fresh evening air could not restore him; his breathing felt oppressed and stifled, and his heart began throbbing slowly and violently as though it would have burst his breast. At last he saw that he really had lost his strangers—they were neither in the main street nor in the alley. But already a thought had come to Ordynov, and in his mind was forming one of those strange, decisive projects, which almost always succeed when they are carried out, in spite of their wildness. At eight o'clock next morning he went to the house from the side of the alley and walked into a narrow, filthy, and unclean backyard which was like an open cesspool in a house. The porter, who was doing something in the yard, stood still, leaned with his chin on the handle of his spade, looked Ordynov up and down and asked him what he wanted. The porter was a little fellow about five and twenty, a Tatar with an extremely old-looking face, covered with wrinkles.

"I'm looking for a lodging," Ordynov answered impatiently.

"Which?" asked the porter, with a grin. He looked at Ordynov as if he knew all about him.

"I want a furnished room in a flat," answered Ordynov.

"There's none in that yard," the porter answered enigmatically.

"And here?"

"None here, either." The porter took up his spade again.

"Perhaps they will let me have one," said Ordynov, giving the porter ten kopecks.

The Tatar glanced at Ordynov, took the ten kopecks, then took up his spade again, and after a brief silence announced that: "No, there was no lodging." But the young man did not hear him; he walked along the rotten, shaking planks that

lay in the pool towards the one entrance from that yard into
the lodge of the house, a black, filthy, muddy entrance that
looked as though it were drowning in the pool. In the lower
storey lived a poor coffin-maker. Passing by his cheering work-
shop, Ordynov clambered by a half-broken, slippery, spiral
staircase to the upper storey, felt in the darkness a heavy,
clumsy door covered with rags of sacking, found the latch
and opened it. He was not mistaken. Before him stood
the same old man, looking at him intently with extreme
surprise.

"What do you want?" he asked abruptly and almost in a
whisper.

"Is there a room to let?" asked Ordynov, almost forgetting
everything he had meant to say. He saw over the old man's
shoulder the young woman.

The old man began silently closing the door, shutting
Ordynov out.

"We have a lodging to let," the young woman's friendly
voice said suddenly.

The old man let go of the door.

"I want a corner," said Ordynov, hurriedly entering the
room and addressing himself to the beautiful woman.

But he stopped in amazement as though petrified, looking at
his future landlord and landlady; before his eyes a mute and
amazing scene was taking place. The old man was as pale as
death, as though on the point of losing consciousness. He
looked at the woman with a leaden, fixed, searching gaze. She
too grew pale at first; then blood rushed to her face and her
eyes flashed strangely. She led Ordynov into another little
room.

The whole flat consisted of one rather large room, divided
into three by two partitions. From the outer room they went
straight into a narrow dark passage; directly opposite was the
door, evidently leading to a bedroom the other side of the
partition. On the right, the other side of the passage, they
went into the room which was to let; it was narrow and pokey,
squeezed in between the partition and two low windows; it was
blocked up with the objects necessary for daily life; it was
poor and cramped but passably clean. The furniture consisted
of a plain white table, two plain chairs and a locker that ran
both sides of the wall. A big, old-fashioned ikon in a gilt
wreath stood over a shelf in a corner and a lamp was burning
before it. There was a huge, clumsy Russian stove partly in

'this room and partly in the passage. It was clear that it was impossible for three people to live in such a flat.

They began discussing terms, but incoherently and hardly understanding one another. Two paces away from her, Ordynov could hear the beating of her heart; he saw she was trembling with emotion and, it seemed, with fear. At last they came to an agreement of some sort. The young man announced that he should move in at once and glanced at his landlord. The old man was standing at the door, still pale, but a quiet, even dreamy smile had stolen on to his lips. Meeting Ordynov's eyes he frowned again.

"Have you a passport?" he asked suddenly, in a loud and abrupt voice, opening the door into the passage for him.

"Yes," answered Ordynov, suddenly taken aback.

"Who are you?"

"Vassily Ordynov, nobleman, not in the service, engaged in private work," he answered, falling into the old man's tone.

"So am I," answered the old man. "I'm Ilya Murin, artisan. Is that enough for you? You can go . . ."

An hour later Ordynov was in his new lodging, to the surprise of himself and of his German, who, together with his dutiful Tinchen, was beginning to suspect that his new lodger had deceived him.

Ordynov did not understand how it had all happened, and he did not want to understand. . . .

CHAPTER II

HIS heart was beating so violently that he was giddy, and everything was green before his eyes; mechanically he busied himself arranging his scanty belongings in his new lodgings: he undid the bag containing various necessary possessions, opened the box containing his books and began laying them out on the table; but soon all this work dropped from his hands. Every minute there rose before his eyes the image of the woman, the meeting with whom had so troubled and disturbed his whole existence, who had filled his heart with such irresistible, violent ecstasy—and such happiness seemed at once flooding his starved life that his thoughts grew dizzy and his soul swooned in anguish and perplexity.

He took his passport and carried it to the landlord in the

hope of getting a glance at her. But Murin scarcely opened
the door; he took the paper from him, said, "Good; live in
peace," and closed the door again. An unpleasant feeling came
over Ordynov. He did not know why, but it was irksome for
him to look at the old man. There was something spiteful and
contemptuous in his eyes. But the unpleasant impression
quickly passed off. For the last three days Ordynov had, in
comparison with his former stagnation, been living in a whirl
of life; but he could not reflect, he was, indeed, afraid to. His
whole existence was in a state of upheaval and chaos; he dimly
felt as though his life had been broken in half; one yearning,
one expectation possessed him, and no other thoughts troubled
him.

In perplexity he went back to his room. There by the stove
in which the cooking was done a little humpbacked old woman
was busily at work, so filthy and clothed in such rags that she
was a pitiful sight. She seemed very ill-humoured and
grumbled to herself at times, mumbling with her lips. She was
his landlord's servant. Ordynov tried to talk to her, but she
would not speak, evidently from ill-humour. At last dinner-
time arrived. The old woman took cabbage soup, pies and beef
out of the oven, and took them to her master and mistress.
She gave some of the same to Ordynov. After dinner there
was a death-like silence in the flat.

Ordynov took up a book and spent a long time turning over
its pages, trying to follow the meaning of what he had read
often before. Losing patience, he threw down the book and
began again putting his room to rights; at last he took up his
cap, put on his coat and went out into the street. Walking at
hazard, without seeing the road, he still tried as far as he could
to concentrate his mind, to collect his scattered thoughts and to
reflect a little upon his position. But the effort only reduced
him to misery, to torture. He was attacked by fever and chills
alternately, and at times his heart beat so violently that he
had to support himself against the wall. "No, better death,"
he thought; "better death," he whispered with feverish,
trembling lips, hardly thinking of what he was saying. He
walked for a very long time; at last, feeling that he was soaked
to the skin and noticing for the first time that it was pouring with rain, he returned home. Not far from home he saw
his porter. He fancied that the Tatar stared at him for some
time with curiosity, and then went his way when he noticed
that he had been seen.

"Good-morning," said Ordynov, overtaking him. "What are you called?"

"Folks call me porter," he answered, grinning.

"Have you been porter here long?"

"Yes."

"Is my landlord an artisan?"

"Yes, if he says so."

"What does he do?"

"He's ill, lives, prays to God. That's all."

"Is that his wife?"

"What wife?"

"Who lives with him."

"Ye-es, if he says so. Good-bye, sir."

The Tatar touched his cap and went off to his den.

Ordynov went to his room. The old woman, mumbling and grumbling to herself, opened the door to him, fastened it again with the latch, and again climbed on the stove where she spent her life. It was already getting dark. Ordynov was going to get a light, when he noticed that the door to the landlord's room was locked. He called the old woman, who, propping herself on her elbow, looked sharply at him from the stove, as though wondering what he wanted with the landlord's lock; she threw him a box of matches without a word. He went back into his room and again, for the hundredth time, tried to busy himself with his books and things. But, little by little, without understanding what he was doing, he sat down on the locker, and it seemed to him that he fell asleep. At times he came to himself and realised that his sleep was not sleep but the agonising unconsciousness of illness. He heard a knock at the door, heard it opened, and guessed that it was the landlord and landlady returning from evening service. At that point it occurred to him that he must go in to them for something. He stood up, and it seemed to him that he was already going to them, but stumbled and fell over a heap of firewood which the old woman had flung down in the middle of the floor. At that point he lost consciousness completely, and opening his eyes after a long, long time, noticed with surprise that he was lying on the same locker, just as he was, in his clothes, and that over him there bent with tender solicitude a woman's face, divinely beautiful and, it seemed, drenched with gentle, motherly tears. He felt her put a pillow under his head and lay something warm over him, and some tender hand was laid on his feverish brow. He wanted to say "Thank you," he

wanted to take that hand, to press it to his parched lips, to wet
it with his tears, to kiss, to kiss it to all eternity. He wanted
to say a great deal, but what he did not know himself; he
would have been glad to die at that instant. But his arms
felt like lead and would not move; he was as it were numb,
and felt nothing but the blood pulsing through his veins, with
throbs which seemed to lift him up as he lay in bed. Somebody gave him water. . . . At last he fell into unconsciousness.

He woke up at eight o'clock in the morning. The sunshine
was pouring through the green, mouldy windows in a sheaf of
golden rays; a feeling of comfort relaxed the sick man's limbs.
He was quiet and calm, infinitely happy. It seemed to him that
someone had just been by his pillow. He woke up, looking
anxiously around him for that unseen being; he so longed to
embrace his friend and for the first time in his life to say, "A
happy day to you, my dear one."

"What a long time you have been asleep!" said a woman's
gentle voice.

Ordynov looked round, and the face of his beautiful landlady was bending over him with a friendly smile as clear as
sunlight.

"How long you have been ill!" she said. "It's enough;
get up. Why keep yourself in bondage? Freedom is sweeter
than bread, fairer than sunshine. Get up, my dove, get up."

Ordynov seized her hand and pressed it warmly. It seemed
to him that he was still dreaming.

"Wait; I've made tea for you. Do you want some tea?
You had better have some; you'll be better. I've been ill
myself and I know."

"Yes, give me something to drink," said Ordynov in a faint
voice, and he got up on his feet. He was still very weak. A
chill ran down his spine, all his limbs ached and felt as though
they were broken. But there was a radiance in his heart, and
the sunlight seemed to warm him with a sort of solemn, serene
joy. He felt that a new, intense, incredible life was beginning
for him. His head was in a slight whirl.

"Your name is Vassily?" she asked. "Either I have made
a mistake, or I fancy the master called you that yesterday."

"Yes, it is. And what is your name?" said Ordynov, going
nearer to her and hardly able to stand on his feet. He
staggered.

She caught him by the arm, and laughed.

"My name is Katerina," she said, looking into his face with

262

her large, clear blue eyes. They were holding each other by the hands.

"You want to say something to me," she said at last.

"I don't know," answered Ordynov; everything was dark before his eyes.

"See what a state you're in. There, my dove, there; don't grieve, don't pine; sit here at the table in the sun; sit quiet, and don't follow me," she added, seeing that the young man made a movement as though to keep her. "I will be with you again at once; you have plenty of time to see as much as you want of me." A minute later she brought in the tea, put it on the table, and sat down opposite him.

"Come, drink it up," she said. "Does your head ache?"

"No, now it doesn't ache," he said. "I don't know, perhaps it does. . . . I don't want any . . . enough, enough! . . . I don't know what's the matter with me," he said, breathless, and finding her hand at last. "Stay here, don't go away from me; give me your hand again. . . . It's all dark before my eyes; I look at you as though you were the sun," he said, as it were tearing the words out of his heart, and almost swooning with ecstasy as he uttered them. His throat was choking with sobs.

"Poor fellow! It seems you have not lived with anyone kind. You are all lonely and forlorn. Haven't you any relations?"

"No, no one; I am alone . . . never mind, it's no matter! Now it's better; I am all right now," said Ordynov, as though in delirium. The room seemed to him to be going round.

"I, too, have not seen my people for many years. You look at me as . . ." she said, after a minute's silence.

"Well . . . what?"

"You look at me as though my eyes were warming you! You know, when you love anyone . . . I took you to my heart from the first word. If you are ill I will look after you again. Only don't you be ill; no. When you get up we will live like brother and sister. Will you? You know it's difficult to get a sister if God has not given you one."

"Who are you? Where do you come from?" said Ordynov in a weak voice.

"I am not of these parts. . . . You know the folks tell how twelve brothers lived in a dark forest, and how a fair maiden lost her way in that forest. She went to them and tidied everything in the house for them, and put her love into everything.

263

The brothers came home, and learned that the sister had spent the day there. They began calling her; she came out to them. They all called her sister, gave her freedom, and she was equal with all. Do you know the fairy tale?"

"I know it," whispered Ordynov.

"Life is sweet; is it sweet to you to live in the world?"

"Yes, yes; to live for a long time, to live for ages," answered Ordynov.

"I don't know," said Katerina dreamily. "I should like death, too. Is life sweet? To love, and to love good people, yes. . . . Look, you've turned as white as flour again."

"Yes, my head's going round. . . ."

"Stay, I will bring you my bedclothes and another pillow; I will make up the bed here. Sleep, and dream of me; your weakness will pass. Our old woman is ill, too."

While she talked she began making the bed, from time to time looking at Ordynov with a smile.

"What a lot of books you've got!" she said, moving away a box.

She went up to him, took him by the right arm, led him to the bed, tucked him up and covered him with the quilt.

"They say books spoil a man," she said, shaking her head thoughtfully. "Do you like reading?"

"Yes," answered Ordynov, not knowing whether he were asleep or awake, and pressing Katerina's hand tight to assure himself that he was awake.

"My master has a lot of books; you should see! He says they are religious books. He's always reading to me out of them. I will show you afterwards; you shall tell me afterwards what he reads to me out of them."

"Tell me," whispered Ordynov, keeping his eyes fixed on her.

"Are you fond of praying?" she said to him after a moment's silence. "Do you know, I'm afraid, I am always afraid . . ."

She did not finish; she seemed to be meditating. At last Ordynov raised her hand to his lips.

"Why are you kissing my hand?" (and her cheeks flushed faintly crimson). "Here, kiss them," she said, laughing and holding out both hands to him; then she took one away and laid it on his burning forehead; then she began to stroke and arrange his hair. She flushed more and more; at last she sat down on the floor by his bedside and laid her cheek against his cheek; her warm, damp breath tickled his face. . . . At last Ordynov felt a gush of hot tears fall from her eyes like molten lead on his cheeks. He felt weaker and weaker; he was too faint to move a hand. At that moment there was a knock at the door, followed by the grating of the bolt. Ordynov could hear the old man, his landlord, come in from the other side of the partition. Then he heard Katerina get up, without haste and without listening, take her books; he felt her make the sign of the cross over him as she went out; he closed his eyes. Suddenly a long, burning kiss scorched his feverish lips; it was like a knife thrust into his heart. He uttered a faint shriek and sank into unconsciousness. . . .

Then a strange life began for him.

In moments when his mind was not clear, the thought flashed upon him that he was condemned to live in a long, unending dream, full of strange, fruitless agitations, struggles and sufferings. In terror he tried to resist the disastrous fatalism that weighed upon him, and at a moment of tense and desperate conflict some unknown force struck him again and he felt clearly that he was once more losing memory, that an impassable, bottomless abyss was opening before him and he was flinging himself into it with a wail of anguish and despair. At times he had moments of insufferable, devastating happiness, when the life force quickens convulsively in the whole organism, when the past shines clear, when the present glad moment resounds with triumph and one dreams, awake, of a future beyond all ken; when a hope beyond words falls with life-giving dew on the soul; when one wants to scream with ecstasy; when one feels that the flesh is too weak for such a mass of impressions, that the whole thread of existence is breaking, and yet, at the same time, one greets all one's life with hope and renewal. At times he sank into lethargy, and then everything that had happened to him the last few days was repeated again, and passed across his mind in a swarm of broken, vague images; but his visions came in strange and enigmatic form. At times the sick man forgot what had happened to him, and wondered that he was not in his old lodging with his old landlady. He could not understand why the old woman did not come as she always used at the twilight hour to the stove, which from time to time flooded the whole dark corner of the room with a faint, flickering glow, to warm her trembling, bony hands at the dying embers before the fire went out, always talking and whispering to herself, and sometimes looking at him, her strange lodger, who had, she thought, grown mad by sitting so long over his books.

Another time he would remember that he had moved into another lodging; but how it had happened, what was the matter with him, and why he had to move he did not know, though his whole soul was swooning in continual, irresistible yearning. . . . But to what end, what led him on and tortured him, and who had kindled this terrible flame that stifled him and consumed his blood, again he did not know and could not remember. Often he greedily clutched at some shadow, often he heard the rustle of light footsteps near his bed, and a whisper, sweet as music, of tender, caressing words. Someone's moist and uneven breathing passed over his face, thrilling his whole being with love; hot tears dropped upon his feverish cheeks, and suddenly a long, tender kiss was printed on his lips; then his life lay languishing in unquenchable torture; all existence, the whole world, seemed standing still, seemed to be dying for ages around him, and everything seemed shrouded in a long night of a thousand years. . . .

Then the tender, calmly flowing years of early childhood seemed coming back to him again with serene joy, with the inextinguishable happiness, the first sweet wonder of life, with the swarms of bright spirits that fluttered under every flower he picked, that sported with him on the luxuriant green meadow before the little house among the acacias, that smiled at him from the immense crystal lake beside which he would sit for hours together, listening to the plashing of the waves, and that rustled about him with their wings, lovingly scattering bright rainbow dreams upon his little cot, while his mother, bending over him, made the sign of the cross, kissed him, and sang him sweet lullabies in the long, peaceful nights. But then a being suddenly began to appear who overwhelmed him with a childlike terror, first bringing into his life the slow poison of sorrow and tears; he dimly felt that an unknown old man held all his future years in thrall, and, trembling, he could not turn his eyes away from him. The wicked old man followed him about everywhere. He peeped out and treacherously nodded to the boy from under every bush in the copse, laughed and mocked at him, took the shape of every doll, grimacing and laughing in his hands, like a spiteful evil gnome: he set every one of the child's inhuman schoolfellows against him, or, sitting with the little ones on the school bench, peeped out, grimacing, from every letter of his grammar. Then when he was asleep

the evil old man sat by his pillow . . . he drove away the
bright spirits whose gold and sapphire wings rustled about his
cot, carried off his poor mother from him for ever, and began
whispering to him every night long, wonderful fairy tales,
unintelligible to his childish imagination, but thrilling and tormenting him with terror and unchildlike passion. But the
wicked old man did not heed his sobs and entreaties, and would
go on talking to him till he sank into numbness, into unconsciousness. Then the child suddenly woke up a man; the years
passed over him unseen, unheeded. He suddenly became aware
of his real position. He understood all at once that he was
alone, an alien to all the world, alone in a corner not his own,
among mysterious and suspicious people, among enemies who
were always gathering together and whispering in the corners
of his dark room, and nodding to the old woman squatting on
her heels near the fire, warming her bony old hands, and pointing to him. He sank into perplexity and uneasiness; he wanted
to know who these people were, why they were here, why he
was himself in this room, and guessed that he had strayed into
some dark den of miscreants, drawn on by some powerful but
incomprehensible force, without having first found out who and
what the tenants were and who his landlord was. He began to
be tortured by suspicion—and suddenly, in the stillness of the
night, again there began a long, whispered story, and some old
woman, mournfully nodding her white, grizzled head before
the dying fire, was muttering it softly, hardly audibly to herself. But—and again he was overcome with horror—the story
took shape before him in forms and faces. He saw everything,
from his dim, childish visions upwards: all his thoughts and
dreams, all his experiences in life, all he had read in books,
things he had forgotten long ago, all were coming to life, all
were being put together, taking shape and rising up before him
in colossal forms and images, moving and swarming about him;
he saw spread out before him magnificent, enchanted gardens,
a whole town built up and demolished before his eyes, a whole
churchyard giving up its dead, who began living over again;
whole races and peoples came into being and passed away
before his eyes; finally, every one of his thoughts, every immaterial fancy, now took bodily shape around his sick-bed;
took bodily shape almost at the moment of its conception: at
last he saw himself thinking not in immaterial ideas, but in
whole worlds, whole creations, saw himself borne along like an
atom in this infinite, strange world from which there was no

escape, and all this life in its mutinous independence crushing and oppressing him and pursuing him with eternal, infinite irony; he felt that he was dying, dissolving into dust and ashes for ever, and even without hope of resurrection, he tried to flee, but there was no corner in all the universe to hide him. At last, in an access of despair, he made an intense effort, uttered a shriek and woke up.

He woke up, bathed in a chill, icy sweat. About him was a deadly silence; it was the dead of night. But still it seemed to him that somewhere the wonderful fairy tale was going on, that some hoarse voice was really telling a long story of something that seemed familiar to him. He heard talk of dark forests, of bold brigands, of some daring bravoes, maybe of Stenka Razin himself, of merry drunken bargemen, of some fair maiden, and of Mother Volga. Was it not a fairy tale? Was he really hearing it? For a whole hour he lay, open-eyed, without stirring a muscle, in agonising numbness. At last he got up carefully, and joyfully felt that his strength had come back to him after his severe illness. The delirium was over and reality was beginning. He noticed that he was dressed exactly as he had been during his talk with Katerina, so that it could not have been long since the morning she had left him. The fire of resolution ran through his veins. Mechanically he felt with his hand for a big nail for some reason driven into the top of the partition near which stood his bed, seized it, and hanging his whole weight upon it, succeeded in pulling himself up to the crevice from which a hardly perceptible light stole into his room. He put his eye to the opening and, almost breathless with excitement, began peeping in.

There was a bed in the corner of the landlord's room; before it was a table covered with a cloth and piled up with books of old-fashioned shape, looking from their bindings like devotional books. In the corner was an ikon of the same old-fashioned pattern as in his room; a lamp was burning before it. On the bed lay the old man, Murin, sick, worn out with suffering and pale as a sheet, covered with a fur rug. On his knees was an open book. On a bench beside the bed lay Katerina, with her arm about the old man's chest and her head bent on his shoulder. She was looking at him with attentive, childishly wondering eyes, and seemed, breathless with expectation, to be listening with insatiable curiosity to what Murin was telling her. From time to time the speaker's voice rose higher, there was a shade of animation on his pale face; he frowned, his eyes began to flash, and Katerina seemed to turn pale with dread and expectation. Then something like a smile came into the old man's face and Katerina began laughing softly: Sometimes tears came into her eyes; then the old man tenderly stroked her on the head like a child, and she embraced him more tightly than ever with her bare arm that gleamed like snow, and nestled even more lovingly to his bosom.

At times Ordynov still thought this was part of his dream; in fact, he was convinced of it; but the blood rushed to his head and the veins throbbed painfully in his temples. He let go of the nail, got off the bed, and staggering, feeling his way like a lunatic, without understanding the impulse that flamed up like fire in his blood, he went to the door and pushed violently; the rusty bolt flew open at once, and with a bang and a crash he suddenly found himself in the middle of the landlord's bedroom. He saw Katerina start and tremble, saw the old man's eyes flash angrily under his lowering brows, and his whole face contorted with sudden fury. He saw the old man, still keeping close watch upon him, feel hurriedly with fumbling hand for a gun that hung upon the wall; then he saw the barrel of the gun flash, aimed straight at his breast with an uncertain hand that trembled with fury. . . . There was the sound of a shot, then a wild, almost unhuman, scream, and when the smoke parted, a terrible sight met Ordynov's eyes. Trembling all over, he bent over the old man. Murin was lying on the floor; he was writhing in convulsions, his face was contorted in agony, and there was foam upon his working lips. Ordynov guessed that the unhappy man was in a severe epileptic fit. He flew, together with Katerina, to help him . . .

CHAPTER III

THE whole night was spent in agitation. Next day Ordynov went out early in the morning, in spite of his weakness and the fever that still hung about him. In the yard he met the porter again. This time the Tartar lifted his cap to him from a distance and looked at him with curiosity. Then, as though pulling himself together, he set to work with his broom, glancing askance at Ordynov as the latter slowly approached him.

"Well, did you hear nothing in the night?" asked Ordynov.

"Yes, I heard."

"What sort of man is he? Who is he?"

"Self took lodgings, self should know; me stranger."

"Will you ever speak?" cried Ordynov, beside himself with an access of morbid irritability.

"What did me do? Your fault—you frightened the tenants. Below lives the coffin-maker, he deaf, but heard it all, and his wife deaf, but she heard, and in the next yard, far away, they heard. I go to the overseer."

"I am going to him myself," answered Ordynov; and he went to the gate.

"As you will; self took the room. . . . Master, master, stay." Ordynov looked round; the porter touched his hat from politeness.

"Well!"

"If you go, I go to the landlord."

"What?"

"Better move."

"You're stupid," said Ordynov, and was going on again.

"Master, master, stay." The porter touched his hat again and grinned. "Listen, master: be not wrathful; why persecute a poor man? It's a sin to persecute a poor man. It is not God's law—do you hear?"

"You listen, too: here, take that. Come, what is he?"

"What is he?"

"Yes."

"I'll tell you without money."

At this point the porter took up his broom, brandished it once or twice, then stopped and looked intently, with an air of importance, at Ordynov.

"You're a nice gentleman. If you don't want to live with a good man, do as you like; that's what I say."

Then the Tatar looked at him still more expressively, and fell to sweeping furiously again.

Making a show of having finished something at last, he went up to Ordynov mysteriously, and with a very expressive gesture pronounced—

"This is how it is."

"How—what?"

"No sense."

"What?"

"Has flown away. Yes! Has flown away!" he repeated in a still more mysterious tone. "He is ill. He used to have a barge, a big one, and a second and a third, used to be on the Volga, and me from the Volga myself. He had a factory, too, but it was burnt down, and he is off his head.''

''He is mad?''

''Nay! . . . Nay! . . .'' the Tatar answered emphatically. ''Not mad. He is a clever man. He knows everything; he has read many books, many, many; he has read everything, and tells others the truth. Some bring two roubles, three roubles, forty roubles, as much as you please; he looks in a book, sees and tells the whole truth. And the money's on the table at once—nothing without money!''

At this point the Tatar positively laughed with glee, throwing himself into Murin's interests with extreme zest.

''Why, does he tell fortunes, prophesy?''

''H'm! . . .'' muttered the porter, wagging his head quickly. ''He tells the truth. He prays, prays a great deal. It's just that way, comes upon him.''

Then the Tatar made his expressive gesture again.

At that moment someone called the porter from the other yard, and then a little, bent, grey-headed man in a sheepskin appeared. He walked, stumbling and looking at the ground, groaning and muttering to himself. He looked as though he were in his dotage.

''The master, the master!'' the porter whispered in a fluster, with a hurried nod to Ordynov, and taking off his cap, he ran to meet the old man, whose face looked familiar to Ordynov; he had anyway met him somewhere just lately.

Reflecting, however, that there was nothing remarkable in that, he walked out of the yard. The porter struck him as an out-and-out rogue and an impudent fellow.

''The scoundrel was practically bargaining with me!'' he thought. ''Goodness knows what it means!''

He had reached the street as he said this.

By degrees he began to be absorbed in other thoughts. The impression was unpleasant, the day was grey and cold; flakes of snow were flying. The young man felt overcome by a feverish shiver again; he felt, too, as though the earth were shaking under him. All at once an unpleasantly sweet, familiar voice wished him good-morning in a broken tenor.

''Yaroslav Ilyitch,'' said Ordynov.

Before him stood a short, sturdy, red-cheeked man, apparently about thirty, with oily grey eyes and a little smile, dressed . . . as Yaroslav Ilyitch always was dressed. He was holding

out his hand to him in a very amicable way. Ordynov had
made the acquaintance of Yaroslav Ilyitch just a year before
in quite a casual way, almost in the street. They had so easily
become acquainted, partly by chance and partly through Yaroslav Ilyitch's extraordinary propensity for picking up everywhere good-natured, well-bred people, and his preference for
friends of good education whose talents and elegance of behaviour made them worthy at least of belonging to good society.
Though Yaroslav Ilyitch had an extremely sweet tenor, yet
even in conversation with his dearest friends there was something extraordinarily clear, powerful and dominating in the
tone of his voice that would put up with no evasions; it was
perhaps merely due to habit.

"How on earth . . . ?" exclaimed Yaroslav Ilyitch, with an
expression of the most genuine, ecstatic pleasure.

"I am living here."

"Have you lived here long?" Yaroslav Ilyitch continued on
an ascending note. "And I did not know it! Why, we are
neighbours! I am in this quarter now. I came back from
the Ryazan province a month ago. I've caught you, my old
and noble friend!" and Yaroslav Ilyitch laughed in a most
good-natured way. "Sergeyev!" he cried impressively, "wait
for me at Tarasov's, and don't let them touch a sack without
me. And stir up the Olsufyev porter; tell him to come to the
office at once. I shall be there in an hour. . . ."

Hurriedly giving someone this order, the refined Yaroslav
Ilyitch took Ordynov's arm and led him to the nearest
restaurant.

"I shall not be satisfied till we have had a couple of words
alone after such a long separation. Well, what of your doings?"
he pronounced almost reverently, dropping his voice mysteriously. "Working at science, as ever?"

"Yes, as before," answered Ordynov, struck by a bright
idea.

"Splendid, Vassily Mihalitch, splendid!" At this point
Yaroslav Ilyitch pressed Ordynov's hand warmly. "You will
be a credit to the community. God give you luck in your
career. . . . Goodness! how glad I am I met you! How often
I have thought of you, how often I have said: 'Where is he,
our good, noble-hearted, witty Vassily Mihalitch?'"

They engaged a private room. Yaroslav Ilyitch ordered
lunch, asked for vodka, and looked feelingly at Ordynov.

"I have read a great deal since I saw you," he began in a

timid and somewhat insinuating voice. "I have read all Pushkin . . ."

Ordynov looked at him absent-mindedly.

"A marvellous understanding of human passion. But first of all, let me express my gratitude. You have done so much for me by nobly instilling into me a right way of thinking."

"Upon my word . . ."

"No, let me speak; I always like to pay honour where honour is due, and I am proud that this feeling at least has found expression."

"Really, you are unfair to yourself, and I, indeed . . ."

"No, I am quite fair," Yaroslav Ilyitch replied, with extra-ordinary warmth. "What am I in comparison with you?"

"Good Heavens!"

"Yes. . . ."

Then followed silence.

"Following your advice, I have dropped many low acquaint-ances and have, to some extent, softened the coarseness of my manners," Yaroslav Ilyitch began again in a somewhat timid and insinuating voice. "In the time when I am free from my duties I sit for the most part at home; in the evenings I read some improving book and . . . I have only one desire, Vassily Mihalitch: to be of some little use to the fatherland. . . ."

"I have always thought you a very high-minded man, Yaro-slav Ilyitch."

"You always bring balm to my spirit . . . you generous young man. . . ."

Yaroslav Ilyitch pressed Ordynov's hand warmly.

"You are drinking nothing?" he said, his enthusiasm sub-siding a little.

"I can't; I'm ill."

"Ill? Yes, are you really? How long—in what way—did you come to be ill? If you like I'll speak . . . What doctor is treating you? If you like I'll speak to our parish doctor. I'll run round to him myself. He's a very skilful man!"

Yaroslav Ilyitch was already picking up his hat.

"Thank you very much. I don't go in for being doctored. I don't like doctors."

"You don't say so? One can't go on like that. But he's a very clever man," Yaroslav Ilyitch went on imploringly. "The other day—do allow me to tell you this, dear Vassily Mihalitch —the other day a poor carpenter came. 'Here,' said he, 'I hurt my hand with a tool; cure it for me. . . .' Semyon Pafnut-

yitch, seeing that the poor fellow was in danger of gangrene,
set to work to cut off the wounded hand; he did this in my
presence, but it was done in such a gener . . . that is, in such
a superb way, that I confess if it had not been for compassion
for suffering humanity, it would have been a pleasure to look
on, simply from curiosity. But where and how did you fall
ill?"

"In moving from my lodging . . . I've only just got up."

"But you are still very unwell and you ought not to be out.
So you are not living where you were before? But what induced you to move?"

"My landlady was leaving Petersburg."

"Domna Savishna? Really? . . . A thoroughly estimable,
good-hearted woman! Do you know? I had almost a son's
respect for her. That life, so near its end, had something of
the serene dignity of our forefathers, and looking at her, one
seemed to see the incarnation of our hoary-headed, stately old
traditions . . . I mean of that . . . something in it so poetical!"
Yaroslav Ilyitch concluded, completely overcome with shyness
and blushing to his ears.

"Yes, she was a nice woman."

"But allow me to ask you where you are settled now."

"Not far from here, in Koshmarov's Buildings."

"I know him. A grand old man! I am, I may say, almost
a real friend of his. A fine old veteran!"

Yaroslav Ilyitch's lips almost quivered with enthusiasm.
He asked for another glass of vodka and a pipe.

"Have you taken a flat?"

"No, a furnished room in a flat."

"Who is your landlord? Perhaps I know him, too."

"Murin, an artisan; a tall old man . . ."

"Murin, Murin; yes, in the back court, over the coffin-
maker's, allow me to ask?"

"Yes, yes, in the back court."

"H'm! are you comfortable there?"

"Yes; I've only just moved in."

"H'm! . . . I only meant to say, h'm! . . . have you
noticed nothing special?"

"Really . . ."

"That is . . . I am sure you will be all right there if you are
satisfied with your quarters. . . . I did not mean that; I am
ready to warn you . . . but, knowing your character . . . How
did that old artisan strike you?"

"He seems to be quite an invalid."

"Yes, he's a great sufferer. . . . But have you noticed nothing? Have you talked to him?"

"Very little; he is so morose and unsociable."

"H'm! . . ." Yaroslav Ilyitch mused. "He's an unfortunate man," he said dreamily.

"Is he?" ˜

"Yes, unfortunate, and at the same time an incredibly strange and interesting person. However, if he does not worry you . . . Excuse my dwelling upon such a subject, but I was curious . . ."

"And you have really roused my curiosity, too. . . . I should very much like to know what sort of a man he is. Besides, I am living with him. . . ."

"You know, they say the man was once very rich. He traded, as most likely you have heard. But through various unfortunate circumstances he was reduced to poverty; many of his barges were wrecked in a storm and lost, together with their cargo. His factory, which was, I believe, in the charge of a near and dear relation, was equally unlucky and was burnt down, and the relation himself perished in the flames. It must be admitted it was a terrible loss! Then, so they say, Murin sank into tearful despondency; they began to be afraid he would lose his reason, and, indeed, in a quarrel with another merchant, also an owner of barges plying on the Volga, he suddenly showed himself in such a strange an unexpected light that the whole incident could only be accounted for on the supposition that he was quite mad, which I am prepared to believe. I have heard in detail of some of his queer ways; there suddenly happened at last a very strange, so to say momentous, circumstance which can only be attributed to the malign influence of wrathful destiny."

"What was it?" asked Ordynov.

"They say that in a fit of madness he made an attempt on the life of a young merchant, of whom he had before been very fond. He was so upset when he recovered from the attack that he was on the point of taking his own life; so at least they say. I don't know what happened after that, but it is known that he was several years doing penance. . . . But what is the matter with you, Vassily Mihalitch? Am I fatiguing you with my artless tale?"

"Oh no, for goodness' sake . . . You say that he has been doing penance; but he is not alone."

"I don't know. I am told he was alone. Anyway, no one else was mixed up in that affair. However, I have not heard what followed; I only know . . ."

"Well?"

"I only know—that is, I had nothing special in my mind to add . . . I only want to say, if you find anything strange or out of the ordinary in him, all that is merely the result of the misfortunes that have descended upon him one after the other. . . ."

"Yes, he is so devout, so sanctimonious."

"I don't think so, Vassily Mihalitch; he has suffered so much; I believe he is quite sincere."

"But now, of course, he is not mad; he is all right."

"Oh, yes, yes; I can answer for that, I am ready to take my oath on it; he is in full possession of all his faculties. He is only, as you have justly observed, extremely strange and devout. He is a very sensible man, in fact. He speaks smartly, boldly and very subtly. The traces of his stormy life in the past are still visible on his face. He's a curious man, and very well read."

"He seems to be always reading religious books."

"Yes, he is a mystic."

"What?"

"A mystic. But I tell you that as a secret. I will tell you, as a secret, too, that a very careful watch was kept on him for a time. The man had a great influence on people who used to go to him."

"What sort of influence?"

"But you'll never believe it; you see, in those days he did not live in this building; Alexandr Ignatyevitch, a respectable citizen, a man of standing, held in universal esteem, went to see him with a lieutenant out of curiosity. They arrive and are received, and the strange man begins by looking into their faces. He usually looks into people's faces if he consents to be of use to them; if not, he sends people away, and even very uncivilly, I'm told. He asks them, 'What do you want, gentlemen?' 'Well,' answers Alexandr Ignatyevitch, 'your gift can tell you that, without our saying.' 'Come with me into the next room,' he says; then he signified which of them it was who needed his services. Alexandr Ignatyevitch did not say what happened to him afterwards, but he came out from him as white as a sheet. The same thing happened to a well-known lady of high rank: she, too, came out from seeing him as white

276

as a sheet, bathed in tears and overcome with his predictions and his sayings."

"Strange. But now does he still do the same?"

"It's strictly prohibited. There have been marvellous instances. A young cornet, the hope and joy of a distinguished family, mocked at him. 'What are you laughing at?' said the old man, angered. 'In three days' time you will be like this!' and he crossed his arms over his bosom to signify a corpse."

"Well?"

"I don't venture to believe it, but they say his prediction came true. He has a gift, Vassily Mihalitch. . . . You are pleased to smile at my guileless story. I know that you are greatly ahead of me in culture; but I believe in him; he's not a charlatan. Pushkin himself mentions a similar case in his works."

"H'm! I don't want to contradict you. I think you said he's not living alone?"

"I don't know . . . I believe his daughter is with him."

"Daughter?"

"Yes, or perhaps his wife; I know there is some woman with him. I have had a passing glimpse of her, but I did not notice."

"H'm! Strange . . ."

The young man fell to musing, Yaroslav Ilyitch to tender contemplation of him. He was touched both at seeing an old friend and at having satisfactorily told him something very interesting. He sat sucking his pipe with his eyes fixed on Vassily Mihalitch; but suddenly he jumped up in a fluster.

"A whole hour has passed and I forgot the time! Dear Vassily Mihalitch, once more I thank the lucky chance that brought us together, but it is time for me to be off. Will you allow me to visit you in your learned retreat?"

"Please do, I shall be delighted. I will come and see you, too, when I have a chance."

"That's almost too pleasant to believe. You gratify me, you gratify me unutterably! You would not believe how you have delighted me!"

They went out of the restaurant. Sergeyev was already flying to meet them and to report in a hurried sentence that Vilyam Emelyanovitch was pleased to be driving out. A pair of spirited roans in a smart light gig did, in fact, come into sight. The trace horse was particularly fine. Yaroslav Ilyitch pressed his best friend's hand as though in a vice, touched his hat and set off to meet the flying gig. On the way he turned round once or twice to nod farewells to Ordynov.

Ordynov felt so tired, so exhausted in every limb, that he could scarcely move his legs. He managed somehow to crawl home. At the gate he was met again by the porter, who had been diligently watching his parting from Yaroslav Ilyitch, and beckoning him from a distance. But the young man passed him by. At the door of his flat he ran full tilt against a little grey-headed figure coming out from Murin's room, looking on the ground.

"Lord forgive my transgressions!" whispered the figure, skipping on one side with the springiness of a cork.

"Did I hurt you?"

"No, I humbly thank you for your civility. . . . Oh, Lord, Lord!"

The meek little man, groaning and moaning and muttering something edifying to himself, went cautiously down the stairs. This was the "master" of the house, of whom the porter stood in such awe. Only then Ordynov remembered that he had seen him for the first time, here at Murin's, when he was moving into the lodging.

He felt unhinged and shaken; he knew that his imagination and impressionability were strained to the utmost pitch, and resolved not to trust himself. By degrees he sank into a sort of apathy. A heavy oppressive feeling weighed upon his chest. His heart ached as though it were sore all over, and his whole soul was full of dumb, comfortless tears.

He fell again upon the bed which she had made him, and began listening again. He heard two breathings: one the heavy broken breathing of a sick man, the other soft but uneven, as though also stirred by emotion, as though that heart was beating with the same yearning, with the same passion. At times he heard the rustle of her dress the faint stir of her soft light steps, and even that faint stir of her feet echoed with a vague but agonisingly sweet pang in his heart. At last he seemed to distinguish sobs, rebellious sighs, and at last, praying again. He knew that she was kneeling before the ikon, wringing her hands in a frenzy of despair! . . . Who was she? For whom was she praying? By what desperate passion was her heart torn? Why did it ache and grieve and pour itself out in such hot and hopeless tears?

He began to recall her words. All that she had said to him was still ringing in his ears like music, and his heart lovingly responded with a vague heavy throb at every recollection, every word of hers as he devoutly repeated it. . . . For an instant a thought flashed through his mind that he had dreamed all this. But at the same moment his whole being ached in swooning anguish as the impression of her hot breath, her words, her kiss rose vividly again in his imagination. He closed his eyes and sank into oblivion. A clock struck somewhere; it was getting late; twilight was falling.

It suddenly seemed to him that she was bending over him again, that she was looking into his eyes with her exquisitely clear eyes, wet with sparkling tears of serene, happy joy, soft and bright as the infinite turquoise vault of heaven at hot midday. Her face beamed with such triumphant peace; her smile was warm with such solemnity of infinite bliss; she leaned with such sympathy, with such childlike impulsiveness on his shoulder that a moan of joy broke from his exhausted bosom. She tried to tell him something, caressingly she confided something to him. Again it was as though heartrending music smote upon his hearing. Greedily he drank in the air, warm, electrified by her near breathing. In anguish he stretched out his arms, sighed, opened his eyes. . . . She stood before him, bending down to his face, all pale as from fear, all in tears, all quivering with emotion. She was saying something to him, entreating him with half-bare arms, clasping and wringing her hands; he folded her in his arms, she quivered on his bosom . . .

PART II

CHAPTER I

'WHAT is it? What is the matter with you?" said Ordynov, waking up completely, still pressing her in his strong, warm embrace. "What is the matter with you, Katerina? What is it, my love?"

She sobbed softly with downcast eyes, hiding her flushed face on his breast. For a long while she could not speak and kept trembling as though in terror.

"I don't know, I don't know," she said at last, in a hardly audible voice, gasping for breath, and scarcely able to articulate. "I don't know how I came here . . ." She clasped him even more tightly, with even more intensity, and in a violent irrepressible rush of feeling, kissed his shoulder, his hands, his chest; at last, as though in despair, she hid her face in her hands, fell on her knees, and buried her head in his knees. When Ordynov, in inexpressible anguish, lifted her up impatiently and made her sit down beside him, her whole face glowed with a full flush of shame, her weeping eyes sought forgiveness, and the smile that, in spite of herself, played on her lip could scarcely subdue the violence of her new feeling. Now she seemed again frightened, mistrustfully she pushed away his hand, and, with drooping head, answered his hurried questions in a fearful whisper.

"Perhaps you have had a terrible dream?" said Ordynov. "Perhaps you have seen some vision . . . Yes? Perhaps *he* has frightened you. . . . He is delirious and unconscious. Perhaps he has said something that was not for you to hear? Did you hear something? Yes?"

"No, I have not been asleep," answered Katerina, stifling her emotion with an effort. "Sleep did not come to me, he has been silent all the while and only once he called me. I went up, called his name, spoke to him; I was frightened; he did not wake and did not hear me. He is terribly sick; the Lord succour him! Then misery came upon my heart, bitter misery! I prayed and prayed and then this came upon me."

"Hush, Katerina, hush, my life, hush! You were frightened yesterday. . . ."

"No, I was not frightened yesterday! . . ."

"Has it ever been like this with you at other times?"

"Yes." And again she trembled all over and huddled up to him like a child. "You see," she said, repressing her sobs, "it was not for nothing that I have come to you, it was not for nothing that I could not bear to stay alone," she repeated, gratefully pressing his hands. "Enough, enough shedding tears over other people's sorrows! Save them for a dark day when you are lonely and cast down and there is no one with you! . . . Listen, have you ever had a love?"

"No. . . . I never knew a love before you. . . ."

"Before me? . . . You call me your love?"

She suddenly looked at him as though surprised, would have said something, but then was silent and looked down. By degrees her whole face suddenly flushed again a glowing crimson; her eyes shone more brightly through the forgotten tears still warm on her eyelashes, and it could be seen that some question was hovering on her lips. With bashful shyness she looked at him once or twice and then looked down again.

"No, it is not for me to be your first love," she said. "No, no," she said, shaking her head thoughtfully, while the smile stole gently again over her face. "No," she said, at last, laughing; "it's not for me, my own, to be your love."

At that point she glanced at him, but there was suddenly such sadness reflected in her face, such hopeless sorrow suddenly overshadowed all her features, such despair all at once surged up from within, from her heart, that Ordynov was overwhelmed by an unaccountable, painful feeling of compassion for her mysterious grief and looked at her with indescribable distress.

"Listen to what I say to you," she said in a voice that wrung his heart, pressing his hands in hers, struggling to stifle her sobs. "Heed me well, listen, my joy! You calm your heart and do not love me as you love me now. It will be better for you, your heart will be lighter and gladder, and you will guard yourself from a fell foe and will win a sister fond. I will come and see you as you please, fondle you and take no shame upon myself for making friends with you. I was with you for two days when you lay in that cruel sickness! Get to know your sister! It is not for nothing that we have sworn to be brother and sister, it is not for nothing that I prayed and wept to the Holy Mother for you! You won't get another sister! You may go all round the world, you may get to know the whole earth and not find another love like mine, if it is love your heart wants. I will love you warmly, I will always love you as I do now, and I will love you because your soul is pure and clean and can be seen through; because when first I glanced at you, at once I knew you were the guest of my house, the longed-for guest, and it was not for nothing that you wanted to come to us; I love you because when you look at me your eyes are full of love and speak for your heart, and when they say anything, at once I know of all that is within you and long to give my life for your love, my freedom, because it is sweet to be even a slave to the man whose heart I have found. . . . But my life is not mine but another's . . . and my freedom is bound! Take me for a sister and be a brother to me and take me to your heart when misery, when cruel weakness falls upon me; only do so that I have no shame to come to you and sit through the long night with you as now.

Do you hear me? Is your heart opened to me? Do you understand what I have been saying to you? . . ."

She tried to say something more, glanced at him, laid her hand on his shoulder and at last sank helpless on his bosom. Her voice died away in convulsive, passionate sobbing, her bosom heaved, and her face flushed like an evening sunset.

"My life," whispered Ordynov; everything was dark before his eyes and he could hardly breathe. "My joy," he said, not knowing what he was saying, not understanding himself, trembling lest a breath should break the spell, should destroy everything that was happening, which he took rather for a vision than reality: so misty was everything around him! "I don't know, I don't understand you, I don't remember what you have just said to me, my mind is darkened, my heart aches, my queen!"

At this point his voice broke with emotion. She clung more tightly, more warmly, more fervently to him. He got up, no longer able to restrain himself; shattered, exhausted by ecstasy, he fell on his knees. Convulsive sobs broke agonisingly from his breast at last, and the voice that came straight from his heart quivered like a harp-string, from the fulness of unfathomable ecstasy and bliss.

"Who are you, who are you, my own? Where do you come from, my darling?" he said, trying to stifle his sobs. "From what heaven did you fly into my sphere? It's like a dream about me, I cannot believe in you. Don't check me, let me speak, let me tell you all, all! I have long wanted to speak . . . Who are you, who are you, my joy? How did you find my heart? Tell me; have you long been my sister? . . . Tell me everything about yourself, where you have been till now. Tell me what the place was called where you lived; what did you love there at first? what rejoiced you? what grieved you? . . . Was the air warm? was the sky clear? . . . Who were dear to you? who loved you before me? to whom did your soul yearn first? . . . Had you a mother? did she pet you as a child, or did you look round upon life as solitary as I did? Tell me, were you always like this? What were your dreams? what were your visions of the future? what was fulfilled and what was unfulfilled with you?—tell me everything. . . . For whom did your maiden heart yearn first, and for what did you give it? Tell me, what must I give you for it? what must I give you for yourself? . . . Tell me, my darling, my light, my sister; tell me, how am I to win your heart? . . ."

Then his voice broke again, and he bowed his head. But when he raised his eyes, dumb horror froze his heart and the hair stood up on his head.

Katerina was sitting pale as a sheet. She was looking with a fixed stare into the air, her lips were blue as a corpse's and her eyes were dimmed by a mute, agonising woe. She stood up slowly, took two steps forward and, with a piercing wail, flung herself down before the ikon. . . . Jerky, incoherent words broke from her throat. She lost consciousness. Shaken with horror Ordynov lifted her up and carried her to his bed; he stood over her, frantic. A minute later she opened her eyes, sat up in the bed, looked about her and seized his hand. She drew him towards her, tried to whisper something with her lips that were still pale, but her voice would not obey her. At last she burst into a flood of tears; the hot drops scalded Ordynov's chilly hand.

"It's hard for me, it's hard for me now; my last hour is at hand!" she said at last in desperate anguish.

She tried to say something else, but her faltering tongue could not utter a word. She looked in despair at Ordynov, who did not understand her. He bent closer to her and listened. . . . At last he heard her whisper distinctly:

"I am corrupted—they have corrupted me, they have ruined me!"

Ordynov lifted his head and looked at her in wild amazement. Some hideous thought flashed across his mind. Katerina saw the convulsive workings of his face.

"Yes! Corrupted," she went on; "a wicked man corrupted me. It is *he* who has ruined me! . . . I have sold my soul to him. Why, why did you speak of my mother? Why did you want to torture me? God, God be your judge! . . ."

A minute later she was softly weeping; Ordynov's heart was beating and aching in mortal anguish.

"He says," she whispered in a restrained, mysterious voice, "that when he dies he will come and fetch my sinful soul. . . . I am his, I have sold my soul to him. He tortures me, he reads to me in his books. Here, look at his book! here is his book. He says I have committed the unpardonable sin. Look, look . . ."

And she showed him a book. Ordynov did not notice where it had come from. He took it mechanically—it was all in manuscript like the old heretical books which he had happened to see before, but now he was incapable of looking or concentrating

283   K

his attention on anything else. The book fell out of his hands. He softly embraced Katerina, trying to bring her to reason. "Hush, hush," he said; "they have frightened you. I am with you; rest with me, my own, my love, my light."

"You know nothing, nothing," she said, warmly pressing his hand. "I am always like this! I am always afraid. . . . I've tortured you enough, enough! . . ."

"I go to him then," she began a minute later, taking a breath; "sometimes he simply comforts me with his words, sometimes he takes his book, the biggest, and reads it over me —he always reads such grim, threatening things! I don't know what, and don't understand every word; but fear comes upon me; and when I listen to his voice, it is as though it were not he speaking, but someone else, someone evil, someone you could not soften anyhow, could not entreat, and one's heart grows so heavy and burns. . . . Heavier than when this misery comes upon me!"

"Don't go to him. Why do you go to him?" said Ordynov, hardly conscious of his own words.

"Why have I come to you? If you ask—I don't know either. . . . But he keeps saying to me, 'Pray, pray!' Sometimes I get up in the dark night and for a long time, for hours together, I pray; sometimes sleep overtakes me, but fear always wakes me, always wakes me and then I always fancy that a storm is gathering round me, that harm is coming to me, that evil things will tear me to pieces and torment me, that my prayers will not reach the saints, and that they will not save me from cruel grief. My soul is being torn, my whole body seems breaking to pieces through crying. . . . Then I begin praying again, and pray and pray until the Holy Mother looks down on me from the ikon, more lovingly. Then I get up and go away to sleep, utterly shattered; sometimes I wake up on the floor, on my knees before the ikon. Then sometimes he wakes, calls me, begins to soothe me, caress me, comfort me, and then I feel better, and if any trouble comes I am not afraid with him. He is powerful! His word is mighty!"

"But what trouble, what sort of trouble have you?" . . . And Ordynov wrung his hands in despair.

Katerina turned fearfully pale. She looked at him like one condemned to death, without hope of pardon.

"Me? I am under a curse, I'm a murderess; my mother cursed me! I was the ruin of my own mother! . . ."

Ordynov embraced her without a word. She nestled

tremulously to him. He felt a convulsive shiver pass all over
her, and it semed as though her soul were parting from her
body.

"I hid her in the damp earth," she said, overwhelmed by the
horror of her recollections, and lost in visions of her irrevocable
past. "I have long wanted to tell it; he always forbade me
with supplications, upbraidings, and angry words, and at times
he himself will arouse all my anguish at though he were my
enemy and adversary. At night, even as now—it all comes
into my mind. Listen, listen! It was long ago, very long ago,
I don't remember when, but it is all before me as though it had
been yesterday, like a dream of yesterday, devouring my heart
all night. Misery makes the time twice as long. Sit here, sit
here beside me; I will tell you all my sorrow; may I be struck
down, accursed as I am, by a mother's curse. . . . I am
putting my life into your hands . . ."

Ordynov tried to stop her, but she folded her hands, beseeching his love to attend, and then, with even greater agitation
began to speak. Her story was incoherent, the turmoil of her
spirit could be felt in her words, but Ordynov understood it
all, because her life had become his life, her grief his grief, and
because her foe stood visible before him, taking shape and
growing up before him with every word she uttered and, as
it were, with inexhaustible strength crushing his heart and
cursing him malignantly. His blood was in a turmoil, it flooded
his heart and obscured his reason. The wicked old man of
his dream (Ordynov believed this) was living before him.

"Well, it was a night like this," Katerina began, "only
stormier, and the wind in our forest howled as I had never
heard it before . . . it was in that night that my ruin began!
An oak was broken before our window, and an old grey-headed
beggar came to our door, and he said that he remembered that
oak as a little child, and that it was the same then as when the
wind blew it down. . . . That night—as I remember now—my
father's barge was wrecked on the river by a storm, and though
he was afflicted with illness, he drove to the place as soon as the
fishermen ran to us at the factory. Mother and I were sitting
alone. I was asleep. She was sad about something and weeping
bitterly . . . and I knew what about! She had just been ill,
she was still pale and kept telling me to get ready her shroud.
. . . Suddenly, at midnight, we heard a knock at the gate; I
jumped up, the blood rushed to my heart; mother cried out.
. . . I did not look at her, I was afraid. I took a lantern and

285   K*

went myself to open the gate. . . . It was *he!* I felt frightened, because I was always frightened when he came, and it was so with me from childhood ever since I remembered anything! At that time he had not white hair; his beard was black as pitch, his eyes burnt like coals; until that time he had never once looked at me kindly. He asked me, 'Is your mother at home?' Shutting the little gate, I answered that 'Father was not at home.' He said, 'I know,' and suddenly looked at me, looked at me in such a way . . . it was the first time he had looked at me like that. I went on, but he still stood. 'Why don't you come in?' 'I am thinking.' By then we were going up to the room. 'Why did you say that father was not at home when I asked you whether mother was at home?' I said nothing. . . . Mother was terror-stricken—she rushed to him. . . . He scarcely glanced at her. I saw it all. He was all wet and shivering; the storm had driven him fifteen miles, but whence he came and where he lived neither mother nor I ever knew; we had not seen him for nine weeks. . . . He threw down his cap, pulled off his gloves—did not pray to the ikon, nor bow to his hostess—he sat down by the fire . . ."

Katerina passed her hand over her face, as though something were weighing upon her and oppressing her, but a minute later she raised her head and began again:

"He began talking in Tatar to mother. Mother knew it, I don't understand a word. Other times when he came, they sent me away; but this time mother dared not say a word to her own child. The unclean spirit gained possession of my soul and I looked at my mother, exalting myself in my heart. I saw they were looking at me, they were talking about me; she began crying. I saw him clutch at his knife and more than once of late I had seen him clutch at the knife when he was talking with mother. I jumped up and caught at his belt, tried to tear the evil knife away from him. He clenched his teeth, cried out and tried to beat me back; he struck me in the breast but did not shake me off. I thought I should die on the spot, there was a mist before my eyes. I fell on the floor, but did not cry out. Though I could hardly see, I saw him. He took off his belt, tucked up his sleeve, with the hand with which he had struck me took out the knife and gave it to me. 'Here, cut it away, amuse yourself over it, even as I insulted you, while I, proud girl, will bow down to the earth to you for it.' I laid aside the knife; the blood began to stifle me, I did not look at him. I remember I laughed without opening my lips and looked threateningly straight into mother's mournful eyes, and the shameless laugh never left my lips, while mother sat pale, deathlike . . ."

With strained attention Ordynov listened to her incoherent story. By degrees her agitation subsided after the first outburst; her words grew calmer. The poor creature was completely carried away by her memories and her misery was spread over their limitless expanse.

"He took his cap without bowing. I took the lantern again to see him out instead of mother, who, though she was ill, would have followed him. We reached the gates. I opened the little gate to him, drove away the dogs in silence. I see him take off his cap and bow to me, I see him feel in his bosom, take out a red morocco box, open the catch. I look in—big pearls, an offering to me. 'I have a beauty,' says he, 'in the town. I got it to offer to her, but I did not take it to her; take it, fair maiden, cherish your beauty; take them, though you crush them under foot.' I took them, but I did not want to stamp on them, I did not want to do them too much honour, but I took them like a viper, not saying a word. I came in and set them on the table before mother—it was for that I took them. Mother was silent for a minute, all white as a handkerchief. She speaks to me as though she fears me. 'What is this, Katya?' and I answer, 'The merchant brought them for you, my own—I know nothing.' I see the tears stream from her eyes. I see her gasp for breath. 'Not for me, Katya, not for me, wicked daughter, not for me.' I remember she said it so bitterly, so bitterly, as though she were weeping out her whole soul. I raised my eyes, I wanted to throw myself at her feet, but suddenly the evil one prompted me. 'Well, if not to you, most likely to father; I will give them to him when he comes back; I will say the merchants have been, they have forgotten their wares . . .' Then how she wept, my own. . . . 'I will tell him myself what merchants have been, and for what wares they came. . . . I will tell him whose daughter you are, whose bastard child! You are not my daughter now, you serpent's fry! You are my accursed child!' I say nothing, tears do not come me to me. . . . I went up to my room and all night I listened to the storm, while I fitted my thoughts to its raging.

"Meanwhile, five days passed by. Towards evening after five days, father came in, surly and menacing, and he had been stricken by illness on the way. I saw his arm was bound up,

I guessed that his enemy had waylaid him upon the road, his enemy had worn him out and brought sickness upon him. I knew, too, who was his enemy, I knew it all. He did not say a word to mother, he did not ask about me. He called together all the workmen, made them leave the factory, and guard the house from the evil eye. I felt in my heart, in that hour, that all was not well with the house. We waited, the night came, another stormy, snowy one, and dread came over my soul. I opened the window; my face was hot, my eyes were weeping, my restless heart was burning; I was on fire. I longed to be away from that room, far away to the land of light, where the thunder and lightning are born. My maiden heart was beating and beating. . . . Suddenly, in the dead of night, I was dozing, or a mist had fallen over my soul, and confounded it all of a sudden—I hear a knock at the window: 'Open!' I look, there was a man at the window, he had climbed up by a rope. I knew at once who the visitor was, I opened the window and let him into my lonely room. It was *he!* Without taking off his hat, he sat down on the bench, he panted and drew his breath as though he had been pursued. I stood in the corner and knew myself that I turned white all over. 'Is your father at home?' 'He is.' 'And your mother?' 'Mother is at home, too.' 'Be silent now; do you hear?' 'I hear.' 'What?' 'A whistle under the window!' 'Well, fair maid, do you want to cut your foe's head off? Call your father, take my life? I am at your maiden mercy; here is the cord, tie it, if your heart bids you; avenge yourself for your insult.' I am silent. 'Well? Speak, my joy.' 'What do you want?' 'I want my enemy to be gone, to take leave for good and all of the old love, and to lay my heart at the feet of a new one, a fair maid like you. . . .' I laughed; and I don't know how his evil words went to my heart. 'Let me, fair maid, walk downstairs, test my courage, pay homage to my hosts.' I trembled all over, my teeth knocked together, but my heart was like a red-hot iron. I went. I opened the door to him, I let him into the house, only on the threshold with an effort I brought out, 'Here, take your pearls and never give me a gift again,' and I threw the box after him.''

Here Katerina stopped to take breath. At one moment she was pale and trembling like a leaf, at the next the blood rushed to her head, and now, when she stopped, her cheeks glowed with fire, her eyes flashed through her tears, and her bosom heaved with her laboured, uneven breathing. But suddenly she

,turned pale again and her voice sank with a mournful and tremulous quiver.

"Then I was left alone and the storm seemed to wrap me about. All at once I hear a shout, I hear workmen run across the yard to the factory, I hear them say, 'The factory is on fire.' I kept in hiding; all ran out of the house; I was left with mother; I knew that she was parting from life, that she had been lying for the last three days on her death-bed. I knew it, accursed daughter! . . . All at once a cry under my room, a faint cry like a child when it is frightened in its sleep, and then all was silent. I blew out the candle, I was as chill as ice, I hid my face in my hands, I was afraid to look. Suddenly I hear a shout close by, I hear the men running from the factory. I hung out of the window, I see them bearing my dead father, I hear them saying among themselves, 'He stumbled, he fell down the stairs into a red-hot cauldron; so the devil must have pushed him down.' I fell upon my bed; I waited, all numb with terror, and I do not know for whom or what I waited, only I was overwhelmed with woe in that hour. I don't remember how long I waited; I remember that suddenly everything began rocking, my head grew heavy, my eyes were smarting with smoke and I was glad that my end was near. Suddenly I felt someone lift me by the shoulders. I looked as best I could; he was singed all over and his kaftan, hot to the touch, was smoking.

" 'I've come for you, fair maid; lead me away from trouble as before you led me into trouble; I have lost my soul for your sake, no prayers of mine can undo this accursed night! Maybe we will pray together!' He laughed, the wicked man. 'Show me,' said he, 'how to get out without passing people!' I took his hand and led him after me. We went through the corridor—the keys were with me—I opened the door to the store-room and pointed to the window. The window looked into the garden, he seized me in his powerful arms, embraced me and leapt with me out of the window. We ran together, hand-in-hand, we ran together for a long time. We looked, we were in a thick, dark forest. He began listening: 'There's a chase after us, Katya! There's a chase after us, fair maid, but it is not for us in this hour to lay down our lives! Kiss me, fair maid, for love and everlasting happiness!' 'Why are your hands covered with blood?' 'My hands covered with blood, my own? I stabbed your dogs; they barked too loud at a late guest. Come along!'

"We ran on again; we saw in the path my father's horse, he had broken his bridle and run out of the stable; so he did not want to be burnt. 'Get on it, Katya, with me; God has sent us help.' I was silent. 'Won't you? I am not a heathen, not an unclean pagan; here, I will cross myself if you like,' and here he made the sign of the cross. I got on the horse, huddled up to him and forgot everything on his bosom, as though a dream had come over me, and when I woke I saw that we were standing by a broad, broad river. He got off the horse, lifted me down and went off to the reeds where his boat was hidden. We were getting in. 'Well, farewell, good horse; go to a new master, the old masters all forsake you!' I ran to father's horse and embraced him warmly at parting. Then we got in, he took the oars and in an instant we lost sight of the shore. And when we could not see the shore, I saw him lay down the oars and look about him, all over the water.

" 'Hail,' he said, 'stormy river-mother, who giveth drink to God's people and food to me! Say, hast thou guarded my goods, are my wares safe, while I've been away?' I sat mute, I cast down my eyes to my bosom; my face burned with shame as with a flame. And he: 'Thou art welcome to take all, stormy and insatiable river, only let me keep my vow and cherish my priceless pearl! Drop but one word, fair maid, send a ray of sunshine into the storm, scatter the dark night with light!'

"He laughed as he spoke, his heart was burning for me, but I could not bear his jeers for shame; I longed to say a word, but was afraid and sat dumb. 'Well, then, be it so!' he answered to my timid tnought; he spoke as though in sorrow, as though grief had come upon him, too. 'So one can take nothing by force. God be with you, you proud one, my dove, my fair maid! It seems, strong is your hatred for me, or I do not find favour in your clear eyes!' I listened and was seized by spite, seized by spite and love; I steeled my heart. I said: 'Pleasing or not pleasing you came to me; it is not for me to know that, but for another senseless, shameless girl who shamed her maiden room in the dark night, who sold her soul for mortal sin and could not school her frantic heart; and for my sorrowing tears to know it, and for him who, like a thief, brags of another's woe and jeers at a maiden's heart!' I said it, and I could bear no more. I wept. . . . He said nothing; looked at me so that I trembled like a leaf. 'Listen to me,' said he, 'fair maid,' and his eyes burned strangely. 'It is not a vain word I say, I make you a solemn vow. As much happiness as you give me, so much will I be a gentleman, and if ever you do not love me—do not speak, do not drop a word, do not trouble, but stir only your sable eyebrow, turn your black eye, stir only your little finger and I will give you back your love with golden freedom; only, my proud, haughty beauty, then there will be an end to my life too.' And then all my flesh laughed at his words. . . .

At this point Katerina's story was interrupted by deep emotion; she took breath, smiled at her new fancy and would have gone on, but suddenly her sparkling eyes met Ordynov's feverish gaze fixed on her. She started, would have said something, but the blood flooded her face. . . . She hid her face in her hands and fell upon the pillow at though in a swoon. Ordynov was quivering all over! An agonising feeling, an unbearable, unaccountable agitation ran like poison through all his veins and grew with every word of Katerina's story; a hopeless yearning, a greedy and unendurable passion took possession of his imagination and troubled his feelings, but at the same time his heart was more and more oppressed by bitter, infinite sadness. At moments he longed to shriek to Katerina to be silent, longed to fling himself at her feet and beseech her by his tears to give him back his former agonies of love, his former pure, unquestioning yearning, and he regretted the tears that had long dried on his cheeks. There was an ache at his heart which was painfully oppressed by fever and could not give his tortured soul the relief of tears. He did not understand what Katerina was telling him, and his love was frightened of the feeling that excited the poor woman. He cursed his passion at that moment; it smothered him, it exhausted him, and he felt as though molten lead were running in his veins instead of blood.

"Ach, that is not my grief," said Katerina, suddenly raising her head. "What I have told you just now is not my sorrow," she went on in a voice that rang like copper from a sudden new feeling, while her heart was rent with secret, unshed tears. "That is not my grief, that is not my anguish, not my woe! What, what do I care for my mother, though I shall never have another mother in this world! What do I care that she cursed me in her last terrible hour? What do I care for my old golden life, for my warm room, for my maiden freedom? What do I care that I have sold myself to the evil one and abandoned my soul to the destroyer, that for the sake of happiness I have committed the unpardonable sin? Ach, that is not my grief, though in that great is my ruin! But what is bitter to me and rends my heart is that I am his shameless slave, that my shame and disgrace are dear to me, shameless as I am, but it is dear to my greedy heart to remember my sorrow as though it were joy and happiness; that is my grief, that there is no strength in it and no anger for my wrongs! . . ."

The poor creature gasped for breath and a convulsive, hysterical sob cut short her words, her hot, laboured breath burned her lips, her bosom heaved and sank and her eyes flashed with incomprehensible indignation. But her face was radiant with such fascination at that moment, every line, every muscle quivered with such a passionate flood of feeling, such insufferable, incredible beauty that Ordynov's black thoughts died away at once and the pure sadness in his soul was silenced. And his heart burned to be pressed to her heart and to be lost with it in frenzied emotion, to throb in harmony with the same storm, the same rush of infinite passion, and even to swoon with it. Katerina met Ordynov's troubled eyes and smiled so that his heart burned with redoubled fire. He scarcely knew what he was doing.

"Spare me, have pity on me," he whispered, controlling his trembling voice, bending down to her, leaning with his hand on her shoulder and looking close in her eyes, so close that their breathing was mingled in one. "You are killing me. I do not know your sorrow and my soul is troubled. . . . What is it to me what your heart is weeping over! Tell me what you want— I will do it. Come with me, let me go; do not kill me, do not murder me! . . ."

Katerina looked at him immovably, the tears dried on her burning cheek. She wanted to interrupt him, to take his hand, tried to say something, but could not find the words. A strange smile came upon her lips, as though laughter were breaking through that smile.

"I have not told you all, then," she said at last in a broken voice; "only will you hear me, will you hear me, hot heart? Listen to your sister. You have learned little of her bitter grief. I would have told you how I lived a year with him, but I will not. . . . A year passed, he went away with his comrades down the river, and I was left with one he called his mother to wait for him in the harbour. I waited for him one month, two, and I met a young merchant, and I glanced at him and thought of my golden years gone by. 'Sister, darling,' said he, when he had spoken two words to me, 'I am Alyosha, your destined betrothed; the old folks betrothed us as children; you have forgotten me—think, I am from your parts.' 'And what do they say of me in your parts?' 'Folk's gossip says that you behaved dishonourably, forgot your maiden modesty, made friends with a brigand, a murderer,' Alyosha said, laughing. 'And what did you say of me?' 'I meant to say many things when I came here'—and his heart was troubled. 'I meant to say many things, but now that I have seen you my heart is dead within me, you have slain me,' he said. 'Buy my soul, too, take it, though you mock at my heart and my love, fair maiden. I am an orphan now, my own master, and my soul is my own, not another's. I have not sold it to anyone, like somebody who has blotted out her memory; it's not enough to buy the heart, I give it for nothing, and it is clear it is a good bargain.' I laughed, and more than once, more than twice he talked to me; a whole month he lived on the place, gave up his merchandise, forsook his people and was all alone. I was sorry for his lonely tears. So I said to him one morning, "Wait for me, Alyosha, lower down the harbour, as night comes on; I will go with you to your home, I am weary of my life, forlorn.' So night came on, I tied up a bundle and my soul ached and worked within me. Behold, my master walks in without a word or warning. 'Good-day, let us go, there will be a storm on the river and the time will not wait.' I followed him; we came to the river and it was far to reach his mates. We look: a boat and one we knew rowing in it as though waiting for someone. 'Good-day, Alyosha; God be your help. Why, are you belated at the harbour, are you in haste to meet your vessels? Row me, good man, with the mistress, to our mates, to our place. I have let my boat go and I don't know how to swim.' 'Get in,' said Alyosha, and my whole soul swooned when I heard his voice. 'Get in with the mistress, too, the wind is for all, and in my bower there will be room for you, too.' We got in; it was a dark night, the stars were in hiding, the wind howled, the waves rose high and we rowed out a mile from shore—all three were silent.

" 'It's a storm,' said my master, 'and it is a storm that bodes no good! I have never seen such a storm on the river in my life as is raging now! It is too much for our boat, it will not bear three!' 'No, it will not,' answered Alyosha, 'and one of us, it seems, turns out to be one too many,' he says, and his voice quivers like a harp-string. 'Well, Alyosha, I knew you as a little child, your father was my mate, we ate at each other's boards—tell me, Alyosha, can you reach the shore without the boat or will you perish for nothing, will you lose your life?' 'I cannot reach it. And you, too, good man, if it is your luck to have a drink of water, will you reach the shore or not?' 'I cannot reach it, it is the end for my soul. I cannot hold out against the stormy river! Listen, Katerina, my precious pearl! I remember such a night, but the waves were not tossing, the stars were shining, and the moon was bright. . . . I simply want to ask you, have you forgotten?' 'I remember,' said I. 'Well, since you have not forgotten it, well, you have not forgotten the compact when a bold man told a fair maiden to take back her freedom from one unloved—eh?' 'No, I have not forgotten that either,' I said, more dead than alive. 'Ah, you have not forgotten! Well, now we are in hard case in the boat. Has not his hour come for one of us? Tell me, my own, tell me, my dove, coo to us like a dove your tender word . . .'"

"I did not say my word then," whispered Katerina, turning pale. . . .

"Katerina!" A hoarse, hollow voice resounded above them. Ordynov started. In the doorway stood Murin. He was barely covered with a fur rug, pale as death, and he was gazing at them with almost senseless eyes. Katerina turned paler and paler and she, too, gazed fixedly at him, as though spellbound.

"Come to me, Katerina," whispered the sick man, in a voice hardly audible, and went out of the room. Katerina still gazed fixedly into the air, as though the old man had still been standing before her. But suddenly the blood rushed glowing into her pale cheek and she slowly got up from the bed. Ordynov remembered their first meeting.

"Till to-morrow then, my tears!" she said, laughing strangely; "till to-morrow! Remember at what point I stopped: 'Choose between the two; which is dear or not dear to you, fair maid!' Will you remember, will you wait for one night?" she repeated, laying her hand on his shoulder and looking at him tenderly.

"Katerina, do not go, do not go to your ruin! He is mad," whispered Ordynov, trembling for her.

"Katerina!" he heard through the partition.

"What? Will he murder me? no fear!" Katerina answered, laughing: "Good-night to you, my precious heart, my warm dove, my brother!" she said, tenderly pressing his head to her bosom, while tears bedewed her face. "Those are my last tears.

Sleep away your sorrow, my darling, wake to-morrow to joy."
And she kissed him passionately.

"Katerina, Katerina!" whispered Ordynov, falling on his
knees before her and trying to stop her. "Katerina!"

She turned round, nodded to him, smiling, and went out of
the room. Ordynov heard her go in to Murin; he held his
breath, listening, but heard not a sound more. The old man
was silent or perhaps unconscious again. . . . He would have
gone in to her there, but his legs staggered under him. . . .
He sank exhausted on the bed. . . .

CHAPTER II

FOR a long while he could not find out what the time was
when he woke. Whether it was the twilight of dawn or of
evening, it was still dark in his room. He could not decide how
long he had slept, but felt that his sleep was not healthy sleep.
Coming to himself, he passed his hand over his face as though
shaking off sleep and the visions of the night. But when he tried
to step on the floor he felt as though his whole body were shattered, and his exhausted limbs refused to obey him. His head
ached and was going round, and he was alternately shivering
and feverish. Memory returned with consciousness and his heart
quivered when in one instant he lived through, in memory, the
whole of the past night. His heart beat as violently in response
to his thoughts, his sensations were as burning, as fresh, as
though not a night, not long hours, but one minute had passed
since Katerina had gone away. He felt as though his eyes were
still wet with tears—or were they new, fresh tears that rushed
like a spring from his burning soul? And, strange to say, his
agonies were even sweet to him, though he dimly felt all over
that he could not endure such violence of feeling again. There
was a moment when he was almost conscious of death, and was
ready to meet it as a welcome guest; his sensations were so over-
strained, his passion surged up with such violence on waking,
such ecstasy took possession of his soul that life, quickened by
its intensity, seemed on the point of breaking, of being shattered, of flickering out in one minute and being quenched for
ever. Almost at that instant, as though in answer to his anguish,
in answer to his quivering heart, the familiar mellow, silvery
voice of Katerina rang out—like that inner music known to

man's soul in hours of joy, in hours of tranquil happiness. Close beside him, almost over his pillow, began a song, at first soft and melancholy . . . her voice rose and fell, dying away abruptly as though hiding in itself, and tenderly crooning over its anguish of unsatisfied, smothered desire hopelessly concealed in the grieving heart; then again it flowed into a nightingale's trills and, quivering and glowing with unrestrained passion, melted into a perfect sea of ecstasy, a sea of mighty, boundless sound, like the first moment of the bliss of love.

Ordynov distinguished the words, too. They were simple, sincere, composed long ago with direct, calm, pure, clear feeling, but he forgot them, he heard only the sounds. Through the simple, naïve verses of the song flashed other words resounding with all the yearning that filled his bosom, responding to the most secret subtleties of his passion, which he could not comprehend though they echoed to him clearly with full consciousness of it. And at one moment he heard the last moan of a heart swooning helplessly in passion, then he heard the joy of a will and a spirit breaking its chains and rushing brightly and freely into the boundless ocean of unfettered love. Then he heard the first vow of the beloved, with fragrant shame at the first blush on her face, with prayers, with tears, with mysterious timid murmuring; then the passion of the Bacchante, proud and rejoicing in its strength, unveiled, undisguised, turning her drunken eyes about her with a ringing laugh . . .

Ordynov could not endure the end of the song, and he got up from the bed. The song at once died away.

"Good-morning and good-day are over, my beloved," Katerina's voice rang out, "Good-evening to you; get up, come in to us, wake up to bright joy; we expect you. I and the master, both good people, your willing servants, quench hatred with love, if your heart is still resentful. Say a friendly word!" . . .

Ordynov had already gone out of his room at her first call and scarcely realised that he was going into the landlord's bedroom. The door opened before him and, bright as sunshine, the golden smile of his strange landlady flashed upon him. At that instant, he saw, he heard no one but her. In one moment his whole life, his whole joy, melted into one thing in his heart —the bright image of his Katerina.

"Two dawns have passed," she said, giving him her hands, "since we said farewell; the second is dying now—look out of the window. Like the two dawns in the soul of a maiden,"

Katerina added, laughing. "The one that flushes her face with its first shame, when first her lonely maiden heart speaks in her bosom, while the other, when a maiden forgets her first shame, glows like fire, stifles her maiden heart, and drives the red blood to her face. . . . Come, come into our home, good young man! Why do you stand in the doorway? Honour and love to you, and a greeting from the master!"

With a laugh ringing like music, she took Ordynov's hand and led him into the room. His heart was overwhelmed with timidity. All the fever, all the fire raging in his bosom was quenched and died down in one instant, and for one instant he dropped his eyes in confusion and was afraid to look at her. He felt that she was so marvellously beautiful that his heart could not endure her burning eyes. He had never seen his Katerina like this. For the first time laughter and gaiety were sparkling on her face, and drying the mournful tears on her black eyelashes. His hand trembled in her hand. And if he had raised his eyes he would have seen that Katerina, with a triumphant smile, had fastened her clear eyes on his face, which was clouded with confusion and passion.

"Get up, old man," she said at last, as though waking up; "say a word of welcome to our guest, a guest who is like a brother! Get up, you proud, unbending old man; get up, now, take your guest by his white hand and make him sit down to the table."

Ordynov raised his eyes and seemed only then to come to himself. Only then he thought of Murin. The old man's eyes, looking as though dimmed by the approach of death, were staring at him fixedly; and with a pang in his heart he remembered those eyes glittering at him last time from black overhanging brows contracted as now with pain and anger. There was a slight dizziness in his head. He looked round him and only then realised everything clearly and distinctly. Murin was still lying on the bed, but he was partly dressed and had already been up and out that morning. As before, he had a red kerchief tied round his neck, he had slippers on his feet. His attack was evidently over, only his face was terribly pale and yellow. Katerina was standing by his bed, her hand leaning on the table, watching them both intently. But the smile of welcome did not leave her face. It seemed as though everything had been done at a sign from her.

"Yes! it's you," said Murin, raising himself up and sitting on the bed. "You are my lodger. I must beg your pardon, sir;

I have sinned and wronged you all unknowingly, playing tricks with my gun the other day. Who could tell that you, too, were stricken by grievous sickness? It happens to me at times," he added in a hoarse, ailing voice, frowning and unconsciously looking away from Ordynov. "My trouble comes upon me like a thief in the night without knocking at the gate! I almost thrust a knife into her bosom the other day . . ." he brought out, nodding towards Katerina. "I am ill, a fit comes, seizes me—well, that's enough. Sit down—you will be our guest."

Ordynov was still staring at him intently.

"Sit down, sit down!" the old man shouted impatiently; "sit down, if that will please her! So you are brother and sister, born of the same mother! You are as fond of one another as lovers!"

Ordynov sat down.

"You see what a fine sister you've got," the old man went on, laughing, and he showed two rows of white, perfectly sound teeth. "Be fond of one another, my dears. Is your sister beautiful, sir? Tell me, answer! Come, look how her cheeks are burning; come, look round, sing the praises of her beauty to all the world, show that your heart is aching for her."

Ordynov frowned and looked angrily at the old man, who flinched under his eyes. A blind fury surged up in Ordynov's heart. By some animal instinct he felt near him a mortal foe. He could not understand what was happening to him, his reason refused to serve him.

"Don't look," said a voice behind him.

Ordynov looked round.

"Don't look, don't look, I tell you, if the devil is tempting you; have pity on your love," said Katerina, laughing, and suddenly from behind she covered his eyes with her hands; then at once took away her hands and hid her own face in them. But the colour in her face seemed to show through her fingers. She removed her hands and, still glowing like fire, tried to meet their laughter and inquisitive eyes brightly and without a tremor. But both looked at her in silence—Ordynov with the stupefaction of love, as though it were the first time such terrible beauty had stabbed his heart; the old man coldly and attentively. Nothing was to be seen in his pale face, except that his lips turned blue and quivered faintly.

Katerina went up to the old man, no longer laughing, and began clearing away the books, papers, inkstand, everything that was on the table and putting them all on the window-sill.

Her breathing was hurried and uneven, and from time to time she drew an eager breath as though her heart were oppressed. Her full bosom heaved and fell like a wave on the seashore. She dropped her eyes and her pitchblack eyelashes gleamed on her bright cheeks like sharp needles. . . .

"A maiden queen," said the old man.

"My sovereign!" whispered Ordynov, quivering all over. He came to his senses, feeling the old man's eyes upon him— his glance flashed upon him for an instant like lightning— greedily spiteful, coldly contemptuous. Ordynov would have got up from his seat but some unseen power seemed to fetter his legs. He sat down again. At times he pinched his hand as though not believing in reality. He felt as though he were being strangled by a nightmare, and as though his eyes were still closed in a miserable feverish sleep. But, strange to say, he did not want to wake up!

Katerina took the old cloth off the table, then opened a chest, took out of it a sumptuous cloth embroidered in gold and bright silks and put it on the table; then she took out of the cupboard an old-fashioned ancestral-looking casket, set it in the middle of the table and took out of it three silver goblets— one for the master, one for the visitor, and one for herself; then with a grave, almost pensive air, she looked at the old man and at the visitor.

"Is one of us dear to someone, or not dear," she said. "If anyone is not dear to someone he is dear to me, and shall drink my goblet with me. Each of you is dear to me as my own brother: so let us all drink to love and concord."

"Drink and drown dark fancies in the wine," said the old man, in a changed voice. "Pour it out, Katerina."

"Do you bid me pour?" asked Katerina, looking at Ordynov.

Ordynov held out his goblet in silence.

"Stay! If one has a secret and a fancy, may his wishes come true!" said the old man, raising his goblet.

All clinked their goblets and drank.

"Let me drink now with you, old man," said Katerina, turning to the landlord. "Let us drink if your heart is kindly to me! Let us drink to past happiness, let us send a greeting to the years we have spent, let us celebrate our happiness with heart and with love. Bid me fill your goblet if your heart is warm to me."

"Your wine is strong, my love, but you scarcely wet your

lips!'' said the old man, laughing and holding out his goblet again.

"Well, I will sip it, but you drink it to the bottom . . . why live, old man, brooding on gloomy thoughts; gloomy thoughts only make the heart ache! Thought calls for sorrow; with happiness one can live without thinking; drink, old man,'' she went on; "drown your thoughts.''

"A great deal of sorrow must have fermented within you, since you arm yourself against it like this! So you want to make an end of it all at once, my white dove. I drink with you, Katya! And have you a sorrow, sir, if you allow me to ask?''

"If I have, I keep it to myself,'' muttered Ordynov, keeping his eyes fixed on Katerina.

"Do you hear, old man? For a long while I did not know myself, did not remember; but the time came, I remembered all and recalled it; all that has passed I have passed through again in my unsatisfied soul.''

"Yes, it is grievous if one begins looking into the past only,'' said the old man dreamily. "What is past is like wine that is drunk! What happiness is there in the past? The coat is worn out, and away with it.''

"One must get a new one,'' Katerina chimed in with a strained laugh, while two big tears like diamonds hung on her eyelashes. "One cannot live down a lifetime in one minute, and a girl's heart is eager for life—there is no keeping pace with it. Do you understand, old man? Look. I have buried my tear in your goblet.''

"And did you buy much happiness with your sorrow?'' said Ordynov—and his voice quivered with emotion.

"So you must have a great deal of your own for sale,'' answered the old man, "that you put your spoke in unasked,'' and he laughed a spiteful, noiseless laugh, looking insolently at Ordynov.

"What I have sold it for, I have had,'' answered Katerina in a voice that sounded vexed and offended. "One thinks it much, another little. One wants to give all to take nothing, another promises nothing and yet the submissive heart follows him! Do not you reproach anyone,'' she went on, looking sadly at Ordynov. "One man is like this, and another is different, and as though one knew why the soul yearns towards anyone! Fill your goblet, old man. Drink to the happiness of your dear daughter, your meek, obedient slave, as I was when first I knew you. Raise your goblet!''

"So be it! Fill yours, too!" said the old man, taking the wine.

"Stay, old man! Put off drinking, and let us say a word first! . . ."

Katerina put her elbows on the table and looked intently, with passionate, kindling eyes, at the old man. A strange determination gleamed in her eyes. But all her movements were calm, her gestures were abrupt, unexpected, rapid. She was all as if on fire, and it was marvellous; but her beauty seemed to grow with her emotion, her animation; her hurried breath slightly inflating her nostrils, floated from her lips, half-opened in a smile which showed two rows of teeth white and even as pearls. Her bosom heaved, her coil of hair, twisted three times round her head, fell carelessly over her left ear and covered part of her glowing cheek, drops of sweat came out on her temples.

"Tell my fortune, old man; tell my fortune, my father, before you drown your mind in drink. Here is my white palm for you—not for nothing do the folks call you a wizard. You have studied by the book and know all of the black art! Look, old man, tell me all my pitiful fate; only mind you don't tell a lie. Come, tell me as you know it—will there be happiness for your daughter, or will you not forgive her, but call down upon her path an evil, sorrowful fate? Tell me whether I shall have a warm corner for my home, or, like a bird of passage, shall be seeking among good people for a home—a lonely orphan all my life. Tell me who is my enemy, who is preparing love for me, who is plotting against me; tell me, will my warm young heart open its life in solitude and languish to the end, or will it find itself a mate and beat joyfully in tune with it till new sorrow comes! Tell me for once, old man, in what blue sky, beyond far seas and forests, my bright falcon lives. And is he keenly searching for his mate, and is he waiting lovingly, and will he love me fondly; will he soon be tired of me, will he deceive me or not deceive me, and, once for all and altogether, tell me for the last time, old man, am I long to while away the time with you, to sit in a comfortless corner, to read dark books; and when am I, old man, to bow low to you, to say farewell for good and all, to thank you for your bread and salt, for giving me to drink and eat, for telling me your tales? . . . But mind, tell all the truth, do not lie. The time has come, stand up for yourself."

Her excitement grew greater and greater up to the last word, when suddenly her voice broke with emotion as though her heart were carried away by some inner tempest. Her eyes flashed, and her upper lip faintly quivered. A spiteful jeer could be heard hiding like a snake under every word, but yet there was the ring of tears in her laughter. She bent across the table to the old man and gazed with eager intentness into his lustreless eyes. Ordynov heard her heart suddenly begin beating when she finished; he cried out with ecstasy when he glanced at her, and was getting up from the bench. But a flitting momentary glance from the old man riveted him to his seat again. A strange mingling of contempt, mocking, impatient, angry uneasiness and at the same time sly, spiteful curiosity gleamed in his passing momentary glance, which every time made Ordynov shudder and filled his heart with annoyance, vexation and helpless anger.

Thoughtfully and with a sort of mournful curiosity the old man looked at his Katerina. His heart was stung, words had been uttered. But not an eyebrow stirred upon his face! He only smiled when she finished.

"You want to know a great deal at once, my full-fledged nestling, my fluttering bird! Better fill me a deep goblet! and let us drink first to peace and goodwill; or I may spoil my forecast, through someone's black evil eye. Mighty is the devil! Sin is never far off!"

He raised his goblet and drank. The more wine he drank, the paler he grew. His eyes burned like red coals. Evidently the feverish light of them and the sudden deathlike blueness of his face were signs that another fit was imminent. The wine was strong, so that after emptying one goblet Ordynov's sight grew more and more blurred. His feverishly inflamed blood could bear no more: it rushed to his heart, troubled and dimmed his reason. His uneasiness grew more and more intense. To relieve his growing excitement, he filled his goblet and sipped it again, without knowing what he was doing, and the blood raced even more rapidly through his veins. He was as though in delirium, and, straining his attention to the utmost, he could hardly follow what was passing between his strange landlord and landlady.

The old man knocked his goblet with a ringing sound against the table.

"Fill it, Katerina!" he cried, "fill it again, bad daughter, fill it to the brim! Lay the old man in peace, and have done with him! That's it, pour out more, pour it out, my beauty! Let us drink together! Why have you drunk so little? Or have my eyes deceived me? . . ."

Katerina made him some answer, but Ordynov could not hear quite what she said: the old man did not let her finish; he caught hold of her hand as though he were incapable of restraining all that was weighing on his heart. His face was pale, his eyes at one moment were dim, at the next were flashing with fire; his lips quivered and turned white, and in an uneven, troubled voice, in which at moments there was a flash of strange ecstasy, he said to her—

"Give me your little hand, my beauty! Let me tell your fortune. I will tell the whole truth: I am truly a wizard; so you are not mistaken, Katerina! Your golden heart said truly that I alone am its wizard, and will not hide the truth from it, the simple, girlish heart! But one thing you don't see: it's not for me, a wizard, to teach you wisdom! Wisdom is not what a maiden wants, and she hears the whole truth, yet seems not to know, not to understand! Her head is a subtle serpent, though her heart is melting in tears. She will find out for herself, will thread her way between troubles, will keep her cunning will! Something she can win by sense, and where she cannot win by sense she will dazzle by beauty, will intoxicate men's minds with her black eye—beauty conquers strength, even the heart of iron will be rent asunder! Will you have grief and sorrow? Heavy is the sorrow of man! but trouble is not for the weak heart, trouble is close friends with the strong heart; stealthily it sheds a bloody tear, but does not go begging to good people for shameful comfort: your grief, girl, is like a print in the sand—the rain washes it away, the sun dries it, the stormy wind lifts it and blows it away. Let me tell you more, let me tell your fortune. Whoever loves you, you will be a slave to him, you will bind your freedom yourself, you will give yourself in pledge and will not take yourself back, you will not know how to cease to love in due time, you will sow a grain and your destroyer will take back a whole ear! My tender child, my little golden head, you buried your pearl of a tear in my goblet, but you could not be content with that—at once you shed a hundred; you uttered no more sweet words, and boasted of your sad life! And there was no need for you to grieve over it—the tear, the dew of heaven! It will come back to you with interest, your pearly tear, in the woeful night when cruel sorrow, evil fancies will gnaw your heart—then for that same tear another's tear will drop upon your warm

303

heart—not a warm tear but a tear of blood, like molten lead; it will turn your white bosom to blood, and until the dreary, heavy morning that comes on gloomy days, you will toss in your little bed, shedding your heart's blood and will not heal your fresh wound till another dawn. Fill my goblet, Katerina, fill it again, my dove; fill it for my sage counsel, and no need to waste more words." His voice grew weak and trembling, sobs seemed on the point of breaking from his bosom, he poured out the wine and greedily drained another goblet. Then he brought the goblet down on the table again with a bang. His dim eyes once more gleamed with flame.

"Ah! Live as you may!" he shouted; "what's past is gone and done with. Fill up the heavy goblet, fill it up, that it may smite the rebellious head from its shoulders, that the whole soul may be dead with it! Lay me out for the long night that has no morning and let my memory vanish altogether. What is drunk is lived and done with. So the merchant's wares have grown stale, have lain by too long, he must give them away for nothing! but the merchant would not of his free will have sold it below its price. The blood of his foe should be spilt and the innocent blood should be shed too, and that customer should have laid down his lost soul into the bargain! Fill my goblet, fill it again, Katerina."

But the hand that held the goblet seemed to stiffen and did not move; his breathing was laboured and difficult, his head sank back. For the last time he fixed his lustreless eyes on Ordynov, but his eyes, too, grew dim at last, and his eyelids dropped as though they were made of lead. A deadly pallor overspread his face . . . For some time his lips twitched and quivered as though still trying to articulate—and suddenly a big hot tear hung on his eyelash, broke and slowly ran down his pale cheek. . . .

Ordynov could bear no more. He got up and, reeling, took a step forward, went up to Katerina and clutched her hand. But she seemed not to notice him and did not even glance at him, as though she did not recognise him. . . .

She, too, seemed to have lost consciousness, as though one thought, one fixed idea had entirely absorbed her. She sank on the bosom of the sleeping old man, twined her white arm round his neck, and gazed with glowing, feverish eyes as though they were riveted on him. She did not seem to feel Ordynov taking her hand. At last she turned her head towards him, and bent upon him a prolonged searching gaze. It seemed as though at last she understood, and a bitter, astonished smile came wearily, as it were painfully, on her lips. . . .

"Go away, go away," she whispered; "you are drunk and wicked, you are not a guest for me . . ." then she turned again to the old man and riveted her eyes upon him.

She seemed as it were gloating over every breath he took and soothing his slumber with her eyes. She seemed afraid to breathe, checking her full throbbing heart, and there was such frenzied admiration in her face that at once despair, fury and insatiable anger seized Ordynov's spirit. . . .

"Katerina! Katerina!" he called, seizing her hand as though in a vice.

A look of pain passed over her face; she raised her head again, and looked at him with such mockery, with such contemptuous haughtiness, that he could scarcely stand upon his feet. Then she pointed to the sleeping old man and—as though all his enemy's mockery had passed into her eyes, she bent again a taunting glance at Ordynov that sent an icy shiver to his heart.

"What? He will murder me, I suppose?" said Ordynov, beside himself with fury. Some demon seemed to whisper in his ear that he understood her . . . and his whole heart laughed at Katerina's fixed idea.

"I will buy you, my beauty, from your merchant, if you want my soul; no fear, he won't kill me! . . ." A fixed laugh, that froze Ordynov's whole being, remained upon Katerina's face. Its boundless irony rent his heart. Not knowing what he was doing, hardly conscious, he leaned against the wall and took from a nail the old man's expensive old-fashioned knife. A look of amazement seemed to come into Katerina's face, but at the same time anger and contempt were reflected with the same force in her eyes. Ordynov turned sick, looking at her . . . he felt as though someone were thrusting, urging his frenzied hand to madness. He drew out the knife . . . Katerina watched him, motionless, holding her breath. . . .

He glanced at the old man.

At that moment he fancied that one of the old man's eyes opened and looked at him, laughing. Their eyes met. For some minutes Ordynov gazed at him fixedly. . . . Suddenly he fancied that the old man's whole face began laughing and that a diabolical, soul-freezing chuckle resounded at last through the room. A hideous, dark thought crawled like a snake into his head. He shuddered; the knife fell from his hands and dropped with a clang upon the floor. Katerina uttered a shriek as though awaking from oblivion, from a nightmare, from a heavy, immovable vision. . . . The old man, very pale, slowly got up from the bed and angrily kicked the knife into the corner of the room; Katerina stood pale, deathlike, immovable; her eyelids were closing; her face was convulsed by a vague, insufferable pain; she hid her face in her hands and, with a shriek that rent the heart, sank almost breathless at the old man's feet. . . .

"Alyosha, Alyosha!" broke from her gasping bosom.

The old man seized her in his powerful arms and almost crushed her on his breast. But when she hid her head upon his heart, every feature in the old man's face worked with such undisguised, shameless laughter that Ordynov's whole soul was overwhelmed with horror. Deception, calculation, cold, jealous tyranny and horror at the poor broken heart—that was what he read in that laugh, that shamelessly threw off all disguise.

"She is mad!" he whispered, quivering like a leaf, and, numb with terror, he ran out of the flat.

CHAPTER III

WHEN, at eight o'clock next morning, Ordynov, pale and agitated and still dazed from the excitement of that day, opened Yaroslav Ilyitch's door (he went to see him though he could not have said why) he staggered back in amazement and stood petrified in the doorway on seeing Murin in the room. The old man, even paler than Ordynov, seemed almost too ill to stand up; he would not sit down, however, though Yaroslav Ilyitch, highly delighted at the visit, invited him to do so. Yaroslav Ilyitch, too, cried out in surprise at seeing Ordynov, but almost at once his delight died away, and he was quite suddenly overtaken by embarrassment half-way between the table and the chair next it. It was evident that he did not know what to say or to do, and was fully conscious of the impropriety of sucking at his pipe and of leaving his visitor to his own devices at such a difficult moment. And yet (such was his confusion) he did go on pulling at his pipe with all his might and indeed with a sort of enthusiasm. Ordynov went into the room at last. He flung a cursory glance at Murin, a look flitted over the old man's face, something like the malicious smile of the day before, which even now set Ordynov shuddering with indignation. All hostility, however, vanished at once and was smoothed away, and the old man's face assumed a perfectly unapproachable and reserved air. He dropped a very low bow to his lodger. . . . The scene brought Ordynov to a sense of reality at last. Eager to understand the position of affairs, he looked intently at Yaroslav Ilyitch, who began to be uneasy and flustered.

"Come in, come in," he brought out at last. "Come in, most precious Vassily Mihalitch; honour me with your presence, and put a stamp of . . . on all these ordinary objects . . ." said Yaroslav Ilyitch, pointing towards a corner of the room, flushing like a crimson rose; confused and angry that even his most exalted sentences floundered and missed fire, he moved the chair with a loud noise into the very middle of the room.

"I hope I'm not hindering you, Yaroslav Ilyitch," said Ordynov. "I wanted . . . for two minutes . . ."

"Upon my word! As though you could hinder me, Vassily Mihalitch; but let me offer you a cup of tea. Hey, servant. . . . I am sure you, too, will not refuse a cup!"

Murin nodded, signifying thereby that he would not.

Yaroslav Ilyitch shouted to the servant who came in, sternly demanded another three glasses, then sat down beside Ordynov. For some time he turned his head like a plaster kitten to right and to left, from Murin to Ordynov, and from Ordynov to Murin. His position was extremely unpleasant. He evidently wanted to say something, to his notions extremely delicate, for one side at any rate. But for all his efforts he was totally unable to utter a word . . . Ordynov, too, seemed in perplexity. There was a moment when both began speaking at once. . . . Murin, silent, watching them both with curiosity, slowly opened his mouth and showed all his teeth. . . .

"I've come to tell you," Ordynov said suddenly, "that, owing to a most unpleasant circumstance, I am obliged to leave my lodging, and . . ."

"Fancy, what a strange circumstance!" Yaroslav Ilyitch interrupted suddenly. "I confess I was utterly astounded when this worthy old man told me this morning of your intention. But . . ."

"*He* told you," said Ordynov, looking at Murin with surprise.

Murin stroked his beard and laughed in his sleeve.

"Yes," Yaroslav Ilyitch rejoined; "though I may have made

307

a mistake. But I venture to say for you—I can answer for it on my honour that there was not a shadow of anything derogatory to you in this worthy old man's words. . . ."

Here Yaroslav Ilyitch blushed and controlled his emotion with an effort. Murin, after enjoying to his heart's content the discomfiture of the other two men, took a step forward.

"It is like this, your honour," he began, bowing politely to Ordynov: "His honour made bold to take a little trouble on your behalf. As it seems, sir—you know yourself—the mistress and I, that is, we would be glad, freely and heartily, and we would not have made bold to say a word . . . but the way I live, you know yourself, you see for yourself, sir! Of a truth, the Lord barely keeps us alive, for which we pray His holy will; else you see yourself, sir, whether it is for me to make lamentation." Here Murin again wiped his beard with his sleeve.

Ordynov almost turned sick.

"Yes, yes, I told you about him, myself; he is ill, that is this *malheur*. I should like to express myself in French but, excuse me, I don't speak French quite easily; that is . . ."

"Quite so . . ."

"Quite so, that is . . ."

Ordynov and Yaroslav Ilyitch made each other a half bow, each a little on one side of his chair, and both covered their confusion with an apologetic laugh. The practical Yaroslav Ilyitch recovered at once.

"I have been questioning this honest man minutely," he began. "He has been telling me that the illness of this woman. . . ." Here the delicate Yaroslav Ilyitch, probably wishing to conceal a slight embarrassment that showed itself in his face, hurriedly looked at Murin with inquiry.

"Yes, of our mistress . . ."

The refined Yaroslav Ilyitch did not insist further.

"The mistress, that is, your former landlady; I don't know how . . . but there! She is an afflicted woman, you see . . . She says that she is hindering you . . . in your studies, and he himself . . . you concealed from me one important circumstance, Vassily Mihalitch!"

"What?"

"About the gun," Yaroslav Ilyitch brought out, almost whispering in the most indulgent tone with the millionth fraction of reproach softly ringing in his friendly tenor.

"But," he added hurriedly, "he has told me all about it.

And you acted nobly in overlooking his involuntary wrong to you. I swear I saw tears in his eyes."

Yaroslav Ilyitch flushed again, his eyes shone and he shifted in his chair with emotion.

"I, that is, we, sir, that is, your honour, I, to be sure, and my mistress remember you in our prayers," began Murin, addressing Ordynov and looking at him while Yaroslav Ilyitch overcame his habitual agitation; "and you know yourself, sir, she is a sick, foolish woman; my legs will hardly support me . . ."

"Yes, I am ready," Ordynov said impatiently; "please, that's enough, I am going directly . . ."

"No, that is, sir, we are very grateful for your kindness" (Murin made a very low bow); "that is not what I meant to tell you, sir; I wanted to say a word—you see, sir, she came to me almost from her home, that is from far, as the saying is, beyond the seventh water—do not scorn our humble talk, sir, we are ignorant folk—and from a tiny child she has been like this! A sick brain, hasty, she grew up in the forest, grew up a peasant, all among bargemen and factory hands; and then their house must burn down; her mother, sir, was burnt, her father burnt to death—I daresay there is no knowing what she'll tell you . . . I don't meddle, but the Chir—chir-urgi-cal Council examined her at Moscow. You see, sir, she's quite incurable, that's what it is. I am all that's left her, and she lives with me. We live, we pray to God and trust in the Almighty; I never cross her in anything."

Ordynov's face changed. Yaroslav Ilyitch looked first at one, then at the other.

"But, that is not what I wanted to say . . . no!" Murin corrected himself, shaking his head gravely. "She is, so to say, such a featherhead, such a whirligig, such a loving, headstrong creature, she's always wanting a sweetheart—if you will pardon my saying so—and someone to love; it's on that she's mad. I amuse her with fairy tales, I do my best at it. I saw, sir, how she—forgive my foolish words, sir," Murin went on, bowing and wiping his beard with his sleeve—"how she made friends with you; you, so to say, your excellency, were desirous to approach her with a view to love."

Yaroslav Ilyitch flushed crimson, and looked reproachfully at Murin. Ordynov could scarcely sit still in his seat.

"No . . . that is not it, sir . . . I speak simply, sir, I am a peasant, I am at your service. . . . Of course, we are ignorant folk, we are your servants, sir," he brought out, bowing low; "and my wife and I will pray with all our hearts for your honour. . . . What do we need? To be strong and have enough to eat—we do not repine; but what am I to do, sir; put my head in the noose? You know yourself, sir, what life is and will have pity on us; but what will it be like, sir, if she has a lover, too! . . . Forgive my rough words, sir; I am a peasant, sir, and you are a gentleman. . . . You're a young man, your excellency, proud and hasty, and she, you know yourself, sir, is a little child with no sense—it's easy for her to fall into sin. She's a buxom lass, rosy and sweet, while I am an old man always ailing. Well, the devil, it seems, has tempted your honour. I always flatter her with fairy tales, I do indeed; I flatter her; and how we will pray, my wife and I, for your honour! How we will pray! And what is she to you, your excellency, if she is pretty? Still she is a simple woman, an unwashed peasant woman, a foolish rustic maid, a match for a peasant like me. It is not for a gentleman like you, sir, to be friends with peasants! But she and I will pray to God for your honour; how we will pray!"

Here Murin bowed very low and for a long while remained with his back bent, continually wiping his beard with his sleeve.

Yaroslav Ilyitch did not know where he was standing.

"Yes, this good man," he observed in conclusion, "spoke to me of some undesirable incidents; I did not venture to believe him, Vassily Mihalitch, I heard that you were still ill," he interrupted hurriedly, looking at Ordynov in extreme embarrassment, with eyes full of tears of emotion.

"Yes, how much do I owe you?" Ordynov asked Murin hurriedly.

"What are you saying, your honour? Give over. Why, we are not Judases. Why, you are insulting us, sir, we should be ashamed, sir. Have I and my good woman offended you?"

"But this is really strange, my good man; why, his honour took the room from you; don't you feel that you are insulting him by refusing?" Yaroslav Ilyitch interposed, thinking it his duty to show Murin the strangeness and indelicacy of his conduct.

"But upon my word, sir! What do you mean, sir? What did we not do to please your honour? Why, we tried our very best, we did our utmost, upon my word! Give over, sir, give over, your honour. Christ have mercy upon you! Why, are we infidels or what? You might have lived, you might have eaten our humble fare with us and welcome; you might have lain there—we'd have said nothing against it, and we wouldn't have dropped a word; but the evil one tempted you. I am an afflicted man and my mistress is afflicted—what is one to do? There was no one to wait on you, or we would have been glad, glad from our hearts. And how the mistress and I will pray for your honour, how we will pray for you!"

Murin bowed down from the waist. Tears came into Yaroslav Ilyitch's delighted eyes. He looked with enthusiasm at Ordynov.

"What a generous trait, isn't it! What sacred hospitality is to be found in the Russian people."

Ordynov looked wildly at Yaroslav Ilyitch.

He was almost terrified and scrutinised him from head to foot.

"Yes, indeed, sir, we do honour hospitality; we do honour it indeed, sir," Murin asserted, covering his beard with his whole sleeve. "Yes, indeed, the thought just came to me; we'd have welcomed you as a guest, sir, by God! we would," he went on, approaching Ordynov; "and I had nothing against it; another day I would have said nothing, nothing at all; but sin is a sore snare and my mistress is ill. Ah, if it were not for the mistress! Here, if I had been alone, for instance; how glad I would have been of your honour, how I would have waited upon you, wouldn't I have waited upon you! Whom should we respect if not your honour? I'd have healed you of your sickness, I know the art. . . . You should have been our guest, upon my word you should, that is a great word with us! . . ."

"Yes, really; is there such an art?" observed Yaroslav Ilyitch . . . and broke off.

Ordynov had done Yaroslav Ilyitch injustice when, just before, he had looked him up and down with wild amazement.

He was, of course, a very honest and honourable person, but now he understood everything and it must be owned his position was a very difficult one. He wanted to explode, as it is called, with laughter! If he had been alone with Ordynov— two such friends—Yaroslav Ilyitch would, of course, have given way to an immoderate outburst of gaiety without attempting to control himself. He would, however, have done this in a gentlemanly way. He would after laughing have pressed Ordynov's hand with feeling, would genuinely and justly have assured him that he felt double respect for him and that he could make allowances in every case . . . and, of course, would have made no reference to his youth. But as it was, with his habitual delicacy of feeling, he was in a most difficult position and scarcely knew what to do with himself. . . .

"Arts, that is decoctions," Murin added. A quiver passed over his face at Yaroslav Ilyitch's tactless exclamation. "What I should say, sir, in my peasant foolishness," he went on, taking another step forward, "you've read too many books, sir; as the Russian saying is among us peasants, 'Wit has over-stepped wisdom.'. . ."

"Enough," said Yaroslav Ilyitch sternly.

"I am going," said Ordynov. "I thank you, Yaroslav Ilyitch. I will come, I will certainly come and see you," he said in answer to the redoubled civilities of Yaroslav Ilyitch, who was unable to detain him further. "Good-bye, good-bye."

"Good-bye, your honour, good-bye, sir; do not forget us, visit us, poor sinners."

Ordynov heard nothing more—he went out like one distraught. He could bear no more, he felt shattered, his mind was numb, he dimly felt that he was overcome by illness, but cold despair reigned in his soul, and he was only conscious of a vague pain crushing, wearing, gnawing at his breast; he longed to die at that minute. His legs were giving way under him and he sat down by the fence, taking no notice of the passing people, nor of the crowd that began to collect around him, nor of the questions, nor of the exclamations of the curious. But, suddenly, in the multitude of voices, he heard the voice of Murin above him. Ordynov raised his head. The old man really was standing before him, his pale face was thoughtful and dignified, he was quite a different man from the one who had played the coarse farce at Yaroslav Ilyitch's. Ordynov got up. Murin took his arm and led him out of the crowd. "You want to get your belongings," he said, looking sideways at Ordynov. "Don't grieve, sir," cried Murin. "You are young, why grieve? . . ."

Ordynov made no reply.

"Are you offended, sir? . . . To be sure you are very angry now . . . but you have no cause; every man guards his own goods!"

"I don't know you," said Ordynov; "I don't want to know your secrets. But she, she! . . ." he brought out, and the tears rushed in streams from his eyes. The wind blew them one

312

after another from his cheeks . . . Ordynov wiped them with his hand; his gesture, his eyes, the involuntary movement of his blue lips all looked like madness.

"I've told you already," said Murin, knitting his brows, "that she is crazy! What crazed her? . . . Why need you know? But to me, even so, she is dear! I've loved her more than my life and I'll give her up to no one. Do you understand now?"

There was a momentary gleam of fire in Ordynov's eyes.

"But why have I . . . ? Why have I as good as lost my life? Why does my heart ache? Why did I know Katerina?"

"Why?" Murin laughed and pondered. "Why, I don't know why," he brought out at last. "A woman's heart is not as deep as the sea; you can get to know it, but it is cunning, persistent, full of life! What she wants she must have at once! You may as well know, sir, she wanted to leave me and go away with you; she was sick of the old man, she had lived through everything that she could live with him. You took her fancy, it seems, from the first, though it made no matter whether you or another . . . I don't cross her in anything— if she asks for bird's milk I'll get her bird's milk. I'll make up a bird if there is no such bird; she's set on her will though she doesn't know herself what her heart is mad after. So it has turned out that it is better in the old way! Ah, sir! you are very young, your heart is still hot like a girl forsaken, drying her tears on her sleeve! Let me tell you, sir, a weak man cannot stand alone. Give him everything, he will come of himself and give it all back; give him half the kingdoms of the world to possess, try it and what do you think? He will hide himself in your slipper at once—he will make himself so small. Give a weak man his freedom—he will bind it himself and give it back to you. To a foolish heart freedom is no use! One can't get on with ways like that. I just tell you all this, you are very young! What are you to me? You've come and gone—you or another, it's all the same. I knew from the first it would be the same thing; one can't cross her, one can't say a word to cross her if one wants to keep one's happiness; only, you know, sir"—Murin went on with his reflections—"as the saying is, anything may happen; one snatches a knife in one's anger, or an unarmed man will fall on you like a sheep, with his bare hands, and tear his enemy's throat with his teeth; but let them put the knife in your hands and your enemy bare his chest before you—no fear, you'll step back."

313

They went into the yard. The Tatar saw Murin from a distance, took off his cap to him and stared slyly at Ordynov.

"Where's your mother? At home?" Murin shouted to him. "Yes."

"Tell her to help him move his things, and you get away, run along!"

They went up the stairs. The old servant, who appeared to be really the porter's mother, was getting together their lodger's belongings and peevishly putting them in a big bundle.

"Wait a minute; I'll bring you something else of yours; it's left in there. . . ."

Murin went into his room. A minute later he came back and gave Ordynov a sumptuous cushion, covered with embroidery in silks and braid, the one that Katerina had put under his head when he was ill.

"She sends you this," said Murin. "And now go for good and good luck to you; and mind now, don't hang about," he added in a fatherly tone, dropping his voice, "or harm will come of it."

It was evident that he did not want to offend his lodger, but when he cast a last look at him, a gleam of intense malice was unconsciously apparent in his face. Almost with repulsion he closed the door after Ordynov.

Within two hours Ordynov had moved into the rooms of Schpies the German. Tinchen was horrified when she saw him. She at once asked after his health and, when she learned what was wrong, at once did her best to nurse him.

The old German showed his lodger complacently how he had just been going down to paste a new placard on the gate, because the rent Ordynov had paid in advance had run out, that very day, to the last farthing. The old man did not lose the opportunity of commending, in a roundabout way, the accuracy and honesty of Germans. The same day Ordynov was taken ill, and it was three months before he could leave his bed.

Little by little he got better and began to go out. Daily life in the German's lodgings was tranquil and monotonous. The old man had no special characteristics: pretty Tinchen, within the limits of propriety, was all that could be desired. But life seemed to have lost its colour for Ordynov for ever! He became dreamy and irritable; his impressionability took a morbid form and he sank imperceptibly into dull, angry hypochondria. His books were sometimes not opened for weeks together. The future was closed for him, his money was being spent, and he gave up all effort, he did not even think of the future. Sometimes his old feverish zeal for science, his old fervour, the old visions of his own creation, rose up vividly from the past, but they only oppressed and stifled his spiritual energy. His mind would not get to work. His creative force was at a standstill. It seemed as though all those visionary images had grown up to giants in his imagination on purpose to mock at the impotence of their creator. At melancholy moments he could not help comparing himself with the magician's pupil who, learning by stealth his master's magic word, bade the broom bring him water and choked himself drinking it, as he had forgotten how to say, "Stop." Possibly a complete, original, independent idea really did exist within him. Perhaps he had been destined to be the artist in science. So at least he himself had believed in the past. Genuine faith is the pledge of the future. But now at some moments he laughed himself at his blind conviction, and—and did not take a step forward.

Six months before, he had worked out, created and jotted down on paper a sketch of a work upon which (as he was so young) in non-creative moments he had built his most solid hopes. It was a work relating to the history of the church, and his warmest, most fervent convictions were to find expression in it. Now he read over that plan, made changes in it, thought it over, read it again, looked things up and at last rejected the idea without constructing anything fresh on its ruins. But something akin to mysticism, to fatalism and a belief in the mysterious began to make its way into his mind. The luckless fellow felt his sufferings and besought God to heal him. The German's servant, a devout old Russian woman, used to describe with relish how her meek lodger prayed and how he would lie for hours together as though unconscious on the church pavement . . .

He never spoke to anyone of what had happened to him. But at times, especially at the hour when the church bells brought back to him the moment when first his heart ached and quivered with a feeling new to him, when he knelt beside her in the house of God, forgetting everything, and hearing nothing but the beating of her timid heart, when with tears of ecstasy and joy he watered the new, radiant hopes that had sprung up in his lonely life—then a storm broke in his soul that was wounded for ever; then his soul shuddered, and again the anguish of love glowed in his bosom with scorching fire; then his heart ached with sorrow and passion and his love seemed to grow with his grief. Often for hours together, forgetting himself and his daily life, forgetting everything in the world, he would sit in the same place, solitary, disconsolate; would shake his head hopelessly and, dropping silent tears, would whisper to himself:

"Katerina, my precious dove, my one loved sister!"

A hideous idea began to torment him more and more, it haunted him more and more vividly, and every day took more probable, more actual shape before him. He fancied—and at last he believed it fully—he fancied that Katerina's reason was sound, but that Murin was right when he called her "a weak heart". He fancied that some mystery, some secret, bound her to the old man, and that Katerina, though innocent of crime as a pure dove, had got into his power. Who were they? He did not know, but he had constant visions of an immense, overpowering despotism over a poor, defenceless creature, and his heart raged and trembled in impotent indignation. He fancied that before the frightened eyes of her suddenly awakened soul the idea of its degradation had been craftily presented, that the poor *weak* heart had been craftily tortured, that the truth had been twisted and contorted to her, that she had, with a purpose, been kept blind when necessary, that the inexperienced inclinations of her troubled passionate heart had been subtly flattered, and by degrees the free soul had been clipt of its wings till it was incapable at last of resistance or of a free movement towards free life . . .

By degrees Ordynov grew more and more unsociable and, to do them justice, his Germans did not hinder him in the tendency.

He was fond of walking aimlessly about the streets. He preferred the hour of twilight, and, by choice, remote, secluded and unfrequented places. On one rainy, unhealthy spring evening, in one of his favourite back-lanes he met Yaroslav Ilyitch.

Yaroslav Ilyitch was perceptibly thinner. His friendly eyes looked dim and he looked altogether disappointed. He was racing off full speed on some business of the utmost urgency, he was wet through and muddy and, all the evening, a drop of rain had in an almost fantastic way been hanging on his highly decorous but now blue nose. He had, moreover, grown whiskers.

These whiskers and the fact that Yaroslav Ilyitch glanced at him as though trying to avoid a meeting with an old friend almost startled Ordynov. Strange to say, it even wounded his heart, which had till then felt no need for sympathy. He preferred, in fact, the man as he had been—simple, kindly, naïve; speaking candidly, a little stupid, but free from all pretensions to disillusionment and common sense. It is unpleasant when a foolish man whom we have once liked, just on account of his foolishness, suddenly becomes sensible; it is decidedly disagreeable. However, the distrust with which he looked at Ordynov was quickly effaced.

In spite of his disillusionment he still retained his old manners, which, as we all know, accompany a man to the grave, and even now he eagerly tried to win Ordynov's confidence. First of all he observed that he was very busy, and then that they had not seen each other for a long time; but all at once the conversation took a strange turn.

Yaroslav Ilyitch began talking of the deceitfulness of mankind in general. Of the transitoriness of the blessings of this world, of the vanity of vanities; he even made a passing allusion to Pushkin with more than indifference, referred with some cynicism to his acquaintances and, in conclusion, even hinted at the deceitfulness and treachery of those who are called friends, though there is no such thing in the world as real friendship and never has been; in short, Yaroslav Ilyitch had grown wise.

Ordynov did not contradict him, but he felt unutterably sad, as though he had buried his best friend.

"Ah! fancy, I was forgetting to tell you," Yaroslav Ilyitch began suddenly, as though recalling something very interesting. "There's a piece of news! I'll tell you as a secret. Do you remember the house where you lodged?"

Ordynov started and turned pale.

"Well, only fancy, just lately a whole gang of thieves was discovered in that house; that is, would you believe me, a regular band of brigands; smugglers, robbers of all sorts, goodness knows what. Some have been caught but others are still being looked for; the sternest orders have been given. And, can you believe it! do you remember the master of the house, that pious, respectable, worthy-looking old man?"

"Well?"

"What is one to think of mankind? He was the chief of their gang, the leader. Isn't it absurd?"

Yaroslav Ilyitch spoke with feeling and judged of all mankind from one example, because Yaroslav Ilyitch could not do otherwise, it was his character.

"And they? Murin?" Ordynov articulated in a whisper.

"Ah! Murin, Murin! no, he was a worthy old man, quite respectable . . . but, excuse me, you throw a new light . . ."

"Why? Was he, too, in the gang?"

Ordynov's heart was ready to burst with impatience.

"However, as you say . . ." added Yaroslav Ilyitch, fixing his pewtery eyes on Ordynov—a sign that he was reflecting—"Murin could not have been one of them. Just three weeks ago he went home with his wife to their own parts . . . I learned it from the porter, that little Tatar, do you remember?"